The Only Thing Necessary

A Tale from the Cameron Line

D.C. SHEPHERD

The Only Thing Necessary
Copyright © 2024 by D.C. Shepherd

All rights reserved. No part of this publication may be reproduced, distributed, or transmitted in any form or by any means, including photocopying, recording, or other electronic or mechanical methods, without the prior written permission of the author, except in the case of brief quotations embodied in critical reviews and certain other non-commercial uses permitted by copyright law.

Tellwell Talent
www.tellwell.ca

ISBN
978-1-77941-979-8 (Hardcover)
978-1-77941-978-1 (Paperback)
978-1-77941-980-4 (eBook)

Foreword and Dedication

We will never know how many fugitive slaves who sought freedom in British North America were kidnapped and returned to the United States by bounty hunters. Historians estimate the number was in the hundreds.

When abductions reached a crescendo in the 1850's, some concerned citizens said, "Not on my watch!" This novel is dedicated to those people in what is now Ontario who formed vigilance committees to put a stop to the practice.

"The Only Thing Necessary: A Tale from the Cameron Line" is a work of historical fiction based on several real people and several historic events. It reflects the language and circumstances of their time. In our politically correct time, when everyone is a victim, some may not understand the difference between a book which includes racists and a racist book. Dear Reader, if that applies to you, please set this book down and walk away.

d.c.s.

THE ONLY THING NECESSARY

"The only thing necessary for evil to triumph is for good men to do nothing," is a quote generally attributed to Edmund Burke.

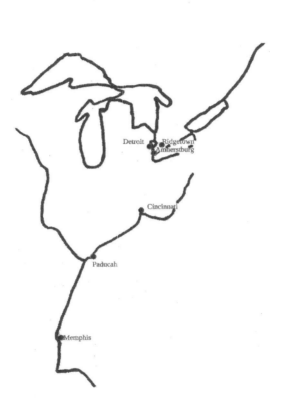

A TALE FROM THE CAMERON LINE

Table of Contents

Foreword and Dedication iii

Part One: Decisions

The Third Choice 2
The Die is Seized 8
Sunday Afternoon 17
The Die is Cast 24
Lonnegan Flags a Boat 30
The Business of Bounty Hunting 34
A Thorn in the Foot 43
Fleeing South 48
Miles and Miles 56
The Kindness of Strangers 62
Socks and Shingles 69
Constance Lonnegan Has Coffee 73
The Exchange 78
The Offer 82
The Lady in the Wheeled Chair 86
The Cabin 93
A Collar of Yarn 99
The Rock 105

Part Two: The Illusion of Safety

Freight Crosses the Jordan 112
An Eye for the Grain 117
Routines 120
The Messenger 123
The Last Sunday 128
The Fort 133
Conspirators 141
Mister Cork Talks to Mrs. Duffy 145

Part Three: North

Kentucky 150
The Contract 159
Rot and Vinegar 163
Ten Weeks 166
Ellie Washes a Platter 172
Paducah 174
A Whiff of Brimstone 182
The Deacon Talks Cattle 189
The Friends 192
The Package Goes North 195

Part Four: Action

Detroit 200
Fast... and Final 203
An Investigation and a Report 209
A Quite Satisfactory Outcome 215

Part Five: Gideon Sounds a Trumpet

Gideon Chooses His Warriors 220
Mrs. Hedley Disapproves 224
Daniel Talks to Jessie, Jacob and Susan 229
Daniel and Archie Talk Horses 240
The Flock Suffers 247
The Argument 251
Amherstburg 256

Part Six: Immersion

Mrs. Hedley Reports 266
Two Worlds Intersect 270
Day One 279
The First Week 283
Aeneas Ragg Encourages His Associates 293
Metamorphosis 297
Mrs. Hedley Entertains 306
John Duffy Recruits 311
Fort Malden Revisited 316
Noah Hedley Makes a Deal 320
Mrs. Hedley Enlightens 324
Constance Recruits an Ally 331
A Message for Aeneas Ragg 335
Archie's Plan 340
The Mariners Return 348
Local Heroes Safe After Rescue Attempt 351
Shorter Days 353
Winter Realities, Spring Plans 361
The Best-laid Schemes... Gang Aft Agley 368

Part Seven: On Her Majesty's Secret Service

Emmett Explains 374
Cameron and Taylor: Horse Traders 385
A Letter to Aeneas 393
The Team Practises 395
A Letter From the Ferret 406
To Mayfield and Deacon's Mill 408
Into Tennessee 416
The Hamlet 422
Aeneas Revisits the Sawmill 428
Spoils Divided 432
Constance Acts 437
God Rewards the Deacon 442
The Dam Bursts 447

Part Eight: Prices To Be Paid

The Understanding 458
Messages 462
Ellie Runs Away 465
Lonnegan Returns From Memphis 470
At the Lonnegan Plantation 474
Master Lonnegan Gives a Tour 482
Lunch, Supper and Breakfast 491
At the Sleepy Goat 499
Clothes for Ellie 503
Lonnegan Learns of the Conspiracy 510
The Raggs Visit 516
Heading South, Heading North 518
The Gunfight at the Bridge 525

To The Sleepy Goat 530
Aeneas Returns to the Plantation 537

Part Nine: Justice

Running North 542
The Billie Jo Sails North 552
Reports to be Written 562
Home 568
Two Tables 574
Gettysburg 582
Author's Notes 587

Part One

DECISIONS

The Third Choice

As one quarter year cycled into another, the plantation shifted its priorities. Cotton bales and freshly coopered barrels of a new crop, sorghum, were readied for their float down to New Orleans. In the cobblestone storehouse, ceramic jars, topped up with the life's work of countless bees and sealed with waxed cheesecloth, awaited transport to the master's kitchen. This day, the female field hands were piling dry wood near the smokehouse in preparation for the pig slaughter which marked the end of the harvest season. Bindle, the overseer, had assigned the men to clearing forest, a Herculean task that had been started the previous year to expand the east fields.

It all began with one stubborn stump. Little Seth pushed and pulled and pulled and pushed what remained of a red oak so Joseph could cut the individual roots. It rocked and twisted under Seth's attack but tenaciously resisted all efforts from his diminutive frame to break it free. Axe at the ready, sweat dripping from his face, Joseph circled his victim. "What's holdin' it d'ere? I has cut every root I could see. D'ere's gotta be one right underneaf dat we cain't get at."

Malachi wandered over to assess the problem. "Joseph, let's wrap a rope around it, an' wif me and Seth pulling t'gether maybe we can pop dat out like a rotten toof. Gimme a minute. We can use da rope I'se usin' to haul branches to da burnin' pile."

Before he could walk ten yards, Bindle rode up on his white horse and stopped beside Malachi. "Weren't you told to work on the loose branches?" he asked.

"Yas suh, I was, but I see'd dem two," and he gestured toward the stump, "having a pa'ticlar hard time wif dat one so I thought..."

Bindle brought the butt end of his whip down the side of Malachi's head with such force he recoiled a step and put a hand up to his face as if to check that it was still there. Blood trickled a path through the dirt on his right cheek. He looked at the ground and shook his head like a skunk-sprayed dog.

"I'se jus' tryin' ta..."

Bindle struck him again beside the head, and again Malachi took a backward step. Bindle unravelled the whip and with a flick of his wrist snaked it out beside his horse. "Shut your mouth! Are you talkin' back to me? You talkin' back? You thought... You don't think! You do what I fucking well tell you! And I told you to pile those goddamn branches over there! I see you doing any more thinking, by God, I'll skin you with this," and he shook the whip handle in Malachi's face.

There was focused hatred in Malachi's look; for a brief moment it seemed he might pull Bindle from his horse. The two huge men glared at one another. One of the other supervisors trotted over, his hand resting on his sidearm. "Trouble here, Boss?" he asked.

"Taken care of. For now. But if you see this goddamned malingerer so much as fuckin' look sideways from what he's supposed to be working at, you can have a go at him. Just leave enough so's I get the bones."

Malachi shambled back to the brush pile, head down. After a half hour with pick, shovel, and axe, the resistant roots finally broke free. Seth, Joseph and the rest of the stump detail tackled two more before quitting time. Knowing Bindle would be watching, they avoided Malachi on the walk back to the barns.

The extent of the wound became more evident once they had washed the day's grime from hands and faces in preparation for supper. As Malachi lined up with his tin plate and cup at the food dispensing table, Old Mose pulled him to one side. Too ancient for field work, Old Mose made himself useful in the field kitchen cutting vegetables, packing lunches, doing dishes, or administering first aid, the job of the moment. He dabbed the cut with cotton lint soaked in horse liniment.

"Best leave dat one to da air. Yesirree... Dat one startin' ta scab over already. After supper, I'll rub some honey on it. At da rate you'se irritatin' Mister Bindle, he be requirin' a new whip soon."

"He sure as hell won't want ta use da old one when I shove it up his ass firs' chance dat comes."

"Now what good gonna come from talkin' like dat? Ever'body know Mister Bindle be one nasty customer. Yeah, you be big and strong as him, sure, but he got doze two supervisors dat's never far away, an' what you gonna do? You kill 'im, you be hanged 'fore da sun sets. You break him up bad, you gets whipped or worse, an' d'en you'se on da block in Memphis."

"I cain't take much more wif'out doin' somethin', but I cain't see no altern'tive."

"D'ere ain't one. Dat's what I'se tryin' to make ya see. You was borned to dis life, an' ya cain't change it all by you'self. Now, ya take dis here cotton and squeeze da blood on it inta a dried up lake. When dat lake is overflowin', dat's how much blood it gonna take ta change what's goin' on here."

The old man stopped talking to let his patient's anger drain away a little more. Malachi resumed his place in the chow line. Before he hobbled back into the field hands' kitchen, Old Mose said, "You get angry, ya talk it outta yer system wif me, or yer friends, Joseph, Seth. Ya gotta promise me dat. Promise? Promise me dat?"

Malachi nodded and shuffled forward.

Malachi one powerful bull of a man an' once his blood get hot, cain't be nuthin' but grief come of it, Old Mose thought. *Ain't no way to tell Bindle I jus' might a saved his life tomorra. More important ta drain dat invisible anger boil outta Malachi d'an ta wipe up a bloody face.*

He added more wood to the fire under the cauldron where dirty dishes were washed and wallowed in the smug warmth of the peacemaker.

After supper and clean-up, there was little conversation in the cramped, ramshackle clapboard cabin Joseph, Seth, and Malachi shared. Tired work boots were placed at the end of each bed, faded blue dungaree overalls, blue cotton shirts, and brown broadcloth jackets hung on nails. They stretched out on the wooden slats of their pine bunks in their nightshirts, waiting for sleep to cart away the fatigue from the day's labours.

"T'was my fault," Malachi said, just as the others thought he had fallen asleep. He turned onto his side and re-positioned his single blanket and a straw-filled pillow sewn from a flour sack. "It was my fault, all of it. I should've known Bindle was jus' lookin' fer a chance ta pounce on me. He bin ridin' my ass f'rever. I'm gonna kill him tomorra," he said matter-of-factly.

"An what'll dat do, except give ya da satisfaction a sendin' his soul ta Hell?" Joseph asked. "Dat be suicide fer you. New overseer for us, worse d'an Bindle maybe, 'cause now dis plantation got a reputation for trouble. Maybe da master sell us all off, buy new field hands. Maybe promote one of da fresh supervisors, turn out meaner'n Bindle maybe."

"I'se got no choice," Malachi said. "I cain't spend another day livin' like dis. I either rip dat man's win'pipe out or I hang myself. D'ems da choices I got. Either way, I end up hangin'."

There was silence for a few minutes, then Seth said, "Ya could run away. Dat'd give ya another choice, an' cause consid'able trouble fer Bindle in da bargain."

The silence lasted longer this time.

Seth said, "I would run wif ya, if dat be yer choice."

More silence.

Joseph's voice broke the darkness. "Ain't no future here but da graveyard. We be lucky to end up like Old Mose, jus' hangin' on."

Silence.

Joseph continued. "1856. Accordin' ta Old Mose, dat's where we be. Where we gonna be in five, ten years, I ask ya? Still be in 1856, dat's where. Da numbers will change, but we'll be sufferin' da same year ag'in and ag'in. Don't matter if d'ere's a new Bindle, it'll be da same whip. For months I bin tossin' aroun' da idea a shovin' off, takin' my chances. Today, what happen to you, Malachi, well, dat jus' help me see dat I gotta go 'fore I'se too old ta travel hard."

A long silence.

Finally, Malachi said, "Seth, you be right about dat third choice. I'll sleep on it. If I doan kill Bindle tomorra, then you two know I plan on leavin'. Dat's my las' word on da matter."

"I doan need ta sleep on it. I bin sleepin' on it fer too long. I is goin' firs' chance I get," Joseph muttered.

"Da only thing keepin' me from runnin' off is dat I have abs'lutely no idea how ta take on such a enterprise. I doan know how ta go 'bout it or where ta go if I did get away," Seth added.

Malachi said, "If Bindle be 'live tomorra night, then we talk about jus' what we 'tend to do."

No one drifted off to sleep right away.

The Die is Seized

At quitting time, Bindle was still alive. He had watched Malachi in particular that day, searching for an excuse to torment him, but Malachi focused on piling branches as though yesterday and all the previous yesterdays had never existed.

As darkness fell and the three retreated to their cabin, no one broached the forbidden topic, as if merely mentioning the crime was equivalent to committing it. Finally, Joseph said, almost whispering, "I bin thinkin', an' I've come ta my decision. Even if you two doan leave, I be goin' soon's I can. 1857 ain't gonna catch me here. If I gotta die, I'se gonna die a hunted man, not a slave."

Malachi chuckled. "Good ta hear, Joseph. Good ta hear. I has come to da same conclusion, but I didn' wanna mention it 'cause I doan want you two ta get punished fer knowin' an' not tellin'"

"Y'all ain't leavin' wif'out me," Seth added. "I tole ya I was comin' wif ya. I tole ya!"

In the following days, the bleakness of a pathetic existence waned. They coped with Bindle's cruel domination, long hours of back-wrenching labour, food that would be thrown to the pigs if served at the big house. Without complaint they bore whatever misery an indifferent heaven threw their way. Hope elbowed resignation aside.

Resolve jelled in the short intervals between supper and the body's relentless demand for sleep. Here the magnificent idea crystallized, safe from the ever-watchful eye of Bindle. Here they swore secrecy, pledged loyalty, convinced the others of their steel, argued in hushed tones, minutely examined options, fantasized, shivered with the audacity, shuddered at the thought of failure. It was here they realized they had no plan, no timeline, no course of action. No plan meant no chance of success. Without a plan, there was only despair. There had to be a plan.

Saturdays were not good for conspiring. At three in the afternoon, tools cleaned and stacked, the men scrubbed up at the stable pump while the women washed from wooden buckets carried to the nearest rickety cabin. After supper, there would be a bonfire and singing and dancing that would last well into the night. If Bindle reported the week's labours had been satisfactory, there would be rum. But there would be no pairing off for the unmarried. Not without Master Lonnegan's permission. The master was mighty particular about his breeding stock. You talked to Bindle about that first, and if Bindle was in a benevolent frame of mind, he might mention your interest in the girl to Master Lonnegan, although to recall a time when Bindle was in a benevolent mood was a challenge. Once he had enjoyed the girl himself, just to remind them what they were. It was safer to let the master orchestrate the couplings.

They would be noticed if they broke Saturday's routine. Sunday would be better. Sundays were a different kind of special from Saturdays. No matter the weather, Sundays were always beautiful. There was no work. None. After breakfast, both field hands and servants — Master Lonnegan liked to call the house slaves "servants" — clustered around the ear tree on the front lawn or in the granary if it was raining. Mothers straightened up small children and cuffed them beside the head at the least squirming inattention. No interruption was tolerated when the master read from the scriptures. An unsuppressed cough or a fidgety child diverting his focus earned a baleful eye that threatened retribution. He usually ended with several verses from Ephesians Six or Matthew Six and a passage from a Psalm. Then he would exhort them to be of good cheer and reminded them of God's love and mercy for the righteous in the world to come. Everyone joined in the singing of the hymn chosen and led by Cicero, the master's house steward. The master would then retreat with the servants, Cicero leading, into the imposing white plantation house to enjoy a hearty brunch with his wife and any guests.

Even though the house was set a furlong and half again from the road, no passer-by could fail to notice its size, its grandeur. The lane formed a horseshoe, the open end to the road, the apex rounding at the east-facing front porch where four fluted Greek columns supported the protruding second story. The shaded afternoon porch often found the master and mistress enjoying a libation while they took the air. Only guests and house servants catering to their unpredictable whims ever used the bevel-windowed, double French doors.

The view from the porch was idyllic. The arms of the lane embraced a sheep-manicured lawn, where mature trees led the eye to the road and to more of the Lonnegan fields and forest beyond. The southern arm of the horseshoe boasted a westward extension that took service traffic to a cluster of essential buildings: the overseers' cottages, a cotton-processing workshop, a blacksmith's and a carpenter's workshop, a smokehouse, storehouses, a barn with adjacent stable, a pigsty, the granary, a partially roofed kitchen for the field hands, slave cabins, and outhouses. None of these could be seen from the porch.

After Sunday service, the field hands gathered in the dappled shade of the ear tree to enjoy the best meal of the week. Once the men had wrestled live-edge pine trestle tables into a rough semi-circle, the women set out chipped and cracked ceramic plates, plates so ancient most could recollect no pattern. The older women doled from antediluvian pots and pans. When all heads were bowed, Old Mose intoned, "Lord, we thank you for this food" in a voice more feeble than stentorian, and the chorus of "Amen" was the signal to begin the feast. In season, their garden plots provided potatoes, cabbages, onions, tomatoes, turnips, beans, beets, peas, sweet potatoes, okra, pumpkins and melons. There was always cornbread and molasses, and maybe they might get an opportunity to sample the new sorghum syrup soon. The master supplied surplus from the house garden and salt and meat, usually sausages or chitlins or hogs' feet or ox tails or organ meats, occasionally topped up with a chicken or two.

When there was more talking than eating, Cicero, in his white linen suit, bald head glistening with perspiration in the mid-day sun, would emerge from the plantation house, his stride purposeful and efficient, reminding them yet again of his importance, the delegate of the master and mistress. He would say the mistress wished to know if their repast was sufficient and if anyone required any medical attention. Old

Mose would push himself laboriously to his feet and entreat Cicero, on behalf of the field hands, to thank the master and mistress for their kind concern. No one ever had any ailments; any medical attention would come from the old folk's natural remedies. To mention an infirmity was to invite Bindle's scrutiny in the fields. No one wished to be sold. There were worse masters than Beauregard Lonnegan.

Once Cicero transported himself with an air of self-importance back to the house and tables and dishes were looked to, everyone drifted off to laze or repair exhausted bodies by revelling in an afternoon of sleep. Sunday was a holiday from Bindle's menacing horse and Bindle's menacing frown and Bindle's menacing shouts and Bindle's delivered whip.

For planning an escape, Sunday was optimal.

It was Malachi who proposed taking Old Mose into their confidence. "What we know 'bout what we do next, once we fly da coop? Old Mose all crippled up and 'crepit, so he ain't gonna say he gonna tag along. He only got da one ear and cain't scaresly walk. He bin 'round long time. He ain't about ta tell no one."

Joseph agreed. "We be three frogs swimmin' in milk. Cain't see far 'nough ahead. Even if he cain't help, he won't sing. Mama said he run away hisself once, but he don't talk about it. Yessiree, we need ta have a long conflab wif Mister Old Mose."

"We gotta do dis quick and we gotta do dis right or we not gotta do dis at all," Seth said. "Best spot? Cemetery. Old Mose, he hobble over d'ere ever'day ta talk wif his wife. Anybody come, we just say we helping Old Mose get back to his rockin' chair 'cause he ain't walkin' good t'day."

They nonchalantly wandered out to the hands' cemetery at the edge of the pasture behind the horse paddocks. Where mature oak trees from the adjacent woodlot did not shade the grassy mounds, rough split-board crosses cast shadows creeping to mark the passage of eternity. As Seth predicted, they found the frail old man at his wife's grave. His skeletal frame slouched on an old, yellow painted chair that had been rescued from the woodpile, and he was napping under a tattered, brown felt hat that might have been new when Andrew Jackson was a pup. He roused slowly at their approach.

"Now what you boys want? You'se disturbin' a man's repose wif his missus."

Malachi said, "Old Mose, we muchly need your assistance. We three is aiming ta run off, but we don't know nuthin' 'bout where ta go or what ta s'pect."

Joseph added, "We need ya ta help us get up a plan 'bout how to run off da best way."

The old man took a deep breath and blew it slowly out a gap-toothed mouth. "I ain't got nuthin' for ya. Run off? You askin' for nuthin' but trouble talkin' such tripe."

Joseph said, "We be going no matter. We be going better if you 'vise us wif what ya know, cause we ain't never run off before. Mama said you run off once."

"Well, she wrong. I wish she was alive so I could tell her dat myself. I run off twice. And I got catched twice. So maybe ya best converse wif someone who run off and wasn't catched if ya want ta know how ta do it proply."

There was silence. Finally Seth said, "Old Mose, please. You is all we got. We goin'. We goin' for certain. We jus' need to know when's da best time and where ta go."

"Ya better think real long and real hard 'bout dis. Runnin' off is serious business, an' ya better give it serious consid'ration."

He pulled the pant legs of his ragged overalls halfway up his bony shins to better display calloused feet. "I ain't gonna talk no more about my 'scape now, but ya look here. Runnin' off? Look at my feet. I can still feel 'em, but da big toes has run off. Ain't d'ey run off? Jus' run off. Well, d'ey run off at da end of a axe da second time I was catched."

He dropped his pant legs and rubbed his left temple, then smoothed the scraggly whiskers on his chin. "Ya go ta da ear tree. Ya'll find da spike if ya look. Still d'ere. Dat's where da old Massa Lonnegan had 'em tie me up on dis here chair afta my first run and he nailed my ear ta dat tree. D'en he handed the young massa his skinnin' knife and told him what ta do. D'ey hold me so I couldn't interfere wif him, and the massa, him jus' a boy d'en, he slice' off my ear real slow, enjoyin' every minute. I couldn't do nuthin' but yell. So 'fore ya even think a leavin', ya best think 'bout what happen if ya is catched."

The three said nothing. Seth and Malachi stretched the straps on their overalls with their thumbs and studied their bare feet. Joseph glanced back at the barn to ensure no one was watching.

"Ya meet me here nex' Sunday aft'noon if ya is still fixin' on 'scapin'. We talk d'en. If ya doan show, d'en I knows you'se got some sense. Joseph, yer mama's gone, an' y'other two got no one d'ey can pour hell down on if ya run. But if ya 'cide ta run, you'se got ta act not ta give suspicion, or ya never get yer chance."

"We already 'cided. We be real careful. In da fields we talk real low, mumble if Bindle near, move apart if he lookin' at us," Malachi said.

"We done be real careful to keep dis jus' wif us. We be lookin' o'er our shoulder all da time," Seth added.

"An' ya don't reckon dat Bindle he not watchin' ya lookin' for someone watchin' ya? Him and Cicero got dis whole operation under control. We be like mice under a blanket and d'ey got da hammer. If I can see Joseph here staring at da big house windows, hankerin' for a glimpse of dat l'il scullery wench Ellie, d'en I figure Cicero see him staring too. Joseph, dis is what I'm talkin' about. When he notices ya longin' fer Ellie he pays attention ta ya, and when he pays attention ta ya, you is under suspicion."

"Cicero don't care nuthin' 'bout da field hands," Joseph argued. "Ellie make it plain she got eyes for me too. She smile and nod, and she even wave ta me if she see me at da pump or muckin' da stables. I talk ta her more'n a dozen times when da missus send her out to feed her prize chickens. I bin thinkin' a talkin' ta Bindle."

"You aimin' ta give dat sweetheart ta dat brute? You boys sure is green corn. Cicero want dat pretty l'il girl for hisself, and he only waitin' 'cause he figures she too young ta bleed. What he doan know is dat she already bleedin', and dat's a secret da women is guardin' so's ta keep him off her."

"How you know all dis?" Seth asked.

"Not dead yet. Still got one good ear. I sit in my rockin' chair and rock and rock and listen ta da clatter of woman-talk while'st d'ey boiling da laundry on Monday mornins. So you boys got some thinkin' ta do. You go look for dat spike in da ear tree, and ya think long and hard 'bout runnin' and longer and harder 'bout gettin' catched."

The old man looked directly at Joseph and in a slow voice said, "If Cicero think you interested in Ellie, maybe he get rid of the competition, maybe have Master Lonnegan cull ya from da breedin' stock. Maybe he have Bindle sep'rate off more d'an toes or a ear. You best think about dat too. Now, leave me wif my missus, and I doan want ta see ya here next Sunday aft'noon."

Sunday Afternoon

Old Mose was slouched on his rescued yellow chair when they met at the cemetery the following Sunday. He wasn't asleep. He looked the three up and down and said nothing. They rocked nervously back and forth on their heels and studied the ground, reluctant to break the silence. Finally, the old man rubbed the grey fuzz on his head with his ancient sweat-stained hat, hitched his bones more vertical, and said, "I was hopeful ya wouldn't show today. I truly was. But I reckoned ya would. Why doan ya jus' sit down and make a smaller target for anyone checkin' up on ya? Do I gotta do da thinkin' for all of us? You gotta start thinkin' like you is prey. You is gonna be prey."

"Thank you, Old Mose," Malachi said.

"Doan thank me yet. In my mind I bin forkin' over what ta tell you boys ta do, and it do seem ta me my advice is pretty slim pickin's. So... Ya have no set plan for leavin'?"

"We was thinkin' a maybe heading out da first autumn storm dat comes along," Joseph answered. "We figure da dogs would have more trouble trackin' in da wet. Make a run for the Mississippi, steal a skiff, head upstream, travel at night until we can get ta a free state. Take a line an' hooks. If da fishin' don't keep our bellies full, we'll need ta sneak around and lift a chicken or two."

Old Mose shook his head slowly from side to side. "Pitiful. Jus' pitiful. You boys'll be back here in three days. You relyin' on luck too much. Storm doan come when it be convenient for runaways. No, you best leave afta supper on Satu'day night. Everybody hear ya laughin' and singin' and no one pay no mind when d'ey doan see ya ag'in. Dat way ya got two nights an a full day between 'til ya doan show up when Bindle assign' da work at Monday mornin's bell. We can move aroun' a bit ta cover dat ya ain't d'ere at Sunday service, and if Cicero notices ya missing from da tables, I'll tell him ya tole me ya shared sumpin bad and now cain't keep food in ya, so you'se off somewhere feelin' sorry for yourselves. If he appear doubtful, I'll git someone ta say d'ey think yer in da shitters yet ag'in, and I'll wager he won't wanna check d'ere in his purty white linen suit."

"We cain't let you put yourself in danger for us. T'aint right." Malachi said.

"Doan worry 'bout me. Anythin' I can do ta help we'll jus' call a down payment on da price of a toe."

"What's wrong wif our plan, 'ceptin' a storm don't arrive on time?" Joseph asked.

"Let's see. Boat missin'... D'ey went dis way boys. D'ey sure as hell ain't floatin' south. No freedom nowheres d'ere. Even more misery south. Three Black men in a boat, d'ey gotta be rowin' in da dark. Ag'inst da current. Cain't get too far in a night, an' d'ey'll need ta fish, and d'ey'll get mighty hungry and d'en d'ey'll rouse someone's dog when d'ey try ta lift a chicken and da whole country'll know ta be on da look-out, an' even a dimwit can figure out Massa Lonnegan be mighty gen'rous wif a reward. Huntin' you three down'll be da best ent'ainment dis part of da country seen in years. 'Sides, ya think people jus' tie up a good skiff and leave da oars lying 'bout for ya ta help you'selves?"

"What if we steal a skiff, an' sink it where it cain't be seen?" Seth asked. "People figurin' we on da river, d'ey lookin' at ever' boat in da moonlight, but we headin' inta da back country 'stead."

Old Mose nodded his approval. "Dat's more like it. Now yer thinkin'. How you gonna 'vade da dogs?"

"Follow da main creek upstream 'til it peters out," Joseph answered. "Walkin' in water 'll slow us for sure, but I cain't see no other way ta 'vade dogs. One of us could maybe set a false trail off'n da bank ever' now an' ag'in, but I reckon dat won't throw off experience' dogs for long."

"See. Now yer thinkin' like prey. Dat's what'll keep ya alive. Bindle won't use our'n 'cause d'ey too friendly, too used to ya feedin' 'em an' making a fuss over 'em. Once't d'ey catched you, d'ey just 'spect a pet an' a belly rub an' off d'ey go afta squirrels. Ya can bet Massa Lonnegan will hire in da bounty hunters. He cain't tolerate ta lose three young field hands all at once't, an' he sure as hell gotta guarantee none of his other proptee get inspired by yer example an' start thinkin' a takin' a holiday from bondage."

"What's da moon at?" Malachi asked. "We want it waxin', not wanin'."

"No moon t'all las' night," Joseph said. "Good reason to leave nex' Satu'day. It waxin' by nex' Satu'day."

Old Mose nodded again. "Water only good ya keep in it. Jus' keep goin' ag'inst da flow. Even a swamp is fed by sumpin'. Find what feeds it and jus' keep goin' to da higher ground. Dat always take ya away from here. We's the low ground here, 'side the river. But if ya is truly goin', sooner is better. It gettin' cold fartha' north ya go. Take yer jackets an' yer hats. Goes wif out sayin'. Cold rains comin'. Snow up d'ere. Easy ta track ya in snow. Ya got no 'sperience wif snow dat stays on da ground. Snow a fearsome enemy on a empty belly. Ya got a long list of enemies. Rain, snow, cold, hunger, dogs, bounty hunters, ever'body scrabblin' fer Massa Lonnegan's reward, every slave owner out to make ab'slutely postive ya get catched and punished so bad... so bad..."

The old man paused to let this sink in.

Seth gave a little chuckle. "If we could get somma dat bad food inta Bindle, might give us a extra day."

"Now ya jus' fantasizin'," Old Mose said. "What ya gotta do is get north fast as ya can." Arthritic fingers fumbled three small pieces of crumpled paper from the top pocket of his overalls and gave one to each.

"I made these ta help ya nav'gate. Now pay 'tention. D'ose top dots is da constlation Orion. Two bright stars fer his head, three bright ones make his belt. See da star on da right side a his belt? Dat one's important. If the head tilt left, ya make a 'maginary line from da left top bright star through da star on da right side of his belt. Where dat 'maginary line touch da horizon, dat be south. If da head tilt right, ya make a 'maginary line from da right top bright star through da same star on da right side of da belt. Where dat line touch da horizon, dat be south."

"We'll practise every night," Joseph said. Seth and Malachi nodded their affirmation.

"Good. Now d'ose dots at da bottom of da paper... Dat constlation be da Drinkin' Gourd. It wheels an' tilts like

Orion, but it da best tool ta find Polaris, da North Star. Dat da one ya follow, da one ya wanna see all da time. See da two stars at da end of da gourd? Follow a line from da star at da bottom of da gourd's end ta da star at da top edge. Now heave your eye 'bout five times dat distance 'long dat same line and ya see da North Star. It ain't da brightest, but it always says north."

The three nodded again to show they understood.

"If anybody see you boys standin' in da dark, lookin' at a piece of paper an' studyin' da heavens, ya ain't smart enough ta run away."

"We be cautious as a cat sneakin' up on a alligator. We won't lose d'ese here instructions," Seth said.

"'Deed you won't! 'Cause while I take a break from jawin', you boys is gonna mem'rize d'ose dots, d'en you is gonna give me back d'ose papers in l'il bitty pieces and recite how ya gonna find north an' south."

Joseph was the first to give Old Mose his ripped up sky chart, followed by Malachi, then Seth. Old Mose had each precisely recite how to determine direction, then turned their attention to other practical considerations.

"Shoes. Ya ain't use' ta wearin' shoes in da fields much, but where you goin', ya need shoes. Take what ya got. D'ey slow ya down at first, 'specially in da water, but by-an'-by you be real happy ya got 'em. Bare feet jus' scream out 'Runaway!' Shoes say, 'Maybe I be on a errand for my massa.' Any meat ya leave wif, eat it first. Meat's heavy, goes bad easy. Potatoes? Too heavy. Take corn meal or oat meal. Meal doan weigh much, but a drink a water will make a han'ful of it swell in yer stomach, trick it inta thinkin' you'se eaten."

The old man was silent again for so long the three thought he might have dozed off. Eventually he stirred and asked, "What you doin' 'bout travellin' vittles?"

Malachi said, "We plannin' ta ration our field lunches so's ta have some travellin' food, but if we 'scape on Satu'day night, we maybe could raid da food put by fer Sunday's noon meal. Ever'body busy singin', dancin' at da bonfire, nobody notice us in da field hands' kitchen loadin' up."

"More good thinkin'. Wrap yer blankets round some straw, leave 'em on your beds, might fool somebody for ten minutes. D'ose blankets too thin, too ragged. Lift a horse blanket, cut it down to size if need be. Wrap whatever ya got in it, carry it on a stout stick, a stick thick 'nough ta stun a pig. Even a blanket piece help keep out da cold. Dat stick got a dozen uses. A old hoe handle serve good. Let yer shoulder carry da weight, not yer hand. An' doan forget somethin' dat holds water. A canteen from da field wagon be best. Steal some a d'em Lucifer matches from da hands' kitchen an' grease 'em wif a candle an' carry 'em in a roll of waxed cheesecloth in yer blanket."

"How we know when we's arrived in a free state?" Seth asked. "It wouldn't do ta ask someone if we wasn't there yet."

"First, ya gotta cross a mighty big river. Ohio. Ohio River. Some call it da River Jordan 'cause on t'other side is da Promise' Land. Doan you believe it! Yes, d'ere's abolitionists d'ere, but d'ere's a mighty powerful lot of bounty hunters lurkin' in Ohio too, jus' itchin' ta haul yer sorry ass back to Tennessee and make d'eir fortune on da back a Massa Lonnegan. Da real River Jordan, dat be a good ways farther north yet. Once ya cross dat one, you is truly free 'cause ya ain't in this country no more. You is where there ain't no slaves now. There was once, some, not as many as here, but some. But not now. Not now."

"How you know all dis?" Seth asked.

"Picked up some here, some d'ere. A runaway from down river got all way ta somewheres called Sandusky 'fore d'ey catched him, carted him back. He tole Tom an' Tom tole Dick an' Dick tole Harry an' Harry tole me."

"What happen' ta him?" Joseph asked.

"First d'ey whipped him 'til he was past feelin', d'en d'ey hanged him from a tree near da slave cabins. Left da body ripenin' in da hot sun. Dat massa, he said he chop a hand off anyone cuttin' him down."

Old Mose scratched his left shoulder, readjusted his hat, and let the ensuing silence drive the message home. Malachi looked off into the woodlot, Joseph bit at a thumbnail, and Seth worried a pebble with his foot. They avoided looking at each other.

"So, whatcha' gonna do? Stick t'gether an' get catched all at once, or split up an' get catched one at a time?"

"We was thinkin' a stayin' t'gether, sorta lookin' out for one 'nother," Seth said. "An' we ain't plannin' ta get catched at all. Ever!"

"I 'magine every wretched soul dat got catched said da same goddamn noble speech 'fore he set off. If ya travel three sep'rate ways... Alone, one might 'rouse less suspicion. Doan tell me no more details. What Old Mose doan know Old Mose cain't tell. Lemme know if ya change yer mind. Now leave me be so I can talk wif my missus."

"Thank you," they said, and each put a hand on the old man's shoulder as they left, as if touching a treasured talisman for good luck.

The Die is Cast

Saturday night went well at first. Malachi drew the short straw and left at dark to sneak down to the landing. With a small clasp knife liberated from the stable, he cut the painter on a skiff and pushed it into the main current to be miles downstream by first light. While Seth stood watch, ready to distract any wanderers, Joseph surreptitiously recovered the travelling bundles from their hiding place in the haymow and shoved them under his wooden bunk in the cabin. The singing and dancing was well underway when Malachi returned. Each made a point of being seen at various points around the bonfire before fading into the darkness. In half an hour, they had crossed the east fields and were heading upstream in the creek.

Cloud cover diffused the weak moonlight and suggested a possibility of rain. Rain would be an ally once they left the creek, but coming now, it would quench the bonfire and drive the revellers into the cabins earlier. Everyone would pretend not to notice their absence. Old Mose would make certain of that. Still, it was better to be long gone before the whispers began.

Within twenty yards, they realized they had greatly overestimated their rate of progress. The weight of water in wet shoes slowed them to a plod, each step demanding significantly more energy than its dry land equivalent. Every slip and fall added weight to clothing and bundles. When the creek flowed through fields, ambient light permitted quicker speed. Forest cover blanketed them in total darkness. They tried not to touch the banks, to leave no trace of their passage for the dogs they knew must come, but this was impossible. So was silence. Some noise was necessary to keep the group together. Branches whipped their faces where the creek narrowed. Fallen trees impeded them most; an ankle snapped in the traverse would be disastrous. Biting insects, rustlings, animal calls, slitherings in the night — each a reminder they had exchanged one unwelcoming world for another. By first light, they had travelled only a few inadequate miles.

On their right, a small stream gurgled its contribution to the creek. They sloshed up it for a couple of minutes, then separated into a triangle about a hundred yards apart to relieve themselves and make the job of the dogs more difficult. They had considered evacuating bowels and bladders in the water, then realized that the malodorous ribbon diffusing down the watercourse would be a gift to the dogs. Back in the creek, they pushed on. There was no alternative.

Sunday. The day they hoped to leave Lonnegan's plantation many miles behind. It was not to be. The creek bottlenecked to a few yards, then widened into the marsh it drained. To wade in waist deep water near the left bank was the only way forward, the sucking mud halfway to their knees. They clambered over fallen timbers, bulled through head high cattails, frightened mud turtles from favourite sunning logs, and were in turn startled by rattlesnakes and cottonmouths lethargic with cold. Pondweed, coontail and water lilies dripping from their feet, avoiding masses of water willow, they foolishly congratulated themselves on slogging through terrain which would be an extreme challenge to pursuing dogs until they looked behind and saw the trail they had created through the wetland vegetation.

"Dis be Hell," Seth muttered as they plodded on. "I always figured Hell ta be hot, but dis water so goddamn cold it surely be givin' us a ordeal."

"Dis ain't Hell", Joseph argued. "It be a Calvary for sure, but it ain't Hell. You wanna see Hell, you wait 'til we is caught an' dragged back ta Massa Lonnegan. D'en you be in Hell." They stopped for a moment to determine the optimum path forward. Each assessed their collective condition. Eyes betrayed the level of fatigue. Each surveyed the others' bite-swollen, splotchy faces, scratched hands, muddy clothes. Each was exhausted, yet in the others he saw a reflection of his own intransigent determination.

They took a five minute break on a blowdown tree, its branches fingering pickerelweed in deeper water. A high sun confirmed what their stomachs already knew, but this was not the place to eat. Canteens lighter by too much, they pushed on.

A slow mile later, sedges replaced water lilies as the water near the edge became shallow. Greater speed brought higher spirits, spirits which deflated once they entered the upper creek that fed the marsh. Through gloomy forest they followed its twisting, snaking, frustrating course for miles, accomplishing little straight line distance. It was Malachi who first noticed the difference in the bottom. He pointed to his feet. "Sand, not mud."

Gradually the sand became pebbles, then increasingly larger rocks until they were walking through clear water burbling over small rock ledges. Canteens replenished, on they trudged under the dark canopy. Half an hour later, they rounded a bend to find a primitive, square timbered bridge across the creek. With a dreamlike slowness, they removed squelching work boots from pruned feet and stretched out on the sun-warmed planks in the full gold open to give aching legs a respite. Rest was trumped by a need for sustenance. Swishing slabs of pork in the water to remove the salt and retrieving soggy cornpone from their bundles, they savoured their first true meal since leaving the plantation. Too tired to set a watch, they dozed, stinking in their freedom, until Seth roused them from their stupor and goaded them back into their boots, into the water, and into the forest.

By the sun, they knew they were travelling mostly east. Their only strategy was to put as many watery miles as possible between themselves and Lonnegan's plantation. Where they bordered two small swamps the footing was once again mud, but they knew from the quicker current and the pebblier bottoms of the intake streams that the land was rising. At dusk, in a tiny meadow at the edge of a pond encircled by mature trees, they constructed a rough lean-to from fallen branches and fanned out their horse blankets over top to dry.

Malachi baited a hook with grubs found under a rotting log. In five throws of the line he landed three fish a foot long, scaled and gutted them with the stolen knife, and within ten minutes had them skewered and steaming above Joseph's small fire. A handful of corn meal and an apple completed their meal.

"Should be fartha' 'long by now, but cain't be helped," Malachi pointed out. "Lucifers was good 'vice from Old Mose. Never did have much luck scarin' up a flame wif a flint an' steel."

"Me neither," Seth agreed. "We sure did pick a in-between time ta run off. Some bugs still bitin', snakes jus' tryin' ta get d'emselves stepped on, an' yet dat water freezin' da blood in my feet."

"We gotta make distance tomorrow," Joseph said. "We gotta make a decision 'bout when we leave da water an' head nort'. Travellin' cross country mighty tirin', but we gonna meet people on a road."

"Depends if the moon is shinin', don't it?" Malachi asked. "Make better time on a road, slip off d'edge inta da woods, somebody come. Course, we cain't always count on travellin' where da gitting off an' hidin' is good."

"Maybe we ain't far enough east to start nort'. Maybe we should stay wif da water tomorra, see what da weather does. Ain't much use headin' nort' if we cain't see da sun or da stars," Joseph added. "Agreed?"

"'Greed," they said in unison.

Despite their fatigue, they slept poorly, using hats for pillows and thankful for the slim warmth of their jackets. They daren't maintain a smoky fire to discourage the ubiquitous chiggers and late season mosquitoes. Malachi dreamt of wolves coursing through a foggy forest, Seth of a sun-dried black corpse slowly revolving at the end of a hangman's rope. In Joseph's dream he was sitting beside Ellie at a Sunday noon meal attended by no one else but Cicero.

They woke to a thin sun failing to drive away a grey mist over the pond. While Seth and Joseph disassembled the lean-to, Malachi tried several throws of the line; no fish were interested. Last night's cold ashes were hidden beneath the log where he had searched for grubs. Flattened grass was finger-combed to hide where they had slept. A handful of corn meal washed down with water and half a loaf of soggy bread already starting to mould sufficed for breakfast.

Dulled by the reality of their travails, they pictured Bindle searching the assembly of field hands as they awaited their daily tasks, him walking up to the plantation house, hat in hand, to inform Master that three field hands were missing.

They shouldered their bundles. There was no talk.

Lonnegan Flags a Boat

Cicero let Bindle, hat in hand, enter through the side door and motioned for him to wait there. "Mister Lonnegan is finishing his morning ablutions and will attend upon you shortly," he explained. "I shall inform him you wish to conference."

"No need, Cicero. Mister Lonnegan is here," the master said, entering the room while wiping away the last vestiges of shaving soap lather with a white towel. His grey trousers were perfectly pressed to a sharp crease, his white linen shirt immaculate, but he had not yet donned his waistcoat. "A visit this early in the morning can only mean trouble. Tell me I'm wrong, Mister Bindle."

"You are not wrong, sir."

"Step into my office. Cicero, we will not be disturbed. Coffee, the morning meal, they can wait. Inform Mrs. Lonnegan she may commence breakfast without me. I shall join her soon."

Cicero bowed ever so slightly and left the room. Lonnegan led Bindle into a mahogany-panelled room lighted by large windows on two sides, sat in a swivel chair behind a six foot long mahogany desk, retrieved a cigar from a pasteboard box on its left front corner, scratched a match on the box lid, puffed the cigar into life, and blew fragrant blue smoke toward the tin ceiling. He leaned back in the chair and took two more long draws from his cigar. Bindle, still standing, hat in hand, was not offered a chair or a cigar.

Lonnegan moved a massive accounts book with a faded green leather cover from its place of honour in the center of the desk and leaned on his elbows, thumbs touching his lips, fingers arched, the cigar pointing to a window. He looked unblinking at Bindle.

"Leave nothing out," he said.

"Three missing from the morning bell. Malachi, the big one. Joseph, and little Seth. They bunk together in cabin seven. Me and my boys interrogated the field hands one by one. Every goddamn one spewed out the same story. Malachi, Joseph and Seth were at the gathering on Saturday night. No one remembers seeing them on Sunday, but Old Mose says that's because everyone thought they had eaten something gone off and had the shits. No one has reported anything missing except horse blankets from the stables. That's it."

The master said nothing. He rubbed the top of his left ear, a habitual gesture, leaned back in his chair, and savoured two more slow draws on his cigar. He leaned forward and looked out a window. He stubbed out the cigar in a black glass ashtray, placed his hands palms down on the desk, looked at Bindle, and in a calm voice began.

"Three at once. One is a toll I will not pay. This plantation can not afford to lose one. Not one, goddamn it. But three... The loss of property is always painful, but what really stings is the ingratitude. Jesus H. Christ, do these simpletons think they can survive outside my care? You, Mister Bindle, you have not been in my employ overly long, but I see in you the very model of the perfect overseer, and I applaud you for it. Be assured your position here is safe. This is a straightforward problem with a straightforward solution. They must be returned to face a harsh punishment, a public punishment, a retribution so convincing, so final, so... so... so... so brutal the others will be inoculated against this contagion. Otherwise, it will spread like a plague. So, what's to be done?"

Mister Bindle considered this a rhetorical question and said nothing.

Lonnegan stood, pushed his chair back, walked over to the north window, and studied the view. He hooked his thumbs in his trouser pockets. There was a long silence. Finally, Lonnegan pulled on a red cord with a gold tassel hanging from the ceiling in the corner of the room. Almost instantly, Cicero appeared.

"Cicero, send a boy down to the dock to put up the flag for a downstream boat. Pack an overnight bag for me and one for yourself; we have business in Memphis. Inform Mrs. Lonnegan we may be gone two days or longer, and tell her Mister Bindle will be visiting the neighbours to spread the word about three runaways. No... On second thought, tell her one of his subordinates will do it."

Cicero bowed ever so slightly again and left as silent as a cat. Bindle was about to leave as well when Lonnegan closed his office door. "Have a seat, Mister Bindle. There is one other item of business that requires our attention."

Lonnegan resumed his swivel chair. Bindle pulled a chair from the corner and sat opposite the desk. Lonnegan slid the cigar box toward himself, took a fresh cigar, and offered the open box to Bindle. He lit Bindle's cigar before his own. They smoked in silence for several minutes.

Finally, Lonnegan said, "Truly, there is no need for you to visit the neighbours today. You and I both know who is behind this discontent. He was recalcitrant in his prime, and he continues to stir up trouble in his dotage, always the malcontent, always picking at the sore. Frankly, Bindle, I am tired of feeding that old son of a bitch. I think you'll find him down at the hands' cemetery sometime today, once he's talked to his bees and everyone's gone to the fields. Take a close weave sack with you, and be quick. You can piss on it if you like; it will work better if it's wet. Are we agreed he died of a heart attack?"

Bindle took a long draw from his cigar and exhaled slowly toward the gold tassel. He gazed a thousand yards through its smoke, then mashed the cigar stub in the ashtray. "A heart attack it is," he said, and closed the office door behind him as he left.

The Business of Bounty Hunting

They did not wait long for a downstream boat. A field hand assigned to carry their bags rowed them out to a large sternwheel whose first mate huffed something about leaving the channel for only two until Cicero added two silver dollars to their fare. Upon a late arrival at Beau Lonnegan's favourite hotel in Memphis, they found the desk clerk in a fluster. "We weren't expecting you on such short notice, sir. If you would be good enough to have a seat in the bar, we will have two adjoining rooms cleared as soon as possible for you and your manservant. Do you wish to enjoy the usual amenities during your stay with us?"

"Our business here will be expeditious, so we will forego the pleasure of the ladies on this occasion. My man will require a boy to deliver a message. Find one immediately. We have not enjoyed noteworthy gastronomic fare in our travels, therefore the dining room will be preferable to the bar."

"Very good, sir. I believe the dining room is serving a delightful galantine this week and the orange duck is always popular. I shall inform you myself when the rooms are prepared." With a stiff bow from the waist reciprocated by a small nod from Lonnegan, the clerk returned to his post.

While Lonnegan ordered their meal and brandies, Cicero sent a messenger to inform Ragg and Associates their establishment could expect a visit first thing in the morning.

Aeneas Ragg, a short, muscular, barrel chested man, was fast becoming a Memphis institution. Tiny craters in a fleshy face spoke of smallpox in the distant past. Always dishevelled, his greying hair greasy and unkempt, his personal hygiene questionable, Ragg was a more prosperous businessman than his appearance would suggest. His uniform was a brown leather vest over a food-stained white shirt and a wide brown belt which held up fawn breeches that disappeared into knee-high brown riding boots. He habitually carried a short riding crop with which he accentuated conversations. His first appointment of the day found him stretching the crop between two hands, feet on a cluttered desk, and lounging back in a captain's chair. He did not rise when Lonnegan and his servant entered. Cicero assumed a station just inside the door.

By way of greeting, Ragg motioned to a matching captain's chair in front of his desk. Lonnegan sat, relaxed, crossed his left leg over his right, and studied the man behind the desk.

"Who, when, where, why and how?" Ragg asked.

"Three males. Field hands. Two late teens, one mid-twenties. Probably Saturday night last. Possibly Sunday morning. No idea where. You know why. Either snagged a skiff or took to the woods."

"Three is expensive."

"I know. I also know you have a reputation for getting results. I want results. The results are more important to me than the money."

"What exactly are the results you want?"

"Dead or alive. Alive is better but dead if necessary. Alive, I will ensure no one on my plantation will have the slightest inclination to follow their example. In brief, my present intention is to hang one, cauterize the tongues of the other two. Amputations limit their work usefulness, as my father and I have discovered. My manservant suggests one should be gelded. We'll see."

With his left arm, Ragg swept the desk clutter enough to create a level area, pulled open the top right drawer, removed two smudged glasses and a bottle of whiskey, poured three fingers, and offered one to Lonnegan.

"Bit early," Lonnegan said.

Ragg waved a dismissive hand. "Property doesn't get returned until they gets caught. They doesn't get caught until me and my crew know where to find 'em. We won't know where to find 'em until we have discussed circumstances. Also, they doesn't get caught — or returned — unless I has my money. So, you see Mister Lonnegan, the whiskey is a toast to our mutually beneficial business relationship. I am assuming we can do business, you and me."

Lonnegan raised his glass to some point above Ragg's head and took a drink. Seeing there was no room on his side of the desk, he placed the glass on the floor beside his chair, withdrew an envelope from an inner pocket of his morning coat with his left hand, and tossed it onto the desk. "You will find my bank draft for one thousand dollars in that envelope. Think of it as your retainer. I said I want results.

I expect results. Does that fit into your assumption we can do business?"

"Yes, I think we can, I think we can. Of course, my fee will ultimately depend on what transpires in the hunt, but we seem to be off to a good beginning. Details now. Bought or bred on your plantation? Any hint of unrest, rebellion, a lack of servile attitude evident before this?"

"Malachi is over six feet tall, two hundred sixty, maybe two hundred seventy pounds or more, probably about twenty-five years old. He requires a firm hand from time to time. Mister Bindle, my overseer, keeps a close watch on him. I purchased Malachi from Nathan Forrest here in Memphis for top money — but he's strong, worth two regular field hands for heavy work. He's quick and agile for such a big man.

Joseph and Seth are home stock, bred on the plantation. Joseph is nineteen, as is Seth. Joseph is about five ten, of medium build, in good health, good musculature, good teeth, sturdy, intelligent, a fine-looking specimen of his race. His mother died in the fields three, maybe four years ago. Seth's mother died in childbirth; he never did thrive. Seth is small in stature, a wiry little man, wouldn't be more than five three, five four tops. He's not as physically strong as the other two, but he's clever, and I would have moved him from the fields into the household if I did not already have enough house servants. I planned to have him take over the beehives when I'm through with the old man who presently looks after them, assuming Seth could learn his secrets. This old man has a way of superimposing a skep on a gum log that fools the bees into leaving the honey chamber when he smokes them. I thought Seth could apply himself to beekeeping; Joseph is better suited for field labour."

"Any experience outside the plantation? What I mean is, have any of the three travelled far enough to acquire an understanding of the lay of the land?" Ragg asked.

"Joseph and Seth have been no more than five, maybe eight miles — only when I day-rented them out to neighbours. Malachi came from a plantation below Memphis."

"Where is your plantation?"

"On the river, Tennessee side, half day or so by steamboat to Memphis downstream, depending on the current. Much of a day upstream, more when the river's in flood."

"Three together. Not coupled. Married don't run off much and leave a spouse or little ones behind. No chance they've been stolen by abolitionists. Not here. Not three. In your opinion, will they stay together? Did they steal anything from you when they left?"

"They stole themselves, goddamn it. They're my property, and I want my property back! Will they stick together? Joseph might try to run alone, but Seth would never have left on his own. They had a push from someone, but that is being looked after."

Ragg drained his glass and said nothing. "Any other theft? Horses, a wagon?" he prodded.

"Some old blankets. Nothing consequential." Lonnegan pointed with a thumb over his left shoulder. "My man thought to ask if anything was missing while we waited for the boat. A skiff has disappeared, but the oars weren't in it."

"That is an important item. Now, Mister Lonnegan, this is the process. There are only two ways runners can escape on their own. They may have stole a boat and are heading up the river, but in my experience that is highly unlikely. The current will limit their progress and they must travel in the dark. They sure as hell ain't drifting south. Field hands won't have much competence with river matters. I'll have one of my men post bills and spread the word up the river just in case I'm wrong. But I'm not wrong.

They are most certainly headed into the bottom-land marshes. They will have picked up the notion we will chase them down with the dogs — which we would have if the trail was day old fresh. The fear of dogs will keep them in the wet, and that's slow goin'. However, there's a lot of wet for pursuers to splash around in, so the best way to hunt 'em down now is to advertise in the back country what we're lookin' for. Maybe me and my crew will be unlucky and some locals will apprehend them, but I expect any push from the amateurs will just spur 'em to greater speed. That's good for us, 'cause they'll run out of steam and make mistakes."

Lonnegan picked up his whiskey from the floor, finished it, and let Ragg talk on.

"They're heading for the Ohio, of course. Runners usually head east, then north, thinkin' they'll reach the higher country where it dries out. That's good for us too, 'cause they don't realize the river wanders westerly nearer the Kentucky border, so they'll bog down in the same wet hell they thought they'd escaped. They go north, they hit water. They go northeast, they hit water. There's enough water for Noah to get nostalgic any which way they choose. Better to go south a bit first, then east a long ways before cuttin' north, but they won't know that, bein' homebodies. They gotta get food from somewheres. People 'll notice when somethin' goes missing. If they don't, their dogs will. See where I'm goin' with this, Mister Lonnegan? There's a natural bottleneck on the Kentucky border near the Mississippi. That's where we intercept them. That's where we get most."

"Dead or alive," Lonnegan said.

"Dead or alive. They'll be so worn down to a nub with their little holiday in the back country, won't take much more'n a horse runnin' at 'em and a tap on the head. Chains seal the runnin' game."

Lonnegan rubbed his left ear. "And if they get help?"

"Abolitionists, you mean? Not all that many active between here and the Ohio. It's not just me in the business, Mister Lonnegan. I'm in touch with a dozen or more professional hunters who will keep an eye open. They'll uncover information — for a fee. My profit will be reduced if they catch your property, so I'd rather catch 'em myself."

"I want this simple and straightforward. I don't intend to squander money on sightings or hearsay."

Ragg chuckled. "It don't work like that, Mister Lonnegan. You post an attractive reward. Anyone who claims it has to work through me, so I get a cut — to be negotiated with whomever. My network knows they get fair recompense from me — that's looking after business with the long view. My crew is good and my network is good. That's why you are dealing with 'Ragg and Associates' rather than 'Ragg'. If I catch 'em, I get the whole reward plus my fees."

"Which are what, precisely?"

"Precisely fifteen dollars a week for each of my employees active in the chase and thirty dollars a week for me. Plus expenses."

"Tell me about the expenses."

"All our cash outlay. Expenses for up to three months. If they aren't caught by then, we renew our agreement, or you may cancel it. Outlay could be anything from steamboat tickets to hotel meals. All expenses. I warned you this would be expensive."

"It's only too steep if I don't get results."

"You understand I can not give you a guarantee we'll catch these three. But I can guarantee you will find no fault with our effort. Trust me, sir. Our record is good, our net is good. I keep our associates sweet with three little tricks I got up my sleeve. Number one, pay well. Number two, pay promptly. Number three is the clincher. I pay in English pounds. None of your here-today-gone-tomorrow state banknotes for my people. Internationally recognized and good in any state. And our net is spread wide. Example: we've got some on the Ohio, some as far as the Canadas. We've got an old codger up on the state border who has accumulated a sizeable nest egg from working for me. He's only got one leg, but he's caught his share and more. He pretends to be an abolitionist and helps out runaways, then he either signals while they're asleep or he sends them right into our people waitin' for 'em."

"The reward. I was thinking a thousand dollars for Malachi, seven hundred for Joseph, two hundred for Seth."

"Generous. More than generous. I appreciate that you appreciate what gets results. It is truly easy to spend other people's money, but may I suggest three hundred for the little one? That makes the total two thousand for the bunch. Two thousand dollars is a powerful dose of motivation. I'll personally see my printer this afternoon if we have a deal. Do we have a deal?"

"We have a deal." Lonnegan began to rise and stretch out his hand to complete the transaction. Ragg waved him back down into his chair and reached for the whiskey.

"It is a pleasure to do business with a gentleman of your refinement, sir. Of course you understand there would be an extra fee should you require our services for the hanging or the gelding. It's best done off-site. Stirs up resentment, like ringing your own bull."

"Thank you, but that won't be necessary. I can handle the details myself."

A Thorn in the Foot

Always they chose the left side of any wetland they encountered, hoping it was the north side. The streams became narrower and faster as they climbed away from the Mississippi bottom-lands. By mid-morning the mist was burned off, the sun promised a cloudless day, and a breeze from their backs cooled their push through mile after mile. At noon, they halted for the other half of the loaf and another handful of meal. After refilling the canteens, they stripped down to wash the mud out of their filthy overalls and shirts, then plodded on again, thankful for the breeze that dried them above the waterline.

Following the stream around a curve and out of the forest, they discovered another pond flanked by meadows and tall trees. A better night's sleep might have prevented their inattention. They were almost to the far end when they heard feminine laughter. Dropping flat, then taking cover behind a stand of cattails, they peered from their refuge. Not forty yards away were two naked women, about twenty years old, cavorting in the cool water, giggling, splashing each other with the heels of their hands, floating, diving, twisting, with glistening breasts and legs and buttocks white as a trout's belly. Just ahead were two heaps of garments piled on the bank, poorly guarded by two horses, horses that were tethered to a sapling, horses that were looking straight at them, ears pricked in curiosity.

The three gazed, transfixed. Numbingly beautiful, naked, young white women were as far beyond their limited experience as aliens. Treading water, the mermaids paused in their frolic to catch their breath. One looked to see what drew the horses' attention. She screamed and pointed.

Seth whispered, "Stay down! Back off from da bank. They'll be lookin' at me while you'se makes a run for it. If you'se stay low, away from da edge, d'ey cain't tell how many we be. I'll catch ya up real soon."

He didn't wait for an answer but half ran, half stumbled toward the piles of clothes. Scooping them up, he threw them into the pond, then turned to untie the horses and shoo them away. The screaming and his unfamiliarity made them dance skittishly, so he abandoned the idea and ran toward the denser trees at the end of the pond as fast as wet clothes, saturated shoes, and fatigue would allow. Not until he found Joseph and Malachi waiting for him behind trees shading a tiny stream did he realize he had left his bundle behind.

Wordlessly, they sloshed upstream through more floodplain until the water was below the top of their shoes. A fallen timber across the little stream offered an excuse to sit and assess their situation. They did not look at one another, and no one spoke.

"Bad!" Joseph said finally. "Bad! Back d'ere was bad luck. Bad luck."

"What we gonna do now?" Malachi asked. "We got no idea how soon d'ose girls gonna be to where d'ey gonna tell somebody d'ey see'd us an' we doan know what d'ey's gonna say. Sure as fleas on a dog d'ey knows we ain't where we b'long, 'specially d'ey stumble on Seth's trappin's."

Seth nodded slowly. "It t'was only me what got see'd. Maybe. Maybe you two should cut north. I'll keep on goin' east and leave sign so dat I be da one gettin' chased, and you two can get away clean. Maybe safer we split up anyway."

Joseph waved the idea away. "Too soon to split up. An' we be findin' drier, higher groun' da further east we go. Let's go on 'til we comes across a road, d'en we decide what ta do next. Dat way Malachi and me can share provisions — whatever we got left — wif you, Seth. Dat okay wif you, Malachi?"

"Yup. Ain't no need to worry 'bout sharin' cause d'ere's precious little ta share. All we got is da two canteens and 'bout a pound and a half, maybe two, of meal. Salt pork's gone mostly. Got some withered apples. I think we should eat a han'ful of meal right now, keep us going 'til dark, push on far an' fast as we can. You knows we be missed by now."

There was no argument. On they trudged, cursing their luck to be discovered so soon. At a spring burbling from a hillside, the tiny stream ended. They refilled canteens. The forest thinned. The more the country opened, the more they missed the cover of dense trees and the more vulnerable they felt. North and south, they could see farms and plantations. They picked their way through more forest directly in their path, only to find it was a woodlot at the bottom end of a harvested corn field.

Voices. They halted a few yards in from the edge of the trees to watch two Black men, one substantially older than the other, repair a fence with cedar rails stacked on a nearby wagon, at the front of which an ancient draft horse dozed peacefully in the late afternoon sun. The three relaxed, and Joseph stepped out of the forest.

"We's lost and on da run. We be mighty grateful if ya could help us." As soon as he uttered the words he thought, *damn, I should have said, "I'm lost."*

There was no reaction. The older of the two did not look in his direction. He carried a fragment of broken rail to the edge of the woodlot and said, "We heard ya comin' through the woods. How many be ya?"

"Three. We's run off an' gettin' powerful hungry. We be travellin' east mostly, from down on da river, an' we not sure where ta go next."

The older man said nothing as he placed a new rail on the fence. The younger positioned a diagonal, pretending not to know a dialogue was going on.

"It go pretty hard with us helpin' runaways, anyone find out," the old man said.

"Ain't no one here gonna mention any help, but we is in tight straits and we sure could use any food you is willin' to part wif."

The younger stared at a faraway house while the other said nothing as he unloaded rails from the wagon.

"This is how it must be," the older one said, once the wagon was empty. He did not make eye contact and stared into the distance as well. "You stay in these here woods an' I'll send a boy with what we can scare up. Look at the sack he packin'. Strap o'er the right shoulder, coast is clear an' ya can push on away from the big river. Strap o'er the left shoulder, trouble pokin' aroun', ya best stay in the woods fer another day. No fire, hear? You get caught, no one here see'd you or talked to you. You got all that? Left mean stay where you is at."

Joseph nodded and sat down in the tall weeds behind the fence as the workers left. In his exhausted state, all he could mutter was "We is mighty grateful. Mighty grateful."

A few yards into the woods, they stretched out under a red oak with nothing to do but wait. At dusk, a small boy about eleven years old ambled along the fence line. Barefoot, clothed in an overlong faded blue shirt of a slave, he reached into the bordering weeds periodically to forage specific plants, which from a distance would appear to drop into a dirty canvas sack whose single strap hung from his left shoulder.

When he neared the latitude of the runners, he sat down facing into the field, apparently to remove a thorn from his left foot. He dumped the contents of the sack into the weeds, stood, and resumed his foraging, never looking beyond the fence.

They waited until the boy was out of sight before Seth crawled to the field's edge to retrieve the offering. In the dying twilight, they surveyed their wealth. There were three bags of rice, each tied with twine. Wrapped in brown paper twists in a yard square of cotton they discovered black beans, dried peas, pumpkin seeds, corn meal, and three small loaves of hardtack bread. There was a small jar of honey. And most wonderful of all, a chicken. A whole roasted chicken.

Malachi divided this miracle into thirds with the clasp knife. No sound except the chewing of the glorious fowl and the sucking of greasy fingers was heard for the next quarter hour. Soon the oily juice triggered their bowels and prompted a dash behind neighbouring trees. No one complained. No one could remember a tastier meal.

Fleeing South

No shelter and no fire meant a damp, toss and snort, chill night. It was Joseph who heard whistling at first dawn and shook the others awake. Seth crawled through the dewy field-side weeds to see last night's small boy opposite their bed-down. There was no pretence of secrecy. The boy was looking straight at them.

"Pa, he say ta run. Run right now, 'fore the house up. The missus got suspect when she saw vittles bein' squirreled. Pa says she added a chicken and honey herself, so's you'd think you'se safe. Massa gone to rouse some neighbours. Ya gotta run! Ya gotta run right now, fore you'se gets caught."

"Where to? Which direction best?" Seth asked, but the boy was already in full retreat.

In less than a minute, they were on the move. Cold, stiff, wet as Seth with dew, they half ran, half stumbled along the edge of the woodlot away from the distant buildings. They stopped to catch their breath only when they reached the cover of a tangle of bushes a mile or more from their bed-down.

"We be headin' south, but no matter, we's gotta be headin' somewheres dat doan be dangersome, and we got ta run smart. Specially if d'ey's got dogs — or horses," Malachi said.

Joseph agreed. "Let's keep movin' 'til full sun-up, put some distance 'tween our bed-down spot and us. D'en we can decide our next move."

Seth and Malachi just nodded their heads and followed him as he fought his way out of the tangle.

About mid-morning, they stopped to drink from a small creek. Seth created a shoulder stick from a broken branch while the other two fashioned a new bundle from the square of cotton and divided their provisions into three.

"What we gonna do?" Seth asked. "By da sun, we goin' south. We doan wanna go south."

"Maybe we do, least for a little while," Joseph said. "Chasers 'spectin' us ta go east or nort'. Maybe we gain more time if we go sout' fer a day, maybe two."

"Don't much matter if d'ey's got dogs. Dogs ain't 'spectin' us ta go any pa'ticlar direction 'cept da one we's takin'," Malachi said. "I figure it dis way. We can follow dis here creek, but it'll peter out once we get past any feeder streams. I doubt it'll fool dogs too much. We gotta be somewheres dogs get confused."

"Where's dat?" Seth asked.

"I dunno. But it's gonna be near where dis creek get too narrow to be any use ta us. So we might as well get movin'."

Malachi was right. About noon the stream was so diminished they knew they were leaving scent as they brushed foliage on the bank. A huge pine on a nearby grassy knoll dominated an open glade. Seth used a leaning log to access a bottom branch, then climbed higher to get a view of the surrounding country and listen for sounds of pursuit. "D'ere's a marsh up ahead, maybe four, five hundred yards. Dat's what dis l'il creek drain. If we could maybe lure d'em dogs inta thinkin' we's gone inta dat marsh, maybe d'ey get confused like Malachi said."

There was no more reasonable option. Seth dropped down out of the tree and the three of them followed the creek into the deeper water, touching nearby bushes as they went. They voided bladders on a cluster of water willows, then backtracked, brushing away their trail from the creek to the pine with broken branches, and rubbed the tree all round with vegetation they had harvested from the marsh. Joseph wrapped the water weeds around a stick and threw it as far away from the tree as he could. Seth ascended the propped log first and caught the bundles as Joseph chucked them up to him. Then he offered a hand to Malachi, who was less clumsy than Joseph in reaching a sit-able branch. With great difficulty, Malachi pulled up the log, and the three manhandled it to lean on some supporting branches. It didn't appear completely natural, but they didn't want to leave evidence of their scent at the bottom of the pine.

"Gonna be here 'til we sure nobody comin', so better get comf'table," Malachi said. He climbed higher until he found two branches he could use as a chair and made sure there was sufficient foliage to obscure his bulk from the ground. Seth and Joseph followed his example. All were hungry but feared food smells might be detected by dogs. Joseph broke into the supply of pumpkin seeds, and these and water from a canteen somewhat appeased empty stomachs.

They munched in silence, listening for any hint of dogs or horses, then tried to nap on their respective perches, backs against the massive trunk, to relieve the monotony. The sun was past mid-afternoon when Joseph said, "I'm stiff and sore and dis branch, it be growin' inta my ass. Cain't stay here much longer. Sure as hell cain't sleep up here t'night. Don't need no dogs to smell us. I can smell us, we so stale. I'se gonna use dat creek water to unstale once I'se hit da ground."

Malachi agreed. "Dis a poor s'cuse fer a campout. I doan reckon I'm much good ta las' more'n a hour more. Seems d'ere ain't no one chasin' us after all."

Seth stretched and said, "We doan know how d'eys got d'emselves organized, dat master and da neighbours. We got maybe an hour, maybe two or three, jump on 'em, an' maybe d'eys gotta round up a herd a dogs an' we ain't bein' told as a courtesy what's happenin', so I is gonna sit here 'til dat sun touches d'ose trees over d'ere 'fore I resettle my hurtin' body onta dat comfo'table ground down d'ere."

Two more wretched, miserable hours passed as they fidgeted on their respective branches, backs against the trunk. Malachi woke from a doze, yawned, and stretched his arms. Joseph hunched his shoulders, stretched his arms in front with fingers intertwined, and stood on a lower branch to regain circulation in his legs. He took another swig from the canteen and passed it to Malachi. "Don't drink too much," he advised. "A yella piss stream gonna tell anybody below ta look up." Above them in upper branches, Seth remained motionless, apparently asleep. A light breeze from the west stirred the pine needles.

Malachi had just said, "Cain't stand any more a dis. I gotta get down," when Seth lowered his head and put a finger to his lips.

Joseph and Malachi glanced at each other to confirm the faintest of dreaded sounds, the baying of hounds following a trail.

There was nothing to do but wait. Joseph and Malachi pulled the handles out of their bundles. Seth snorted. "You gonna fight off hunters wif a stick? Hell, boys, d'ey can shoot us outta dis tree an' we ain't gonna be able ta do nuthin' 'bout it. We jus' gotta stay still as mice an' trust da false trail inta da marsh works ta addle d'ose dogs. If it don't, sticks ain't gonna be much help."

They waited, each minute an hour. Joseph saw that Malachi was frozen in his perch, eyes squinted shut, his face contorted, as if by not letting in the light he could keep the sound out as well. Seth was trembling with fear.

"Seth," Joseph said, "you be shiverin' like you'se cold. You get yer shiverin' over when da dogs get here. We gotta not make any distraction t'all. Ya said so yerself. 'Still as mice,' ya said."

Seth nodded but made no reply. The dogs were nearer now. Soon they could hear the baying of individuals. *It don't sound like a big pack*, Joseph thought. *It don't need to be a big pack to bring us grief. It jus' need to have one smart dog.*

Above the cacophony of canine pursuit, their ears picked up the drum of horses' hooves. The dogs did not come in a straight line but followed the banks of the little creek, crossing and recrossing, the momentum of the scent carrying them past the glade. A quarter minute later, five horsemen trotted past, wearing slouch hats, blue cotton shirts, and broadcloth work pants held up with suspenders. Three had muskets, one a pistol, the fifth a coil of rope.

"We knows d'ere ain't no scent trail outa dat marsh, but d'ey doan know it. Wonder how long it take for d'em dogs to tell 'em," Malachi muttered in a low voice.

"We has gotta stay put 'til we's positive d'ey has left da neighbourhood. We doan want no surprises," Seth replied.

"I ain't got no argument wif dat," Joseph said.

Straining their ears to pinpoint the whereabouts of their enemy, they shifted on their perches, ready to freeze movement at the slightest sound.

The sun was an hour and some from setting when the entourage of men, dogs, and horses returned. Their hope that the group would simply trot by in failure evaporated when the lead rider reined in and alighted from his horse on the grassy knoll right under the pine.

"My horse will thank me if I lighten the load," he said, as he relieved himself against the huge pine. Two others followed suit. The man with the rope lit a pipe and blew the aromatic smoke into the air, looking after it as it dissipated. The dogs milled about slowly, heads down in fatigue and shame that their quarry had eluded them. One sniffed at the tree near to the dribble of urine from the first rider. With his foot, the rider with the pistol pushed it away and urinated on the tree. "The creek's right there if you're thirsty," he said, and the other men laughed.

"Can't quite figure out where we lost the spoor," the man with the rope said. "My dogs are as good as any, and if they can't find a trail, then hell, there ain't one to be found. You would think they're still in the marsh, but they ain't, or we could've seen 'em."

"It's possible they doubled back on their trail," the pistol said.

"I doubt it," the lead rider replied, shaking his head. "If they doubled back, the dogs would've picked up the new trail or we would've over-run 'em coming back. No, I'm wondering if maybe they were in the water all along, breathing through hollow reeds. We shoulda spread out more, 'cause they couldn't have stayed under long. Water's too cold. I wish we'd thought of that earlier."

"And I wish we knew what they was worth," the man with the rope said. "On reflection, maybe it's better we don't know how much money we lost today. We'll just pretend this excursion was to exercise the dogs and horses." The others laughed again. "This jaw wagging ain't gonna get us home before dark. I gotta let the boy out of the cellar; I promised him I wouldn't whup him if he told me the truth."

As they mounted, the dog which had been kicked away from the urine looked into the tree and whined, but the hunters had already begun to move, and no one noticed but the three above.

The quarry waited until the sound of the horses had completely disappeared before they slowly alighted from the pine. Seth was the least affected by the hours of discomfort, but his descent was far from nimble. After they had walked about to waken inactive muscles, they stretched out beneath the tree on its bed of needles. Nothing was said for several minutes. There was no need to share words about the recent danger. It had been too immediate, too real.

Joseph stirred first, propping himself on one elbow to study the setting sun. "Not much chance anyone comin' back. Dark soon. Might as well maybe sleep here. We got beans an' rice an' water from da creek to soften 'em, an' some honey to dip da hardtack inta."

"Da way I sees things, we best eat good tonight, bed down right here, travel east again tomorra as fast as we is able," Malachi said. "We gotta put miles an' miles an' miles 'tween us an' Lonnegan. We talked 'bout dat in da plan, but we ain't done it yet. We bin travellin' a lot slower than we figured ta do." Seth and Joseph just nodded and said nothing.

Despite a fall coolness in the air, this was their most comfortable night since they had run. Shrinking bellies appreciated the victuals brought by the boy, the pine needles provided a soft bed, and as adrenaline drained from their bodies, they slept the sleep of those who have passed to the other side of danger. In Joseph's dream, Ellie smiled at him as she tossed grain to Mrs. Lonnegan's chickens.

Seth shook the others awake at first light. Breakfast was black beans and rice. Despite the early morning chill, they stripped and washed themselves and their clothes in the refreshing waters of the creek and skirted their saviour marsh as soon as the sun was high enough to point them east.

Miles and Miles

Each time the three needed to pass an obstacle, whether it be a farm or a body of water, they chose the northern side, hoping to curve back to their original latitude. Progress was frustratingly slow, and they never had sufficient food. Joseph stole some cobs from a field of unharvested corn, shelled them into a bandana, and smashed the kernels with a rock, but it was a poor substitute for milled grain. They gorged on wild apples until the acidic juice made stomachs raw. Four days out from the pine, Seth rescued a chicken with a broken leg from its tall grass hiding place. It met its next incarnation on a skewer rotated over a small fire dug into sandy soil behind a stump. Several times they wandered dangerously close to a habitation, and each time a watchdog announced their presence to the world.

"We is gonna starve ta death unless we kin find some adequate victuals," Malahi lamented. "Can't fight da cold wif an empty belly. Da land only rising slowly. Old Mose said it'd turn inta hill country, an' d'en we know ta go due north, but what is we seein'? Plantations and more bottom-land and scattered farms, dat's what we's seein'."

"What you want? Towns?" Joseph answered. "Least dis way, rail fences warn us when we gettin' close ta people, and we can usually walk 'round 'em. I figure we bin real lucky so far ta not get see'd. How much longer you figure dat can happen? Sooner, later, somebody gonna see us 'fore we sees d'em, an' what happen? Trouble, dat's what happen."

"We could make more miles if we had a horse 'neath us," Seth observed.

"Might as well bang on pots 'n pans an' yell, 'Here we is, ready ta go back ta Massa Lonnegan!' if we was ta steal horses. Nuthin'll stir up a neighbourhood like huntin' down horse thieves. An' what you know 'bout horse ridin'? You know 'bout followin'' a horse, not 'bout bein' top a one," Joseph pointed out.

"Well, all's I know is dat we is gettin' weaker every day," Malachi said. "We ain't sleepin' good, what wif da hard ground and da night chills an da dew. Bin lucky it ain't raining. Rain's comin' soon. Ain't even mentioned bugs dat chew on ya, but forget about d'em. Dat cold rain what's comin' will knock 'em back some. You boys might be able to carry on wif what rations we bin on, but I cain't. First chance I git ta grab some real nourishment, I gotta take it."

On they marched, east and north. Malachi's prediction came true. The following day, a cold rain blew in from the north in the early afternoon and soaked them to their shivering skin in seconds. Unable to use the sun as guide, they plodded on for miles, wet, cold, stoic in the knowledge there was no alternative, hoping the rain would drive unwelcome eyes indoors. As they muttered and swore against their miserable circumstance, Joseph leading, they suddenly pushed through bushes onto a rutted road. Not sixty feet away stood two horses, dripping in the rain, hitched to a buckboard that had once enjoyed a coat of emerald green paint, and on the buckboard's seat sat a boy of thirteen or fourteen, dripping from a wide brimmed hat and an oilskin slicker. The runners froze, aware they had been seen, not sure what to do next.

"Lucky I found you," the young man said, waving a partially-eaten apple. "Providence maybe that I just stopped to grab an apple when you waltzed out of the bushes. Real lucky. Hop in the back, I'll take you up to the farm."

They did not know what to do. Dispirited, tired, wet, cold, hungry, they couldn't summon the energy to retreat into the forest, so they simply stood on the road in the pouring rain and looked at the team and the buckboard and the boy as if they had never seen any one of them before.

"Hop in the back. I'll take you up to the farm," the young man repeated. "You're welcome to sleep in the barn. Darn sight drier than here. I was dropping off grain sacks in town when I got caught out in this. I would appreciate if you'd hurry before our horses drown."

They stood immobile, assessing the situation, uncertain what to do. The boy clicked his tongue and the team pulled the buckboard alongside, where he stopped it with a pull on the reins.

"You sure don't want to go into that town. You're safer with us. Providential it was us that found you."

Malachi was the first to break out of his stupor. He threw his meagre bundle into the box, placed one foot on the rear wheel hub, and in slow motion hoisted his bulk over the side. Two equally small bundles followed. He extended a hand to help Seth and Joseph into the buckboard. The boy flicked the reins, the wheels began to turn, and the three looked at each other in silence, wondering if captive was their new status. The boy talked on.

"You can call me George. That's my pa's name too. Best you not know anything else. The reverend asked everyone yesterday at Sunday meeting to keep an eye out for you. Never thought it would be me who would find you. Never figured anyone would find you, come to that. You look like rats drowned twice. S'pose I might too. Not too far now. Two more bends and three hills and we're there. We got a hundred acres we're working. Well, the bank's got a hundred acres and we're looking after it for 'em, I guess."

"Doan seem like George see many people, he prattlin' on so," Seth whispered.

"Maybe he jus' tryin' ta keep us distracted, let our guard down," Joseph whispered back. "Gotta chance there ain't no rope-wieldin' welcomin' committee waitin' fer us. Look at us. We ain't in no condition to run further."

The cold rain continued. Eventually the boy haw'ed the team into a curving, tree-lined lane. They passed a small frame house with two windows looking out onto a porch with a sloping roof. Only the porch side had been whitewashed. Two sows with their piglets oinked about, oblivious to the rain, while five thin cows and a young bull laid in a small, rail-fenced field that boasted a ten duck pond.

"Sure sign it gonna las' long time, cattle lying down in da rain like dat," Malachi observed.

As they passed a ramshackle shed, they could see old harness, a crosscut saw, a pickaxe, logging chains hanging from spikes, and at the back, a gig. Wider wheel tracks suggested the shed served as shelter for the buckboard as well.

Beyond the shed a barn, five times the size of the house, leaned toward it in poor health. No two walls enjoyed the same exact altitude top or bottom, the pigeon-grey boards at the corner nearest the house were warping open, half the shingles were missing from the far quarter of the roof, and a double-wide sliding barn door was off its track and leaning against the near wall. George drove the team up a dirt ramp and through the open door into the nave, panicking the black and white chickens taking refuge in the doorway, and reined in on an uneven plank floor that flexed under the weight. A similar opening at the back of the drunken structure boasted it had been designed to permit a wagon and horses to pass through.

The boy jumped down from the driver's seat and stood with fingers in his pockets, looking them over. "I have never seen runaways before," he said. "You are a sight. You've been sleeping on the ground, haven't you? I reckon you could use a good bed and a bath. Pa will be along presently. He's over at the neighbours, talking weather no doubt. Can't get much done when it's raining as t'is. Here, pass your belongings down."

He piled the bundles against hay that filled the left half of the barn. "You stay on this side," he said, gesturing toward the hay. "The other side, 'hind that wall there, that's the stable and a pen for the pigs. You'll sleep better in the hay. You can dry yourself off with it too." He climbed back onto the buckboard seat and said, "I'll go tell Ma I've found you. Be back in a jiffy, once the horses are unhitched and I've rubbed them down."

Seth pulled some hay onto the plank floor and flopped down in his sodden clothes. Malachi and Joseph didn't bother with the hay, just stretched out in exhaustion.

"Still doan know whether we gotta be fearful or grateful," Joseph said.

"D'at young man got some education," Seth observed. "Who says, 'I would appreciate if you'd hurry before our horses drown,' or, 'I have never seen runaways before?' We would'a said, 'I ain't never see'd runaways b'fore'."

"His pa at da neighbours worries me some. Last time neighbours was visited, a chase party was involved an' hounds got invited," Malachi muttered.

"I cain't speak for you, but I feels we gotta jus' hang on, see what happens. What we got here? A roof, a bed, chickens... We also got empty bellies an' no prospect a gettin' any proper food if we leave. My feet's so chawed up, I ain't good for another mile," Joseph said.

"D'ese here feet will heal real quick, we hear a passel a riders comin', I betcha," Seth added.

"You had best stay right where you are," said a female voice, and they looked around to see a woman in her late thirties standing in the doorway. Chestnut brown hair braided around her head matched her full sleeved brown dress that had trailed through the brown mud, and over it she wore a stained, flowered gingham apron. Later, they would notice her temples sported a few grey hairs and her face was beginning to wrinkle, but at the moment the focus of their attention was a musket carried in a relaxed manner, as if she had mastered its use long ago.

The Kindness of Strangers

No one moved. The woman took two steps into the barn to get out of the rain. The muzzle dropped an inch. "Well, the boy was right. You don't look like much of a threat. George says he picked you up on the road. He told me it's Providence. Possibly. For sure, we don't want trouble here. You hear?" The three men nodded. "We got enough trouble for two families. My husband broke his leg bad half a year ago, and has not mended properly. The fracture pains him in the body and pains him in his mind, because the boy has to take up the slack around the farm." She paused to let this information sink in.

"You stay in the barn, you hear? If anyone comes, you hide in the hay. Understood? We don't need any more trouble." They nodded again. "You may sleep there too. There's a pump in the yard back of the house. It stays primed. Water's good, but don't use it until after dark. You know why." As she turned to go she added, "I'll send out the boy's pa as soon as he's back."

No one uttered a word for a full minute. They simply wilted onto the hay in relief.

"She wouldn't a said ta hide in da hay if she was 'spectin' hunters to show up an' catch us," Malachi observed. Joseph and

Seth nodded agreement. The pathetic remnants of their shoe leather they stuffed with hay, then leaned backs against the fragrant pile. They were not stretched out for more than twenty minutes when the woman reappeared, followed by a small man wearing a straw hat, amber with rain, and the uniform of the male countryside, blue overalls. He looked them over, said nothing, turned in the doorway, and limped toward the house.

"I will want your clothes tomorrow, once the rain stops."

The three looked at her in silence.

"I'll want your clothes tomorrow," she repeated. "I want to boil them. You smell." She laughed. "What did you think, that I wanted to wear them?"

The small man returned, carrying a cast iron pot full of stew and half a loaf of bread. As he retrieved three pewter tablespoons out of his pocket, he said, "Rain's letting up a little. Should clear out overnight. You boys eat up now and get a good night's rest. We'll talk tomorrow while your clothes are drying on the line."

There were carrots in the stew, and potatoes and peas and stewed tomatoes and onions and a few kernels of corn for colour, but best of all were the plentiful chunks of pork. They used the bread to scour the last dregs of juice from the pot, then collapsed on the hay, hands clasped over bellies, saying nothing.

The small man suddenly reappeared. "Here, I'll take that pot, give it a scour. Always easiest to clean up when it's fresh. I forgot to tell you, there's an outhouse behind the shed when you need it."

Joseph said, "Suh, you have no idea t'all how grateful we is. Mighty 'ppreciative, suh. We has eaten yer supper, ain't we?"

"Never mind. You needed it more. The missus has cooked up some eggs for the boy and me. We'll do fine. We don't have any spare blankets. Pull some hay over you. Rest up now, and like I said, we'll talk tomorrow."

They were accustomed to rising with the sun, but even so, they resented the rooster that evicted them from the first refreshing sleep they had enjoyed since the pine glade. Stiff from sleeping in wet clothes and their arduous travels, they found the outhouse, watched a fresh breeze wash away the last of yesterday's clouds while each waited his turn, then retreated into the barn to be out of sight.

Through the barn door they could see young George hitching the horses to the gig, and soon he and his mother disappeared down the lane. The small man brought a honey pail full of hard boiled eggs, the better part of a loaf of bread, and the cast iron pot half full of oatmeal porridge. While this was consumed as if last night's stew was a childhood memory, the small man retrieved some kindling and six or eight quarter-rounds of dry wood from behind the house and lit a fire under an iron cauldron hanging from a tripod about forty feet from the pump. He half-filled the cauldron with water from the pump and returned to the barn while the water heated.

"Strip down and give me your clothes. I'll boil them for an hour and hang 'em to dry. I'll bring a wash basin and soap so you can start fresh." They stripped. Looking to the side, George senior carried their garments at arms length to the cauldron, threw them in, and stirred them with a wooden paddle. He added a handful of what looked like salt and returned to the barn.

"No work here today, so George is off to the school with his mother. She teaches there — all the forms. Not much profit in it, really. Still, it's something so long as folks pay their share in cash and not crops."

"That s'plains it. We figured on a well-schooled boy when we hear young George speak — an' your missus too," Joseph said. "I notice she say, 'you may sleep in da barn,' 'stead a, 'you can sleep in da barn,' like she givin' permission. Dat sign of a education."

"She does what she can with what she's given. Now, what are we going to do about you?"

"Suh, we doan wanna give you or your fam'ly any more inconvenience. We be gone soon as ya say. We remains mighty grateful for ever'thing you'se done for us, an' we thanks ya. Malachi here was most starved to death 'cause he so big he eat a lot an'—"

The small man held up his hand to stop him. "We don't need to know your names. When did you leave the Lonnegan plantation?" he asked.

Seth started to say, "Satu'day night after..." when Joseph interrupted. "How did ya know we was from Lonnegan's?"

The small man pulled a damp paper from the left top pocket of his overalls, unfolded it, smoothed it on his knee, and handed it to Joseph. "My wife ripped this off a tree when she was returning from church on Sunday. It was near the bank." Joseph looked at it quizzically, turned the paper over and back, straightened the ripped corners, and returned it to the small man.

"Suh, we cain't read. What's dat?"

"It says *Cash Reward Paid for Return of Three Runaway Negro Slaves from Lonnegan's Plantation. $2 000.00 for All Three. Single Rewards Pro Rata. Dead or Alive! Contact Ragg and Associates, Memphis, Tennessee*"

There was silence. Finally Malachi muttered, "Dead or alive" and Seth said, "Two t'ousand dollar. Oh lord... Two t'ousand dollar..." and he exhaled air through his mouth at the rafters.

"Pro Rata mean fer just one?" Joseph asked.

The small man said, "That's about it. You are as safe here as anywhere at the moment. Today is Tuesday, so you've been on the run for about ten days, and obviously living rough has taken its toll. You best get your feet and your stomachs near normal before we send you on your way. We figured you were nearby, least the reverend did."

"The reverend?" Seth asked.

"Someone saw some smoke a few days ago, found chicken bones and ashes behind a stump, figured it must be you when they saw the posters nailed up in town. Told the reverend. At Sunday meeting he asked the congregation to keep an eye out for you. My wife's congregation is small, but generally they're good people. Not all abolitionists, mind you, not slave owners either. Still, you know how folks talk. So, we'll harbour you until we can find a way to get you safely out of here. You are travelling north, of course."

They nodded.

"Sorry. If ever there was a stupid question..."

"Mista...?" Malachi began.

"You don't need to know the family name. George will do. Safer."

They nodded again. "Mista George, how far we be from da big river?" Seth asked.

"The Mississippi? Maybe forty, maybe forty-five miles. Not more than fifty."

They sat in stunned silence. Heat, cold, sun, rain, blisters, insects, creeks, marshes, swamps, ponds, lakes, fields, forests — evasions for ten days, and they were within forty miles of the Mississippi! It was spirit breaking news.

The small man attempted to soothe their disappointment. "You cannot have progressed in a straight line. Most likely you have travelled over a hundred miles or more, back and forth. The bald truth is, you must not continue as you have. You will be captured, sure as thunder follows lightning. The countryside is crowded with eyes eager to claim that reward."

"What we gonna do?" Joseph said, more to himself than the others.

"You? Nothing. Not many visitors, but you gotta burrow into that there hay if anyone comes up the lane. On Saturday morning, I'll send young George to see the reverend, take him some produce, maybe a chicken, get his advice. It would look suspicious if he was to skip school, his mother being the schoolmarm and all. I'd go myself, except George and the missus need the horses. Besides, the reverend and I don't always see eye-to-eye on how the Good Book should be interpreted, but he'll talk to George, figuring his mind is still malleable."

"What town we be near?" Seth asked.

"It's better if you don't know names of people or places. That way, if they do catch you, you would be unable to give information that could lead to retribution. Understand?"

They nodded. The small man limped away to hang their clothes on the line, and when he returned he brought a wash basin, a jar of soft, white soap, and a small brush. The pump water was closer to cold than refreshing. At supper time the woman brought rashers of bacon and eggs to the barn and served bread pudding for dessert. They tore through another loaf of bread. Malachi and Seth rinsed off the dirty dishes at the pump and left them on the porch to be washed.

Just before they drifted off to sleep in their hay cocoons, Joseph said, "Clean clothes, clean bodies, full bellies, kind folks. How we ever gonna repay dis?"

Socks and Shingles

"Ya got shingles for dis here barn roof?" Joseph asked the small man when he brought breakfast the next morning.

"Didn't expect to need any, so I was waiting for winter to split some. Hard to do with a bad leg. I haven't been able to do much extra, even with George's help. We had a twister frolic through a month or so ago, only touched the end of the barn. It knocked a tree down in the orchard behind the house, though. I can't say it did much good for the fence, either, when it ripped into the woods on the far side of the pasture."

By late afternoon, Malachi had shaved a cedar round into usable shingles and straightened a honey pail of bent nails. Seth and Joseph mucked out the stables and put fresh straw down for the livestock. Twice they heard horses on the road and prepared to hide, but they were false alarms. For supper they were brought sausages, corn bread and tea.

The following day, they tackled the barn roof. The ladder the small man provided was far too feeble to hold Malachi's weight, so he stabilized it while Seth climbed onto the roof to nail down the new shingles. With the axe Malachi had used, Joseph limbed the storm-broke apple tree, chopped the trunk into manageable lengths, and stacked them beside the covered woodpile at the back of the little house. Before supper, they had reset the barn door on its track, repaired the roof, cleaned up the dead apple tree, and repaired a sixty foot section of pasture fence where the winds had scattered rails. Joseph noticed dozens of wood rounds on the other side of the fence at the edge of the woodlot. "D'ose got sawed last year, b'fore Mista George busted his leg, an' he ain't had da time or strength to get 'em to da woodshed," he said.

The rounds, too far from the woodshed to carry individually, were a challenge, and a flimsy, dying wheelbarrow bogged down in soil still wet from the recent deluge. When young George and his mother returned from school, the horses were hitched to the buckboard and the rounds were ferried in multiple trips until they ran out of daylight. They left the buckboard near the woodlot, ready to be filled the next morning and retrieved once the horses came back from school.

Sitting in the dark, gazing out the barn door at the flickering light from the little frame house, they felt bonded to this family. "Doan know how many more dis kind a people we's gonna meet," Seth said.

There was silence for a few minutes. Joseph pointed toward the house. "We sure bin eatin' mighty fine, mighty fine. But look. D'ey is usin' a tallow candle. Look aroun'. Look at da shabby buildin's. House ain't never bin painted. Not wif real paint. D'ose cows gonna be fat as d'em fence rails b'fore spring. Da pig's 'll get'em through da winter. Just. Can't count on chickens always, not if a fox or weasel comes visitin'. D'ese here be poor people. Can ya imagine Massa Lonnegan sittin' in da big house wif one tallow candle?"

"You sayin' dis fam'ly got use fer two t'ousand dollar?" Malachi asked.

"If d'ey had wanted da reward money from Lonnegan, we be in chains by now. No, what I'se saying is dat we gotta be real careful when we leaves here, 'cause d'ere ain't gonna be many more like dis."

Saturday brought surprises. The rounds from the woodlot were finally transported to the woodshed about an hour after the job got tiresome. Malachi had the axe in his hand to start splitting them when they heard a horse turn into the lane. A few minutes later, the visitor had departed and the small man beckoned them out of their aromatic hiding place.

"You're leaving us tomorrow," he said bluntly. "That was the reverend. He's made arrangements to get you north." He looked at each. "You must follow the instructions exactly, no questions asked. Understand?" They nodded, but said nothing. "You will be in the buckboard tomorrow, under sacks of corn. Corn is lighter than wheat, so you'll be okay. Young George will ride in the box with you, on top of the corn. I will drive George and the missus to church. Usually they take the gig and I don't fret the reverend with my presence, so if anyone notices the change in routine, I'll say I'm dropping off seed corn. If they ask where, I won't hear them. I'll just say I gotta hurry, be back in time to pick up the folks after the service. You boys still with me?"

Again they nodded and said nothing.

"Now you gotta stay below the edge of the box 'til we make the exchange. We will be met at a crossroads just north of town by an empty buckboard. I don't expect anyone nearby. People will either be in church or sleepin' it off. You will climb over without looking at the driver. That's the deal.

He won't look at you; you won't be able to identify him. I'll throw the corn sacks in on top of you and off you go. You'll be in that buckboard for hours, so take those canteens with you. The missus will pack some dried peas and hardtack for you. Food that travels well. You can carry it in those bundles you brought. But I must emphasize: if the driver sees you looking at him, he will drop you off at the side of the road immediately."

"Suh, where we goin'?"

"I have no idea. North. That's all I know. I don't even know who will meet us, just the crossroads. Here, I brought you some socks as a going away present, seeing as how you don't have any. Where you're headed, you'll need 'em. Young George's feet are about the same size as yours," and he pointed to Seth. "My socks will fit most men, but the missus, she had to knit up a new pair for Malachi."

Sleep came late that night.

Constance Lonnegan Has Coffee

As usual, in her languid life of privilege, Constance Lonnegan lingered over her mid-morning coffee in the drawing room. There was no reason not to. Later, she would inspect her flock of exotic chickens, scatter some grain, try to determine their pecking order. If she fancied a bit of air before her constitutional nap in the afternoon, she would enjoy the soothing rhythm of Bellerophon, her favourite horse, as she rode the perimeter of the plantation. So there was no real sense of urgency to leave the table; no responsibilities demanded attention. With Cicero in charge, the household ran like clockwork. The cook had mastered poached eggs on toast with crisp bacon and English style muffins laden with jam, a breakfast enjoyed by Beau as well. He had retired to his office. Through the open door she could see him meticulously writing in this year's ledger.

She really could not fathom why she was in such a reflective mood this morning. Possibly Beau's demeanour had influenced her on some subconscious level. He was a stabilizing influence on her, she acknowledged, yet since those three field hands had run away there was a tension, an anger, a sublimated fury that bubbled just below his normally sanguine composure. It couldn't be the money that upset him so. Beau Lonnegan could afford to buy new slaves to replace the ingrates. Cotton was selling high, the plantation was prospering, otherwise why would he have chosen a prestigious school like The Citadel in Charleston for their sons? The river exacted its annual dues, nibbling away at the rich bottom-land each flood, but it gave back too; that was nature and to be expected. If the ledgers warned of the depletion of the soil, well, Beau was his father's son and was already clearing forest for new fields.

Had the death of the old man triggered his anger? No, that alone would not explain his recent short temper. The loss of a slave was unfortunate only if he was still productive, so Constance understood why Beau had expressed little sadness when Old Mose passed. There was nothing Old Mose had been doing that could not be assumed by someone younger, although he had been good with the bees. She had heard the story of the severed ear and how her husband had chopped off the big toe on each foot after Old Mose's second escape attempt. As the mistress of the plantation, she would have no hand in such retributions, but she appreciated why they were necessary. It was business. How could anyone profit if your cattle or your slaves just decided to leave? For Beau or Mister Bindle, a studied cruelty was as much a tool as a hammer or a hoe.

Ellie cleared the breakfast dishes. Constance watched her as she retreated to the kitchen to scrape plates into the slop bucket for the hogs. Filling a dishpan with hot water from the stove, she put in the dishes to soak. As she readied fresh tea towels for the drying, she gazed wistfully out the window, looking left and right of the lane to the road, smiled at some private humour, hummed some nondescript song, and began to sway her hips to a hidden rhythm.

That girl is budding out into quite a beauty, she thought. *Pretty face. Lovely breasts. Small, but give them time. Yes, a real beauty. In N' Orleans they would call her statuesque. And so light skinned for a Negro. Odd how that turned out, her mother being of such a dark complexion. Beau will be marrying that girl off soon so she can throw some babies. I wonder who gets her. Certainly not a field hand. Even though she shamelessly trotted out to speak to Joseph every time he worked near the house, there's no chance Beau would let him near her, even if he hadn't run off. Ellie's features are too delicate and her carriage too refined to be a field hand's wife. Maybe Beau will have cook teach her some culinary skills, give her a future as a sous chef...*

Cicero warmed her cup from the coffeepot, and with his back to the office door, surreptitiously topped it up with a shot of brandy. She nodded a *thank you;* Cicero nodded a *you're welcome.* Beau didn't approve of alcohol consumption this early in the day; he claimed it made her fuzzy-headed, but what he didn't know... She had started taking her coffee black when Beau noticed the brandy curdling the cream.

In anticipation of an encore, the coffeepot retired to the kitchen. She had never warmed to Cicero. Old Master Lonnegan had purchased Cicero for Beau when he came of age. Beau appreciated his quiet efficiency, yet to her there was something sinister, something threatening in his silent, humourless, detached manner. He was already a fixture on the estate when she, the blushing bride of unimpeachable lineage, had arrived, so it seemed natural Beau sought his counsel before her own and trusted him implicitly. It was not uncommon for Cicero to conduct business on behalf of the Lonnegan plantation as far away as Jackson or even Natchez.

She tried to put an analyzing finger on her reticence. Was it because Cicero's smooth face never registered any emotion? Because he had mastered the running of the household with military efficiency? Maybe because, without speaking, he radiated authority? Possibly because no one had ever seen him smile, or laugh, or enjoy convivial conversation? Because his only diversion was to study the scriptures and in his immaculate white linen suit lead the hymn sing on Sundays? She could not pinpoint with precision why she did not like him. *If the house catches fire*, she thought, *Beau will rouse Cicero before he thinks to mention it to me.*

Through the kitchen door she could see Ellie laughing as she and the other kitchen girl finished up the breakfast dishes. At a preparation table behind them sat Cicero, his Bible open in front of him, his gaze riveted on Ellie. With her left hand Ellie passed the last of the clean dishes to the other girl to dry, studied the sky on the other side of the window, smiled at her private joke, became aware of Constance watching her, smiled in Constance's direction, dried her hands on a towel, and rubbed her ear.

Very slowly, like water percolating through coffee, one drop at a time, Constance began to understand. What reason did Ellie have to smile, to be happy, to hum a tune in her drudgery? What joy could she find in washing someone else's dishes, boiling someone else's laundry, slopping someone else's hogs? No, she wasn't happy for herself. She was thinking of the runaways, she was happy for the runaways, she was jubilant that some of her kind were escaping the station they had been born into. Damn, she was thinking about Joseph,

Constance realized. Ellie's smile was so familiar, she hadn't seen behind it before. That little bitch wasn't smiling. She was smirking. That not one of those boys had yet been hunted down was a triumph for her. Her smile was a defiance, a way to say, "You only have control over our bodies. And sometimes..."

Gradually, Constance Lonnegan became aware of a second unwelcome revelation. Blossoming, nubile Ellie, in the humblest of circumstances, had found something outside her own pitiful existence to nurture her spirits. Ellie's irrational, unmerited contentment began to irritate Beau Lonnegan's double chinned wife, she who wore a dove-grey dress with lace at the wrists to breakfast, she who enjoyed brandy in her coffee and afternoon rides and raising exotic chickens. She would speak to Beau, have him take steps to douse Ellie's happiness, expel this festering sore from her household. That would put a stop to songs and smiles and swaying hips. Yes, she would speak to Beau. Field work under Bindle's whip was one remedy. On the other hand, she would be worth good money on the block down in Memphis...

A suspicion began to darken her mind, casting a longer shadow each second. Straight ahead, Mrs. Lonnegan could see her husband writing in the ledger — with his left hand. Absentmindedly, he touched his left ear, looked up, saw her watching him, and smiled. Her sons' smile. Ellie's smile. With a gut wrenching suddenness, she realized why Beau Lonnegan had incorporated Ellie into the household staff, why he would never condemn her to field work, why he would never sell her, and to whom Beau Lonnegan would give her.

The Exchange

Nine burlap bags of shelled corn covered the three prone in the bottom of the buckboard. Young George rode in the box with them, behind his father. "Good luck," he whispered as he and his mother were dropped off at the church. George Sr. greeted several churchgoers as he wheeled the wagon away from the churchyard and headed for open countryside.

Bags of corn were shifted so they could breathe better. No one spoke. Discomfort was setting in when the buckboard suddenly stopped under trees. "Get out and stretch, then hop in t'other," the small man said. "There's no one here, but you best keep your eyes on the ground all the same."

Even with heads bowed, they could see the small man had stopped beside another buckboard, its horses standing with Job-like patience, waiting for their driver. The small man was piling the corn sacks into the empty box before Joseph was completely horizontal. He rapped on the side of the box as a good-bye, and they heard him turn his horses in the crossroads and drive away. Under his breath, Seth said, "We is mighty grateful."

A full five minutes after the sound of the small man's horses had died away, someone heavy creaked the springs of the buckboard's seat, clicked a giddy-up to the horses, and off they trotted. From a slit between two bags, Joseph could see the broad shouldered back of a long-haired man in a green coat. Only the sound of horses' hooves, wheels on a dirt road, and the groaning of the buckboard broke the silence. There was no wind. The sun arced for a large fraction of its daytime journey before the horses were reined to a stop. In a low voice their driver said, "I'm going into the trees on the left to take a piss. Count to thirty, slowly, then do what you have to do in the trees to the right. Drink some water. I will return in fifteen minutes. I will drive away whether you are in the box or not. If I see you, you walk."

They heard the seat springs creak and felt the buckboard lean. Having no way to tell precise time, they could take no chances. In ten minutes they had stretched, relieved themselves, and were back under the corn.

Several times they heard the driver exchange greetings with oncoming traffic. Lying flat on the wooden floor under bags of corn, heads, shoulders, hips, and heels absorbing every bump, vision blocked, discomfort morphed into pain and pain became agony. When a second rest stop was provided at a river bank near sunset, they were so stiffened by their unnatural posture they had difficulty climbing out of the buckboard.

"Longer break this time. Horses need water. Anybody comes, get into those trees. I'm gonna give the horses some oats. You eat something too."

"We's gotta remember dat every mile we be hurtin' here, we not gotta walk. Every turn a da wheel, every bump in da road get us closer to dat north star," Malachi reminded them.

The sun set. The driver stopped for a third time when it was truly dark. "Get out. Stay on the road behind the buckboard. I have no way to find you if you lose yourself in the forest."

They walked in a tight circle to restore circulation and pushed elbows toward their backs and tried to touch their toes. Stomachs had expanded from the meals at the farm, so a handful of dried peas washed down with water did little to assuage their hunger. They relieved themselves.

Before they set off again, their driver said, "The moon will be up soon. Don't matter when 'cause my horses know this road. You can sit on those bags now, but don't look up front when the moon rises. Next time we stop, you'll hear what you'll do next."

Sitting on the corn was a blessed relief. Wispy clouds partially obscured a gibbous moon. Absentmindedly, Malachi said, "Gonna rain ag'in," and the driver hissed, "Silence!"

The buckboard journey was tolerable now that they could sit up. Each thought of how many miserable steps they were avoiding, how far they must be from the big river, how fortunate they had been to encounter young George.

On their right came the promise of dawn. Fifteen minutes later, their driver stopped at the end of a farm lane. He remained facing the horses. "I leave you here. Follow my instructions exactly. A quarter mile up that lane is a sizeable house with a half cellar underneath. You can access it through the root cellar door on the near side. That's where you will stay until someone comes for you with a wagon or a buckboard similar to this one. You will be seen by no one, and you will see no one. You will only hear them; pay attention to what they have to say. The dog will tell them you have arrived. He is a vicious brute, but he's on a chain, so pass him close in to the house where his chain can't reach, and you best pray that chain doesn't break."

Their bundles dropped first, then they climbed out with an inflexibility purchased with long hours in a confined space. Before they could express their thanks, the buckboard was gone into the faint light.

The Offer

George Sr. limped out of the barn, leaned on his pitchfork, and watched strangers ride up his lane. The lead horse, a dappled grey, carried a muscular man wearing a brown vest and high brown boots. Two bays, ridden by hard looking, slender, sinewy men, stopped a respectful distance behind. The grey circled the small man, its rider studying him, studying his modest house, the livestock, the lay of the place, saying nothing for a full minute.

"The wife and boy home?" the grey's rider asked.

"School. Is there something I can do for you?"

"There certainly is. Ragg. Aeneas Ragg. Pleased to make your acquaintance. Me and my associates here are looking for three Nigras what run off from a plantation on the river. Know anything about 'em?"

"Why would you think I would know anything about them?"

"Seems a neighbour of yours saw 'em cookin' somethin' a few days ago, back of her farm, headed this way. Says you'd be the sort what might get it in your head to harbour fugitives, you being the religious sort what thinks it can meddle with other people's property."

The small man said nothing.

"Then there's the matter of you leavin' town with a load of something. On the Sabbath no less. That don't sound to us like the Christian way, workin' on a holy day like that."

"You seem to know a lot about my family and my business, Mister Ragg."

"Sir, it's my business to know about your business if it interferes with my business. We've made our inquiries. People around here are real helpful. Some don't seem to like you much 'cause you march to your own drum, we're told. Do you know where the three runaways are?"

"No. I do not."

"But you and your missus helped them on their way."

The small man said nothing.

Ragg circled his horse again, studied the house, the barn, the fields and woods behind. "Hard to make any kind of livin' farming, ain't it? So much depends on the weather — and luck — and a man needs good neighbours. I don't need to tell you he needs his health too. Now, you help me track those three down, I cut you in. Even if we only catch one, there's cash money comin' your way."

The small man remained silent.

"How long was they here?"

"I never said they were here."

"Don't game me! You best keep me and my boys civil. Fresh shingles on that there barn roof. Reckon you didn't do that yourself, what with that bum leg. Wouldn't a sent a boy up there, now would ya? Wagon tracks comin' across that field from the forest, multiple times. Deep. Carryin' something heavy. Wood maybe? You and a boy cartin' wood that many times in a short space, well, does seem rather beyond your capacity, don't it?"

The small man made no reply.

"Ain't no substitute fer cash."

"That's true," the small man said. "There is no substitute for water either, but it doesn't do your system any good if it's fouled."

"You sayin' my money's dirty? You tryin' to get me riled?"

"No, Mister Ragg. I'm just saying if I accepted money for betraying a fellow human being, well, that would make me a Judas, wouldn't it? No matter where the money started, no matter how pure, my betrayal would make it dirty."

"You best consider my offer a mite longer. Me an' my boys, we're beddin' down at the hotel in town. We're real easy to find, should you have any pertinent information. Information such as who you off loaded to, and where, and if they're still journeying together. Those sorts of details are worth money. This place looks like you could use some. If we don't hear from you by, let's say eight o'clock, well... Sir, we'll have to assume you are being deliberately uncooperative."

The small man said nothing.

Ragg wheeled his horse around and cantered with his associates down the lane.

The woman turning grey at the temples roused some time after midnight, unsure of the noise that woke her. It sounded like a cow bawling in labour. The sound was repeated, then came the high-pitched whinny of a terrified horse. She rolled onto her side. The window glass shimmered with gold.

Together, they were able to get the horses out of their stalls and all the cows from the stable. Intense heat prevented them from rescuing the pigs and the bucking bull from his pen.

The woman, the boy, and the small man stood on the porch, water buckets ready in case the fire spread to the house. The woman cried as she watched the barn burn. The boy and the small man said nothing.

The Lady in the Wheeled Chair

Trees and untrimmed bushes encroached onto the lane, creating a dark tunnel. They were barely off the road when they heard a large dog rouse the county. Barks became growls and snarls as they approached the house. A fearsome beast with a flattened head and massive snapping jaws lunged at them, straightening a logging chain secured to an iron stake anchored between the house and the lane. With one eye on the chain and one eye looking for any sign of life from inside, they reached the near corner of the house, found the root cellar doors unlocked, felt their way down stone steps, and in the faint light passed shelves of preserves and porcelain crockery until they came to a wooden door open to a stone-walled cellar that extended about half the length of the house. Here were two straw palliasses and a canvas cot beside a small table on which a pale yellow beeswax candle sputtered. More candles tied with string and a box of Lucifer matches lay beside it.

"Just lit. No wax drips," Joseph observed. He returned through the root cellar to close the doors. A harvest table on the far wall supported a silver pitcher of water, a warm ceramic pot of beans, a loaf of bread, a jar of pickles, strips of beef jerky wrapped in cheesecloth, and a small lidless wooden box of spoons. A pail for sewage rested directly under the landing of the stairs to their left.

Despite fatigue, food was their priority. Within twenty minutes all that remained was a half jar of pickles. Malachi and Joseph stretched out on the straw mattresses while Seth took the cot. They slept. Joseph was the last to wake, roused by the sound of Seth lighting a fresh candle. He lifted the root cellar doors slowly to avoid alerting the dog and reported that the sun was far into the afternoon.

"Starting ta cloud up," he said. "Malachi's right. Rain 'll be here by tomorra."

The new candle was half gone when they heard the door at the top of the stairs open. Light from above lit a small portion of the cellar. A woman's voice said, "Move out of the light. You get caught, I can honestly swear on the Bible I never saw you." The voice belonged to an old woman, but it was assertive, not feeble. *This one used ta giving orders*, Malachi thought. There was a sound like a cannon ball rolling across the floor above them, right onto the stairs' landing. Seth looked quizzically at Joseph. "Wheeled chair," he whispered.

"Choose one to talk. No one else speaks."

Joseph and Malachi pointed at Seth simultaneously. Seth shrugged and said to the landing, "We mighty grateful..."

"Of course you are," the old woman interrupted. "But gratitude is not going to save you. I am going to save you. Now, respond in one word answers. How many arrived?"

"Three," Seth said.

"Does anyone require the services of a physician?"

Seth looked at Malachi and Joseph quizzically.

"A doctor. Does anyone need a doctor?"

"No, ma'am."

"One word answers. Did we leave enough to eat?"

"Yes, ma'am."

"I said to answer with one word. Do you know where you are?

"No, ma'am."

There was an audible sigh of exasperation. "You are in the northwest corner of Tennessee. Sometime tomorrow, probably in the evening, I or my maid will open this door behind me and indicate that you are to leave immediately, that we have received the signal. Be ready. No more than fifteen minutes later a buckboard or wagon filled with straw or hay will pass by the lane. It will not stop, so you will need to jump lively so as to be on board and burrowed down before anyone sees you. Although few travel this road, I do not relish having to explain to neighbouring folk why fugitives chose my habitation for a rendezvous. Do you know what a rendezvous is?"

"No, ma'am."

"It's of no importance. You will not look at the driver or talk to him. If you are captured, he will say he had no idea you had jumped in the back. You will not contradict his protestation of innocence. Do you understand?"

"Yes, ma'am. Absl'utely, ma'am."

"You will be conveyed to a station just a stone's throw from our border with Kentucky."

She was silent for a moment. "Do you know what a station is?"

"No, ma'am."

Another sigh of exasperation. "This house is a station. You are in a station. Think of yourselves as freight that is transported by a railroad, from one station to another."

"We got no 'sperience wif railroads, ma'am. We from da river. Got no need for a railroad on da river."

"Where are you heading?"

"North, ma'am."

Another sigh. "I know that. What is your intended terminus?"

"Doan know what terminus mean, ma'am."

"Your terminus — or terminal — is where you hope to end your journey to freedom. Where exactly do you hope to escape to?"

"North far enough dat d'ere ain't no more slave bondage, ma'am. We was tole to get north a Ohio ta where da Britishers live cause d'ere ain't no slavery d'ere no more."

"The Canadas then."

"If dat be where da Britishers live, d'en dat's where we's headed."

"The Canadas are a very long way north. Ohio is a free state. If we could get you to Ohio, get you a job..."

"We is worth two t'ousand dollar ta anybody what fetches us back home. Dat's a powerful 'centive for anybody, even in a state where d'ey ain't got no slaves."

"True. And then there's the *Fugitive Slave Law*... Well, one step at a time, one station at a time. Let's get you through Kentucky first." She paused. "I suppose you know nothing of the railroad, how to find folks sympathetic to our cause. How did you find help in the past? Do not tell me any names."

"We was travellin' cross country, steerin' by da sun and da stars, in da water mos'ly ta 'vade da dogs, trying ta get far, far from da river. We was most worn down ta bone when we stumble' 'cross a family dat took us in an' fed us an' 'ranged for us ta get ta here. Wifout d'em we woulda starve' ta death, an' dat's da truth. We was truly lucky, dat's for sure."

"Yes, indeed you were. You will not be able to count on luck all the time. The Mississippi is not very far away. It bends west hereabouts. You say you know how to navigate at night?"

"If da stars be out an' we can see 'em, yes, ma'am."

"A conductor will transport you to the next station tomorrow. I do not know where it is, and it will not know about me and my maid — and you will not mention any details about this station or about us. Is that very clearly understood?"

"Yes, ma'am. Clear understood."

"It is imperative that you find folks with abolitionist sympathies. At night, look for coal oil lanterns or candles in a particular pattern, two in a window, two on opposite corners of a table in the same room as the window. Look for quilts hanging on a clothesline. If you see blue or green stars in a pattern, sometimes like the Big Dipper, that place is probably friendly. The same is true if there is a large star, usually green or blue, at the top of the quilt. It will always be hung with the star at the top. For confirmation, you knock on the door and say your master has sent you with a message for Mister Polaris, but you have lost your way and could they please give you directions. Are you comprehending all this?"

"Yes, ma'am. Quilt, stars, lanterns, Mister Polaris."

"In an hour my maid will leave ample food and two buckets of fresh water on this landing from which I speak. One of you will empty the ordure pail. Throw the waste from the corner of the house farthest from the dog. Try not to wake him. He can be disruptive. Use the water from the second bucket to rinse the pail. My maid should not find its retrieval distasteful. Do you have any questions?"

"Yes, ma'am. Why ya helping us? Ya can get two t'ousand dollar for us."

There was a long silence. Finally, in softer tones, the old woman said, "My husband and I worked this farm with two male children and some hired help, and we made a good life here without having to buy slaves. We even took on extra land. Of course, we didn't raise cotton or tobacco on a grand scale, just crops we could use and sell the extra when there was some, so I guess I don't see the need for slaves like some do. Up north, folks would call me a Free Soiler. We prospered enough I can afford to let out shares on the farms and hire house help now that my legs don't work. The boys are gone, husband's passed — pneumonia — and maybe I'm looking for some way to help others in my dotage."

"You doan talk like..." Seth began.

"Like a Southerner?" the old lady interjected. "I'm not. New England. Married one, but never quite adopted the South. Maybe the South never got around to adopting me. It's suspicious of Northerners. And rightly so, I suppose."

Seth said nothing. The assertive voice returned. "No more talk. You know far too much about this station as it is. You will be gone tomorrow night. Farewell."

The wheels rumbled back, the door closed, and the three relaxed, thankful to know they would soon be on their way again.

A deck of cards helped pass a few hours the next day. The inaction was enervating. Seth paced, Malachi consumed whatever food was left from their dinner, and each half hour when he peeked out the root cellar doors, Joseph brought back weather reports of a light rain. In the late afternoon, it was he who pulled the low card and emptied the sewage bucket. "Rainin' still, but just soft like. Just enough ta get us soaked through in a hour an' not let us dry out for a day," he grumbled.

They packed, then repacked their bundles with the hardtack bread, jerky, rice, beans, and cookies left on the landing, anxious to get moving again and fearful of the unknown.

Total darkness had arrived when the door above opened, an unfamiliar female voice said, "Now," and they closed the root cellar doors quietly behind them as they left. There was no sound of dog or chain. As they emerged from the tunnel of foliage, they could hear horses approaching. A fully-loaded wagon plodded by; they climbed over the rear rack and made dens in straw, each hoping his was deep enough to hide from probing lantern light.

The Cabin

For hours, the wagon wheels rolled over roots, banged against rocks, and splashed through puddles. They spoke in whispers. "Dawn cain't be more'n three days away," Seth grumbled.

"No complainin' from me, so long as we's puttin' miles 'tween us and Lonnegan," Joseph said.

The rhythm of the wheels and the soft straw lulled them to nod off, losing sense of time, but each was instantly alert when the wagon suddenly stopped.

Their driver walked to the back of the wagon. A voice said. "It's an hour or two short of dawn. We have heard of riders waiting to intercept freight, so this is the most dangerous part of my route. If I see or hear anything the least suspicious, I will call my horses 'darlings.' That's your signal to get out pronto. Leave on the right side where I am and get into cover just as soon as you can. Mostly forest around here. Get down and stay down. Try not to leave a trail of straw. Do ya hear?"

In unison each said, "Yes, suh."

"The road forks just ahead, once we get past an inn. We'll stay to the right 'cause I know the people at the next station.

I've heard we have a friend in a station to the left, but I have no knowledge of it."

The driver resumed his seat, and they were in motion. No one snoozed now. A few minutes later, they heard a horse nicker to their right, but the wagon maintained a constant speed. A quarter hour on they heard another nicker, and this time, "Won't be long now, my darlings!"

Over the side they tumbled, into the dark, brushing straw from bundles, clothes, and hair as if stung by bees. As they scrambled off the road, each encountered bushes which he immediately sheltered under, face first pressed into dew-moist weeds, then turned to watch the drama unfold. The wagon had stopped at the divergence.

Ahead of it horses snuffled and snorted. Someone said, "You're out at a very early hour, neighbour. Boys, check the load."

A match flared, a lantern was lit, and they could see two tall men emerge from the darkness and walk to the back of the wagon, thrusting long knives into the straw as they went. They heard their driver say something about bedding for his chickens. There was derisive laughter from the darkness.

"Pickin' up or droppin' off?" and "Would those be black chickens that's flown the coop?" Their driver pretended not to know what they were talking about, which earned more laughter.

"Sure as hell ain't no one in that straw, 'less he's in deep, but maybe we better make real sure," the first voice said. "Cut the reins and use them to wrap his hands behind his back."

The two with the knives obeyed without a word. "Now, light the way so our neighbour here can enjoy the beauty of the countryside."

There was more laughter from the darkness. As the lantern moved to the side nearer the fugitives, they could see someone throw liquid into the straw. Another match flared; this one was tossed into the wetted straw, which immediately began to burn. Fearing light from the flames might betray him, Joseph was about to wriggle farther from the road when one of the men with the knives smacked a horse on the rump and off the team bolted, trailing a wagon on fire, its hunched driver desperately attempting to keep his balance.

"Goddamn meddling abolitionist! That son of a bitch won't be able to make us out in daylight, even if he takes a notion to, not after his ride," the first speaker said. The fugitives waited until all sounds of laughter and horses had faded down the road to the right before they emerged from the bushes.

"What we gonna do now?" Malachi asked. "I cain't see no way ta help dat man. He halfway ta Jerusalem by now, if he still on da wagon, maybe dead. Gotta jump ta get away from dat fire. Hurt bad if his horses doan wanna stop an' d'ey won't wanna wif a fire chasin' em. He in a tub a grief, no two ways ta look at it."

"We knows d'ere be a passel a horses an' trouble on da right. We see'd d'em go dat way. D'ey was waitin' for us — for him anyways. Only one way for us ta go, dat be take da left road. Chains waitin' for us on da right," Joseph said.

"An' d'ere's da dawn jus' startin' ta creep," Malachi pointed out. "We gotta get off dis road onta da left fork an' find us a proper hidin' spot ta spend da day. Ain't no tellin' when d'ose riders gonna come back."

They followed the left fork, keeping to the side of the winding road, prepared to dash into the trees and bushes of a bordering forest at the first hint of danger. Morning had broken when they heard horses' hooves. A lone carriage passed their hiding trees.

"We gotta hole up. Dis place be as good as any 'cause d'ere's a little stream right over d'ere," Seth said, pointing. "Cain't bet on no more traffic comin' round da next bend. We is too exposed on da road in da day."

They followed the stream into the forest and settled down in a tiny glade to wait until sunset, using up their food, taking turns on watch while the others dozed. As light faded, they ventured back onto the road and cautiously set off, ears and eyes alert, no one speaking. Until it became too dark to see a signal, one would walk a hundred yards ahead to wave the others on as he discovered no threat around each bend. Several times they hurried past an isolated cabin, a barking dog, or a window glimmering with candle light bravely trumpeting its presence to the world. Light cloud diffused moonlight sufficiently to allow a slow progress but prevented any sense of direction. Hearts almost stopped when a horse plodded up behind them. Fearing to make any noise, they froze at the edge of the road; the lone rider slouched past, asleep or drunk.

After an hour at this inefficient pace, they were barked through a darkened hamlet of seven houses. A lone ancient log cabin bordered the road about a quarter mile past the last house. Pale orange light spilled from a single small window. From inside, a small dog yipped, and they would have hurried past it like all the others except a candle was placed in the window by an unseen hand, then a second.

They halted. Malachi whispered, "I doan like it. We is still too close ta d'ose riders dat fired da wagon an' prob'ly killed dat driver. We bin too lucky so far, findin' good people ta feed us, shelter us, help us on our way."

"How long we gonna have good luck we keep walking all da way ta Ohio?" Joseph asked. "You got enough food ta not start stealing some soon? Then where we be? Right where Old Mose said. Catched."

"You two walk up da road a ways, not so far ya cain't hear. I'll knock on da door an' run like hell if dat cabin ain't friendly," Seth volunteered. "Dog don't sound too big."

The knock produced more barks and a door opened by an unshaven old man in a filthy cap and nightshirt. Holding a small, orange coal oil lamp in one hand and a scruffy white terrier in the other, he peered up and down the road before looking at Seth. The old man, the dog, and the cabin were dirty and dishevelled; food encrusted dishes covered an unpainted wooden table and blankets were tossed on the floor. A miasma of dog, sweat, mouldy food, and urine wafted into the night air. The old man said nothing. He left the door open, retrieved the candles one at a time from the window, and placed them on opposite corners of the cluttered table, then he hung the lamp from its ceiling chain and returned to the door.

"My massa has sent me wif a message fer Massa Polaris, but I has lost my way in da dark. If ya could tell me where ta find Massa Polaris, I'd be mighty obliged ta ya."

The old man looked at Seth suspiciously. Finally, he said, "And why did you think to knock on my door, 'specially this late at night?"

"We see'd two candles in da window, thought it might be a friendly place. A place ta get information, dat is."

"We? How many are you?"

Seth cursed himself for repeating Joseph's obvious mistake with the fence menders, then figured there was an easy escape if they had misjudged. "Three," he said.

"Who told you to look for two candles?"

"Ever'body know two candles in a window show a friendly house."

The old man clumped over to his sagging bed and sat down, the dog still cradled in his arms. "Well, call them in before someone from down the road hears you. It's late. You'll have to sleep on the floor. All I have is bread and beans and a few onions and sweet potatoes. Tomorrow morning, we'll see if we can find Mister Polaris for you."

The noxious atmosphere of the little cabin was stifling after the freshness of the open air. Using their meagre bundles as pillows, they arranged themselves like sausages on the floor, heads to the door, Seth's beside a compressed pile of straw that from the odour he assumed was the dog's bed. Their host blew out the candles. They could hear him fumbling in the dark, then an object hit the floor.

"Wonder how he lost his leg," Joseph whispered.

A Collar of Yarn

In the morning, their host was friendly, almost jovial. On a smoky little stove that did nothing to dilute the staleness, he fried a mess of beans, onions, and slices of bread in pork fat he scooped from a barely translucent glass jar with his fingers. Equal portions were dolloped onto chipped saucers to be consumed using grey wooden spoons. He placed the cast iron frying-pan on the floor by the stove so the dog could lick it clean.

After breakfast, the three found the outhouse behind the cabin so overflowing they slipped into the backing trees. On their return, they discovered the old man boiling a pot of what smelled like chicory coffee.

"Shouldn't leave in daylight. Best stay inside lest someone from the houses sees you. Wouldn't do. Let the coffee cool a mite, get you boys headed in the right direction."

They relaxed, becoming more accustomed to the oppressive stink of the cabin. There weren't enough chairs for four, so Malachi and Seth sat on the floor, backs to the rotting bottom logs. The terrier curled up on his bed of straw, surveying them all, too wary to permit Malachi to pet him.

"Ain't my dog." He gestured toward the hamlet. "He comes from down the road, likes to spend the night with me. I'll send him home in a bit." He seemed to forget his advice about staying indoors. "Wonder if you'd mind topping up that there wood box from the pile out back and fetchin' in a pail of water from the well. Easier for you than me with a peg leg."

When the tasks were completed, they were treated to ersatz coffee with a spoonful of brown sugar added to override the bitterness. Joseph and Seth drank theirs from smudged glass jars because there were only two cups. Malachi and Seth resumed their previous stations on the floor. Malachi attempted to coax the dog over by rubbing his fingers as if he had food for it, but the little terrier continued to eye him with suspicion.

The old man got up from the table and thumped over to the stove. With one leg stiff, he clumsily picked up the unkempt dog and carried him to the open door. "You go home. Be gone now. Get your supper somewheres else." He set the dog down on the threshold and shoved him toward the road. The dog obediently disappeared and the old man returned to his chair.

Their host had turned away from Joseph when he moved the terrier, but from their vantage point on the floor both Malachi and Seth noticed the dog now sported a length of red yarn around his neck.

"Why ya put a yarn collar on da dog?" Seth asked.

The old man dismissed the question with a wave of his hand. "That's to let his real owner know he's bin fed." He changed the subject. "Wanna thank ya for bringin' in the wood and water." He pointed to his wooden leg. "You'd think I'd be used to it by now. Goddamn Redcoat bullet, so I've had it for a time." He moved to his bed, rolled up a pant leg, unbuckled the shiny leather straps that secured his peg leg, let it fall to the floor, and rested his good leg on the vacated chair. "Now, let's talk about how we can help you boys. Headin' north of course. Where ya from? How much are ya worth?"

Joseph felt uneasy. He coughed several times before the others could reply, just to earn some thinking time, and said, "Down sout' a here. Couldn't find it now we's so turned around. Doan know what we's worth."

The old man nodded, seemingly satisfied with Joseph's answer. "Well, you are turned around for going north, that's for sure. You keep on this road far enough, it'll curve you back to the Mississippi. Back a ways, you probably took the left fork in the road, ain't that so?"

When no one said anything, he continued. "Right fork's the one you want. It'll take you north and east, miss the river. Wetlands everywhere, swamps, marshs, hundreds of cricks... Tricky to get around. You go back the way you come, all the way to the fork, that's gonna use up time and energy. No, what we gotta do is get you on the shortcut to find that road you shoulda took in the first place."

The three listened carefully, not to miss any tidbit of information.

"Ain't got much ta give ya for your journey. Some dried navy beans is all I got, an' I can give ya a loaf of bread. Lady down the road sends me some loaves now and again. Moon should be high enough tonight so's ya can see your way through the shortcut. Sky's clear. Still, it'll be rough going for most of the night. Cold too. Shortcut sorta forms the top part of a triangle. It's only used by the folks hereabouts when they need to get to the east road and don't want to backtrack to the fork, so it's pretty much overgrown. Ain't really a road, just a wagon track."

"We is much obliged fer your assistance. Mighty thankful, suh," Seth said, and the others muttered their assent.

"Wish I could do more. Won't be any travelling past here after supper that you can't dodge, so you should be on your way while there's still some light. That way you won't miss the turn-off. You'll see a rope hangin' from a limb a couple of miles from here, and you'll see the path on your right hand side real easy."

They napped in the afternoon in preparation for the night's walk. After a supper of fried bread and beans and a re-expression of gratitude, they set off into the waning light, no one talking, their legs working off the inflexibility of a lethargic day, Joseph ahead to warn of on-comers. They met no one. The old man was right; at the hanging rope the wagon track was easily discernible and the track was rough going as he predicted. Movement kept the damp night cold from taking hold in the first hours. They took turns leading the way, each losing the path at times and necessitating a backtrack. The land began to rise, gently at first, then more dramatically. As the moon threatened to set, the rate of progress slackened with the fatigue of a long walk and the increasing chill of cold air on sweat.

Malachi returned from a false lead and found the main trail again. Suddenly he stopped and stood, silent.

"Hear somethin'?" Seth whispered.

"No. Jus' thinkin'. Why dat old man so int'rested in where we's from an' what we is worth?"

"What got ya wonderin' 'bout dat?" Joseph asked.

"Da dog. Dat dog went home wif a stretch a yarn 'round his neck. Seems like a passel a trouble jus' ta tell da owner it's bin fed. An' d'eres one more thing."

"What's dat?" Seth asked.

"Dat dog wasn't fed. He got ta lick da breakfast fryin'-pan, but dat ain't feedin'. So I'se wonderin' if dat yarn not some kinda code, ta let someone know we's here an' where we is goin'."

They stood dumb in the moonlight. Finally, Joseph said, "We cain't do nuthin' 'cept push on. Cain't go back. We leave dis here track we is lost for sure. We best push on real careful like, be quick but vig'lant." There could be no argument. On they pushed, more uphill than down. As dawn broke, the wagon track became easy to follow through the forest; there was no road to be seen.

Ahead a dog started to bark. "Maybe gettin' close ta dat road, maybe houses near," Seth said.

"Dog don't sound too threatenin'. Sound like same size dog dat was wif dat old man," Joseph whispered.

A quarter mile later, they observed below them a dirt road meandering beside a river farther down in a narrow, forested valley. With rising spirits, they accelerated their pace. Nothing was said. Each looked about for the habitation with the dog.

They were still some distance from the road when the unmistakable sound of a horse hoof stamping the ground in impatience froze them in mid-step. Forty feet into the dense timber was darkness. Mortal danger might be in those trees, yet they could discern nothing. To their right the waiting hoof stamped the ground again. Cautiously they inched forward, each breath a gamble, willing whatever peril lurked in that forest not to awaken. Behind them, as unmistakable as the impatient hoof, they heard the ripple of a horse's quivering flank, followed by the click of a human mouth, then the slap of leather. In terror, they sprinted for the road, dropping their bundles as they ran, as if to attain that open space was to win God's personal protection.

As he turned into the road, Joseph stole a glance behind just as three horses, one a dappled grey, the other two bays, broke out of their timbered lair. Concentrating on staying in the open corridor of the wagon track, the riders whooped their horses on. The fugitives were out of sight for a few seconds, heading for a bend in the road, Seth in front, Joseph a yard behind Malachi, Reason whispering "Get off the road!" while Terror shouted "Run!"

The Rock

In a pure panic, time to witness every sound, every action, becomes a curse. Time elongated for Joseph. He ran in dreamlike slow motion as if swimming in honey, incapable of speed. The riders shouted to each other. One yelled, "I've got the near one!" A bullet furrowed through the left sleeve of his jacket before he heard the shot. There was no pain. A second shot kicked up dirt in front of Seth. The ground trembled as hooves pounded at his heels. A whip wrapped around his legs. He fell hard, sliding in the dirt. The momentum of the grey horse and rider that brought him down carried them past him. Seeing Seth and Malachi still running, the rider dropped the whip and abandoned him, stunned and prone on the road, to gallop after the others.

The lead man reined in his horse, stood upright in the stirrups, levelled his musket, and fired. Malachi stopped running. He stood perplexed, as a man does when he forgets why he has entered a room, then slumped to his knees, face turned toward the north. Through the smoke and dust, Joseph watched a crimson rose ooze out of a crabapple-sized hole below the big man's left shoulder. The shooter rode up to the body, circled it, then pushed it over with the musket barrel.

"Thousand dollars!" he yelled.

Joseph unwound a coil of whip from his legs, crawled over to the edge of the road, and half climbed, half fell down a steep, rocky incline, his descent into the quick current of the river arrested by a massive boulder as large as their shack at Lonnegan's. He scrambled to its upstream side to watch for his pursuers, knowing they must come. There was the stomp of hooves and more shouting. Up above he saw Seth, hands tied in front, blood trickling from a scalp wound through dirt on his face, running stiff-legged behind a horse whose rider scanned the river bank. *I'm next*, he thought. *What had Old Mose said? "...thinkin' like prey. D'at's what'll keep ya alive."*

He eased his legs into the numbing water, planning to be carried by the current, hoping to stay submerged until the riders saw him. Then they would shoot; they had no alternative. He wondered if the bullet would grant a quick death like Malachi's.

The river pinned a ten foot log against the boulder, one end bobbing, the other anchored on the bank. He climbed over it to press himself into a smaller target, and there it was, a glimmer of hope. He blessed the current that through centuries had sculpted out the bottom of that rock. A concave arch under an overhang concealed a shelf about three feet wide. This den might serve until someone searched the river's edge. He snaked under the boulder and pulled the log closer to better cover the entrance to the sanctuary.

The inevitable happened two minutes later. Rushing water overshadowed the sounds of his pursuers, so he did not realize anyone had descended to the river until he saw a pair of brown riding boots on the other side of the log. He stopped breathing, fearing the boots would hear his heart smashing against his ribs. The boots moved on, reappeared, paced back and forth on the bank. "I know bloody well this is where I saw him last."

Another voice said, "Pa, he's probably taken to the river. He'll be shiverin' fine if he did. Won't be able to climb out real easy, 'specially on t'other side. Steep as this one. Maybe we can catch him downstream."

The first voice said, "I can't believe I was so fuckin' stupid. He looked to be out cold, so I set off to help you two with the little one. Goddamn son of a bitch and hell! I left seven hundred dollars on the road to chase down three hundred. Jesus, I'll never live this down." The boots moved a few steps. "By God, he's got to be here somewhere. No goddamn sambo what has never been ten miles from home is gonna cheat me outta my seven hundred dollars!"

The boots returned. One was placed on the log. "Should never had got this far, damn it! Wouldn't have neither, if it weren't for those goddamn Bible thumpin' meddling do-gooders!" The pacing resumed.

Eventually there was no more sign of the boots, but Joseph could not risk emerging to look for his pursuers. Shivering and wet to the knees, he realized he could not survive until dark in this clammy, cramped hole. He would either expire from hypothermia or be discovered when the brown boots did a more thorough search. Malachi dead, Seth captured, he was desperate. *Gotta make my play sooner than later*, he thought. *Sooner, while I still got some feeling in my legs.*

Clumsily, he pulled off his jacket and surveyed the bullet burn from elbow to cuff. He tied the arms around the log as quickly as shivering fingers permitted, anxious lest there be an observer, anticipating a shout or a shot any second. To keep the jacket in place, he attempted to double-knot the arms, then it occurred to him a log carrying a person downstream would look more natural if he buttoned opposite sleeves together. Several small rocks in the pockets might keep the jacket under the log. With his feet, he pushed the log off the bank and into the current.

Within seconds there was a shout from up top. "Pa, he's tryin' to make a run for it! Under that log! See him? Get him before he gets to the bend!" There was a shot, then another from farther away, then a third.

Joseph peeked out from under his sanctuary, saw no one at the top of the incline, and with cramped legs crawled and scrambled and climbed upstream along the river bank, crouching behind trees and rocks whenever possible. Over the noise of the rushing water came three more distant shots. Cold, stiff, hungry and tired, he gained the edge of the road, peered in the direction of the shots, could see no one his side of the bend, and hobbled across the road into sheltering bushes.

Gonna get caught yet I stay here, he said to himself. *Where they not think ta look fer me?* He heard another shot. *Still think I in da water. Dat jacket doin' its job.*

Staying back from the verge and any sight line, he cautiously paralleled the road to the wagon trail. He was about to collect the scattered bundles when it occurred to him the hunters had seen them discarded. *Better leave 'em 'til I knows d'ey has given up on me*, he thought, and entered the forest where hoof marks showed the trio had emerged, being careful to leave no footprints of his own. He backtracked, this time moving parallel to the wagon trail, until he could look down on the rutted dirt road.

The day remained sunny but cold. With his back to a tree, concealed by foliage, numbed by the loss of his friends, Joseph pondered his situation. No help for Malachi. Even if he could stalk his captors, there was nothing he could do to rescue Seth. Seth was smart. Maybe he could figure out some way to escape on his own. Immediately he realized how futile a wish this was. Who ever heard of an escape from bounty hunters?

Wagons and lone travellers passed, more going north than south. He dozed off, as drained by the stresses of the day as from the night's march. When he awoke, the shadows were long and the temperature had dropped. He was about to return to the wagon road to retrieve a morsel of food from his bundle when he heard hooves. The dappled grey led, ridden by a short, barrel-chested man wearing a brown, wide-brimmed hat, a brown leather vest, and high brown leather boots. A short-barrelled musket was scabbarded in front of his left knee. From the right saddle bag hung a canvas sack, its bottom third dark red. The two bays followed several yards behind, each carrying a tall, long-haired, slender man in farmers' broadcloth. The first bay had little Seth slung in front of the saddle, his stomach on the base of its mane, his wrists roped to his ankles. The man on the second cradled two muskets.

There was nothing Joseph could do except watch the procession from his hiding place. He sat leaned against a tree and watched the shadows lengthen. The cold intensified. Several travellers passed, unaware they were observed by a wretched young man who this day had lost his only friends. At dusk, he returned to the bundles, retrieved a match, and lit a small fire in the trees beside the shortcut path, in shock and indifferent to his safety. He ate several mouthfuls of bread, made a primitive bed by mounding pine needles, and stretched out beside his fire. The invasive cold was only partially responsible for his fitful sleep.

Part two

THE ILLUSION OF SAFETY

Freight Crosses the Jordan

The man with the limp had not met the other two before. At early dawn, the latest conductor led the trio to a warped wooden dock on the south Detroit waterfront where two young men rested on their oars in a small skiff that already seemed to ride low in the water. There was no greeting. Fingers pointed to where they were to sit, the boy in the bow, the adults at the stern. The conductor untied the painter and grunted "Godspeed" as he pushed the boat off.

About two hundred yards out, the upstream rower rested on his oar to toss a small canvas bag. "Ham sandwiches. Some muffins and fruit leather too. Better eat, even if you don't feel like it. No tellin' when you get vict'als next, so share with the boy."

The passengers regarded the black water roiling just a few inches below the gunnels with trepidation. When the man with the limp tightened his grip on a gunnel, the other rower chuckled and said, "Just wait. This is nothing. The main current of the Detroit eddies when we pass the point. That's where the pulling gets hard, least 'til we angle into the lee of Fighting Island. If we get swept past that one, there's other islands we can tuck behind. We'll get you across, even if we drift to Bois Blanc."

"Dinna fash yersel'. We've already lost our quota of freight this month," the other added. "Besides, wouldn't you rather drown free in Canada than drown owned in the Great Republic?" and he laughed at his own humour and their discomfiture.

The sun was above the horizon when the skiff nuzzled into the upstream side of a small wharf where a fisherman had secured an optimistic drift line. "Whatcha got for me?" he asked as he caught a tossed rope.

The rower who had thrown the sandwiches said, "Three. Don't like to bring more than two, but the wind is calm this early and one is small. Better get 'em moving though. They've been shivering all the way over."

The fisherman pulled in his line, removed a dead whitefish, and threw it back into the water. As he coiled the line around his hand, he studied the new arrivals. "See that fella sauntering 'long the riverbank. He'll take you two inland," and he pointed to the woman and her son. "You follow me," he said to the man with the limp. "You're going south a few miles. Got a buggy over there 'hind those trees 'cause I don't plan on walking, and it appears you couldn't. Take a piss or whatever you need to. Don't want to get caught short while we're passing through the town, do we? I'm gonna stop for pipe tobacco at the general store. When I do, you stay put."

An hour later the buggy slowed at the far edge of town as it encountered a whitewashed cottage with a small yard held in place by a white picket fence. The fisherman pulled up at an assortment of fresh and veteran wagon wheels leaning against a barn-board workshop on the other side. A wisp of grey smoke lazed from a tin chimney strapped to its side. A substantial woodpile suggested industry and foresight.

"Can you read that sign over the door?" the fisherman asked.

"No, sir."

It says, "*M. Duffy Wheelwright Wagons Custom and Repaired*"

The wheelwright, wiping his hands on a rag, emerged through a smaller door hinged inside a barn door. A thin, beanpole of a man, about forty and already white-haired, he looked up at the newcomer with an appraising eye. "Any experience working with wood or iron?" he asked in an accent that suggested feathers in the mouth.

"Wood. A little, sir. Splitting and burning mostly."

"A start. I'll teach you if you can learn. There's a cot for you in the workshop. 'Most as warm as the house when the fire's on. Baggage? Didn't think so. Now jump yourself down and go round to the back door of the house. You look about my size. Ask my good woman to dig out some old work clothes. They're spark holed but better than what I'm looking at. Tell her you're hungry. No, tell her we're both hungry."

He turned to the fisherman, touched a finger to his forehead, stuck the rag into a back pocket, and returned to his workshop.

The man with the limp knuckled the back door with timorous taps. It was opened immediately by a tiny woman in a full-skirted shiny black dress. Her right hand caressed a small silver cross hanging from a chain about her neck while she examined him. He was amazed at the strength in her little fingers when she squeezed a bicep. She took one of his hands, turned it over and back as if to read his future, then studied his face.

Without a word, she turned and left him standing at the open door. Inside, on a small table under a window, he could see a candle burning beside a bronze crucifix on a pedestal. In front of these were a peaked cap, a pair of leather gloves, a shoe, a book, and a rosary. She returned with a neatly folded bundle of rough clothing. "When you've got these on, come back for the food," she said, with a mouthful of feathers similar to her husband's.

"Accident?" she asked.

"Club foot. Born with it. Doesn't slow me down much."

"We'll see," she said, and closed the door to indicate he was dismissed.

That night, as he stretched out on the cot and listened to the fire crackling, he pondered the vagaries of good and evil.

"Thank you, Lord," he said, and drifted off into the sleep of the righteous.

In the first days, the man with the limp learned that the M stood for Michael and that Michael was ruled totally by his good woman. He learned that Michael Duffy was a poor conversationalist with any subject other than wheels and wagons and that he was an exacting craftsman. Even with customers waiting impatiently, Mister M. Duffy refused to hurry repairs until a damaged wheel was as true and sturdy as new. He learned there was a waiting list for new wheels and that they were usually made in pairs. He learned that the wheelwright's many unfamiliar tools were treated as old, comfortable friends, friends that were always kept clean and sharp and returned safely to their homes. He learned that a wheelwright was a highly respected and essential occupation.

He learned there was a multitude of skills that would require mastering before he could be of much use. Best of all, he learned there was not much walking involved working on wheels and that he enjoyed the smell and orderliness and rhythm of the workshop. He learned to hope.

An Eye for the Grain

"See that browner section in the grain. That's heartwood. Might as well call it firewood. It's not strong enough for our purposes. We need the clean-lined outer wood, straight so it doesn't crack in the steamer. I prefer ash to oak or elm. It's strong and hard and will take a good bend before the grain ruptures.

We'll start you on rough spokes for a pony cart. This is how it was done before we could set up a lathe.

This is a drawknife. You use the two handles to draw the blade towards you. It seems unnatural to cut toward yourself, but that's how this tool works best. Now, what you want is to keep the heel of the wood firm in the vise and with each pass shave some off the blank until it tapers just like this one here. Use this one as a model. See how neatly it slides into the sizing cone. Keep your spine straight and lean backwards with the draw stroke. The power comes from your back and shoulders, not your wrists. When you've finished one, call me to check it for you. If it's done right, we'll need thirty-nine more just like it.

Take your time. You'll get the hang of it better if you work slowly and methodically. Notice the blanks are longer than what we need. Once you have the spokes tapered, we'll shape the tangs and square up the tenons and cut them all at once to the same length. A pony cart isn't expected to handle heavy loads, so we won't need to dish the wheels for lateral support.

A basic pony cart is as good a place to start as any for a novice.

I'm glad you're here. I lost my helper a while back, and there are few jobs in the wheel and wagon trade best done by one man. I want to try making hubs — we called 'em naves back home — from a double-long blank spun on the lathe. On a long piece, I can't pump the lathe and work the chisel too, so if we can get the set-up just right, you could keep her spinning and I would do the cutting. If we sawed the finished blank in half, we'd get two identical hubs with one turning. When the mortise holes are drilled and chiselled for the tenons, with a little fuss they'd be ready for their collars, once we grind the chamfer on 'em.

Don't work so hard you're useless to me tomorrow..."

That night the man with the limp went to sleep mulling the context of unfamiliar words, words like mortise and tangs and chamfer and tenons and naves and blanks and "I'm glad you're here."

"My good woman suggests a raw day like this might do for you to learn how the steamer works. Cold wind, always damp when it's from the east, so I think she's right. Smart woman. Smarter than me. Always thinking two steps ahead.

You know those staves I've had soaking out back of the pump... Well, while I'm dragging a couple in, you fill the steamer's reservoir, and get a fire going underneath. Don't spare the fuel, 'cause we need a hot one.

You will be amazed how much bend we can coax into a straight-grained piece of hardwood if it's completely saturated and we can get the steam to it. The fewer splices in the felloes the better, I always say.

I see you've a talent working with wood. My last helper had an eye for it too, before he left us. Not everyone has. Maybe it can't be taught."

"Why did he leave?"

The wheelwright busied himself straightening tools on the wall before he answered.

"He was needed somewhere else."

"Where did he go?"

"St. John's churchyard."

He turned to face the man with the limp. "You're not ready for the metal work yet, but you're comin'."

He took a long time to retrieve the staves.

Routines

Winter months brought new challenges. Pitch warmed in the brazier was forced into the larger spaces between the workshop planks to slow the wind. Cold metal demanded gloves. The horse shared with a neighbour required a skilled farrier to replace a broken shoe that had contributed to a split hoof. The good woman was annoyed when Mister Duffy was reluctant to tackle the job himself, explaining to the novice he was not particularly good with animals. Occasionally they left the property to fetch formed iron from the blacksmith. A firkin of nails the blacksmith had so effortlessly placed on the wagon took both of them to wrestle into the shop. The wheelwright was unimpressed by the flat iron ordered for wheel rims. "Careful of your hands," he said. "These have more burrs than a Scotsman's tongue."

On colder days, the wheelwright focused on metal work and showed him how to stack charcoal and maximize the bellows for a white heat. The novice learned how to roll a hot metal strip into a ring and hammer the join smooth on the anvil's horn. Using tongs, they dropped the hot ring over the wooden rim, banged it home, then drizzled pails of water on it to cool and contract before it could burn the wood below.

The shop became frigid at night. The tiny woman sent out a buffalo robe blanket, a heavy longcoat, a knitted hat, wool mitts, and three pairs of wool socks. The wheelwright helped him stack boards behind his cot to reflect heat from the stove, helped him string a cord from his corner of the workshop to dry wet laundry, and donated a washstand complete with basin and pitcher and drawers for washcloths and towels. As a token statement of independence, he used the basin and water jug to scrub dirty dishes before they were returned to the house.

At Christmas, the wife gave him a teakettle, a jar of loose tea, and an absolutely new enamelled tin mug. From the wheelwright came the best present of all — a chamber pot. It granted luxurious freedom. No more would he need to visit the outhouse behind the shop in total darkness and piercing cold. On New Year's Eve, Michael Duffy brought a half-finished bottle of whisky to the workshop, and together they drank a goodbye to 1856 and a second glass to a prosperous 1857.

The wheelwright's wife ignored him, but he had no complaints; she provided simple but ample fare. His diet included root crops and potatoes, dried apples, and fruits in sugar syrup preserved in glass jars sealed with wax. They enjoyed fresh bread twice a week. A chicken coop at the rear of the property supplied protein.

The woman wore the same full length black dress whether she was hanging out laundry or sweeping the front step or setting off for church. Except for mass on Sundays, she never left the property. The couple enjoyed no social life with the community beyond church and business dealings. A local farmer kept the house and workshop topped up with hardwood, cut, split, and piled with precision, delivered dressed lumber by the wagon load, and brought food supplies every Tuesday.

Several times each week the novice wheelwright got a peek inside the cottage when the master craftsman sent him for their lunch. A candle always burned in the little shrine on the small table opposite the back door, the table with the cap, the gloves, the shoe, the book, and the rosary. Only the rosary ever changed its position. He reasoned the woman used it when she attended church.

Despite the pressing need for his skill and products, the wheelwright permitted nothing to disturb his week-end routine. Work was halted at three o'clock sharp on Saturday afternoon, although another hour of labour would have completed a job. On Sunday morning, he walked to church in even the most intemperate weather, his tiny woman on his arm. After mass, the couple enjoyed a leisurely late meal and always shared the leftovers.

Visitors were invariably customers, so the club-foot was surprised one work day when a middle-aged Black man, dressed in go-to-meeting finery and a top hat, dropped in to chat, not with the wheelwright about wheels or conveyances, but with him.

The Messenger

"I'll see what the mice left for lunch while you two converse," the wheelwright said, and as he was closing the door behind him, the Black man replied, "Thank you, sir. I doubt we will be long."

He surveyed the workshop, wandered into the novice's corner, noted the washstand and cot, looked for a surface free of sawdust, and, delicately placing his top hat on the anvil, he perched on a nearby stool after he had flicked it with a handkerchief.

"I am a confidant of Isaac Shad and a member of our True Band. It has been my honour to submit, on occasion, contributions to *The Provincial Freeman*. You will not be familiar with that publication, so my name is of no consequence," he said by way of introduction. "You cannot read, can you?"

"Not yet."

"Do not entertain any illusions that I have come to help you post-haste in your situation." He surveyed the workshop disdainfully before he continued. "We will almost certainly have no further discourse. My role is to enlighten the raw humanity, such as yourself, which continues to pour across the border. My purpose in coming here today is to advise you are not yet a candidate for aid, assistance, benevolence, support, or encouragement in any way from organizations I represent and to which I belong."

"I haven't asked for or required any aid, assistance, benevolence or whatever since I was taken in. Sir... What makes you think I need your help?"

"You fit into a pattern. A recent escapee from oppression and bondage comes here thinking he has crossed the Jordan, reached the Promised Land, that he's now free. He brings no capital, no education, no marketable talents, no prospect of adding value. He faces a limited future, an exclusion from the greater society, based on his race. Even if he appreciates that the whites are much divided in their attitude to his arrival, he will nurture a natural expectation that the Black community will automatically welcome him with open arms. I am here to disavow him of any such fantastical hopes."

"Sir, I resent your prejudices. I was a cook before..."

"Warming grits and frying chitlins does not make you a cook."

"I'm starting a new life here! I'm learning new skills, I intend to..."

"You intend! You'll intend what your new master intends for you. Have you received any more money for your labours than when you were a slave?"

"There is no comparison between then and now. Mister Duffy took me in the day I crossed. He and his missus have been good to me. I have a roof over my head, food in my belly — not as good as I could cook, but they don't know that — and I am learning a trade. The Duffys have never called me Boy."

"Is this a template for your future? No money, food scraps, no opportunity to strike out on your own?"

"What right do you have to march in here and...?"

"Don't be a simpleton! The Black community is established, respectable. We are contributors. We are thrifty. We work hard. We value education. We abhor drunkenness and sloth and discourtesy in any of its forms..."

"Your command of language reflects formal schooling, but I don't see..."

"That's exactly it! You don't see! You don't see that every ragged fugitive assails our hard-earned status and dilutes what charitable help we can muster. There exists an element that will always say, 'No more. They will never fit in. They will bring crime and alcoholism and debauchery. They will never be us. They will work for less. They will take our jobs.' That element thrives on your arrival."

"So my own race makes me unwelcome. I am not a thief or a drunk or..."

"But they will say the wheelwright could have trained a white man when his son died. A white man who would get paid wages he would spend at the general store to buy shoes to support the cobbler or a lantern to help the tinsmith feed his family. Do you spend money at the general store? Do you even know where the general store is? They will say you have stolen someone's job."

"I told you. I'm just getting established in a new life — in a new occupation — in a new country. I'll get to needing things at a general store by-and-by. The Duffys have been kind to me, kinder than you, who I have known for ten minutes. You know nothing about me, about my tribulations, about my character, yet you fear my 'raw humanity' will shatter your mirror of respectability."

"Yes, the Duffys have been kind, I'll grant you that. Yet haven't you been a benefit to them as well?"

"I would like to think so."

"Maybe the Duffys' introverted lifestyle is to keep you under surveillance so you don't think of striking out to make your fortune on your own."

"That is ridiculous! Work to Mister Duffy is like alcohol to some men — a necessity. The missus stays close to what reminds her of her lost son. Maybe what you call surveillance is them keeping an eye out that I'm not snatched back into slavery."

"Maybe. But enough of this idle banter. My mission is complete. I repeat: until you have earned a respectable reputation through hard work and the exhibition of a high moral standard, you must expect little help from the Black community. Many newcomers have gone into the back country to practise the agricultural arts and avoid recapture and repatriation to their former hellish existence. You might wish to emulate their example."

"I am not a farmer," and he pointed to his deformed foot.

"Our skin may have the same hue, but here we are not what you left. We have our own newspaper, our own church, our own teachers, our own school. We have a literary and debating society. We are loyal subjects of the Crown. We obey the law. We condemn anyone who betrays our values. So I advise you and I warn you against doing anything which would bring disrepute upon our people or our community. If you do nothing to tarnish our standing, then possibly we can be of some assistance in the future."

The visitor stood, dusted off the seat of his trousers, and retrieved his hat from the anvil. "You will thrive or perish as your own efforts or fortunes dictate," he said as he closed the workshop door behind him.

"Any idea who that was?" the wheelwright asked upon his return. "He didn't buy those clothes from any tailor around here."

"A messenger with a warning," the novice replied. "He wants to ensure I don't besmirch the Black community."

"Not much chance of that."

"Thank you," the sample of raw humanity said as he accepted the proffered lunch. "I'm glad the mice aren't partial to roast beef."

The Last Sunday

He heard the cottage door close and the squeak of shoe leather on fresh snow. *The mercury must be trying to bust out the bottom of the thermometer if the snow talks back when the tiny woman treads on it,* he thought. The workshop was so cold he could see his breath. Eventually he would need to rouse himself and start a fire, but for the moment he was content to pull the buffalo robe higher and luxuriate in a day of rest. He dozed off.

A half hour later, a cold nose and a full bladder forced him off his cot. He dressed quickly, tossed some kindling into the stove to catch on last night's embers, and shook the teakettle. No sound. Solid ice. He stretched and was rubbing his hands together for warmth when there was a rapid knock on the workshop door. He opened it to find a huge man with a scarf over his ears and tied under his chin against the cold. He stood with knuckles raised to knock again.

"Got a bit of an emergency. Seized hub. The wheelwright in?"

"No, sir. The missus and him, they're at church."

"Yeah, I know," the man smirked, and caught him full on the jaw with a fist the size of a turnip. He staggered back into the shop, reeling toward the work bench. A second blow caught him above a kidney. Fighting the blackness, he staggered, almost fell, regained his equilibrium, and grabbed a chisel from its home beside the vise. On the periphery of his vision, he detected a second intruder. A single coil of rope lassoed his shoulders. His frantic, shrugging, ducking attempt to throw it off was only partially successful. The rope tightened around his neck and one arm. He swept the chisel back and forth in front with one hand while the other tried to get his head out of the loop.

The second man circled behind him and tugged the rope tighter, throwing him off balance. He fell sideways, hitting the stove, his left arm transmitting agony from elbow to shoulder, but his good foot remained on the floor. The man who had punched him waited patiently while the man with the rope tried to pull him completely off his feet.

Pivoting, Michael Duffy's helper spun toward the man who held the rope and slashed and stabbed at him with the chisel. An "Ahhhh!" told of some success. From a half crouching position, he turned to face the first attacker, the one silhouetted against the open door, the one with the club, the club that smashed the raised chisel against his head, the head with the concave cranial fracture.

He drifted in and out of darkness. Each time he surfaced into semi-consciousness his arm, his back, and his head communicated its own unique brand of pain, pains so extreme he had no inclination to move. A stale smell filled his nostrils. The only eye that would open refused to focus on swirls of faded orange flowers on a grey background. Sounds were muffled, distant. It took minutes to comprehend he was in the box of a moving buckboard, loosely rolled in a tattered carpet that reeked of dust and mould and cat urine.

The buckboard stopped. He smelled fish, heard gulls and the plash, plash, plash, plash of waves. Bones grated when they carried the carpet to the ship. He lost consciousness again.

The darkness ebbed enough for him to realize he was on a boat. The gentle rise and fall of its deck was calming compared to the bouncing of the buckboard. An icy breeze penetrated the carpet. He wondered why he wasn't shivering. He was hungry. His mind wandered. *Had the kindling caught?* He hoped the wheelwright wouldn't be angry when he found the chisel not in its home. Michael Duffy was mighty particular about his tools. He drifted away.

The last time he emerged from the darkness, there was a monstrous throbbing in his skull, each pulse a hammer blow on an anvil.

It surprised him that he could be so accepting of the inevitable.

Random visions melded and flowed, interrupting the flowers. He smelled freshly baked bread and corn syrup and ham with his own honey and mustard glaze. He was in a white stuccoed kitchen with gleaming copper pots and pans hanging from a plank behind his head and the mistress was half leaning over a pot, sucking tomato sauce from a wooden spoon. As she nodded approval, the kitchen morphed into a small barn where wheels of all sizes leaned against its walls. He smelled paint and sawdust and smoke from the brazier. His enamelled mug was on the stove. He reached for it and was alone in a rowboat with no oars, being carried out from a foggy shore by the strong and silent energy of a mighty river.

On a dilapidated wharf the last conductor and the fisherman and the wheelwright and a child in a black satin dress waved good-bye as the boat turned its bow downstream toward a distant light. He was unable to raise a hand to acknowledge them. Across the dark waters, the last conductor mouthed "Godspeed," and now someone in white was with him in the boat, steering toward the light. "Dinna fash yersel," the steersman whispered...

The captain thumbed three crew members below and flipped back the blanketing layer of carpet. "Fierce fight from a cripple, judging from that hand," he said to the others without taking his eyes off the corpse. "Bet you clowns didn't expect that, did you? Fee remains the same. The second half in full when we reach Toledo. Quibble, and I'll haul about into British waters before you can think about it."

"We were hoping to pay passage and freight with the reward money," the huge man with the turnip fists said.

"No reward now, is there? Looks like you hit him pretty hard. Too hard. Too hard if there's no compensation for him being dead."

"No. He's worth nothing now. You'll have to wait for the rest of your money. We're not very flush at the..."

"Listen carefully, you horse's ass! For all you know, we could be sailing right back where I picked you up. You wanted a boat no matter the weather. I told you when you hired the *Linda Ann*, I told you this time of year costs extra, and I'm not thinking warm thoughts about you two incompetents when the wind cuts like this. Even with the Detroit current emptying into it, it's cold enough this end of the lake could ice up by tomorrow."

The two said nothing.

"Money at the dock, or you can talk to my crew about how they won't get paid 'cause you're not very flush at the moment. Yes or no."

"Okay," the man with the bandaged hand said reluctantly.

"Good. Enough of this bullshit. Help me roll this poor bugger overboard and we'll break out some grog. And throw that fucking carpet in too. It stinks!"

The Fort

Michael Duffy and his wife ate what the mice left for supper in total silence. While the tiny woman cleared the table and washed their dishes, the wheelwright remained immobile, gazing into the candle flame, his elbows on the table, his jaw resting on clasped hands.

When the dishes were dried and put away, the missus pulled up a chair beside him and rested a hand on his arm. He stirred and said in a matter-of-fact voice, "I try, but it's never enough. First the boy, now... This must be stopped. I'm going up to the fort tomorrow."

The first man he met he recognized from their church. "Well, if it isn't Mister Duffy, the very man himself," the sergeant observed in a brogue as thick as the wheelwright's. "Come to see our old artificer again, have you? You can save your breath if you're still offering employment. His arthritis..."

"Give my regards to the worthy man, Sergeant Madill, but no, no, it's the man in authority I've come to consult about a serious matter."

"Consult, is it? Mister Duffy, the sergeant major is not here. He's gone up the river with a few of the boys for a picnic."

"A picnic?"

"That's what he calls keeping close watch on t'other side. Easier to do once you're upstream of the islands. No telling when he'll be back. You may be in luck though. Just day before yesterday the higher-ups sent an officer to take a peek at the sergeant major's account book. It's an annual routine. If you'll follow me, we should be able to track him down. He's a mere slip of a fresh faced lad, just come out, but he may be of help."

They waded through the flock of sheep that in warmer weather kept the abandoned fort's killing grounds close-cropped and pulled up at what once were officers' quarters to find a young man of about eighteen sitting on a campaign chair, buffing his boots.

"Major Emmett, a Mister Duffy to see someone in authority it is, sir."

In no one's description would Major Emmett be called handsome. Beneath a thick mass of carrot-coloured hair, protruding ears framed a freckled face that sported prominent front teeth. His tall frame might be called slim or lanky by friends and gaunt or skeletal by those less charitable or more concerned with accuracy. Arms and legs had the musculature and overly-long proportions of a puppet and moved in a random and jerky fashion.

The wheelwright expected to find a newly stationed youth just off the boat from England, puffed up with arrogant self-importance and eager to impress with a recently purchased commission. Instead, he found an amiable young man in a fatigue shirt who immediately set him at his ease.

"Authority to check accounts, sergeant. Authority to count beans. The sergeant major who directly oversees the pensioners' scheme is the genuine article, but he is not present at the moment, Mister Duffy, so I'm afraid you're burdened with me. If you could give me a moment to finish smacking these boots about, I'll be with you presently. I wouldn't take a seat if I were you. We haven't yet had the opportunity to make this room habitable again, so the dust..."

The young officer set his brush and buffing cloth aside and leaned against the chair's back. "One would think that since Her Britannic Majesty's Government sees fit to send me dashing about on various errands that could be done by any literate corporal, it would also see fit to provide me with at least an ensign for an *aide-de-camp*," he said jovially. With Madill's assistance, he squirmed his feet into the boots, stood, and ignoring his tunic and reaching for a field jacket instead, he asked, "So, what can we do for you, Mister Duffy?"

"Major, I am come on a serious matter. We have been giving refuge to a fugitive from the republic, a Black man of about thirty, thirty-five years, partially crippled by a clubbed foot. He has been an able and talented student of my craft. Yesterday, the missus and I returned from church to find my workshop in disarray, splattered with a copious quantity of blood. Indeed, a potentially fatal amount of blood. There is no sign of the man. I fear the worst."

"Abduction?"

"Abduction."

"He has no one who shows him personal animosity?"

"He has not had the time or the inclination to interact beyond his work and habitation. Major Emmett, I ask you in plain talk. The men in the pensioners' settlement are the only real authority here. What will be done about this?"

"Mister Duffy, I have yet to take my morning constitutional. Walk with me. Sergeant Madill, please be good enough to inform the sergeant major's wife I shall take her up on her kind offer of a lunch. It will save me a stroll into the town."

"Sir."

"You are familiar with many of the pensioners here? You were greeted by name several times."

"I know quite a few from St. John's, and everyone has need of the blacksmith and the wheelwright from time to time."

"I am told they have been good soldiers, seen more of life and the world than I... so far. Then you know the army considers this a success."

"The pensioner scheme you mean? Yes, everyone seems to benefit, if I understand it correctly. The older men are not cast adrift once their service ends, they receive a quarterly stipend, some a full pension, a parcel of Ordnance Reserve land, enough for a garden, a cabin..."

"Permit me to correct you on one point, Mister Duffy. Their service has not ended. The pensioners may be old soldiers, but they are still soldiers, an experienced if interim military force. You are aware they occasionally act in a constabulary capacity. And if the Americans were to invade again..."

"Is that likely?"

"Quite. But when or what form it will take is anyone's guess. It could be a repeat of 1812. They have many who are convinced God has decreed the whole of North America must be absorbed into their great republic. It would seem that more bloodshed does not dismay God, or He would communicate those wishes to us."

"Major, our conversation is not addressing the abduction of someone who trusted he would find freedom here."

"Actually, we *are* discussing the issue, only in a circuitous fashion. What did we see? Pensioned veterans, cabins, plots of land, a small infirmary maintained by the old doctor who stayed on with the pensioners when the garrison was redeployed and who would starve to death were it not for the maladies of the townsfolk."

He pointed to the parade square. "It's the doctor's little flock of sheep that keep the grounds tidy, not boots practising disciplined drill. Let me tell you what you did not see. You did not see a garrisoned fort protected by sufficient resources to withstand an attack in force. You did not see a fortification Her Majesty's Government is willing to maintain, let alone reinforce. Did you see active regulars? Heavy artillery? What we saw are steadfast, experienced men who are addressed by their last rank, old soldiers who, in the event of an invasion, are our first line of delay until regulars and militia can be mobilized."

"But such a strategic position... Fort Malden must be considered essential."

"By you and me and everyone who understands the ground, yes. But England has other concerns at the moment. The Thirty-fourth was at one time stationed here. I hear they have been sent to Sevastopol to fight the Russians. That's a posting to a real war, not a possible one. What is to be held at all costs? India, Mister Duffy, India. Not this insignificant little finger of the empire."

"Major, I have no love for England or, begging your pardon and with respect, the English, yet I prefer the lesser of two evils. I am no Fenian. If this 'insignificant little finger of the empire' were to be swallowed by..."

"Mister Duffy, just last month an observant friend over the river noticed reprinted copies of *Bald Eagle* surfacing in public houses. That rag openly espouses an attack on British North America. Both Detroit and Cleveland have spawned active Hunters' Lodges. We have received multiple reports of drilling by said Lodges in preparation for God-knows-what mischief. Detroit and Cleveland are not so far away we can sleep easy. So that, sir, is why you are conversing with a green, newly minted officer who has been sent to find out just what the hell is going on and not the real man in charge here, who is, as we speak, patrolling along the river, watching, reconnoitring, and planning how he can slow an incursion with a pathetically small number of old men."

"You are here for a term, then?"

"Ostensibly to check financial records, but in reality to collate observations and information from our friends on the other side. I suppose the army doesn't know just what to do with me. No combat experience, not enough seasoning for a field command. So yes, I shall set up shop in these musty quarters or find a room in the town until I can cobble together a report that sounds plausible."

"Major, to return to why I am here... Am I to understand that the authorities are content to see fugitive slaves kidnapped under our very noses? Am I to understand that nothing will be done to address this outrage? Am I to understand that...?"

"You misspeak Mister Duffy. Calm yourself, sir. I share your frustration — I honestly do — and I have great sympathy for these pathetic refugees, but nothing will be done officially to investigate the tragic circumstance you relate. What you see here is too few burdened with a task beyond the scope of our numbers or ability. Our orders are to defend our sovereign soil, not expend men, time, and energy tracking the disappearance of individuals who most certainly have been returned to bondage in the United States."

"I hear what you are saying, but I find the situation unacceptable."

"As do I, Mister Duffy, as do I. Just yesterday, while I was glancing over the sergeant major's books, all square and in order, I might add, his good wife initiated a similar conversation. It will be no consolation when I tell you your missing man is far from the first case noted in these parts."

"So nothing will be done?"

"On the contrary. I said we can do nothing officially. In our present circumstances, our hands are tied. Nevertheless, if you would consider an alternate course of action... I gleaned much from chatting with that woman. In a circumspect manner, she alluded to a citizens' group which might deflect your impatience in a different direction, a more productive direction."

"I am listening."

"You are obviously acquainted with Madill. Speak to him. Mention I have sent you to inquire about the price of oranges."

"Oranges."

"Oranges. Now Mister Duffy, I must track down a local woman who can supply my meals if I am to thrive here, so I bid you a Good Day."

Conspirators

Michael Duffy expected the meeting to be held after dark in a dank basement hidden from prying eyes. He had not anticipated losing a morning's work in a spacious, well-lit room above the livery stable. He climbed the outside stairs and was met on the landing by a short, burly man who blocked the door. Sounds of conversation and laughter came from within.

"If you wish to rent a horse or buggy, you will find the ostler can be of assistance, sir."

"Thank you, but that won't be necessary. I've come to inquire about the price of oranges."

"There may be someone here who can give that information," the doorkeeper answered, and ushered him into a room filled with tobacco smoke and several tables where two groups of men were playing cards. Several individuals leaned their chairs against a wall and watched with interest. He recognized the harness maker, a miller, two old soldiers from Malden, and most from chance encounters in a small town. As the fisherman escorted him by the elbow to a vacant chair, the doorkeeper returned to his post. Conversation stopped, and all eyes turned on the wheelwright.

The fisherman took a seat at the front of the room. "Now, sir, tell us why you are here. Do not use names, even your own. We may share the same concerns and agreements and commitments concerning actions to be taken. Then again, we may not, and your most welcome visit will be forgotten by everyone." He left a pregnant pause. "Everyone."

Duffy began with "An officer checking on the pensioners directed me to speak with..." and told them how his wife was against him coming, for "she has no faith in the honour of an Englishman and fears he may have directed me into a trap." A low chuckle permeated the room.

"Go on," the fisherman said.

He told them of how the fisherman had brought him a fugitive with a club foot, how the man had become a great help in the workshop, and what he knew of his abduction.

"Why did you bother going to the old fort?" the fisherman asked. "The garrison has been gone for years."

"Gentlemen, I was most distressed by this outrage. I entertained a hope that someone in authority, once informed, would be as incensed as I and help catch the perpetrators and return my apprentice."

"Did anyone offer any assistance?"

"None at all. Which is why I am here. The sergeant... I mean I was informed by someone there are individuals who..."

"Individuals who have had enough of kidnappings and who will act to stop them?"

"Yes."

"And you wish to join them?"

"Yes, I do. Yes, most emphatically. I can not sit idly by, but I have no idea where to begin."

"Sir, at the termination of the information we shall share with you, you will make a decision. Yes, you are one of us, or no, you are unaware of our existence. Do you understand?"

"I understand."

"The men in this room, plus a few who are unable to be in attendance, formed a Vigilance Committee because kidnappings have reached epidemic proportions. We have a singleness of purpose — to stop the abductions of Blacks and punish the abductors. Each time an escaped slave is repatriated by force, it is an affront to our sense of justice, our morality, and our sovereignty. Are you in agreement with our aims?"

"Completely."

"Frankly, our methods require brutality. We do not enjoy the luxury of time to alert the authorities, so we act without the consent of the law and enforce our own brand of justice on those so vile, so contemptible, as to profit from the return of their wretched victims to slavery. As you can well imagine, those returned usually suffer horrific retribution. Unspeakable punishments! We show no mercy to bounty hunters. They are not afforded the benefit of trial, and if that offends your tender conscience, then our conversation terminates here. For emphasis, I repeat: we show no mercy to bounty hunters. We administer justice with vigour and promptitude. There are no exceptions. Are you in agreement with our methods?"

The wheelwright took a deep breath. "Absolutely."

"You must appreciate that as we operate without official sanction, we must remain a secret organization. Our involvement is even kept from spouses in some cases. We could be arrested on charges of conspiracy at any time. No records are kept. Communication is verbal and usually involves the barber or sons and daughters on errands. We use colours or cities instead of names. For example, I am Mister Rose, that man is Mister Scarlet, the man at the door is Mister Madrid, the gentleman to my right is Mister Vienna. Only one on this committee knows the contact person for another Vigilance Committee. Do you understand how the committees are organized, and are you willing to follow the rules?"

"I understand, and I will obey the rules."

"Do you wish to join this Vigilance Committee, in full knowledge it operates outside the law, in full knowledge it uses violence to achieve its aims, and in full knowledge it demands secrecy? Yes or no."

Michael Duffy took another deep breath and crossed the Rubicon. "Yes. Yes I do. Mister Rose, I most assuredly do."

"Since orange is the password of the week, your name will be Mister Orange. We'll take a smoke break, after which we'll tell you what we know of the club-foot's disappearance."

Duffy squirmed in his chair. "Mister Rose, if it's not too impertinent of me... I'm an Irishman born into the Church of Rome persuasion. Orange doesn't seem appropriate for me. Would it be possible to have another name?"

There was laughter. Mister Rose said, "Mister Cork it is then."

Mister Cork Talks to Mrs. Duffy

The tiny woman ladled a second helping of stew into her husband's bowl and began to fish. "You came home with more spring to your step than when you returned from the old fort. The half day's holiday seems to have raised your spirits."

"I returned from the fort having received no encouragement, no help, but this morning I met with neighbours of like mind who prefer action to words. Moreover, I have information now that sheds light on our man's abrupt departure."

"Will you share what actions these neighbours of like mind will take to help the unfortunate Duffys, who are once again left with no one to help in the workshop?"

"Ask me no questions and I'll tell you no lies. Isn't that the way the saying goes?"

"So falling in with neighbours of like mind encourages you to lie to your wife? By all the angels, Michael, whatever have you got yourself mixed up in?"

"I do not wish to compromise any of the like-minded individuals I met this morning. Our approach to the abduction issue must be..."

"Blessed Mother of God, so now it's 'our approach!' Husband, you are being evasive. You are not normally secretive. How soon must I fear a knock on the door from the constabulary?"

"Mrs. Duffy, stop twisting my words. It is actually very simple and straightforward. I met with some people this morning who are concerned about the many abductions of recently arrived fugitives, and they are investigating, of their own volition, the circumstances surrounding each to determine if there is a pattern. That is all. Just that."

"So you have information about our man's disappearance?"

"I said I did before you accused me of being secretive. The day before the club-foot was taken, two men rented a team and buckboard from the livery. The ostler was paid in advance, and in American coin if you please, to retrieve them at supper time on Sunday from the town dock."

"And who told you this?"

"The owner of the livery told me this. Let me finish. There's more. The ostler believes he could identify the two if he ever saw them again. He describes one as a huge brute of a man, the other of a more ordinary size, but wiry. The ostler noticed blood on the tailgate when he returned the buckboard to its place. Suspicious of foul play, the livery owner sent him scurrying down to the dock to question anyone who might have witnessed the departure of the men in question."

"Our livery owner is quite the detective. If he is one of your like-minded neighbours, does that make you a detective too?"

"I will not respond to sarcasm. The ostler could find no one who saw the two suspects with the buckboard, but an old woman walking her dog claims she saw a fair-sized boat with a square foresail and a gaff-rigged main cast off from the dock and run south before the wind. It was a cold, nasty winter's day, if you remember."

"Of course I remember. Why wouldn't I remember?"

"This woman was unable to make out the full name, but the boat is christened *Linda* something or other and has a navy blue hull with a red stripe above the water line. A friend on the other side is checking American records for any boat named *Linda*. Probably a brigantine. She flew no flag. Now you can see why I was walking more sprightly than my return from Fort Malden."

"There is little possibility of rescuing the club-foot though, is there?"

"No chance at all, really. I hope he won't be maltreated excessively. I rather liked him, and he did have an eye for the grain. Possibly Mister... possibly the fisherman can find a replacement soon."

Later, while waiting for sleep, Michael Duffy reviewed his day. There was satisfaction in being accepted as a co-conspirator by men who could help him avenge the club-foot's abduction. He was proud of how he had deftly informed the missus of discoveries about the club-foot's disappearance without revealing any of the conspiratorial details. A letter sent upcountry to his brother to solicit his advice would not be remiss. He fell into a smug sleep, unaware the tiny woman was ruminating about his day as well.

Michael's simple, open mind has always been easy to read, she thought, *yet he has never been so abrupt or assertive with me before this day. How many are there of these like-minded neighbours? He resisted telling details of the meeting, so why the need to be so furtive? Unless these new associates have something to hide... The poor man says "our" instead of "their" and he has met with them but once. How far-reaching their grasp must be to have friends on the other side who can track down a boat's name. What will such men expect of him? The business can only suffer from today's diversion. Yes, the business will suffer.*

Mrs. Duffy fell into a troubled slumber, convinced a talk with Father Daudet could only be helpful.

Part Three

NORTH

Kentucky

Joseph was awakened by the sound of horses and wagon wheels. The sun was clearing morning mists; the ashes were cold. After making sure he could not be seen from the road, he stretched out the night chill, then sat with his back against a tree to assess his dire situation. It did not take long; there was no alternative but to press on.

Carrying their impedimenta into the trees, he added Seth's and Malachi's food shares and fishing line and matches to his own. Keeping the better canteen, he threw all but his own bundle into the forest. He hesitated before stepping onto the road; somehow, this step signified the start of a totally different journey. Even at this early hour, there was occasional traffic. Uncertain what to do if he met anyone, he set off to look for bloodstains in the dirt.

Malachi's body, thrown over the steep incline out of sight of the road, sprawled at the river's edge not far from where Joseph had clambered down. It had come to rest in a half-sitting pose, the back resting against small boulders, the left leg stretched out touching the water, the right twisted under. His huge right arm crossed his broad chest, the left flung wide. A pearl-white bone emerged from the jagged, bloody stump of the neck. Joseph had seen the thousand dollar canvas sack and had expected to find the corpse decapitated, but he shuddered at the gory sight nevertheless.

He sat down beside his old friend, trying to think how he could give him some dignity in death. To bury him was impossible. Rolling him into the river to be carried away seemed unnatural; Malachi would not want a watery grave. He straightened the bottom of Malachi's jacket to cover his rope belt. A round stone nearby he reverently placed above the body to restore some symmetry. He took the clasp knife peeking out of Malachi's right pocket as a memento.

If passersby had looked over the edge, they would have seen the headless corpse of a very large man, a young man sitting beside it, rocking back and forth, sobbing into hands cupped over his eyes. He wept for Malachi and Seth and for himself. Malachi, who always knew when rain was coming. Malachi, the reliable one, the steadfast one, always ready to lend a hand. Their conspiracy had started a day Malachi had tried to help remove a stump. And little Seth, with his huge heart. Seth, who figured out how to set a false trail for dogs. Seth, who was willing to be the decoy when they surprised those frolicking girls. He wept for them, and he wept for what they had lost.

He wiped his eyes on his shirt sleeve, patted Malachi's hand, said, "Rest. You will always be my friend," covered the torso with weeds, picked up the horse blanket bundle that held the sum of his earthly possessions, laboriously climbed up to the road, and began walking.

Meeting the first travellers was the worst. He couldn't dash into hiding each time someone approached or he was overtaken, so he attempted to look as if he were walking with a purpose, a specific destination in mind. He kept his face down, making eye contact with no one. It occurred to him that with the bundle on his shoulder he must be the very picture of the runaway slave, so he entwined his fingers through the knot and carried it at his side. The handle he used as a walking stick. At midday a beckoning rock beside a small stream provided a seat where he could dine on the depressingly scant victuals left. He refilled his canteen and plodded on.

Half an hour later, he was overtaken by an over-sized wagon drawn by four draft horses driven by an aged Black man in a shiny top hat and a long-tailed, burgundy velvet coat with wide black lapels, a coat that had seen better days. "Hop on if yer wantin' ta give yer feet a holiday," the old man yelled as he drew alongside. A younger Black man with a red bandana around his neck caught his bundle and his double with a blue one grabbed his arm to keep him balanced as he tried to hoist himself onto the planks while the empty wagon was still moving.

"Where you headed?" the red bandana asked, once everyone was seated.

"Nort'. Anywhere's nort'."

"We're peeling off on the northeast road where it splits. You can jump off there if it suits you."

"Nort'east would suit my feet just fine. I'm real thankful ya saw fit ta pick me up."

"Pa's done his share a walkin', knows 'bout sore feet, tries ta help the solitary pilgrim when he can."

"Sorta dangerous don't ya think, you travellin' all by yerself?" the blue bandana asked.

Joseph made no reply, just looked at the dirt passing by his dangling legs.

"You on some business?" the blue bandana persisted.

Joseph studied the road beneath his feet.

"Might not turn out comfortable for us if we was caught tryin' ta help a body whose master don't know just where he might be. You free or in bondage?"

"I is free now," Joseph said, without looking up.

"Now?" the blue bandana asked. "Who freed ya?"

"I freed myself," Joseph said, still looking at the road.

There was an uncomfortably long silence. Finally, the red bandana said, "We don't want no trouble. Kentucky's a mighty funny place if you be Black. Some is free, some is not. Don't matter ya be Black or white, it don't be particularly wise ta help runaways, 'cause it stirs up hard feelin's between folks."

"I understand. I kin walk from here so you kind people doan reap dat trouble you'se fearin'."

"Hold up there," the blue bandana said. "Who said anything 'bout us not helpin'? We jus' givin' a footsore traveller a ride, a traveller who never chanced to mention he freed hisself. Don't jump down just yet. Maybe we can nego'shate what our boss calls a symb'otic relationship."

"What about you? You free?" Joseph asked.

"We is sorta free," said the blue bandana.

"Either ya owns yerself or ya don't," Joseph said.

"We is almost free," the red bandana said. "We made a 'greement. Our master is sellin' us to ourselves. We get paid ninety cents a day 'cept Sundays, but he keeps forty cents back for food an' lodging. The other fifty cents goes toward us buying the three of us. We only got three hundred dollars more to go, then we work for cash wages. Unless he find somebody to work cheaper. That ain't gonna happen prob'ly. He can't get hired help to stay on. Work's too hard an' the hours too long."

"Do ya trust him ta keep da bargain?"

"We belongs to a deacon. Church of Christ Come Again, or somethin' like that. Never been in his church 'cause we ain't white. At least he's a deacon on Sundays. Does what he calls lay preachin'. Rest of the week, he owns a sawmill. We'll be there by suppertime tomorrow, day after if the roads ain't dry. Sawmill ain't big, but it turns out squared timbers for barns an' churches an' wherever ya need solid, load-bearing wood. Good market for properly cured square timber, 'specially for post and beam. We jus' comin' home from dropping off a full load. That's why Pa is drivin' four horses 'stead a two. A wagon load of squared timber is heavier than just logs."

"Just 'cause he's a deacon don't mean nothin'. Where I been, da man I trust da least, he read da Bible every day. He read, but he don't listen."

"Deacon, he say this a good bargain for all of us. We get outta bondage, he gets his money for us. He says he figures could be a war comin', or maybe northern folks outvote the southern folks and we all be freed, and then where would he be? This way, everybody's happy."

The blue bandana nodded. "Deacon, he's a smart man, got a good head for business for a man a God. See, we is payin' for our room and board, an' he is gettin' labour every day for half what we is worth. Is you int'rested in a job? The Deacon's always lookin' for help."

"I is int'rested in gettin' nort'. I is worth money, so I cain't trust nobody. Started out three of us. I'se the only one left 'cause we trusted what we thought was a abolitionist."

"Ain't no reason not to talk to Deacon," the red bandana said. "Deacon say he gettin' outta the slave ownin' business, an' I believe him. Never told us nothin' but truth, but if you suspicious of him we look the other way an' you keep on runnin'."

Joseph weighed his options. He didn't want to gamble on his freedom, yet his future on the road was nothing if not a huge risk. "I'm relying on da honesty of strangers," he said. "But I done dat before, an' we paid a mighty high price fer dat mistake."

That night they camped beside the road. The twins secured a rectangle of canvas over a ridge pole held up at one end in the crotch of a tree and the other secured in the fork of a tripod constructed from downed branches. After tending to the horses, the old man boiled some tea and the three shared cold beef sandwiches with Joseph. The bread was getting stale, so they dunked their sandwiches and finished the repast with oatmeal and raisin cookies. To Joseph's shrunken stomach, the meal was a feast. Although the precipitously dropping temperature penetrated his horse blanket cruelly by midnight, Joseph slept more soundly than he expected and was roused at first light by the jangle of harness as the twins prepared the team. The old man fried up some bacon and potatoes and made more tea, and then they were off.

This day there was little talk. A watery sun told Joseph they were travelling north and sometimes east. Despite his night's healing sleep, by the early afternoon the steady clop of the sixteen hooves lulled him into fitful snoozes, although as the team traversed rutted roads through hamlets and little villages, he was rigidly alert. He began to relax as he saw that no one paid any attention to them, nor were the twins or their father in the least apprehensive.

"Sure can tell we ain't near the big river," Joseph remarked. "We got bluffs an' hills, but I ain't ever seen hills like d'ese, squashed t'gether."

The blue bandana laughed. "Wait till we get home. These ain't really hills, just little bumps compared to what we is used to. Better hills than these any which way you look. And if you was to keep going east, I hear the hills get so big it takes most a day to climb over one and come down the other side."

"You tell'n me a stretcher? Doan tell me no stretchers, 'cause I ain't been far from da big river, an' I doan know what ta b'lieve."

The blue bandana just smiled. Joseph leaned against the back rack and watched the miles go by. *Every time I hear a horse foot hit da ground, dat one less foot I got ta put down for myself,* he thought. *An' my foot powerful slow compared to dat horse's foot. We makin' wonderful distance 'tween Massa Lonnegan an' me. Wonderful distance.* He thought of little Seth and Malachi and the stinking old peg-legged Judas and the aloof little terrier with a yarn collar. If only Malachi and Seth could have had his good luck, be here with him. They'd be laughing and joking with him, heading at speed toward the Ohio... He thought of Ellie. There was no chance he would ever again see that spontaneous smile or self-conscious wave of recognition. Impossible to even dream of takin' her with them. Impossible... Hateful ta think of leavin' her to her fate though.

The sun was three hours above the horizon when the old man turned the team off the main road. "Hot food tonight and our own beds," he called out.

Mature hardwoods carpeted hills that sloped into tableland meadow cut by a winding, high banked stream. Joseph noted the absence of near neighbours. The business looked orderly. A substantial timber frame house with precise corners and an overhanging post and beam wraparound porch sat at right angles to a mill powered by an undershot waterwheel in a wooden channel that drained a seven acre millpond. Beyond the pond, an arched bridge, wide enough for a team and wagon, spanned the creek. Squared timbers of varying lengths and widths were stacked in alternating layers beside a pile of slab wood and an equally high mound of sawdust. A small barn sheltering a large haystack and a smaller straw stack boasted an adjacent four rail fenced barnyard where three cows and several pigs watched their arrival with interest. Double doors on a second outbuilding suggested a stable.

A platoon of barn cats scattered at their approach, each vying to be the champion cheater of death from a horse's hoof. The usual flock of chickens concentrated on grain thrown by a strikingly attractive woman of about thirty in a green paisley dress, who smiled and waved and continued her task. She was followed by an old, grey-muzzled yellow dog claimed by no particular breed, a dog so feeble he had difficulty keeping his head erect, his metronome tail hard-pressed to maintain adagio.

The old man introduced Joseph to the Deacon while the red and blue bandanas unhitched the horses and took them to be fed and watered. The conversation was brief and one-sided.

"You bed down in Pa's quarters in the stable. The missus leaves supper on the porch table so the boys can look after themselves when their work is done. We'll talk later."

The Contract

The slaves inhabited half the mill side of the stable. Beside the door, a faded blue ironstone saucer held milk for cats. Opposite the stalls, quilted horse blankets on a wire created the illusion of three small rooms. In the farthest were hay and burlap sacks bulging with oats. The other two housed simple wooden beds with straw mattresses, a raw wood washstand with a mirror, an enamelled pitcher and basin and a small table for each room, and shelves laden with tin plates, chipped ceramic mugs, folded towels, blankets, pants, shirts and socks. Each washstand supported a coal oil lamp.

During the supper of pork, rice, beans, bread, and apple sauce in the first room, which the younger men shared, there was little conversation. The twins washed the dishes at a pump near the house, and by the time they had them stacked on a drying rack at the end of the porch, Deacon had entered the stable. He stayed standing, one boot resting on the end of the nearer bed, where Joseph took the opportunity to study him. Prematurely grey hair cropped short, straight teeth unstained by tobacco, skin leathered by weather, lumberjack arms, work roughened hands, a flat belly, a quick, purposeful stride — each suggested a man confident in himself and in fine physical condition as he entered middle age.

"So, another child of Ham come into misfortune... Name?"

"Joseph, suh."

"Have you been born again?"

Joseph misunderstood the question. "Yes, suh. Borned again when I left where I was borned da first time."

"Amen. Where were you headed when Pa picked you up? Your status is not my concern."

"Canada, suh, where da Britishers live."

"Your journey is ill-fated if you presume you can get even to Ohio this time of year in such rags. It's possible we can arrive at a mutually beneficial arrangement. I offer quarters. You can use the second bed in Pa's section, bunk in with him. It's freed up since the wife died last year. Cholera. Mighta bin yellow fever. Fast and terrible, whatever it was. My missus is almost lost without her.

I offer food. My wife serves enough to keep us working while there's light. I happen to think she's a good cook. Haven't heard these boys complain. I offer a fresh outfitting of clothes, including a quilted jacket. Better throw in some work boots too, judging by the looks of what's left of yours. However, listen now. I offer no money. None. Shall I keep going?"

"Yes suh, please."

"I offer hard work where no one shirks or malingers or complains. We labour from sun-up 'til sundown six days a week, although Wednesday afternoons the boys usually have an earlier quitting time so they can do laundry, now that their mother's passed. The living quarters are to be kept clean and tidy. The coal oil lamp is for light; candles are a fire hazard in a stable. You will not gamble or use alcohol or tobacco. I do not permit card playing. There will be no whistling or frivolity on the Sabbath. I would insist you accompany me to church, but my congregation would not be accepting."

He paused to gauge Joseph's reaction. Seeing none, he resumed.

"I offer to turn you over to the sheriff if you have committed a crime. Have you?"

"No, suh."

"In return, you offer your unstinting labour for ten weeks. After ten weeks, the clothes are yours and you are free to stay or go. This is a contract. Do you accept?"

"Yes, suh."

"The wife will keep the two young 'uns out of your quarters and out of harm's way. You will have nothing to do with her or the children or Butch, her dog. He's getting too old to be much protection, but he won't admit to that — follows her everywhere. He gets nervous if he senses a threat to her or the girls. She will respect your privacy as you will respect hers. You would not understand my wife anyway; she was born deaf, so her communication is unintelligible. She must print what she wants, even to me. Still, the woman is better than I deserve."

He removed his foot from the bed but hesitated as he turned to go.

"Everyone calls the old man Pa. Even Pa can't tell the difference between the twins some days, so he has one wear a red bandana, the other one a blue. We just call them Red and

Blue. Everyone hereabouts calls me Deacon or The Deacon, a title I wear with pride."

As Joseph settled into a real bed with the promise of new clothes to come, it occurred to him that except for the old yellow dog, he had not heard anyone's proper name. He thought of Malachi, of Seth, of men with ropes and muskets, of the man with the knee-high brown boots. He thought of an undercut boulder and a shiny pearl-white bone protruding from a headless neck. He thought of beautiful, blossoming, sweet Ellie. The old man saw the tears and graciously turned toward the blanket wall.

Rot and Vinegar

Bindle leaned against a stable doorpost and idly watched the wheelbarrowing of steaming manure to the pile outside the back door. Rubbing his hands together and blowing on clenched fingers against the cold, he turned at the sound of horses coming up the lane. Leaving his post, he walked out to meet a small, unpainted buckboard. As the horses reined to a stop, he nodded a greeting. The slender, long-haired stranger touched a forefinger to his hat and said nothing.

Bindle motioned to an inquisitive face peering from the barn door. "Go to the back door of the big house. Tell Cicero that Master Lonnegan's presence is required." He knew a field hand's knock would signal urgency.

Lonnegan appeared, buttoning a wool jacket as he strode directly to the buckboard. He said nothing to the stranger, simply looked at the cargo with no hint of anger or disgust, his hands on his hips.

Seth sat barefooted in his rags with legs splayed out on filthy straw, a manacle on his right wrist chained to a staple hammered into the top plank of the buckboard. His hair was matted with dried blood. Dried blood encrusted the corners of his mouth and right ear. His nose had been broken. His left elbow jutted at an unnatural angle. He stared unblinking at a large oak bucket tied to a second staple with no indication he knew where he was or even that the buckboard had stopped.

Without turning his head, in a quiet voice Lonnegan said, "Mister Bindle, when I have finished my business with this gentleman, ring the assembly bell. We'll gather at the ear tree. House servants as well. Everyone. You and your men will be at the rear. I will be attending to this personally."

Hopping down from his seat, the stranger untied the rope from its staple, and looking away, placed the bucket gently beside a front wheel. "Starting to stink real bad. Could be worse, could be summer. We put the head in vinegar to slow the rot, make sure you could recognize your property. Stores better without the flesh, though."

"I appreciate your attention to detail." Still looking at Seth, Lonnegan said, "Mister Bindle, tell Cicero to have water put into the laundry cauldron and fire it up. On your way back, bring me sufficient rope."

"Mister Ragg sends his regards," the slender man said. "My father apologizes for not being able to return the third just yet, but he insists you rest assured he's on the trail and closin' in. I ain't never seen him so enraged that he ain't caught a fugitive 'fore it got this far. Pa don't like failure, he don't. Blames hisself for us not gettin' all three at the interception. He's so hornet stung mad, he's got a business proposition for ya."

"Yes?"

"If you'll increase the reward to one thousand, he'll top it up to twelve hundred out of his own pocket. Twelve hundred would mightily sweeten the motivation for people to be vig'lant, ya see? Like I said, Pa don't tolerate failure, even from hisself."

"Two out of three is not complete failure. It is preferable to none out of three. I detest ingratitude even more than failure. Give my kind regards to Mister Ragg and communicate that one thousand is acceptable."

"He will thank you, sir. He's up in Kentucky at the moment, reelin' in a rumour someone soundin' like your runner was seen riding on an empty wagon pulled by a double team. There were three others, but it's the fourth that fits the description."

Pulling a rusty iron key from his pocket, he unlocked the manacle, dropped the tailgate of the buckboard, pulled Seth out with one hand, and left him in a heap on the ground. He turned the team around, acknowledged Bindle and Lonnegan with a finger to his hat, and disappeared down the lane.

Mister Bindle assembled the slaves.

Ten Weeks

Joseph quickly discovered that a field hand's life on a southern plantation had not prepared him for his new occupation. Over the next weeks he learned the best ways to guide a falling tree with ropes, the intricacies and dangers of notching and felling trees with crosscut saw and axe, how to limb safely and efficiently, the capricious ways of logging chains, how to skid logs with a team of horses without getting mashed in the process, and how to peavey logs onto the mill's "buggy", a wheeled platform on iron rails. He was astounded by how few hardwood logs could be squared cutting with the grain before the saw blade required a sharpening. Pa showed him how to file the teeth without nicking his fingers and how to determine the precise position for the blade to avoid wastage.

In the beginning, using the steel yardstick to measure alternate offsets was frustrating; his knowledge of fractions stopped at halves and quarters. Deacon gave him responsibility for regulating water flow from the millpond into the mill race by raising or lowering damming planks in their grooves, and one of his daily duties was to pour buckets of water over the inventory of piled timbers. It was explained that even in the winter months they must season slowly to prevent warping and cracking. Pa taught him how to establish the edge angle of an axe on a grindstone and finish it with a file. Each day brought new challenges and improved skills. When the missus came back from Mayfield with new clothes, a pair of padded leather gloves was included.

Deacon was as good as his word about respecting his privacy. When the slaves were nearby, the little children and the wife would smile and wave from one world into another. If Butch thought they were too close to his charges, his tail would go still and he would utter a low, thunder-over-the-horizon growl.

Short winter days meant shorter working hours, which gave Joseph's muscles an opportunity to adapt to the new life. Not all labour involved felling, skidding, and squaring timber. Draft horses consumed copious amounts of food and water. The stable required mucking, harness needed to be oiled, hay and straw brought in from the stacks. The work was hard, but the wife's cooking was ample and as tasty as Deacon promised.

Deacon declared no work would be done on Christmas Day; the wife left a roast goose dinner with scalloped potatoes, parsnips, dressing, gravy, and fresh bread on the porch for the crew. As a Christmas present, Pa and the twins received a dollar apiece and Joseph was given a new red handkerchief. New Year's Eve, work was stopped at the sawmill in the early afternoon, and on the first full day of 1857 they only tended to the animals.

After supper one evening, Deacon entered the stable with a sugar pie in one hand and a small notebook in the other. "Reckonin' day," Pa explained. Deacon slid slices onto alligatored china plates, and while they ate he reviewed with the old man and the twins the status of what he referred to as their bondage account. Once each had scratched his X at the bottom of the relevant page he turned his attention to Joseph.

"Ten weeks. So your clothes are paid for. Grub sufficient?"

"Yes, Deacon, better than I'm used ta. Lots of it. Mouthwaterin', every morsel. I ain't had a bad meal yet. Even da field lunches da missus pack for us, she don't skimp on 'em. Yer wife, she a mighty fine cook, suh."

"Glad to hear it. I'll pass on your observation. She'll be pleased. I sometimes wonder if a pretty woman like her would be content here with me if she didn't carry such an affliction. Now, let's talk about the future."

Joseph shifted uncomfortably on his chair.

"I'm trying to see the bigger picture. I'm a businessman first, and I believe there's war fever starting to simmer. This here *Fugitive Slave Act* just puts it on the boil 'cause the Northerners are digging in their heels about returning property. Around these parts that's called theft and a deliberate flouting of the law."

Joseph said nothing.

"Some folks at church last Sunday said there's a man sniffing around south of here, looking for someone who sounds like it could be you. Offers cash for information, he does. You being here could put me and my enterprise on a tender footing with most of the people I do business with — if they find out you belong to someone else. If I don't return you to your owner, that makes me no better than Northern scum who won't honour a contract."

Joseph looked at the floor and clasped his hands to prevent them from shaking.

"Folks are sayin' he's a brutish-looking individual asking after a Black man about your age, a runaway who accosted two young white girls, made them strip naked, stole their clothes before he... before he..." Deacon paused. "Any truth to that? Even a little bit of truth?"

"No, Deacon! No, suh! I swear on da Bible an' all dat's holy d'ere ain't no truth ta dat. No suh, no truth at all, no truth at all! None!"

"I could use your help here. Because you're a good worker, twenty cents a day, if you're interested. But you think through what I just told you before you make any decision about staying for twenty cents a day. You best know, if that man or your owner shows up and asks how you are in my employ, I won't hazard my eternal soul on a lie. You got that?"

Joseph nodded.

Deacon turned his attention to Pa and the twins. "If there's a war coming, as a businessman I want my family to come out the other side in good shape. An army won't want our squared hardwood to build fine buildings. It will want rough lumber for wagons and rail beds. And you know what else it will want, boys? Food, that's what. Food. It will need beef. An army pays good money for beef. So I'm planning on diversifying, 'cause I'm smelling a war. The trees best for squared timber are getting scarcer and farther from the mill and higher on the hills. None at all left in the bottom-land, so I intend to buy some prime breeders, top quality stock, and go into the beef business. We'll use the valley grass to feed 'em."

He paused and waited for a reaction. Seeing none, he continued.

"Here's what we're gonna do. Pa, you'll stay here, look after the chores, keep the place running. Red, Blue, we'll haul a full load of prime timbers north. They'll cover our expenses and more if we can get 'em to Paducah. There are some real big churches planning to be built in Paducah. Real big."

Joseph's ears focused on every syllable after "north".

Pa said, "What we know 'bout cattle? 'Versifying do seem like a cracker idea, but what we know 'bout calvin' an' butcherin' an' ailments and all that? Seems to me we maybe need longer days, what with timberin' in the winter an' ranchin' in the summer. How you gonna keep 'em from just wanderin' off 'less we put up fences here to Jericho or somebody watchin' 'em every minute?"

"There won't be so many we can't handle, least at first. I aim to keep a manageable herd, sell off all but the breeders in the fall. We can throw together some windbreaks and put in more hay before next winter. Animals and people act the same; they'll stay in the bottom-lands where there's water and good grass and not go to the bother of climbing the hills."

Deacon turned to Joseph. "Now you know where this business is headed. Steady work for twenty cents a day. Steady until somebody shows up claiming you. Or you can choose to go north. But if you work your way north with the twins and me, I will feed you only. I'll help you that far, but no more. No profit in it for me, you see."

Joseph nodded. "Deacon, I understan'. You is a businessman. You is prob'ly gonna ask me if I need some time ta think 'bout yer offer. No suh, you and yer missus bin truly kind ta me, offerin' me a job an' a bed an' best food I ever set down ta, but I doan need no time ta think. I best head nort', help ya 'til we get to dis Paducah town. Dat way d'ere ain't no cause for grief wif da neighbours."

Deacon patted him on the shoulder. "Probably a wise decision. For both of us."

At the stable door, Deacon turned and added, "Pa will choose the best timbers tomorrow, and you boys get 'em loaded for an early start the morning after. That 'll give the missus time to pack a few days' grub for us. I don't imagine there's going to be an inn just where we want one between here and Paducah."

"When we throw a couple sacks of oats on top for the horses," Pa added, "I'll tie 'em down and cover 'em good, 'cause my hurtin' feet is saying you boys is gonna be setting off in weather meaner than a jilted badger with a hangover."

Ellie Washes a Platter

A gusting rain furied by an angry north wind had lashed the plantation house since before dawn. Cicero circumnavigated the interior to verify that all shutters had been closed and secured as he had directed. As he glided into the breakfast room, he noticed Ellie, hands on the edge of the dish pan, gazing out the unshuttered window of the adjoining kitchen. Before he could react, Mrs. Lonnegan at her coffee placed a forefinger to her lips and motioned him to sit at the other side of the breakfast table. They watched the girl in silence.

With the slow, fluid motions of a sleepwalker, Ellie began to wash the platter that had transported the breakfast's eggs and bacon, all the while gazing out into a monochromatic greyness. Her head paid no attention to the habits of her hands. The thoroughly spotless platter was stacked in the drainboard, then absentmindedly returned to the dishpan and washed again. And again. And then again.

Unaware she was being observed, the young woman continued her vigil, mesmerized by the drama of the winter storm. The rain deposited accretions of ice on grass and fences and bushes and branches until in minutes all was covered in a translucent sheath.

On the ear tree, the wind buffeted Seth. The torsion of the rope twisted him south and then back to the north. North, then south, then north, then south, north, south, north... As it became encrusted in ice, his emaciated, child-like body swayed in the wind less and less, until Ellie saw the pendulum almost stop. Her gaze dropped to the base of the tree, to an old yellow chair where Malachi's skull had become crystal.

Her hands washed the platter once again. She dropped her eyes to the dishwater, smiled at some private pleasant thought, hummed an unintelligible song, and began to sway her hips and shoulders to its hidden rhythm. Looking up, with a soapy forefinger she traced a J on the window and circled it with a heart.

Constance Lonnegan motioned for Cicero to stay sitting. She walked into the kitchen and slapped Ellie hard, once, twice, three times, right, left, right, across the back of the head. Startled, Ellie put the back of her left hand over her mouth and looked down at the dishpan, not daring to move. Breathing heavily from the exertion, the mistress stood behind her for a full five breaths before she said, "Bitch! Until I give you permission, you do not leave your quarters!"

Ellie fled the kitchen, sobbing. Constance Lonnegan returned to her coffee.

Paducah

They did not set off for Paducah for three days, and even then Deacon wondered if he should have tarried longer. Yesterday's warmer breeze had melted the ice, so the rutted roads were churned into a deeper mud than was usual in March. The ice storm had scattered branches and occasionally fallen trees across their route. Sometimes it took all four men to move the blow-downs, and twice they had to unhitch the lead horses to swing mature trees out of their path. Their speed was inconsistent. Although approaching travellers had done their share to clear the road ahead, the horses tired early from the arduous pull.

No one expected celerity. A local carpenter and wheelwright had custom built the substantial wagon with a reinforced frame to permit heavy loads. To undercut costs, the Deacon's own mill provided the hardwood. With a full load of squared timbers, progress was slow with only four draft horses, even when the road was dry.

Despite minimal speed, spirits were high. Deacon enthused about his new beef herd financed by timber sales, Red and Blue were escaping the drudgery of labour at the mill, and Joseph was heading north. The days journeying to

Paducah were the happiest since he had escaped but tempered by bad memories. As each horse's footfall carried him closer to the Ohio and farther from the spectre of the brown leather vest and the knee-high brown boots, he lamented that Malachi and little Seth could not share in his progress. He thought of Ellie. She would never see as much of the world as he, never see rolling hills like these or villages this big, with dozens of people scurrying about their business or sometimes doing nothing at all. How could she break out of her incarceration unless she ran as well? Maybe Lonnegan would sell her. He thought of Cicero.

As they plodded through one hamlet or village after another, no one wasted a second glance at three Black men proceeding with their master on such an obvious mission. Joseph had never felt safer.

The first night out, a farmer let the horses roam in a two acre meadow he had fenced off for a garden while the humans endured a cold night under the wagon. The Deacon gave him two-bits for his kindness.

On day two, they lost the afternoon detouring around a bridge that was under repair. The banks were too steep to hazard getting the wagon into the water then not being able to haul it up the other side. By pure chance, in the middle of a tiny hamlet they discovered an inn with a livery, just as Deacon was remarking they might need to camp for a second night. Their host permitted the Blacks to throw down bedrolls in the stable, and to stretch their food supplies Deacon brought out bowls of watery stew and a loaf of bread before he retired to his meal and room and Bible inside. All agreed the Deacon's wife made a better stew. Even so, it was warm and filling.

After a hasty breakfast, they discovered the horses weren't all that eager to be harnessed for another day's pull, and for the first hour on the road Deacon complained about his back, his sagging mattress with the mildewed sheets, and the exorbitant fees for food and lodging. He insisted the stable inhabitants must have enjoyed a more comfortable night.

A chilling northeast wind threatened more rain on their third day out. The democratic dampness made no one comfortable, although the Blacks warmed a little when they walked behind the wagon to lighten the load while the Deacon drove up hills. For Joseph, no amount of discomfort could detract from the heaven-sent gift of security. He was heading toward a new life while using someone else's food and someone else's horses and someone else's reasons for being on the road to get him there.

Oncoming travellers advised about washouts or inns to avoid or a mean dog just ahead or where best to rest the horses. The last night before Paducah, they stayed at a small inn where an aged, frail proprietor looked them over circumspectly before giving stable privileges and renting Deacon a room. Deacon wasn't too tired to be irritated when he heard the prices demanded for the various services. "Exploitation of an honest citizen trying to do an honest business, sir. Shameful, sir, that you would attempt to take advantage of a traveller who needs food and shelter for both man and beast and who you very well know you have at your mercy." The grizzled host shrugged a "take it or leave it," and turned back to stacking pint glasses on shelves behind the bar. A deal was struck when Deacon agreed to have his boys carry wood from the woodshed and stack it in the summer kitchen at the rear in return for a reduced fee.

With the horses fed and watered and the wood piled, the boys received their supper of sausages, shrivelled fried potatoes, pickled beets, and stale bread at the back door. They ate in the stable by the dim yellow light of a candle lantern bravely trying to light the world through dust accumulated over a lifetime of neglect. Joseph gathered up the tin plates and returned them to the summer kitchen. Through the grimy window of the inn's back door he could see Deacon sitting at a small table just on the other side, his back to the window. His dirty plate and cutlery had not yet been cleared, and he was in conversation with a plump, ferret-faced man dressed as a farmer or tradesman sitting opposite.

Joseph was about to return to the stable when he heard the stranger ask, "What do you need three of them for, just to deliver one wagon load of wood?"

Deacon explained he owned a sawmill, and wood squared correctly needed muscle, not just for processing but for loading and unloading and so on...

"Beer or whiskey? On me."

"Neither, but thank you. I don't indulge in spirits of any kind. This coffee suits me fine for now."

"You sure? I'm buying."

"I'm sure."

"Don't see how wood needs much more attention than just finding a place for it once it's cut," the ferret face said.

"There's more to milling than that. For lasting constructions, straight-grained wood needs slow, consistent drying once it's cut and stacked, and that has to be done proper. The skeleton of Lord Nelson's *Victory* was cured for three years before the hull planks were added. That's why building projects pay very well indeed for quality timbers."

"Is that right? Even so, you need three? I happen to be in the market for labour. What do you want for the young one?"

"What are you offering?"

Joseph froze.

"Five hundred dollars. I can give you a draft on my bank in Louisville, you cash it in Paducah, I pick him up there when you're finished with him."

"What kind of business are you in that you need more labourers?"

"I provide a service. Think of me as a broker. Buy low, sell high. See, by the time you were to sell the young one, you would need to advertise and guarantee health and delivery and maybe not get a buyer for months. There'd be haggling and inconvenience. Me, I know the right people, men of substance who pay good money, especially for the young ones. And especially for the females. Comely young females can fetch a very attractive price. Got any of them back at your sawmill?"

Deacon sipped his coffee, said nothing, studied the dirty plates, pondered the offer...

"Six hundred. Worth eight hundred to people I know that you don't. At six hundred I make twenty-five per cent. There's God's truth between honest businessmen."

Joseph's mind raced! Until now his future had looked so promising, yet the universe had pivoted between a stable and a summer kitchen door. How many cows would six hundred dollars buy? The Deacon was a businessman... All depended on the next word.

"Not for sale. My business needs skilled labour. It takes years to master the intricacies; there's more to it than most imagine. I would prefer to keep the tested commodity than gamble on the unknown."

"Suit yourself, but the offer is open at six hundred if you change your mind."

Joseph slowly exhaled and tiptoed out of the summer kitchen. At the barn, he sat down on his bedroll, weak in the knees.

"You look like you just see'd a ghost," Red said.

"Ya say ya believe what Deacon tells ya, dat he ain't never lied to ya?" Joseph asked.

"Never lied yet, far as we know. Why you ask?"

"'Cause I overheard Deacon talkin' to a slave trader 'bout me, an' it sure sound like he was thinkin' I was belongin' ta him."

"Did he talk about sellin' ya?" Blue asked.

"Not 'zactly. But he goin' on an' on 'bout how his sawmill business needs skilled labour so I ain't for sale."

Red shook his head and flattened his bedroll in the straw. "Maybe he just sayin' that to de-flect the trader's interest."

"Maybe. Maybe not. Ya best know I'se shovin' off on my own da second I sees dat trader in Paducah or nosin' 'round Deacon, so I'll thank ya now fer lookin' afta me wif such kindness when ya didn't half ta. An' you pass on my gratitude ta Pa too, an' tell him thanks for pickin' me up on da road."

The following morning they entered Paducah. The sights, sounds, and smells of a bustling river port left Joseph's head swivelling. He said nothing to Red or Blue, not wishing to play the country bumpkin, but he could tell they too had never witnessed the frenetic activity of an industrious urban centre. Every back street boasted at least one enterprise catering to the boat-building industry that monopolized the waterfront.

The pastor of the Methodist church directed the wagon to an address several blocks away, explaining the squared timber had been purchased by his congregation as a gift to the Coloured folk so they could establish their own place of worship. Deacon bought sandwiches and soup from a nearby tavern, and by mid-afternoon the timbers were ramped off the wagon and neatly stacked. No one was happier than the horses.

"The pastor recommends an establishment four blocks straight ahead," Deacon said, wiping an arm across his forehead. "Look for green doors. That's what it's called, The Green Door Inn. You can wait for me there. I'll be along presently. I'm going to stretch my legs and walk back to the church to pick up the money owed me."

They waited for almost two hours, lounging on the empty wagon, inhaling the sawdust, tar, and fish smells of a river town, and watching the locals come and go about their business.

"Ya doan suppose he's been robbed a all dat cash, do ya?" Joseph ventured. "We be in a heap a trouble, d'ey find him floatin' face down in da river."

Blue thought for a moment before replying. "He get murdered, that'd be a tragedy for everyone 'cause we be so close to buying us, and him showin' up dead just when Pa's gettin' too old to start somethin' new. We b'long to just the missus then, and maybe she sell the land and the mill and us too. She gotta look after the children somehow, don't she? She ain't gonna..."

Blue stopped talking and pointed down the street. There was Deacon, strolling, studying storefronts that interested him, occasionally chatting with strangers, every inch the tourist. At the inn, he held up a forefinger to indicate he would not be long and entered to register.

By supper time, the horses were unhitched to enjoy the comforts of a spacious livery stable and the slaves had scattered straw beside the end stall in anticipation of a good night's rest. For their repast as the light faded, Deacon brought still-warm bread, fried potatoes, catfish, and a pot of coffee. With cream. And sugar. In celebration of a successful delivery, he had even purchased four iced cinnamon buns. Red stretched out contentedly and patted his stomach. Blue appeared to have dozed off. Deacon offered a morsel of fish to a scrawny barn cat and motioned for Joseph to join him at the stable door.

Joseph had known this conversation was coming. The one about what comes next. The one where one moment he was listening to Deacon and the next he was on the run. The one where he found out Deacon had no intention of letting him continue north. The bun with icing leaded in his gut.

A Whiff of Brimstone

"My plans have changed," Deacon began. Joseph tensed. "The proprietor informs me there's a regular customer of his going to show up soon. He says I should listen to what he has to say. He says it could be profitable. Says this regular customer has influential friends. I told him I'm a businessman on my way to buy quality cattle. No matter what transpires, my offer of twenty cents a day will still hold when we return to the mill."

"When we return to the mill" echoed in Joseph's brain. "When we return to the mill..." So, Deacon thought he could...

The ferret-faced man who had offered Deacon six hundred dollars entered the stable. He grabbed a lantern and held it close to Joseph's face, then replaced it on its nail. With no word of greeting, he unfolded a piece of paper and held it up for Deacon's perusal.

"See what it says here? Eh? Twelve hundred dollars for the capture and return. Name of Joseph. Belongs to a man what has a plantation north of Memphis. Dead or alive. And you were lettin' on that you weren't gonna even entertain sellin' this one 'cause he was so 'skilled' you couldn't part with him. You expect me to swallow that bullshit?"

"There's no need to be crude, Mister..."

"Is he your property or not?"

"What makes you think he is not my property?"

"My business associates, that's what. And your equivocation! This is Joseph what's named on the paper, ain't it?"

"Well, his name certainly is Joseph. As for..."

"And I thought you were an honest, God-fearing man. Turns out you're slipperier than a squashed eel. Of course you had no intention of selling him for six hundred when you can get twelve hundred for him dead or alive. What a goddamned fool I was, thinkin' I could... Well maybe your little game will backfire, eh?"

Deacon moved so he could see if anyone else entered the stable. "You will discover I do not intimidate easily, sir. Your bluster I find offensive."

"Jesus Christ Almighty! Bluster? Where the hell do you think you are? This is Kentucky. And north a' here is Butternut country. Don't matter if some of the folks don't care for slavery 'cause they like Nigras, slave or free, even less. Takin' their jobs, settin' North against South..."

"I will not indulge you with a philosophical discussion on the merits of..."

"Discussion? You'll see how much discussin' we'll be doin' once my associates arrive. Word's out. Travels fast for twelve hundred dollars. I can get a good chunk for doin' nothin' but ringin' the bell."

"I think you should leave, sir. We have had an enervating day."

"Fine. But don't you leave. I'll be back tomorrow, and we'll get this business settled to my satisfaction. And you make certain Joseph don't go for a walk either."

"Your threats fall on deaf ears, sir. I will carry on with my business as I wish. I bid you a good evening."

Deacon looked both ways down the street to make sure the trader was out of earshot before he closed the stable door.

No one said a word. Deacon moved a three-legged stool beside the horse stalls and sat gazing at the stable floor, his elbows on his knees. After several minutes he shook his head to break out of his reverie, emptied his shirt pocket of some loose papers, dropped them at his feet, and motioned for the others to gather round.

Without looking up, he said in a quiet voice, "That was very close. Very close indeed. Breathe in, and you will detect a whiff of brimstone. Six hundred dollars, twelve hundred dollars, thirty pieces of silver... All that ever changes is the amount." He took a deep breath and exhaled slowly through his mouth. "Joseph, I beg your forgiveness. I must confess I was truly, truly tempted by the offer of six hundred dollars. Then I thought of the cattle I could buy for twelve hundred and I... I determined to... I was considering... I have no excuse. It was greed that fuelled my thoughts of betrayal."

The three listened to the penitent as if in a tableau. Downcast, unspeaking, Deacon continued to look at the stable floor. Finally, he took another deep breath and stirred himself more erect. "Did you hear those blasphemous eruptions? I can not, I will not, do business with someone who uses our Lord's name in such a fashion."

Deacon picked up the papers from his feet and stuffed them back into his shirt pocket. "I need to think clearly and act quickly, before anyone shows up to apprehend Joseph. Worse, I will be held accountable for aiding and abetting the escape of another's property. Obviously my only hope will be to plead ignorance, but my business will wither once I am labelled a thief or an abolitionist or a Northern sympathizer. My options are as enticing as pig swill."

He stood up. "I am going out. Kill the lantern and bar the stable door behind me; we cannot trust the landlord. I won't be long."

He was long. It was after midnight when he returned. "I need to see what I'm doing. Put a candle on the stool but don't light the lantern." When Joseph lit a match, he was startled to see a small boy of about twelve waiting deferentially just inside the door.

"Ignore him. Gather 'round. My plans have dramatically changed. In conversation with knowledgeable individuals in Paducah, I have decided to journey to Cincinnati, and then a ways north, where I intend to buy quality livestock and have them shipped by river to where I can herd them home.

Blue, Red, you will hitch up and leave for the mill at first light. Get as early a start as you can. The horses will be rested, so make good time." He pulled the loose papers from his shirt, fished more from a pants pocket, and sorted them in the feeble light. "Here is money for victuals on the road, and in the event you are stopped and questioned, here is a signed letter explaining that with my permission you are returning home from a business trip."

"What you want us say, Deacon?" Blue asked.

"Tell the truth. Say that the last time you saw me I was looking for cattle to buy, and you have absolutely no idea where I am."

"What about Joseph?"

"Again, tell the truth. Joseph has run off. They'll swallow that, knowing he knows there are people after him for the reward. You don't need to mention that the running off you are referring to happened several months ago."

"Deacon, you sure be one smart man," Joseph said.

Red tied his bandana around Joseph's neck. "Won't fool no one close up, but them thinking I'm you from a distance or you're me, well, might get you a few steps on 'em."

Joseph seized his wrist and squeezed it in gratitude. "Da boss, he ain't da only smart one," he whispered.

"While you're hitching up the wagon, Joseph and I will slip out with the boy to guide us," Deacon continued. "We leave now, a conversation with the night watch might prove uncomfortable. Raise suspicions. Leave a trail. So we'll get some rest first. Once I retrieve my Bible and things, I'll bed down here for an early start. The boy will rouse us if anyone comes poking about."

In the grey light before dawn, the boy led them down to the waterfront through a maze of lumber, old clinker-built rowboats with holed hulls, open-air forges, and rusty heaps of discarded metal. For such an early hour, there was much activity. The boy pointed to a wharf where three Black men, barefoot and shirtless even in the cold, trundled coal with wheelbarrows and tipped it down an iron trough into the hold of a small steamboat. Deacon slipped a few coins into an outstretched hand, and they were left alone beside two orange cats sharing a fish head.

Deacon said, "I only purchased one ticket, but I have arranged for you to work your way upriver. This here is a Howard boat, whatever that means, on its way to Cincinnati to pick up hardware and spare parts. You will work in the engine room, fuelling the firebox. You will be fed adequately, so I'm told, and better yet, we will not be stopping in Louisville. That will make any pursuit more difficult. Or you can cut loose from here if you wish. Your choice."

"I is mighty 'ppreciative, Deacon, mighty 'ppreciative, for all dat you has done for me. I will not forget it, suh. Never. I ain't never bin on a steamboat b'fore, 'specially one dat's takin' me ta Cincinnati. I would pull dis here boat wif a rope in my teef b'fore I miss a chance ta go nort'."

Deacon laughed. "Cincinnati is a good ways off. You would have sore teeth before we got away from the wharf. Can you swim?"

"No, suh. Never had no call for swimmin'. But I reckon I could learn real quick if the wrong people comes along."

A middle-aged Black man in a threadbare red shirt bulging with muscles beckoned for Joseph to join him on the aft deck. "You be the new boy what's gonna take my place?" He laughed, puffed up his huge chest, and handed Joseph a pan shovel. "Ain't nobody kin take my place. You're a coal monkey now, like Jefferson. He's already below. I'se the fireman. Today I'se the fireman 'cause our reg'lar fireman busted his arm jist yesterday. Promotion fer me, so what you an' Jefferson is gonna do ta keep me happy is you keep coal comin' from that storage bin ta the hopper 'front of the furnace. Then I take an' scatter it inta the firebox in just the right way so as ta keep the heat even. Takes practice. Today, you'se the brute and I'se the skilled labour," and he laughed again. "Not many boats usin' coal. Most usin' wood. Ya might say we is a experiment. Coal be the future though... Burns hotter an' takes up less space."

Joseph followed the man below, where a Black man in his twenties, muscled like the fireman, was using a glove to open draft vents on the furnace. The firebox was already striving to develop a head of steam. "Hot work," the newly anointed fireman said, "so you keep yerself watered from that jug over there. You and Jefferson let this here hopper get below a third, you be swimmin' to Cincinnati."

'I cain't swim," Joseph said.

"No matter ta me. You just feed that hopper an' don't make me look bad my first fireman day. This little craft, she gonna gobble up lots an' lots of coal 'cause it's high water and we is fightin' the current. Enough jawin'. When we start movin', you know we's built enough pressure."

Engine noise increased until it prohibited conversation. When a shadow passed the head of the stairs and Joseph peered around, fearful of catching sight of a ferret's face, Jefferson banged his shovel, signalling him to get back to work. New vibrations through the hull indicated they had cast off.

A pulse of elation coursed through him. He was hidden from the menacing eyes of Paducah and on his way to a free state. He began to shovel coal into the hopper to match Jefferson's slow and steady rhythm.

The Deacon Talks Cattle

"Herefords, Joseph. Herefords. I've decided on Herefords. I talked to several cattlemen on the boat, and they all say the same thing. Herefords."

Joseph peered down the track to catch a first glimpse of the locomotive that would pull him farther north and said nothing to dim the ardour of the recently converted bovine enthusiast.

"Yes, Joseph, my herd must be Herefords. When the war comes, I want the best cattlebeasts in Kentucky. A war can be beneficial for those in the right business at the right time. Top dollars for top beef, and I'll be ready."

"Ya gotta go all da way ta Columbus ta get d'ese prime Herefords you is salivatin' over? Ain't no Herefords in Kentucky dat ya can drive home wif less fuss?"

"My boy, I have done my research, and I will find the best breeders near Columbus. Columbus, that's where they'll be. A few years back there was an agricultural fair planned for Cincinnati. Well, it never happened because of cholera, so all the farmers that expected to do some wheeling and dealing were either afraid of the outbreak or not willing to go all the way to Cincinnati. But now, Joseph, now the state fair has been relocated to Columbus, and everyone will be getting their stock ready for it, and that is why we are waiting for the train. If this train can take us there, it can bring cattle back."

"Pa and da boys be right when d'ey say you be one smart businessman, Deacon."

"A successful businessman looks for opportunities, listens to knowledgeable people, and trusts in the Lord for guidance. The Good Lord provided a farmer on the Howard boat who told me all about Herefords. Came from England originally. Not the farmer, the cattle. Says the English appreciate good roast beef. Says they're hardy, good breeders, thrifty eaters. The Herefords, not the English. They produce a marbled meat that cooks up tender. Gentle dispositions, so they're easy to work with. Again, the cattle, not the English."

"Dat 'll please Pa an' da boys," Joseph said, "'cause Pa's bin frettin' at knowin' nothin' 'bout cattle. Pa prob'ly never heard tell a Herefords."

"He can learn. Look how much I learned from just one man. Not all is sunshine and roses, though. Herefords may be prone to vaginal prolapse."

"What do prolapse mean?"

"I think it means out when it should be in. See, you were right to inquire about the meaning of an unfamiliar word; we must be open to new ideas and experiences. I intend to learn, as will you, what a ride on a train is like. Naturally, you'll be in the baggage car, but we can compare our journeys when we reach our destination."

"Leastways I won't be workin' my passage all da way, praise da Lord, whilst you was talkin' cattle."

"Look on the bright side, Joseph. How many get the opportunity to learn the intricacies of a steam engine first hand?"

"Deacon, da 'intricacies' I learned was dat heavy coal in Paducah gets a whole lot heavier da closer ya get ta Cincinnati."

The Friends

Deacon stopped the buggy at a church architectured with four classical Greek columns. Joseph waited with the horse while Deacon knocked on a side door, then wandered around the building, peering in windows with hands framing his face when no one answered. He had just completed the circuit when the door opened and a feeble old man emerged, broom in hand. Joseph heard them exchange pleasantries, but their subsequent conversation was inaudible. The old man disappeared back inside for a minute or two, and when he reemerged he handed Deacon a folded piece of paper. Deacon tipped his hat and returned to the buggy. He offered no word of explanation and was uncharacteristically silent as they drove into the countryside.

After several miles, Deacon reined the buggy to a halt at a fork in the road, referred to the paper, and returned it to a breast pocket. "It has been arranged to meet a Friend here. Better to be early than miss the connection."

"Dis connection doan have nothin' ta do wif buying Herefords, does it? You got a friend near Columbus?"

"No Joseph, we aren't here for Herefords. This is where you leave me. Sometime soon, a Quaker will arrive down the left fork. The Quakers call themselves the Society of Friends. The Friends provide safe houses, medicine, transportation, whatever you need to escape. I've got you as far as I can. However, I must not neglect my business any longer, so I'm turning you over to trustworthy people to get you to the Canadas."

Joseph was silent a long minute. "Deacon, you tell me true. Dis here excursion doan have nothin' ta do wif finding da best breeding stock, does it? Ya coulda bought good Herefords in Kentucky if you'd a mind ta look, ain't dat so? And d'ey woulda bin a darn sight easier ta git home d'an livestock from nort' a da Ohio."

Deacon placed a foot on the dashboard and pulled his coat tighter against the cold. "Joseph, are you accusing me of helping a runaway escape from his legal owner? Me, a man who owns three slaves himself. Of course, I don't know for certain you are a runaway, but if you are, I am breaking the *Fugitive Slave Law*, and that would be unconscionable. Should anyone ask, I shall say that my employee left me abruptly and without explanation while I was returning a rented buggy in Columbus. I shall appear suitably mortified when reminded that, had I believed the slave trader and acted earlier, I could have claimed a reward for his capture."

"Deacon, ya take me from Paducah ta Cincinnati when ya had no real need ta go ta Cincinnati, an' ya buy me a ticket ta ride ta Columbus where ya find me a friend dat will git me on my way. D'en ya tell me how you is gonna escape da criticism of yer neighbours when da hunters come. Deacon, you is not only a smart man, you is a good man, and dat be harder ta find."

His voice hitched with emotion. "Deacon, I is so very, very grateful. I doan know how I is ever gonna repay yer kindness, but if I ever git da opportunity... If I ever git da opportunity..." He didn't trust himself to continue.

Deacon fixed his gaze on the horizon. "Joseph, I don't think you are seeing the whole picture. I emerged triumphant from the temptations of Satan. I left the sawmill in capable hands so I could indulge in a bit of an adventure. A holiday of sorts. I had never been on a steamboat. Now I have. I had never travelled on a train. Now I have. I had never been to Cincinnati or Columbus or anywhere north of the Ohio. Now I have. This excursion has been a break from numbing predictability. Don't give me more gratitude than I have earned. My reward awaits at a later date."

He pointed down the road. "That may be our man now."

The Package Goes North

"An evil month, March is. An evil month. Can't make up its mind whether it wants to be winter or spring. Persuades April to be winter too, some years. Looks like this might be one of them."

The conductor refilled Joseph's tin cup with tea, set the pot on a small table, threw a wool blanket onto a low bed constructed from rough lumber, and turned to mount the stairs to the main floor. Changing his mind, he removed a second blanket from its shelf and tossed it after the first.

"You are not accustomed to cold like this, are you?"

"No suh, dis here be as cold as I ever hope ta be. I ain't accustomed ta dis much snow neither. Don't require shovellin' jus' so ya can git outta da house where I come from."

"The closer you get to the lakes, the more snow you can expect. The lakes keep the temperatures from getting too extreme, so there's a trade-off. I imagine Upper Canada — I think they call it Canada West now — will be about the same as here, give or take a bit. You should have chosen a warmer time of year to run."

"Had ta go when da chance come. Wasn't too bad cold-wise at first, but whoever spoons out shivering, well, he made sure we got our share. We was warned. Our friend dat couldn't join us told us d'ere be snow up here. Easy trackin' in snow, he said. Told us we got no 'sperience wif snow. Told us snow a fearsome enemy on a' empty belly. He forgot ta mention dat snow be a fearsome enemy on a full belly too."

"You will leave after dark tomorrow night, on a full belly. You will need them, so keep those blankets with you. I'll get them back from the conductor who takes you to the next station. You know how this works, don't you? I understand you haven't used the Railroad to get yourself this far."

"I was on da real railroad from Cincinnati, but I ain't been what ya call freight since Kentucky. A lady in Tennessee told us how dis all set up so I got da basic idea."

"Ideally each station is a safe house, but it may be a barn or a haystack or a shack in the woods or a cubbyhole in a woodpile. What keeps it safe is total secrecy. You won't be told where you are or the name of your conductor or anything that could betray the system. You absolutely must obey without question the instructions of the conductors. A betrayal endangers not just you. For example, if you were to get uncomfortable in a cold shed and walk about outside to warm yourself and someone were to see you..."

"Suh, da discomfort of a cold shed ain't nothin' compared ta da discomfort a being caught. I swear ta ya I will be da most cautious freight y'all ever sent on its way."

"This close to the end, some think because Ohio is a free state they can get careless. What they don't realize is that this is possibly the most dangerous part of their journey. Lots, maybe most, don't like slavery but care for Negroes even less. The *Fugitive Slave Law* gives a reason to send you back, and there's invariably enough reward for runaways to make the mouth water."

"I knows, suh. I doan wanna tell ya how much I is worth 'cause I doan wanna see ya tempted ta…"

The conductor laughed. "I've probably forwarded more valuable freight than you."

"Ya have no idea how much I appreciate what you is doin', suh. No idea at all."

"Have you had any experience with trapping fish?"

"No, suh. We jus' grab 'em outta da river when we needs 'em."

"Think of stakes hammered into a stream bottom in a shape that funnels fish into a narrow channel. They must get through the narrow spot to escape. Where is the most dangerous place if you're a fish?"

"Da narrow spot."

"You are about to enter the narrow spot. You are the fish. There will be great danger at the narrow spot."

Joseph pondered this for several seconds. "I understand," he said.

Part Four

ACTION

Detroit

The last conductor pulled the wagon up to a warped wooden dock where two young men rested on their oars in a small skiff that already seemed to ride low in the water.

"He's had a tough go of it. Best tell the other side so they can warm him up right away. Frostbite and blistered feet mostly... and fatigue. The usual. Better get him away for now."

The rowers nodded an understanding. "Godspeed" the conductor grunted as he pushed the boat off into the swirling black water. About three hundred yards out, one of the rowers deliberately missed a beat to toss a small canvas bag at Joseph's feet. "Sandwiches. Some biscuits too. Better eat if you can. No tellin' when you'll get grub next."

The rowers angled the little boat diagonal to the current. Joseph's hands were so cold that he extracted a biscuit from the bag with difficulty. By the time he had slowly and methodically consumed the other biscuit and half a sandwich, they had arrived at the other side.

A gusty wind bounced the skiff into the upstream side of a small wharf where a fisherman was watching a drift line. "Whatcha got for me?" he asked as he caught a tossed rope. The rower who had thrown the canvas bag said, "One, but he's travel-worn and chilled through. Frostbitten and blistered they say. His teeth were chattering so bad all the way over, he could scarcely eat."

The fisherman pulled in an empty line, coiled it around his hand, tucked it under his hat, and held the boat steady while a shivering young man stiffly removed himself to the dock. He studied the new arrival.

"You follow me," he said as he helped the newcomer pull tighter a thin blanket thrown over his shoulders. "We're going south a few miles. I've got a buggy over there behind those trees; I don't plan on walking far, and it appears you couldn't. Take a piss or whatever you need to. We don't want to make a poor first impression while we're passing through, now do we?"

The fisherman drove in silence, occasionally casting a sideways glance at his passenger to see how he was faring. "Any warmer now?" he asked as they neared the general store in the centre of town.

"Yes, suh. Mitts and hat do make for a more comfo'table day. I wish I had 'em when…" He interrupted himself to gaze at the general store. "Suh, would it be too much trouble ta stop da buggy for just a moment?"

The horses were duly notified of the request. Joseph continued to stare.

"Are you ill?" the fisherman asked, noticing tears forming.

"Dat flag. It doan have no stars, an' da stripes, d'ey doan all go straight across." Awkwardly, Joseph climbed down from the buggy and knelt beside the road. He kissed the palm of his mitten and held it to the ground.

"I thank Ya," he whispered.

On the far edge of town, the fisherman pulled the buggy up at an assortment of new and old wagon wheels leaning against a barn-board workshop. The wind straightened smoke from a tin chimney strapped to its side.

"Can you read that sign over the door?" the fisherman asked.

"No, suh."

It says, "*M. Duffy Wheelwright Wagons Custom and Repaired*"

The wheelwright emerged through a smaller door hinged inside a barn door and looked up at the newcomer with an appraising eye. "Any experience working with wood or iron?" he asked in an accent that suggested feathers in the mouth.

"Wood. A little, suh. Splittin' and burnin'. I done some fellin' an skiddin' an' I can square timber wif da right tools."

"A start. I'll teach you if you can learn. There's a cot for you in the workshop, and when it's fired up, the stove makes it almost as warm as the house. You go in and thaw out while I ask my good woman to find thicker clothes than what I'm looking at. We had some pork and scalloped potatoes for lunch. I suppose you could use some of that."

"Suh, dat sound won'erful."

"Good. I'll bring us out coffee as well."

Fast... and Final

In the first week, Joseph learned that the M stood for Michael and that Michael was ruled totally by the little woman who fed them adequate amounts but was not as good a cook as Deacon's wife. He learned that Michael Duffy was a taciturn conversationalist until the subject turned to wheels and wagons. An exacting craftsman, Mister Duffy made Pa and Deacon look like clumsy lumberjacks in comparison. His new employer refused to hurry repairs until the damaged wheel was as true and sturdy as new, even for impatient customers. By the end of his first day, he learned he would need to master a range of new skills before he would be of much use in the workshop.

Mid-morning of his fourth day, the ostler poked his head through the small inset door and announced, "Mister Rose has called a meeting tonight, eight o'clock."

The wheelwright nodded, gave him a thumbs up, and continued working.

"That flat iron you're filing, we'll cut that to length for the rear wheels on the wagon the tanner has on order. When you have the edges smooth enough you could run your tongue along them and not get nicked, leave it at the back of the shop so we don't have to root around to find it if it snows again."

"Won't rust as fast inside," Joseph observed.

"Normally you'd have a point, but I intend to tackle those rims tomorrow. They wouldn't have a chance to rust much, even if they were covered in snow, and the fire will burn off any oxidation. Speaking of snow, how are the hands?"

"Good, suh, real good. Da fisherman dat dropped me here tol' me Ole Jack Frost, he jus' nip me, but it sure feel like Massa Frost give a full bite wif possum teeth once't my hands and nose an' ears started warmin' up."

"You were luckier than some. Not everyone crosses on open water as you did. In winter, some try to walk across on the ice, not understanding it may be thick enough for support where they begin but undercut by the current farther out."

"Doan nobody make it dat way?"

"I suppose some do. Of course, there's no way to count the numbers that don't."

"I be real lucky for most a my escape, but I shore feel down when my friends dat couldn't be here come ta mind."

"I'm told the last bit can be the most dangerous."

"Dat's what a conductor dis side a Columbus tole me too. He say we like fish bein' channelled in a fish trap an' da bounty hunters jus' waitin' for us in da narrow part 'fore we get to freedom."

The wheelwright tidied the work bench a little, walked over to the stove, turned to Joseph, and said, "Come over here. I've got something to show you." He knelt down and pointed to where it appeared sunlight dappled the pine planks. "Those blotchy spots, that's where I sanded to get the blood stains out of the wood. You can see I couldn't get them all." As he recounted the events of the fateful Sunday, Joseph sat on his cot, put his head in his hands, and gently rocked back and forth.

"I was tole, over an' over, startin' wif Old Mose, once't I got ta where da Britishers live, d'en I be free. Dis here blood show it ain't so. Dis here man dat bled here, he be a slave again. A slave! Right back where he started, back wif his Bindle an' his Lonnegan. An' here I is, thinkin' I'se free from bondage, afta all da tribulations I bin through..."

"You *are* free. That is, as long as you're here, you're free. Slavery has been outlawed for three generations in Upper Canada — that's what Canada West was called up to a few years back. It's when you're taken from here that you're back in bondage. Joseph, there are good men working on this problem. We *will* put a stop to it."

For the rest of the workday there was little talk.

Some time after supper, Joseph unlocked the workshop door to the wheelwright's voice. "I'm glad to see you put the bar up. Dress as warm as you can and follow me to the livery. You can wait on the landing while we have our meeting. I don't want to leave you here by yourself."

Mister Rose called the meeting to order. "The facts are easily related. A farmer's wife near McGregors' Mills heard a commotion from the barn where she and her husband were sheltering a fugitive mother and son. She roused her husband, who drove off two, possibly more, attempting to seize them. They had muffled the Blacks in blankets and were almost to the road when the farmer let go at one with his musket, but since he had a wad of bird shot in front of the charge he figures he didn't inflict much damage. In the pandemonium, the mother and son fought themselves free and are now sheltering in the summer kitchen. The next day, the good man found three of his heifers with their throats slit, still in their stall — hadn't been let out to spring pasture yet."

He paused to let the information be processed.

Purple put the obvious into words. "So we are hearing of several kidnappings, we have had Mister Cork's apprentice taken from his workshop, and now some kindhearted souls dare not even enter their own barn for fear of..."

"Exactly," Rose said. "The question is, what are we going to do about it?"

"Was the farmer able to give descriptions?" White asked. "Could they be the ones we think absconded with Cork's man?"

"He was unable to get a good look, but he didn't see anything out of the ordinary. He didn't describe one as the huge brute who rented the team and buckboard from my ostler, if that is what you are driving at. The pensioners at the fort were notified, of course."

Vienna leaned forward in his chair, elbows on knees, hands clasped, and talked half to the floor. "This is nothing new. Gentlemen, we are treading water here. We know these vermin will take enormous risks because a successful capture earns them enormous profit. So, first, I think we should move as many of the unestablished inland as soon as it is practical. I will personally send my sons to stir up some sanctuary families where they will be safer. Maybe some of you have family members who can do the same, or do it yourself."

There was a low murmur of assent.

"Second, we know these bastards frequent this very area. Cork's missing man is proof of that. Mister Cork, you have taken in another fugitive recently, have you not?"

"I have. For safety, he accompanied me tonight. He is just outside the door."

"Have you done anything to prevent a second attack?"

"I installed a stout bar — oak, in an oak bracket — so the workshop door cannot be forced easily. Joseph, that's the new arrival's name, Joseph has been instructed to lock himself in after working hours and only open to someone he knows. If I must go out on business, I will take Joseph with me, as I did this evening."

"Those sound to me like wise precautions," Madrid observed.

"Those precautions may be wise, but they are a reaction to what has already transpired," Vienna said testily. "The stable door shut after the horses have fled and all that... For God's sake, the time for thinking defensively is over! We need to catch these fucking sons-a-bitches in the act, then we can deal with them fast and final." He drove his right fist into the palm of his left hand to emphasize his point. "Fast... and final!"

This time the murmur of assent was louder.

"What do you suggest?" Rose asked.

Vienna tracked his points by tapping his right forefinger on the fingers of his left hand, starting with the pinkie. "First, Cork maintains his normal routine. Business as usual, church on Sunday mornings. Second, we take turns keeping an eye on the workshop. Not so close as to be obvious, not so far as to be useless. Third, this Joseph is the perfect target: he's newly arrived, he lives in a shop that wasn't designed by

Vauban, a shop not all that far from the water. Fourth, we know and they know how easy it is to grab and run."

"Does our man know what he's worth?" White asked.

"Twelve hundred dollars, dead or alive," the wheelwright replied. Several made a low whistle, while others shifted in their chairs.

Vienna continued. "Twelve hundred? By God, we couldn't buy better cheese for the trap. If we grab even one, we can make an example of him."

"There will be no need to post sentries when Cork is alert. It will be after dark and on the Sabbath we must be on guard," Rose said. "If you wish to participate, see me at the end of the meeting, and we will draw up a schedule."

Before the door closed behind him, Michael Duffy glanced back into the room to see a cluster around Rose, choosing their preferred sentry time.

At the bottom of the stairs Joseph was jumping up and down, hugging himself, and rubbing his hands together to generate heat. As they began the walk home, the wheelwright said, "You should have waited on the landing. We would have heard you from there."

"I got ta shiverin' an' stompin' my feet to keep warm an' not thinkin' an' I 'preciate yer concern for my safety. Old Mose is right. I gotta be thinkin' like prey, even here."

The wheelwright broke the silence after a few hundred yards. "Well, you said yourself you were like a fish trying not to get caught in the narrows. You have had a change in status."

Joseph looked at him quizzically. "Ya sayin' I ain't a fish no more?"

"Oh, you're still a fish. A very small fish. You are bait."

An Investigation and a Report

The body of a white man was discovered by a little dog of dubious lineage who coincidentally walked the waterside every day with the same shawl-clad old crone who had watched the *Linda Something-or-Other* sail south. A grappling hook and a rowboat soon had the body on the beach, where a blanket protected it from gulls until the fort's aged doctor had the opportunity to examine it and pronounce a cause of death.

"It doesn't take a sawbones to see he got smacked 'longside the head right smartly," the old woman snorted, to the doctor's annoyance.

"Possibly your expertise garnered through long years of medical practice has also noticed the defensive contusions on the left arm, the fractured left wrist, the several broken fingers, all consistent with an attack. This man was bludgeoned, and since the depression in the skull is on the left side, as are the other fractures, we may surmise the attacker was right-handed. Would you not agree, doctor?" he said sarcastically, not looking at the woman. "Was the body floating face up or down?"

"Face down."

"In your learned opinion, would you say the body was floating high in the water, or was it almost completely submerged?"

"Not under the water or we wouldn't have seen it, now would we?"

The doctor took a deep breath to control his impatience and said, "By almost completely submerged, I mean was it level with the water, or did some of the body protrude above the water?"

"Oh, he was easy to see, bobbing in the waves like he was."

"Exactly. This man did not drown. I will examine him more closely in a more appropriate spot, but when I open him, I expect to find no water in the lungs. They will be full of air, resulting in more buoyancy. This man was murdered, and he was dead before his body was thrown into the lake, or possibly the river. The current could have carried him into the lake, and he just happened to wash up here."

The doctor rinsed sand off his hands at the water's edge.

"Due to the preservative nature of cold water, we really have no idea how long this man has been dead, would you not agree?" he said to the old woman.

She ignored him and sat down on a convenient driftwood log to watch as the body was wrapped in the blanket and carried to a wagon. It wasn't every day there was a murder in Amherstburg.

It wasn't every day there was an autopsy at the pensioners' settlement either. A crowd of the curious made way as the major entered the infirmary, where the corpse was laid out on a pine table. Sergeant Madill shooed them away, closed the door, and with the help of an octogenarian corporal began to disrobe the body.

"Major Emmett, sir, you might wish to absent yourself from this, you being of tender years and all," the sergeant said paternally.

"My tender years will remain tender should I absent myself from unpleasantries, Sergeant. Also, unexplained deaths in our jurisdiction must be reported to the governor general, as you are aware, so I will carry on with my duty, as you shall with yours."

"Sir. Thank you, sir."

"Sergeant, when you have the corpse bare, place the clothes on this chair so I may examine them."

"Sir."

Armed with a scalpel, wooden spatulas, a magnifying glass, a wooden screw, a towel, a tin kidney basin, a pail of water, and scientific curiosity, the doctor proceeded to examine the subject from head to toe. With help from the corporal and the wooden screw, he forced the jaws apart to give access to the teeth. He ran a hand down each limb and attempted to flex an arm and the fingers. Other than a muttered "as I thought" when he incised the lungs, he said nothing. The sergeant and corporal helped rotate the body onto its stomach. This time the doctor started at the feet and proceeded to the head. An anomaly near the hair line attracted his attention. He retrieved tweezers from a black leather bag, removed something from the skin of the neck three times, and dropped with a metallic plink whatever he had discovered into the kidney basin.

The doctor held up a forefinger to forestall any conversation, sat down at a small desk, drew a rough outline of a human body on a piece of paper, and proceeded to make notes on the outline with the help of arrows. Meanwhile, the major examined the clothes and turned out the pockets.

Without prompting, the doctor began. "Major, our subject is a man in his early thirties. The cause of death is unequivocally a blow or multiple blows from a blunt instrument to the left side of the skull. The fractures of the left wrist, forearm, and fingers show he raised his arm in defence as he faced his attacker. This man's early years were difficult. Rotten teeth, premature gum recession, two poorly healed fractures from childhood, one a tibia, the other an ulna, and the thickness of skin on the heels plus flattened arches suggest a poverty stricken, barefoot childhood with an inadequate diet. His hands, however, are not the calloused hands of a labourer. I will have a complete written report to you by tomorrow morning. Anything of interest in his clothing?"

"A total of one dollar and seventy-two cents in American coins in his pants pocket, so this unfortunate may be an American citizen. I will communicate to our friends across the river that we may have recovered one of theirs. Corporal, when we have finished here, find a washerwoman to launder these sodden clothes in preparation for the interment. They will get mouldy otherwise. Doctor, what are our next steps?"

"Madill can leave the deceased in someone's icehouse. If we have not heard of anyone missing from their side or ours in four days, I'll arrange for burial in the paupers' yard."

The sergeant and the corporal began to wrap the blanket around the body.

"Doctor," the major continued, "is there any chance this man was a sailor? Possibly he sustained these injuries from a fall, maybe from a yard-arm."

"An interesting hypothesis, one which I shall include in my notes. The clothes suggest nothing nautical... And then there are the hands. A fall is a possible but improbable cause of death, as you shall soon observe." The doctor handed him the tin kidney basin. "For your report."

The newly commissioned, fresh faced young major's report for the governor general described the circumstances of the discovery and noted that the doctor's findings would be appended. He pondered for a brief moment before he wrote his summation: *"Your most humble servant's personal observation of the body leads him to the conclusion that this was an accidental death due to misadventure, consistent with a fall from a height such as a yard-arm and striking a gunnel before hitting water. Upon reading the doctor's post mortem findings, you will find they do not negate this possibility."*

As promised, the doctor's report arrived early the following morning. Once the major had carefully folded and sealed the documents, he handed them to Sergeant Madill. "See these get dispatched immediately," he instructed. "Do you have any personable pensioners who could accompany you when you visit Mister Duffy this afternoon on a social call?"

"He knows Malone, McGuire, and Donnelly from the church."

"Good. Don't be too circumspect. You may tell him with a wink you're taking a break from a patrol. And don't indulge excessively in the hail-fellow-well-met camaraderie you Irish are so fond of. A convivial libation from a flask may loosen his tongue, but do not forget you are on duty. My chit for a bottle of whisky will keep the sergeant major's records square."

"Very kind of you, sir. Yes, sir. And what am I to loosen his tongue concerning, sir?"

"Inquire how the new Darkie is faring and if his new helper has any knowledge of any more coming across. Tell him I would like to know of these things. That is a red herring, because what I actually want to know is if the citizens' group, this vigilance committee the sergeant major's wife mentioned, had anything to do with our guest in the icehouse. When the patrol returns from upriver, the sergeant major will ask how we have been spending our time, and I am confident he will appreciate that we have done all we can to relieve him of the necessity for further inquiry. There is no need to reveal that his wife has shared any information with me. Are we understood, Sergeant?"

"I believe so, sir. We do not wish to burden our already overworked sergeant major with loose ends that might detract from his ability to focus on his primary duties, to supervise the pensioners' scheme and defend our sovereign soil."

"Exactly, Sergeant. Exactly. You have an excellent grasp of our priorities. Carry on, and good luck with Duffy."

There was one more chore before he could enjoy a hot breakfast. He returned to his quarters, picked up the kidney basin from his desk, tilted it until three pieces of bird shot fell into his hand, and tossed them into the fireplace.

A Quite Satisfactory Outcome

The room above the livery stable was uncharacteristically quiet, even before Mister Rose called the meeting to order. If the Vigilance Committee had kept records, they would have shown it was the shortest meeting ever. When Rose asked if the assembled members were in favour of continuing the present course of action, a show of hands indicated unanimity, and then he requested that anyone who wished a change in the schedule see him after the meeting, and it was over.

The conspirators sat in contemplation of their success, some lighting pipes, some helping themselves to the tepid coffee and ginger snap cookies the livery owner's wife had provided. It was Vienna who started the snowball rolling. "Didn't I predict this? Eh? Didn't I? I said we had the best bait for the rat, and I was right, wasn't I?"

Rose said, "Cork's man would have been in a fine pickle if we hadn't set up that watchman's schedule — and kept to it," and Green said, "Thank goodness we had Scarlet on duty. Of us all, he's probably the fleetest of foot." Scarlet added, "I was pungling hard for sure. You would have ripped right along too if it had been you on watch, but the credit goes to White. If he hadn't opened his door to my hammering and sent his boy to rouse the others, both those bastards would have got away, and that's a certainty."

"Who got him?" Cork asked.

"Doesn't matter who got him," Vienna said, after an awkward silence. "He was got, and that's what matters." There was a murmur of agreement.

"We ran the sons of bitches down and cornered them in some trees by the riverside," White explained. "It was dark as a cat's pocket, and everyone was milling around, and we thought we had lost 'em for a minute or two. Then Madrid here saw one thinkin' a taking to the water, and after that it was a mee-lay with a lot of yelling, and so we don't truly know who actually landed the good one on him. It's a crime the accomplice got away, but we got one to set the others thinking, so that's all to the good. So Cork, to answer your question, we all got him."

To change the subject, Rose said, "What happened at your workshop?"

"Our friend Sergeant Madill dropped in on a social call this afternoon. Brought three pensioners from the old sod with him, broke out the whisky, and treated the six of us. Joseph, too. He wanted to know if he knew of more coming across. You will recognize it as a foolish question, as did I. As if conductors would share that information with freight..."

Someone was about to interrupt, but Rose waved him quiet, knowing Cork was building his story.

"About the time the bottle was on its way third time round, our friend wanted to know if anything suspicious had happened in the neighbourhood. I let Joseph talk because he knows nothing of what ultimately transpired and cannot incriminate anyone."

"What did he tell Madill?" White asked.

"The truth. That the missus and I were asleep in the house and he had settled for the night. That he woke when someone tried to force the workshop door, and when they discovered it was barred from the inside, they slipped a knife under the bar and tried to lift it. He says that's when he started yelling, but the missus and I were sound asleep and heard nothing."

"He was one goddamn lucky son of a bitch, that's all I can say," Madrid observed.

"My man says it must have been Samson on the other side, because the blade raised the bar almost high enough to flip it out of its bracket. That was a heavy piece of oak I installed. There is no way I could raise it that high with just a knife, no matter how big, so it was probably the large brute the ostler described, the one that rented the team and wagon the day the club-foot was taken."

"At least your man had the advantage of the dark,"

"True, and he had the presence of mind to grab a hefty spoke from the pile we had been working on and was waiting behind the door. Plucky young man, but he admits he was terrified."

"As we all would be in his shoes," Green said, "knowing what horrors await if we are taken."

"He claims now he should have tried to hold the bar down, but he didn't think of it until later," Cork continued.

"When did he realize the bounty hunters had buggered off?" Vienna asked.

"Not 'til I was roused and went to the workshop to see if he was all right. He didn't hear Scarlet raise the alarm or the bounty hunters skedaddle or anything outside the shop until he heard my voice. He didn't tell the sergeant any of those details because he didn't know them. He thought it was me that scared them off, and I've let him think it was."

"Good thinking," Rose said.

"I feel sorry for him, but my missus is right. He has to go. I thought it best to tell him when we were mellowing with the whisky. It's another dislocation for him. He took it hard and quiet, but he understands. We've tried to help two fugitives now, and where has it got us? The missus can't sleep at night, says we wouldn't be having this bother if we weren't so close to the border or we took on a white apprentice. She's worried about the business, what with these brigands roaming all over the goddamn place, maybe setting fire to the shop in revenge. We have no cows to kill..."

"That boy's seen a lot. What happens to him now?"

"The homegrown Blacks can't help him much, that's for sure. They made that clear with the club-foot. Madill agrees the newcomers should go inland, says maybe there's a temporary job at the fort if he's willing to work for a roof over his head. Madill says he can't promise anything, but he'll float the idea past the newly arrived officer, see if he'll arrange vittles as well. At least he'd be safer there."

"It seems to me this committee is doing its job, wouldn't ya say?" Scarlet said. "One less bounty hunter, maybe one more scared off, and one fugitive Negro kept out of their clutches. That's not bad for this month's work. Let's try for two next month." He turned to face south and raised a middle finger. This generated a laugh, and as the chairs were pushed back and the committee members began to file out of the room, they added their salutes to his.

Part Five

GIDEON SOUNDS A TRUMPET

Gideon Chooses His Warriors

The Reverend Gideon Leeds was an imposing figure in the saddle. Dappled skin stretched drum-tight over a bald skull accentuated unblinking, piercing, discomforting blue eyes. Sun scalded hands and throat boasted only of veins and sinew, as though his Maker had run out of flesh and sent him into the world unfinished. A black suit, shiny in the seat, hung from his gaunt six foot plus frame with the same panache as it would from a nail.

No voice booming from the heavens to announce a man of God was necessary. Righteous indignation emanated from Leeds like ripples from a stone thrown into still water. God had seen fit to dispatch him into a wilderness to preach His word, and He rewarded His humble servant with an over-abundance of sinners to baptize, marry and bury. That their nascent farms were scattered over many miles of maple, oak, beech, and ash forests Leeds regarded as a blessing. Travel on the Carolinian trails and primitive back roads of Canada West gave him time with his horse and his God.

A TALE FROM THE CAMERON LINE

Reverend Leeds knew his sinners. From the Claymore Line in the west to Wallacetown in the east, north to Shetland and Glencoe, south along the Talbot Trail, he had ridden the Ridgetown circuit long enough to wear out two horses, minister to every family, learn every name, lend a sympathetic ear to every sufferer, and pour the healing balm of scripture over every problem. They expected a spiritual leader to preach of a fire and brimstone damnation and God's path to salvation. He delivered nothing less. He had trembled with the awesome responsibility of his vocation, the imperative to communicate the terrible fear of God's wrath on one hand and His bountiful mercy on the other. His flock recognized in him the personification of an iron moral code and an unflinching faith.

And what had been his earthly reward? Deference. Respect. Saddle sores. There was little enough money to keep body and soul together, but every habitation provided a hearty meal for a man of the cloth, hay for his steed, and a bed of straw for both. A Duart family who appreciated the rigours of his circuit had supplied him with his horse. Another had given him his black suit. Others had contributed a spare blanket, boots from a deceased, and a saddle.

Leeds' long days in that saddle were about to end. Ridgetown had provided Anna, a plumpish wife who came with a small house and a dowry that kept her horse in oats, their pantry in preserves, and meat on the table. She taught Sunday school, led the hymn singing, and supplemented his meagre income by teaching the local children their R's. On Sunday afternoons, she visited the sick in her tilbury. He could not quite yet permit himself the pleasures of a settled life, but every day in his devotions, Gideon Leeds gave thanks for the divine benevolence that had provided Anna.

Anticipation of fewer saddle miles brightened his thoughts as he convinced himself that the attraction of a shorter circuit had nothing to do with an ageing body. The diminution of his rounds had more to do with the increasing population of Kent County and the coming of the railroad, which signalled the end of its pioneer status. Various communities were now established enough to construct churches and support a minister. It was possible he might secure an appointment to one of these, although Trinity, built on the highest land in Howard Township, was firmly in the grip of the Anglicans.

Leeds was an imposing man in the pulpit as well. This Sabbath day he was in Morpeth, preaching to dour farm families, not a few of whom were as fluent in Gaelic as English. Many alternated Sundays between Trinity on the Talbot Line and Morpeth, where a few years ago men of vision had constructed a meeting house.

His secondary text today was from Matthew, chapter six, verse thirty-four. *"Take therefore no thought for the morrow: for the morrow shall take thought for the things of itself. Sufficient unto the day is the evil thereof."* He hoped a select few were paying attention as he switched to his primary text in Judges, chapter seven. As his namesake, Gideon, had selected his shock troops, Leeds intended to stir the willing to a holy cause. Some were too old, some too self-centred, some too dull to be worthy, but there might be several suitable candidates on the Cameron Line, a section of the Talbot Trail known locally for the number of families connected to Clan Cameron. Maybe that Desmond boy or Archibald Taylor or Daniel Cameron...

As he shook the hand of each of the worshippers filing out after the service, Reverend Leeds whispered to his chosen, "I must talk to you before you head home." While knots of neighbours coagulated on patches bare of snow on the meeting house lawn and chatted about the weather, last year's crops, deaths and childbirths, he beckoned to three to meet him at the hitching rail.

He had no intention of sharing more than the meat of his conversation with Father Daudet, a Roman priest. Most here would disapprove of his meeting with a Catholic clergyman. He simply passed on a message, certain that God moves in mysterious ways.

Mrs. Hedley Disapproves

Abigail Hedley was ample. She had ample chins, an ample bosom, an ample girth, ample hips, and an ample curiosity about the happenings in her small world. From her front door, Abigail Hedley could look east and west down the Cameron Line. This was fortuitous, because Abigail Hedley needed to see who passed by, where they were going, who they were with, and what they were wearing.

Not much of what transpired on the Cameron Line escaped Abigail Hedley, and not much met with her approval.

She disapproved of the way Mrs. MacPhail double knotted her sun hat under her chin, when any fool could see there was no wind and her old horse was incapable of anything but a plod. She disapproved when the minister's rather plain wife dashed by in her tilbury, as if she were on her way to a frolicsome picnic rather than on an errand involving the Lord's work. She disapproved of how the Chalmers' unhandsome son was always the last of the children to pass her door each school day, both ways, and of how his mother was so vain about the over-baked sawdust she passed off as shortbread. To the inexperienced eye, what she was witnessing today would appear innocent, but Abigail Hedley knew nothing good could come of it.

"Abi, there's still some tea in the pot, but it's quite cooled by now. I can boil up some more," her husband called from the kitchen.

"Thank you, but no."

"Well, you might want to come away from that door and finish your meal before you fade away to a shadow of your former self."

"Noah, there is no cause for sarcasm. You are so blind to the ways of this wicked world. You have no idea, no idea at all, of the carryings-on in this township."

"That's true, and I'll keep it that way. I've got you to look after the carryings-on for the both of us. So what's the trouble now?"

"Mister Cameron has stopped right opposite our front door to talk to someone... I can't quite make out who is in the other..."

"Which Mister Cameron?"

"Daniel. The closest one, the one on the south side, just past the road allowance. The one who married that crazy Susan Green."

"Abi, that's a bit harsh. Susan may be a trifle odd, but she's hardly crazy."

"A trifle odd? More than a trifle, Noah, more than a trifle. Every day the children stop in at the Cameron house on their way home from school. Every day. She maintains milk is unhealthy for the young. Milk! So what does she give them? Wine! Wine and cookies. Now, if that's not crazy, I don't know what is."

"We exchange pleasantries with the Camerons, but we don't know such close neighbours as well as we should. I intend to change that. Maybe I'll drop in for a social call with the school kids. I don't mind the odd cookie or two."

"That's just like you, to joke about something as serious as the destruction of the young."

"Susan Green wasn't so crazy as to miss out on hitching up with Daniel when her parents passed. Word's out he's a good farmer and a better carpenter."

"Daniel Cameron got the better of that match. Now he's got the Green farm as well as his own right next door. How long did it take him to move into the Greens' house, I ask you? Reverend Leeds says he moved lock, stock, and barrel the day of the wedding. Wouldn't it have been more appropriate if she had moved into his house, small though it was? His parents have been dead longer than the Greens. And it wasn't six months before he knocked down his old house and stacked the salvage at his new one, the reverend says."

"I'm pleased Leeds can take a break from throwing coal on the fires of hell long enough to find out these things. Far be it from me to question the solid facts as put forward by our esteemed Reverend Leeds."

"At least Reverend Leeds cares about what goes on in his circuit."

"There wouldn't be a Trinity church if it weren't for the Greens. Maybe Leeds is a bit prejudiced against the Greens because Susan's relatives helped set up the competition. And you, Abi, are you just out of sorts with Mrs. Cameron because she has not joined your ladies' temperance gossip group?"

"I don't know what you mean about gossip, Noah. An exchange of information is not gossip."

"Oh, I see. It's an exchange of information. Is our Mister Cameron driving his buckboard or the buggy?"

"The buggy. And he's wearing his frock coat over a waistcoat. That suggests business. Oh, goodness gracious..."

"What now?"

"I can see who he's talking to. It's... It's... Yes, it is. It's that Irishman, John Duffy. Oh my!"

"Abi, it's not against the law to stop and chat with someone."

"You would apologize for stepping on the viper that bit you. Reverend Leeds and I understand subtleties that you do not. Mister Duffy is not only Irish, but everyone knows he likes the drink. He drinks, and he is a papist, and there's Daniel Cameron talking to him as if it were quite normal."

"Just go out and join the conversation if you want to know what they're discussing. We've had a bit of weather lately, and you could add your two pence about the need for rain."

"Noah, I declare, you are a frivolous man. The very idea... As if I would hazard my standing in the community by being seen conversing with a drunken papist and one of those oatmeal savages. Me, chair of the Temperance Committee. Now, wouldn't that be a fine kettle of fish?"

She opened the door slowly and ever so little, just in case she could pick up the gist of the conversation, but the thread eluded her. She heard Cameron exclaim, "What? That many?" and Duffy reply, "It's a mystery and a damnable disgrace." Then Cameron said, "... down to Fort Malden..." and "no trace?" and "hunters" and Duffy said something indistinct about "friends" and "the authorities" and "what's to be done?", then something about "retribution" and "hanging".

As Daniel Cameron and John Duffy ended their dialogue with a nod and a Good Day to one another, she saw each turn his horses around and proceed in the direction from which he had come. As they parted, she distinctly heard the Irishman say, "Intolerable! It's an intolerable bloody business, and by God, we'll put an end to it," and Cameron say, "Yes, we must!"

Abigail Hedley pondered the significance of this. It was most curious. *Those two are up to something,* she thought. It bothered her for the rest of that week and into the next. She told Noah everything she'd heard, of course, but his interest was feigned. Poor, simple man. He had even chuckled when she told him how Mister Cameron had tipped his hat to her as he drove off.

Daniel Talks to Jessie, Jacob and Susan

Daniel paused to catch his breath, wiped the sweat from his face with a crumpled red handkerchief, and stole a moment to enjoy the quiet end of the day. Carting manure in a wheelbarrow to the pile behind the barn was tedious, hard work. The cattle had just been turned out that morning for their first taste of spring grass. Some kicked up heels in the pure delight of fresh forage. He could appreciate their enthusiasm. *It's a good thing the days are getting longer,* he thought, *because the spring brings more of what needs to be done. Cedar rails must be split to mend fences, the pig pen would benefit from two new boards, lambs are already here, calves on their way... Spring planting will depend on the weather. The garden patch could stand some spading...*

He tried to avoid thinking of the unfinished chairs in the workshop he'd sectioned off in the barn, the chairs he should have assembled in the winter months. He'd clean Jessie's and Jacob's stall tomorrow. The horses weren't as imprisoned as the cattle. They had occasionally escaped their wooden cell to haul next winter's fuel from the woodlot and for Sunday sleigh rides to Trinity and Morpeth.

The draft horses reminded him of his conversation with Duffy. He hung his sweat-stained jacket beside the harnesses and stroked Jessie's chin. "Just what would you recommend we do, old girl?" he asked. "I see you don't have an answer either. It's not that we don't have enough work here to keep us out of mischief, you and I. If you could talk, you'd tell me to mind my own business, and to your everlasting equine credit that would be sage advice. Trouble is, once you know where evil flourishes, you can't just turn your back on it. Well, maybe you can, because you're a horse, in case that slipped your mind, and I suppose we operate under different rules. Still, I almost wish I hadn't told the Reverend Leeds I would talk with the Irishman.

What's to be done, Jessie? Jacob, feel free to enter this discussion at any time. John Duffy may be a papist and not of our stock, but he seems like a solid man — even if his worshipping ways are misguided. You counsel to let things be, is that what I hear? I expect that from a horse. In my defence, my Christian upbringing tells me to follow the righteous path — once I know what the righteous path is. That might take more courage than is in my allotment. I will ask Susan what she thinks. If she agrees with you, so be it. But if she perceives the path as I do, then we're in the thick of it. Tomorrow I'll let the two of you know what she says. That's a promise."

He patted Jacob's neck as he picked up his jacket and headed to the pasture with his dog, Argus, trotting ahead. Argus would do most of the work. Daniel was unclear what breed dominated in the mutt's spectrum of ancestors. His herding abilities were Border Collie, his paws Labrador Retriever, his fur and tail Malamute, and his territorial instincts Staffordshire Terrier. The cows had no inclination to return to the barn, even with Argus's encouragement, so it was dark when he trudged in for supper with slow steps not entirely the product of a full day's labour.

He washed up to dilute the manure odour, changed to a cleaner shirt and trousers, and tucked into supper like a man who has pushed a full wheelbarrow all day. Supper was good. Supper was always good. Susan worked miracles with salt pork and gravy, shrivelled potatoes, and neeps fried in butter. He thought of the joyous cattle and wondered when he would savour the fresh fruits and vegetables of the coming summer's bounty. He speared a second helping of pickles. Odd how he had a terrible craving for pickles at the end of each winter. Yesterday, Susan had used the last of the apples in the root cellar to make apple crisp. *Nothing remotely crisp about withered spring apples,* he thought, but the dessert did not survive another day.

Daniel studied his wife as she cleared the table of dirty dishes, poured hot water over them in a speckled blue enamelled basin, scoured with a horsetail fern, then dried the glasses on a red gingham apron. Pots and stoneware were left to the air. He had been lucky to find Susan. Convenient that she had grown up on the next farm. Prettier than most. Full-bosomed. Plumping up nicely. Long chestnut hair braided and coiled around her head. The tiniest wisp of grey at the temples. A bit early for such a young woman. Chapped hands. Hard working. Charitable to a fault and stubborn as a post. A trifle odd. They never mentioned to neighbours that she had wine fermenting in the root cellar. There would be no notice of whisky. Whisky was expected in the homes of Scottish descent. Whisky was medicinal, the water of life, but homemade wine... Yes, that was different. And it surprised him to realize he was just a little afraid of her.

While Susan put away the dishes, he melted some tallow on the stove, added a clump of chimney soot, a few drops of coal oil, then a dash of vinegar, and muddled the concoction until it looked right. He was working on the second of his Sunday shoes when his wife forestalled any more avoidance.

"Those shoes need blackening again before Sunday service?"

"Susan, I've been giving some thought to buying another horse. Maybe something stylish you could ride or that could pull a gig. Maybe a stepper like the one that makes the rounds for the reverend's wife."

"That would free up Jacob and Jessie, that's the truth. And you need to put shoe black on your Sunday pair to go and buy a horse?"

"Well, I was thinking I might go down to Fort Malden for two or three days or several. Planting's a good way off, and the farm could spare me. Let the calves suckle any cows that freshen 'til I get back. There's bound to be a good horse in a town the size of Amherstburg or thereabouts."

"Amherstburg? That's a frightful ways from home. And you wouldn't be able to find a horse closer? Thamesville has horses, Blenheim has horses, Chatham has horses, Dresden has horses... I know for a fact Mrs. Leeds bought her Canadian filly not fifteen miles from Ridgetown. What does Amherstburg and the fort have that makes for better horses? Or are they an excuse for some other kind of business?"

"Susan, you've always been sharp, but I would prefer you didn't press me for details. I'm of two minds as it is about another kind of business, and I don't want to burden you with worry or anxiety."

Susan said nothing. She brought two small glasses from the cup board and poured them each a generous dram of Scotch whisky from the white ceramic pitcher in the middle of the kitchen table. Pulling up a high-back kitchen chair opposite Daniel, she examined the clarity of her drink against the mantle of the coal oil lamp and let the silence fester.

"Out you went yesterday. Gallivanting on a weekday no less. Today you want to buy a horse in Amherstburg. I promise not to raise my voice, but Daniel Cameron, you should talk to me. Right here, right now. Talk to me. I'm listening."

Daniel began to talk slowly and earnestly. "There are crimes being committed against man and God, and I simply don't know what to do about it. What I do know, and if you call me a fool I'll agree with you, but Susan, I know I must do something."

Susan chucked two more rounds of wood into the kitchen stove, pumped the kettle full, placed it on the stove, and resumed her place opposite her husband. Noticing his whisky had evaporated, she refilled his glass and waited in silence. It took most of a minute for Daniel to resume.

"Susan, there is some serious nastiness afoot. After church last Sunday, Reverend Leeds took Archie and Paul and me aside and suggested we meet with a man who's been down to Amherstburg lately. His name is Duffy. He's an Irishman and a Catholic and maybe it's a sin, but I rather like him. It seems Leeds and a priest, a Father Daudet, have been messaging one another about what's happening west of here. The paddy was to come this way on the Talbot Line yesterday afternoon, and the plan was that we would encounter him on the road. I was the only one who showed up, and wouldn't you know it, we had our conversation right opposite the Hedleys' house. You can just imagine how that damned gossip monger tried to overhear us."

"Yes, I can. Abigail Hedley would want to know every word, even if you were talking to a toad, and then she would inform everyone of her low estimation of toads and anyone who conversed with one. What were you talking about?"

"Evil things. Mister Duffy says there are now hundreds of the Negro race in Malden and the Amherstburg area, and the authorities figure at least two or three dozen or more are smuggled across the border every month. They're a sizeable chunk of the population now, and work and lodgings can not keep up. Quite a few have travelled as far east as Chatham. They're runaway slaves, and many are in a bad way. The rags on their backs is all they own. They have nothing now but their freedom. Duffy says they're a proud people who work hard when given the opportunity."

"You are equivocating, Daniel. You are not giving me news. We've known for years the Friends have been helping runaways. They can't claim all the credit of course, but the Underground Railroad would be a shaky line without them. You're telling me what you know I already know. Do you want to take clothes or food down to Malden? Is that it? Is that why you want to go there? To buy a horse?"

"If it were just as simple as donating a few clothes... Leeds could organize a collection, if that was the issue, and maybe I'll suggest he should. But Duffy has some connection near Malden, so he's up on the latest Devil's work. It's far worse than finding clothes."

"Go on. What did you hear from this Irishman that has you in such a lather?"

"These poor wretches believed they had escaped from the abomination of enslavement — from that hypocritical 'all men are created equal' mob-run republic."

"For God's sake Daniel, get to the point! Put it in a nutshell."

"In a nutshell: runaways are being kidnapped and forcibly taken back across the border."

"What?"

"Kidnapped. Abducted. Abducted by bounty hunters, then returned to the United States. Carted back in shackles to their previous owners in the slave states for a sizeable reward. By all accounts they are then being publicly whipped or mutilated or hanged."

"To set an example to any slave who thinks of running away."

"Exactly. To permeate the slave population with the conviction there is no hope of freedom. That even if, through some miracle, they were to reach British North America, they are still not safe. That even here, they can be secretly and forcefully spirited away by agents from an evil, unfriendly...."

"How does this Mister Duffy know all this?"

"His brother in Amherstburg sheltered a runaway in his workshop, gave him employment. Suddenly he was gone. There were signs of a scuffle and blood on the floor. The runaway did not run away, Susan. He was taken. Duffy told me his brother raised the alarm at the fort with no effect. In short, he discovered that the authorities are aware of incidents in Amherstburg and there have been similar abductions throughout Essex County."

"How many?"

"Kidnappings? No one knows for sure. I first thought three or four. Duffy says dozens and dozens. When the refugees can find sustenance in the back country and away from the border, they're safer, and they tend to look out for one another. It's the newcomer who is most vulnerable, but even children have been abducted. Children, Susan. Children, for God's sake! Duffy told me some people are afraid to get involved for fear of retribution. A farmer sheltering a mother and son near McGregors' Mills drove off some would-be abductors with his musket. Next night, three of his cattle were killed."

"How do we know what happens to those who are taken south?"

"Duffy says the abolitionists have spies as far as the Gulf of Mexico."

"Well, it's obvious we must do something. This is shameful! Absolutely intolerable! Who was it who said, 'The only thing necessary for evil to triumph is for good people to do nothing' or 'When good people do nothing, evil triumphs' or something like that?"

"I disremember at the moment, but I think he said 'for good *men* to do nothing.' Uh... exactly what do you mean by 'we'?"

"I mean we. Us. You and me. We."

"I told Jessie and Jacob your temper might flare up with such news. I know you're passionate about some things, but we need to be sensible about our part in affairs that don't really touch us."

"Don't really touch us? How the man talks, him who's going to Amherstburg, to Fort Malden, to buy a horse!"

"I only said I was thinking of buying another horse."

"You were thinking of poking around to find out about the abductions and figuring out how you could get involved to stop them is what you mean."

"I do admit to some curiosity, but as to what I can do... Whatever action 'we' decide on to right these wrongs, it must be studied, judicious, within our capabilities..."

"And I suppose Reverend Leeds, who started this ball rolling, is much less capable than Daniel Cameron the detective of righting such wrongs."

"That's not fair, Susan. Wouldn't any interest Leeds expressed in this topic be immediately transparent? Leeds is the messenger. The question is, is the message for me?"

"Us."

"We'll see."

"Us. Now, let's look at this rationally. You work dawn to dusk and the farm is doing well. The soil provides. We've got pigs, cattle, sheep, and chickens enough. You harvest deer from the woods and ducks and geese from the lake. We haven't been together all that long, but we are prospering. We're both healthy. Yes, I do my share, and I know you appreciate what I do, but I know you, Daniel. I've known you all my life. Farming can get to be drudgery, even when you take over cleared land, and you are at a point in your life where you need more excitement than just salting down the passenger pigeons you've shot. You are developing an unhealthy capacity for solitude, and most days you talk more to Argus or the team than you do to me."

"After the cows are milked tomorrow morning, I'll visit Archie Taylor. I'm curious why he didn't show up to our rendezvous with the Irishman. I'll find out what he knows and what advice he might have for me."

"For us."

"Us."

"Yes, talk to Archie tomorrow. Maybe he needs a horse in Amherstburg too. If you're interested, the kettle is already on for tea to dilute that whisky before we go to bed."

Daniel placed his freshly blackened go-to-meeting shoes near the woodstove to dry and read his Bible while he sipped his tea. It was more the Bible than the whisky or the tea that fended off sleep.

He lay awake pondering what sort of man could regard another's life so callously that he could force him to labour without pay, whip him for disobedience, hang him for running away, prevent him from learning to read or write, dictate who he must mate with, and then sell his children. He wondered if he was being hypocritical. It was over two decades since slavery had been completely outlawed throughout the British Empire, six since it had been legislated out of existence in Canada West. As it occurred to him that this was exactly the point, that now everyone recognized slavery as a hideous institution, he drifted off to dream of dead cattle bloating in a sun-bathed meadow.

Susan did not drop off to sleep right away either. She thought of what a good choice she had made when she married Daniel. Convenient that he had lived next door. He was hardworking, kind, physically strong, always considerate of her welfare and happiness. Others might see him as a quiet, pious young man slow to anger, but she knew this news of abducted runaways would gnaw at him, chafe against an innate sense of justice. Inaction to her husband was a splinter that worked its way into the mind. So she must send him down to Amherstburg and the fort to at least give him a semblance of doing something. Carpentry had provided some focus other than the farm, but even those skills had been somewhat ignored this winter past. Maybe a ride on the new Great Western Railway would be a diversion, although she would worry. There had been that horrible accident near Baptiste Creek...

Daniel is farming, but he's not yet a farmer, she thought with sudden insight. *It's me that's the farmer. I'm content here, and it's all I've ever known, but maybe he married too young. Now he's married and burdened with a wife and too much land to work before he's had an opportunity to see the world beyond Howard Township. He needs an adventure.*

Daniel and Archie Talk Horses

Breakfast over and morning chores done, Daniel climbed to the second rail of a cedar fence and swung a leg over Jacob's back. Archie lived only a mile away, so there was no need for the buckboard or buggy. A mile riding bareback was not too uncomfortable, even on a work horse. Jessie trotted along behind; the team was inseparable. She would stay nearby when he tied Jacob to a tree at Archie's. Argus wanted to join the outing and only reluctantly accepted a stay-at-home status.

Archie and Daniel had been friends since the Third Book of Lessons, when old Mr. Wickerson had made their proper education inevitable while beating spontaneity out of their young lives. Wickerson, a veteran of Waterloo, knew a thing or two about discipline. Archie, always the lighthearted joker, had received the benefit of the old man's expertise with a switch more often than Daniel, but Daniel had had his share of corrections. Both were now of an age that they looked back on Wickerson with humour and affection.

Physically, the two were a study in contrasts. Daniel's face was more chiselled. He often joked that if he could change anything about his appearance, he would get rid of his Presbyterian mouth, a feature that seemed to disapprove of everything. Archie's mouth always seemed poised to break into a grin. He laughed often and easily, viewing life as a comedy staged for his amusement. Daniel's five foot ten height looked up to Archie's six foot one, and where Daniel carried only muscle, Archie appeared almost portly. To their dismay, would-be schoolyard bullies discovered Archie's thicker appearance was not the product of fat but of a musculature that translated into consistent victories in games and fights. Where Archie relied upon strength, Daniel's speed and agility earned him few pugilistic challenges, and never a second one from the same person.

 Should Mr. Wickerson peer down from his heavenly vantage point, he would see two hardworking men in their mid-twenties sporting farmers' tans, wearing farmers' practical broadcloth, work boots and wide-brimmed hats, and prospering from the fertile soil. He would discover these two friends were mature enough to have married local, solid-minded farm girls but young enough for boisterous fun. Daniel's dry humour was balanced by Archie's propensity for practical jokes. Together, their Hallowe'en pranks and hi-jinks were renowned throughout the township and fell under the umbrella of mischief, a loosely defined word, but the source of much entertainment in rural society.

 When Daniel rode up to the log house, it was apparent why Archie had missed the appointment with Duffy. Archie was relaxing in a rocking chair on his front porch, an oily horse blanket wrapped around his shoulders, trying to find warmth in the spring morning's weak sunshine. An old sheet cut into ribbons kept two tapered wooden splints in place below his left knee. His left leg was supported on a kitchen chair, which also served as a resting place for a crude homemade crutch.

As Daniel tied up Jacob, Archie yelled over his shoulder into the house. "Mrs. Taylor, we'll need some coffee out here and some more of those scones we had for breakfast. And keep the gun handy. There's some ugly-looking travelling salesman gonna try to sell me something. You may have to run him off."

"So, what d' ya know for sure?" Archie said when Daniel reached the porch and took a seat on a second nearby kitchen chair.

"I know coffee would be accepted, and when did I ever turn down any of Catherine's baking? And I know you probably won't be doing the Highland fling tonight, unless that crutch is a ploy for sympathy and an excuse to get out of the little work you do around here."

"I might not do much, but it's good work when I do. So, what brings you to hobnob with the gentry such as myself? And good morning, by the way."

"Good morning to you and the missus as well. Actually, I've come to verify that the rumour is true."

"What rumour would that be?"

"Oh, that a rabbit frightened a neighbour of mine, and while he was in a panic he tripped over a straw and broke his leg."

"Mrs. Hedley wouldn't tell it that way. She would say that a fine, upstanding pillar of the community experienced an unfortunate accident on the way home from church last Sunday. A snake — must of been twenty feet long if it was an inch — startled his horse, and when that pillar of the community alighted from his conveyance to calm the beast, he slipped while attempting to negotiate a muddy rut. Because of this upstanding man's Herculean physique, he only tore some ligaments. Mrs. Hedley would surely add that a lesser man would have a broken leg to show for such efforts."

"So it's not broken?"

"By a serendipitous coincidence, Doctor Monteith passed by in the afternoon, and the missus yelled him in. Cost me three shillings for his learned diagnosis — and I threw in a chicken, because not everyone pays the good doctor's bills as conscientiously as we do."

Catherine Taylor elbowed the door open and set two enamelled tin cups, an ironstone pitcher of cream, a plate of scones with butter and strawberry jam, and a coffee pot — all precariously balanced on a wooden tray — on a stool between the two men.

"Smart you held back on the shortbread," Archie said to his wife. "Daniel might accidentally remark in his sleep that yours is better than Susan's, and then the fat would be in the fire. Jealousy can drive good friends apart."

Daniel righted a teetering cup and said, "Thank you, Catherine. I appreciate the breakfast top-up. So, would you have hailed Doc Monteith if you had known he would tell you to wait on Archie hand and foot until he mends?"

"I'm not seeing anything different from any other day."

Archie looked at his bandaged foot and woefully shook his head from side to side. "A man tries to shield his family from a viper, and this is the thanks he gets."

"A viper? It was a rat snake. I don't feel particularly friendly towards any serpent, and I suppose the horse feels the same, but viper it wasn't. Nor longer than a broomstick either. The poor creature just coming out of hibernation and looking to warm himself in the sun, just like you're doing. So what brings you around, Daniel?"

"Oh, I need some of Archie's advice about horses. I've heard he never has any problem with them, unless there's a twenty foot viper nearby."

"He's so full of advice, you might want to drain some of it out of him before he floats away."

"If he floats away, it won't be advice he's full of," Daniel said. Catherine nodded in agreement and returned to her labours in the house.

Archie waited until Daniel had filled both cups and was munching on a scone before he asked, "Are you really here about horses?"

"Maybe. Actually, I was curious why you didn't show to meet the Irishman, but I can see why now. The Desmond boy didn't make an appearance either."

"Paul has his own problems right now. Monteith was coming from a drop-in at the Desmonds' when Catherine intercepted him. Poor Mrs. Desmond is too feeble to leave her bed now. Consumption. And the old man is so addle-brained he puts his pants on backwards, so Paul has to fetch and carry for them both. But I'm glad you saw the paddy, even if the two of us couldn't. It would have been rude to have no one there. So now sir, your full report."

It took two cups of coffee and a refill of scones before Daniel finished recounting his talks with the Irishman and Susan. For the sake of brevity, he omitted the details of his conversation with Jessie and Jacob.

Coffee drained, they sat in silence. At last Archie said, "Goddamn bastards. Well, the way I see it, the three of you are right."

"How so?"

"Susan. She's right when she says 'Us'. You, when you say 'We must do something.' The Irishman, when he says, 'It's intolerable, and by God, we'll put an end to it!'

"Archie, I just don't understand enough about this whole travesty to know what to do next. I need, we need, your perspective. Where are the authorities in all these abductions? Are they as frequent as Duffy believes? Does anyone give a tinker's dam if a few raggedy ass Blacks disappear? But by God, I won't sit idle and let slavers or their mercenary henchmen steal anything or anyone from our soil."

"Spoken like a true patriot."

"Well, I *am* a patriot. Do you mock me?"

Archie chuckled. "No, I don't mock your love of country. Or your Christian instincts either, for that matter. I aspire to share them with your enthusiasm. What prompts your ardour for such a noble cause when the spring's work is just days away?"

"Knowledge, experience, personal observation, these are uncertainties, subject to change. Only my faith is without error, and my faith tells me I am needed to right a wrong. I'll have an eternity to do nothing, but in this life I'm only given a little time to do everything I'm called to do."

"I'm not sure my faith is as solid as yours. However, I do think we should examine the situation in precise and exquisite detail, before you go off half-cocked."

"Does it appear to you that I would go off half-cocked?"

"Yes. Yes it does. Daniel, I need time to cogitate over what you've told me. Why don't you and Susan drop in for supper tomorrow night? I'll have had time to sleep on all this, and we can put the issues under a magnifying glass. Now, hand me that crutch, if you'd be so kind."

Archie rocked his chair back close to the tipping point and banged on the door with the crutch. As soon as Catherine appeared, drying her hands on her apron, he asked, "Any problem if the Camerons join us for supper tomorrow night?"

"Of course not. Daniel, he's just showing off. You know you're welcome any time."

As Daniel stood to leave, he said, "I appreciate that, Catherine. I'll ride down later to help with tonight's feeding and mucking, if you can handle the milking. I'll do my own chores early tomorrow as well, and then I'll come down to help you do yours. Archie can supervise from wherever, and Susan will help with the supper tomorrow night."

Catherine put a hand on his arm. "Bless you. You're a good neighbour. But don't let Archie pretend he'll be on his pegs in a couple of days and capable of hobbling to the barn."

As he untied Jacob, he heard Catherine say, "That was canny of you to get your chores done by Daniel two nights in a row," and Archie reply, "You know I would do the same for him. It's going to be a tough week for the chickens, though."

The Flock Suffers

The following evening, Daniel had just finished washing his hands in the Taylor's summer kitchen after finishing Archie's chores when he detected the clip-clop of a visitor coming up the lane. As he emptied the wash basin outside, he heard Archie say from his chair at the kitchen table, "Good thing that's a fair-sized hen 'cause the reverend has two hollow legs. One would think he'd thicken up a bit with what that man can consume. He can smell a meal from a league away — and downwind too."

Daniel entered the kitchen from the back door just as Reverend Leeds was greeted by Catherine at the front and pressed into staying for supper. The reverend declined, saying he didn't wish to be a bother on such an unexpected visit, but everyone knew this was just for form's sake. Susan had already added another place at the long pine table, and the minister's feeble protestations were quieted by the delicious aromas emanating from the Taylors' new box stove. Once Susan had finished browning the gravy and Catherine had topped up the meat platter and the serving bowls, the minister led the charge after an unnecessarily protracted blessing of the food, the hands that had prepared it, and the bounties of the land.

The table banter centred on Archie's accident. True to their Scottish roots, there was much humour at his expense, and in return Archie embellished the tale of his rescue of the spooked horse from an enormous reptile until all had done justice to the hearty meal.

In deference to the reverend's admonitions on the evils of tobacco and alcohol, Daniel and Archie did not light their pipes or pour a wee dram while the women were cleaning up. Exposure to dozens of families encouraged a circuit rider to share news, and Leeds did not disappoint.

"There's been a suggestion in the legislature to rename us Ontario," Leeds reported.

"It can't happen too soon," Archie said. "Confusing enough to be Upper Canada, but at least everyone knew we were the colony on the upstream side of the water flow."

Daniel agreed. "That's true. When they changed us to Canada West, that only added to the confusion, because most of us still call this Upper Canada out of habit. 'Ontario' would be better than an upper this or a west that."

The conversation evolved to an evaluation of the recent hard winter, McNabb's future, how John Macdonald was gaining power in the legislature, the impact of the railroad, and if the government would be successful thwarting Britain's attempts to keep her colonies on the pound, shilling, pence system.

The Reverend Leeds was persuaded to spend the night. Catherine made up a cot for him in the front parlour while Susan stacked the dried supper dishes on the cup board. It was while Catherine was adjusting the wick in the coal oil lamp that Leeds made his confession.

"Archie, I did not drop in on any whim of spontaneity. I learned of your accident when I visited the Desmonds yesterday morning to minister to the spiritual wants of that family. The next stop on my circuit was the MacLeods, who graciously invited me for lunch. During that wholesome repast, I heard that the older son, Angus, is looking for work until he heads off to Normal School in London in September. I suggested he stop in here tomorrow and offer his services to you until your leg heals. Despite what you may wish, torn ligaments will plague you for quite some time."

Before Archie could utter a syllable, Catherine said, "Reverend, we are much obliged indeed. Angus MacLeod is a fine young man and experienced in farm work. We can offer him room and board and a shilling a day if that is suitable. Archie is so bull-headed he will say we will only need the help for a few days, but we both know better. The true beneficiary of the arrangement will be Daniel here, who would do chores for both our farms if we let him."

Daniel turned the talk in a new direction before Archie could raise any objections. "I met the Irishman on Monday."

Leeds said nothing for a few moments while he swirled his cup of tea.

"And?"

"And I learned much. I learned much. Thanks to Duffy, I see the problem, but I do not see the solution."

"Nor do I. With the garrison gone, there's more than enough to worry about, what with mutterings about Hunters' Lodges parading on the border. Everyone, myself included, burns daylight and more just to keep body and soul together. And let's not forget that only a few decades ago this was frontier, inflamed by Yankee invasion. When I talked with old Desmond, he couldn't remember what he had for breakfast, but he recalls the fighting like it was yesterday, and he can go on and on about the Indians and how Proctor had to make a stand somewhere."

"It could happen again," Archie pointed out. "I'm thinking, Reverend Leeds, that you have hit the crux of the problem. The authorities are absent or focusing on bigger issues than the disappearance of some pathetic runaways, and just about everyone is tied down with his own needs, wants and demands. But if you, as a man concerned with God's justice, do not see how these abductions may be stopped, then what actions do you expect from us?"

"I'll wager Archie is as curious as I am as to why you chose us and Paul Desmond to meet Duffy," Daniel added. "Why us? What can we possibly do?"

Leeds gazed into his tea. "I thought of you three because you are respected men, young but established, not hardscrabble newcomers clawing for a foothold. You are good people, also concerned with what is right. You are patriots and bristle when you hear of the iniquities practised by our southern neighbours. Above all, I believe you are men of enterprise and action. As to what form that action takes, I have absolutely no idea. Because we can do so little, we may do nothing at all, and that in itself would be a sin. We must let God guide us."

The conversation lightened around a second pot of tea. Susan's raised eyebrows reminded Daniel it was time to go home. He promised to return in the morning once his own chores were done; Angus MacLeod could do the evening ones. They stayed while Leeds read Psalm 118 and ended the evening with an all-too-lengthy prayer. Daniel brought the horses around, Susan thanked their hosts, and under an ivory crescent moon they set off for home.

The Argument

A thin but persistent drizzle set in overnight. By the time Daniel had finished his own and Archie's chores the following morning, he was thoroughly soaked and not in his best humour. "I won't accomplish much of what I'd planned," he grumbled when he entered the kitchen to don dry clothes.

"What you had planned will be right where you left it. Sit and have a cup of coffee once your wet clothes are on the rack. I'll cook us up a second breakfast. I could do with a few wee morsels myself."

Later, Daniel could not explain when the argument started. It may have begun when he fretted about how this year's maple syrup was not as good as usual, or maybe when Susan nicked a finger while slicing the bread, or possibly when he missed some question Susan asked as he absentmindedly gazed through the window at the grey day. Yes, it had to be the question, because Susan was a bit miffed when he asked her to repeat it.

"I said, Now that we've slept on last night's conversation, do you have a clearer picture of what our course of action will be?"

"I don't see what good I can do, even if I were to go down to Amherstburg. The situation — if the paddy is to be believed — is intolerable. If the fort were adequately garrisoned, the answer would be to set the soldiery on this sore, but if the local authorities are unable to address the issue, what can Daniel Cameron hope to accomplish?"

"This issue? It's not an issue, Daniel, it's a crisis. It's a form of invasion, from that rabble again, and you're content to shoot pigeons and mutter, 'What can one man hope to accomplish?' Maybe there are more than you boiling about this *issue*. You won't find them here, now will you?"

"Are you accusing me of shirking my civic duty just because I don't see what, how or when this whole abduction *issue* can be stopped?"

"You missed who and why. The who is once more that republic to our south, and us. You know the why."

"There's that 'us' again! It's me that will be travelling to Amherstburg, not you. What is the impetus that gets you so all riled up? Do you give a tinker's dam about some penniless Darkie who makes it across the river, or has this 'crisis' turned your dislike of the United States into vitriol?"

"Look, Mister Cameron, no one doubts, least of all me, that you are a loyal subject of the Crown and hold solid values, but you seem to have forgotten that you inherited your farm because your grandfather received it 'for meritorious service' in the 1812 war. Daniel, you are in his debt for the land, but you are also in debt to his legacy. You seem to disremember something else too... My Loyalist credentials."

"Susan, I know you despise Yankees down to the marrow in your bones, but there must be some good ones, and it would be unfair to paint them all with the same brush. You are getting me to lose focus on our conversation, and I will not permit your prejudices to cloud my judgment."

"Prejudices? Good God! Prejudices? Let me remind you that my 'prejudices' are well earned and they are indeed bone deep! My Green ancestors, bless them, lost their homes in Connecticut during the Revolution because of their loyalty to the Crown, and they fought to keep the republican mob out during the War of 1812. My Uncle William was personally responsible for our victory at Stoney Creek, and what's more..."

"Now it's you who is telling me what I already know. Whatever action 'we' decide on to right these wrongs, it must be studied, rational, within our capabilities..."

"Oh pish! Studied, rational, my foot! All right, we'll study this issue in a rational way. First, there is our patriotic duty to prevent foreign intervention on our soil. Second, we have a moral duty to prevent injustice, particularly to those who cannot defend themselves. Then there are the personal reasons for our — yes our, and don't interrupt — involvement. You need some excitement, some adventure. Don't you deny it. You have unfinished furniture in the barn you hardly looked at all winter because you are bored, maybe even a bit melancholic. Your world is too small right now, and too predictable. Farming can get to be a monotonous, depressing drudge."

"There's a heap of work waiting for me as soon as..."

"I'm worried there may be little left of you for me, once the livestock and the soil take their share. Daniel, I can manage here until the cows freshen. You know I can. You take Archie with you, and both of you take the new train to Windsor. You can hire horses and a buggy at rail's end to trot down to Amherstburg and find out exactly what is going on. That will give the MacLeod boy a chance to get everything under control without Archie looking over his shoulder and pointing his crutch at what he wants done next."

"I wouldn't feel right about…"

"About what? Finding out just what in tarnation is going on down there? Leave the stable door open so the horses can come and go as they please. Cows out during the day means less mucking. The poultry will be fine; I look after them anyway. I've got Argus and the cats for company, and if there's something urgent that needs an extra pair of hands, then I'll fetch the MacLeod boy or maybe Noah Hedley. I can send a message with the school children. They stop in here every day anyway."

"I'm not sure this isn't a fool's errand, Susan. Where would we start? We can't just walk up to a stranger in the street and ask what he knows about abductions, now, can we?"

"You could start with Mister Duffy's brother. He'll probably know as much as anyone. There may be a public house where you and Archie can sip a beer and listen or maybe buy one for a likely talker. Then there's old Fort Malden. You could…"

"We're sending the wrong detectives. You and Catherine should go, you have all the answers, you're so keen to…"

"Don't be absurd! I would confront the problem myself if I thought anyone would not find a conversation about this issue indecent to discuss with a lady. Women travelling without an escort would attract nothing but the wrong kind of attention and no information. None at all."

"I'll think about…"

"No, you won't. We're done thinking, Daniel. The brother's address you can get from the Irishman. We'll attend church on the Sabbath as usual, just in case Reverend Leeds has any more information for us, then you and Archie are off on your mission. Now enough talk," she said rising. "I have potatoes to peel and shortbread cookies to bake."

With an imperfect expectation as to how he would be received at the Duffy farm, Daniel set off after lunch into a sheepdog wind herding fleecy clouds. As he manoeuvred the buggy around the deeper puddles, he reviewed the morning's argument. Plainly, he had lost. Still, he had put forth valid reasons why he should not indulge in any frivolity just now. The farther he got from home, the more he appreciated Susan's point-of-view. A ride on the new train, a holiday with his best friend, Susan's blessing to quaff a beer or two — all in the spirit of discovery, of course. It would be fun. His wife was right; he did need some adventure in his life and she was quite capable of managing the farm on her own, at least for a little while. Archie would take little persuading; the train might give his leg a chance to heal. Nothing dramatic could come of a little excursion...

By the time Daniel turned into the Duffys' lane, his annoyance at Susan's victory in the debate was evaporating as quickly as the puddles.

Amherstburg

The day of their departure dawned cool and dry and beneficial for everyone. Drier roads meant a lighter pull for the horses. Angus MacLeod established his own routine as a hired man without the over-zealous supervision of Archie. The school children had mentioned that Noah Hedley was going to Thamesville on some errand, so Susan arranged for him to take Daniel and Archie to the Great Western station. In a wicker basket that could hold four litters of puppies, Catherine and Susan had packed a sufficient amount of pigeon pie, potato salad, salt pork sandwiches, scones, strawberry jam, shortbread, cake, and muffins to feed a railway carriage for a week. Each insisted on sending a vinegar jug full of water with her man, as if dehydration loomed as a life-threatening hazard of railway travel. Both women looked forward to a day to themselves, at least until chore time. Noah enjoyed the non-nagging benefit of male company for several hours, and Mrs. Hedley had news to share.

Daniel Cameron and Archie Taylor were taking the train to Windsor, and no one knew why.

A train ride was a novel experience for both. With an exchanged look of silent assent, vinegar jugs were left on the station platform for someone's use. Once underway, fellow passengers enthusiastically lightened the lunch basket. Later, Daniel would say, "Susan, you can not believe how fast that train blurs along until you're on it! It's like sitting in a chair in your own parlour, that's just how comfortable it is, and watching the country go by. We don't have a horse in the county that could keep apace that locomotive for a mile. If you had told me we would be in Windsor and signed into a hotel by suppertime, I wouldn't have believed it possible if I hadn't been there myself."

Archie was sporting a cane and a leather leg brace Doctor Monteith had dropped off for wear in waking hours. A square of stiff leather, held in place by straps stitched top and bottom, stabilized his leg from knee to ankle and made sitting and rising difficult, so he remained at the hotel while Daniel made rental arrangements for a conveyance. Accustomed to farmers' hours and farmers' appetites, they were bathed and breakfasted by seven the next morning and on the front porch just as a stable boy arrived. To demonstrate his healing prowess, Archie insisted on hobbling around the horse and buggy to inspect their rental, and experimented with his leg propped on their overnight bags to ensure there was the requisite room behind the dashboard.

Freed from routine labours, they followed the river road through Sandwich, stopping mid-morning to admire the view of the Detroit River and the American side while divesting themselves of breakfast coffee. A cool northwest wind insisted on gloves and scarves and buttoned coats until early afternoon, when they stopped for lunch and directions at a small hotel with bright yellow shutters and an attached stable.

"Nope, can't help you," they were informed by the proprietor. "I don't recognize the name. We've got plenty of O'Rileys and O'Briens and Maguires, but Duffys are a scarce commodity around here. There's a general store on the other side of the fort. Ask there. They know everyone at a general store. You're no more than an hour's brisk trot away."

Archie sagely suggested they might wish to book a room for the night to avoid a last minute panic searching for accommodation, but frugal Daniel, fearing they would pay in advance for a room they might not use, vetoed the idea. Topped up with tourtiere and raisin pudding and the horse tended to, off they set at the recommended brisk trot, excited to be so far from home.

"South end of town, turn left at the livery stable, you'll see Duffy's sign on your right," were the directions given at the general store.

"From John, you say," Michael Duffy said as he accepted the letter of introduction from Daniel's hand. "Then you had better come in so we can get better acquainted." He made note of Archie's braced leg and the suitcases. Daniel tethered the horse and followed the two into the cottage.

"Have a chair while I read what my brother has to say about you. He visited a while back, but you probably know that. You can see my good woman has already put the water on, and we can share a pipe while I read and the tea steeps."

Daniel worried he had made the wrong decision about reserving a room where they had procured dinner until Duffy placed the letter on the table, re-lit his pipe, and said, "A pipe in the hand makes a man a philosopher." He waved the smoke away. "You'd best stay the night if you don't mind a cot and a plank bed in the workshop. It's almost as warm as the house once the stove's fired up."

His tiny wife added, "Mister Cameron, if you wish to stretch your legs after supper, the livery is not so far away. If you leave right after the ham and potatoes, you can have your horse looked after and be back by the time I've warmed up some pudding for dessert."

During supper, the general conversation was about the weather, the railway, and the new postal service. Daniel sat facing the rosary, the crucifix, the book, the shoe, the gloves, and the cap. The wheelwright noticed him staring at the little table between bites of bread pudding and saw a hint of a smile cross his face.

"Do you find something humorous about our faith, sir?" he asked.

"Not at all, Mister Duffy. Not at all. I was thinking of how prickly our fire and brimstone Reverend Leeds can be when he encounters those who don't appreciate his approach to a vengeful God... And loving one's neighbour — as long as one's neighbour shares his approach."

The wheelwright pointed at the articles. "A reminder the missus keeps of our departed son," he said. "Cholera."

"I'm sorry," Daniel said. "I deduced it was for a loved one passed. I have no intention of offending; it's just I've never dined in a Catholic house before."

"And I don't remember being in a heretic one before, at least not for long. We keep the Devil in the closet, behind the broom," and he laughed.

"Shush, husband," the tiny wife exclaimed as she cleared the table. "You mustn't mention him by name, or he might appear."

"Maybe he's appeared twice now. It's just like him to do his mischief in darkness and not show his face."

That comment plunged the four into a conversation that covered why the visitors had come to Amherstburg, their intention to seek out the authorities at the fort, the details of the abduction and near abduction, an oblique reference to the impatience and anger of the locals who were eager to take matters into their own hands, and a verbatim report of the wheelwright's futile experience when he attempted to get the pensioners to help. Mrs. Duffy explained why the newest fugitive was forced to move on, for everyone's safety. "Joseph was a good worker and might have been as quick to learn as the club-foot," the wheelwright added, "but he wasn't with us long enough for me to find out."

"Where did he go?" Archie asked.

"To Fort Malden. It's on the river, less than a mile. You passed it on the way here. A sergeant sympathetic to our cause persuaded the new major who has taken over the officers' quarters to give him shelter and food in exchange for work. It's anyone's guess how long that arrangement will last, but you may see him when you go up there."

"Your cause?" Archie remarked.

"Don't think we're the only ones trying to help those fortunate enough to escape bondage. The real problem is protecting them once they get here, so a few of us..." He stopped in mid-sentence. With a warning glance to her husband, Mrs. Duffy rose to refill tea cups. "So a few of us," he resumed, "have tried to keep an eye open to help the recent arrivals. They're the most likely to have a feeling of false security."

Daniel stole a glance at Archie to see if he had caught the redirection and received the slightest of nods in return.

Their host showed his visitors to their accommodations in the chilly workshop and started a fire in the stove. As he piled a bundle of heartwood beside it for their convenience, he remarked, "His letter states my brother has a high opinion of you, Mister Cameron, as do I... both of you, and it instructs me to trust you. I wish you lived closer. My friends and I have work only just begun, and we could surely use men with your instincts. That you have seen fit to come all this way..." And he shook his head in disbelief.

He held the lantern close to the dappled floor boards and pointed. "That needs to be avenged, avenged for that poor cripple's sake, and for the damage it's done to my business and my little woman."

As Daniel and Archie examined the bloodstains, Daniel said, "What work are you and your friends engaged in that has only just begun?"

The wheelwright evaded the question. "It's a shame you don't live closer. We could use you to keep an eye out for trouble."

Early next morning, Daniel retrieved the horse and buggy while Mrs. Duffy prepared breakfast. "If you are ever down this way again, you are welcome to stay here," Michael Duffy said as they finished a second cup of coffee. "I would like you to meet several individuals who enjoy action, men who would not hesitate to come to your aid should you require it."

Daniel and Archie thanked him for this thought and dismissed it as a courteous remark. After sincere expressions of appreciation for hospitality, they set off into a chill northwest breeze to Fort Malden.

They had not expected to be directed to the sole officer's quarters as soon as they stopped at the pensioners' community, and they had not expected to find the major so young.

Daniel began to recount the reason for their visit, explaining they had heard that runaway slaves who made it to freedom in Canada West were being abducted in disturbing numbers by bounty hunters and that for patriotic and moral motives the two had... Archie interrupted with "We want to know just what the hell is going on and what's being done about it!"

Major Emmett invited them to accompany him as he walked the perimeters for a casual inspection. For the next twenty minutes he pointed out the missing garrison and artillery, told them of the sergeant major's reconnaissance patrols along the river, explained there was insufficient manpower to protect runaways, confirmed the stories of bounty hunters, and hinted that the local citizenry did what it could to be the eyes and ears of the army. Of course, he pointed out, there was always the danger these people would take matters into their own hands, although nothing of that sort had yet reached his ears.

"We heard much of what you are telling us from Mister Duffy, the wheelwright," Daniel said. "He and Mrs. Duffy were kind enough to put us up for the night. We have been informed already why the military presence seems to be unable..."

"Or unwilling," Archie interjected.

"... seems to be unable to address this travesty. At the very least, couldn't someone monitor traffic going across to Michigan?"

"Impossible. Too many coming and going, and how would we intercept them at night, even if we had the boats and men?"

Emmett stopped on the river path to throw a stick into the water. Several hundred yards away, a young Black man was digging a drainage ditch.

"You can see for yourself how inadequate our defences are. So gentlemen, I laud your motivations. If you have the solution to our situation, I would most gladly entertain it. However, until someone apprises the Colonial Office of the strategic necessity to provide much more of everything, I suspect we shall be pithering about until the other side foments an invasion crisis or rips itself apart over the slavery issue, which could give us some breathing room. Now that you understand why the military cannot be of assistance, what are your plans?"

"Our holiday time is short, but we thought to take a day or two and explore along the river before we return our buggy to its Windsor livery and catch the train home," Archie replied. "My friend here is pondering the purchase of a horse for his wife, so we may inquire of breeders in the area."

"Many have purchased quite satisfactory mounts at the livery in Amherstburg, I'm told. I intend to buy one there myself. The owner is an acquaintance of our local physician, and of Mister Duffy, if I'm not mistaken. It means retracing your steps somewhat, but the doctor maintains you can trust the man's encyclopaedic knowledge concerning all matters equine."

"Thank you, Major," Archie said. "Our horse was bedded there last night, so we are familiar with its location."

"If you find the proprietor absent, check down by the town wharf. Not the main one, the smaller one upstream. He often fishes there."

"Major, you have been very informative," Daniel said. "We came here with our shirt tails in a knot about this bounty hunter business, and we felt compelled to do something to stop it. Your candour has made us appreciate how frustrating the situation is for you, and how powerless we are to help." He looked at Archie, who reluctantly shook his head in agreement.

The major returned his gaze to the young man waist deep in the trench.

"Gentlemen, if you are sincere in your wish to save these unfortunates from bounty hunters... If you truly wish to help... Possibly you might entertain a suggestion that would allow that poor wretch to lick some honey from a thorn."

Part Six

IMMERSION

Mrs. Hedley Reports

The egg salad sandwiches much diminished, the cookie tray began its rounds. Mrs. Hedley helped herself to a wedge of shortbread, and after turning it over and back to complete a thorough, critical inspection, she placed it condescendingly on the saucer beside her teacup. She imbibed a tiny sip of tea, and regarded the wedge with the same enthusiasm she would a maggot.

The Temperance Committee was meeting in Mrs. Chalmers' parlour for an afternoon of righteous railing against alcohol and an update on local goings-on. That the seven attendees had husbands who enjoyed a drink and had never exhibited the slightest inclination to be loutish or permit it to impact their occupation was of no consequence. The general topic of intemperance gave reason for a social gathering. On several recent occasions, a hostess had even provided a raspberry cordial as well as tea, and no one had remarked on it. It had almost become expected.

Abigail Hedley's tongue had no need of cordial lubrication. Thanks to Noah, that dear man, she was the sole proprietor of the facts, facts which she would magnanimously share with the chosen. She made a mental note to refrain from any reference to "oatmeal savages," aware that several of the group, including the hostess, had Scottish origins. She began slowly, as these things were best shared in a circumspect fashion with a dramatic flourish.

"What a wonderful world we live in," she said quite casually. "Imagine sitting on a cushioned seat and being whisked from Woodstock to Windsor in less than a day."

Someone said, "They say the new train is quite expensive," but she ignored her, not wishing to get off topic.

"Did you know, as I did not," she went on self-deprecatingly, "the Great Western provides a car just for the mail service? For the outrageous price of a three penny stamp, you can send a letter from Amherstburg to Chatham or Ridgetown or Thamesville or wherever you wish. Incredible, isn't it?"

The annoying woman who insisted on interrupting said, "I don't think it's the railroad that provides the car. I think it's the postal service that hires —"

"Whoever pays for it is of no importance," Mrs. Hedley said hurriedly, readjusting her ample bottom on the chair. She sipped her tea to re-establish the pace and tone she wished.

"The point is that communication has become incredibly efficient. My stars, remember how we used to send letters with the Reverend Leeds?" She gave a little laugh. "Quite unnecessary in this new age."

Now was the time to sink the hook.

"Why, just yesterday my husband received a letter from Daniel Cameron, advising him there would be no need to meet him and Archie Taylor at the train station on their return from Windsor. It will be Mister Taylor alone who will return by train, and would he please advise the MacLeod boy to be at the station for the eastbound a day later than anticipated, and he intended his own homecoming to be a surprise for Mrs. Cameron."

She took a breath. "Naturally, as a good neighbour, I sent Noah right over there with the message, and told him to tell Mrs. Cameron to be ready for a surprise."

Mrs. Hedley surveyed her salon. The pregnant silence as she sipped more tea told her they were hers.

"Surprise does not begin to describe it. Now, you know my Noah is a man of few words, but I pressed him for all the details. Mister Cameron returned home in a smart new gig, all mid-night blue with red striping and bright red wheels — quite dashing, actually — pulled by a lively filly for Mrs. Cameron. A full-blooded Canadian no less. That in itself would be newsworthy. But he was not alone! No. He brought someone with him, and you now know it was not Archie Taylor. Noah says Mrs. Cameron was taken aback with the suddenness of it, as we all would be, I daresay, because... He brought home a Black man."

She paused to let the enormity of the idea sink in.

"Where he got him and what he intends to do with him is anybody's guess. But he's quite Black. Definitely Black. Imagine meeting that on a dark night." She gave a little voluntary shudder.

Luxuriating in the shocked faces, on she charged. "Noah says he appears to be a quiet young man, quite deferential. Called him 'suh'. He probably doesn't even understand English. Well, watch out for the quiet ones, I always say. I do hope Daniel Cameron knows what he's doing, bringing home someone like that. It wouldn't surprise me to hear they've all been murdered in their beds."

Shortbread cookies were delicately nibbled while silence reigned, although Mrs. Hedley made a show of breaking hers against the teacup, as if it were too tough to simply melt in the mouth. Mrs. Chalmers started the tray around again and said, "I will set out glasses and a decanter of cordial on the table for those who require something more stabilizing than tea. Ladies, please feel free to help yourselves."

Mrs. Hedley tied the ribbon on the package. "We can expect such things from some, I suppose. That clan, Reverend Leeds says, that clan were Children of the Mist after Culloden. The reverend says the Camerons haven't been out of the heather long, whatever that means."

She knew very well everyone in Mrs. Chalmers' parlour knew what that meant.

Mrs. Hedley poured herself a glass of cordial, and not to insult their hostess, took another cookie, all the while congratulating herself on having made her point without reference to savages.

Two Worlds Intersect

Hedley had just delivered his message when who should turn into the lane with a new gig but Daniel, accompanied by a young Black man who was introduced as Joseph. Knowing he would suffer criticism during the coming interrogation for not taking advantage of Susan's offer of a late lunch during which he could glean information, Noah reluctantly declined, thinking his continued presence would constitute an intrusion.

Daniel had ruminated about buying a horse, so his return with a lively young stepper was not unexpected, and anyone could see the gig she pulled was not only sturdily constructed but quite fashionable as well. It had been purchased from the Amherstburg Livery, he informed Susan, and it had been recently made by Michael, John Duffy's brother, a new acquaintance who had shown Archie and him most welcome hospitality. In two sentences, he explained Joseph's presence with the promise of details to follow.

Mrs. Hedley had reported correctly. The delight of being presented with such a conveyance was eclipsed by the arrival of a runaway slave who had escaped capture by the skin of his teeth, and Susan was indeed uncertain how the equilibrium of their lives would be maintained. She had shooed Daniel off on a fact-finding holiday, only to have him get personally involved in what up to now had been abstract and far-off issues.

It pleased Daniel that his wife was enthusiastic about her new horse and gig; they had not been cheap, but he felt it would be in poor taste to disclose the price of a gift. What concerned him was her reaction to Joseph. There was none. She had acknowledged his arrival with a curt "Hello" when Joseph tipped his hat while being introduced, ran an appraising hand over the filly and gig, asked Daniel how he intended to introduce the new horse to Jessie and Jacob, remarked that the travellers must be fatigued after such a long journey in such a light vehicle, and suggested she boil water for tea, make some sandwiches, and fetch wine and cookies for the children.

"Joseph, stretch your legs a bit, take a look around, and get acquainted with the place. I'll keep Argus with me 'til he gets to know you better; he gets his temperament from Mrs. Cameron," Daniel said with a wink and a nod. "We don't trust him not to take a chunk out of strangers. The hay mow will probably be the gig's new home, but fresh eyes may find a better spot," Joseph, subtracting himself from the tension produced by his unannounced arrival, wandered off to take stock of his latest refuge.

He could not resist comparisons to the Lonnegan plantation. The Cameron two storied house, white painted boards over logs, set square to the road and far enough back to avoid dust, was so much smaller than the house in Tennessee. A flagstone path led from the lane across a yard cropped by sheep to the front door, beside which two small cedars stood guard. It occurred to him that light entering the house through a small rectangle of cranberry glass over this visitors' entrance would produce a warm aura of welcome, and although he had never been inside the entertaining part of the plantation house, he wondered if it had been designed not so much to be welcoming as to be imposing.

A basswood eavestrough directed water away from a closed-in porch at the side of the house, and the flagstones leading from it to the lane not twenty paces away were, unlike the front path, well worn. Three wooden steps led from the flagstones into the porch through a faded, well-used door.

Walking down the lane toward an unpainted bank barn, he discovered the rectangular house must have had an addition to the original log cabin. The rear third created an overhang as the back yard dropped away. Under this overhang a single row of firewood, the remnants of the winter's supply, leaned against the farthest support post. Farther down the gently sloping hill he saw a black iron pump sitting atop an enclosed well, a chicken coop, two storehouses, an implement shed housing a buckboard, a buggy, and a plough, and beyond these a hay wagon with red-painted racks waiting at the gate of a five acre, rail-fenced field suitable for a horse paddock or sheep. A set of rusty harrows leaned against the fence nearest the barn. Why two storehouses for only two people, he wondered.

As he entered the barn, he talked softly to introduce himself to its denizens without alarm. It exuded the gentle aroma of hay and cattle and horses and the more acrid smell of pigs. From their common stall, two draft horses eyed him warily, as did several heifers and a bull from its own pen. Feral barn cats shotgunned at his approach. In the far corner of the barn, he found woodworking tools and a workbench, beside which were piled dusty chair pieces and a dismantled table. He smiled to himself, thinking of how Michael Duffy would have an apoplectic fit if he saw dust on a workbench.

He ventured out the back door into the barnyard. Gravel and the slope of the land guaranteed good drainage. A grassy lane separated fields ringed with stump fences and appeared to enter a forest in the distance. *All this done by two,* he mused. *Enough work here for ten.* Then he realized what was missing. Cabins.

Wishing to make himself useful, he walked back to the house, unhitched the filly, and tied her to a tree beside the lane. Wheeling the gig downhill was easy enough, but when he opened the door of the first log storehouse, he discovered it was already filled with a mixture of farm and household items. A side window illuminated an old butter churn, a broken spinning wheel, a rusty scythe, a peavey, logging chains, three empty barrels, an old dresser missing its top drawer, a warped winnowing tray, a wooden box full of stoneware jars, and a small cube of rust that was almost unrecognizable as a wood stove. All spoke of past industry. All languished in disuse on a packed earth floor. On the far side of the storehouse, rocks piled intermittently on top of a shoulder-high pile of weathered lumber limited the warp.

He heard the sound of young voices. Five children of varying ages were replacing glasses on a tray held by Mrs. Cameron. Each took something from a jar and, waving a thank-you, headed back to the road.

The farther outbuilding was windowless and of tighter construction. A four-by-six foot wooden box and a bright red sleigh with a high backrest and a flowing, forward curving dashboard, both on runners, had been abandoned at its rear. Its door was too narrow for the gig, but he opened it out of curiosity and pulled back in surprise at a wall of damp sawdust as high as his chin. When he touched the imprint of the door, some sawdust transferred to his fingers. It was cold. He smelled it, rubbed the aromatic particles between his fingers and thumb, and touched a finger to his tongue. Not recognizing the wood, he spit it out. He shut the door, left the gig at the bottom of the barn ramp, and started back up the hill, puzzling why anyone would store sawdust in a building and fearful lest Mrs. Cameron send him on his way.

She was at the porch door, bent over as if vomiting, and Mister Cameron's hand was on her shoulder as if comforting her in her distress. Joseph stopped walking until Mister Cameron noticed him and waved him on. When he got closer, he could hear Mrs. Cameron gasping for breath. As she straightened, he could see tears running down her cheeks, and she bent over in another spasm of laughter.

"Oh heavens, I haven't had a laugh like that in ages," she managed to say at last. "He tasted it! It's only sawdust... What did he think it was? Did he think we could park the gig in the icehouse?" and she bent over in another fit of laughter. She was finally able to say, "The poor man. He's never seen an icehouse. For goodness sake, come in. The tea will be long past ready."

Daniel followed his wife through the porch door and held it ajar for Joseph, who stood on the last flagstone, hat in hand. "Come in, Joseph. Come in. You, Susan, me... We have much to talk about."

"Massa Cameron, I cain't. Dat d'ere be a foreign country ta me. I ain't never bin in a white house before."

"What? You mean to tell me you have never been inside a house?"

"I bin in cabins an a log shack once an' da basement a houses when I was on da run an' had da railroad people lookin' afta me an' a barn an' a root cellar, once in Tennessee and agin when I was freight in Ohio, an' a workshop and stables like da one where we stopped las' night an' where I catched ma breath in Kentucky and at da fort, an' I bin in da back half a da big house on da plantation when I was truckin' in food and once carryin' a new carpet for da massa's office, but I never bin in a real-ta-goodness white house before, like I was company or sumpin'. I ain't sure I know how ta act in a real house."

"Joseph, that's ridiculous. It's just a house. There's no special way to act."

"Dat ain't so, Massa Cameron. D'ey got a lot a diff'rent ways a actin' in a house. Ya ask any dog — he'll tell ya. Ya gotta act certain ways in certain places, an' dis place I ain't so comf'table wif yet ta know what d'ose ways be. I doan wanna be no embarrassment. I doan want ya ta be sorry ya be helpin' me."

Susan had turned back to see why no one had followed her inside and heard the whole speech. She brushed Daniel aside to stand on the top step with her arms crossed, and looked down on Joseph.

"Joseph, I know nothing about you," she began in a no-nonsense voice. "I don't know your last name, I don't know your history, or where you are from, or where you may be going, or where you are going to sleep tonight. I don't even know if you are welcome here. And I won't know if we don't sit down over a cup of tea and get acquainted. If you don't feel welcome in our house, then we'll sit in the porch, but if you think I intend to stand outside to drink my tea and eat the sandwiches I slapped together while you were exploring, you have another think coming." She returned into the house to fetch a tray of food and the teapot.

"Come sit," Daniel said, waving him inside. "It's best not to get her riled. She laughs easily, but she comes from warrior stock."

"Da porch. But I doan wanna venture inside more, not jus' yet."

"The porch, then."

At first, the conversation focused on practical matters. Argus and Joseph were introduced, and a few discreet morsels of roast beef sandwich under the table sealed their friendship for life. Since Joseph would not enter the house proper, it was decided he would sleep on the workbench in the barn until an empty stall could be cleaned. Susan said she would find extra quilts after supper and grudgingly agreed to leave meals on the table in the porch until Joseph felt accepted enough to join them in the kitchen.

"The two of us are trying to prosper on this land of two farms," Daniel said, "and each day there is more work than we can handle, even when nothing goes wrong. If there was ever a day when nothing went wrong, I didn't recognize it. We are land rich and labour poor. So here's the offer, Joseph. If you wish to stay on as our hired man, we'll pay you whatever Archie Taylor is paying the MacLeod boy, plus room and board. No work on the Sabbath. Or you are free to leave and go whenever you wish, wherever you wish. Sleep on it if you like, and you can give us your answer in the morning. No need to shake on it 'til then."

Joseph took in a deep breath and exhaled through his mouth. "Massa Cameron, I doan need ta sleep on dat offer. Dat's da bes' deal I ever had in my life. I ain't never had a chance ta earn my own money an' be tole I kin go wherever an' whenever I like. Even Deacon couldn't offer me dat. I wish Old Mose an' little Seth an' Malachi an' Ellie be here right now ta hear dis."

"If you go down and get the workbench cleared, Mrs. Cameron can get supper started, and I will draw up a list of the work that's waiting to be tackled. We will prioritize it after supper. We do this every spring, but it will seem less daunting if there are three of us."

"Tomorrow is Saturday," Mrs. Cameron said. "We need a gallon or two of coal oil for the lamp you gave me Christmas past, Daniel, so I think I'll try out my new horse and gig to Morpeth and back. I may stop in to see Catherine Taylor because it would be rude to pass by and not give my regards. Oh, and you should know, I saw skunk tracks near that jagged hole in the southwest corner of the henhouse, so if you want eggs for breakfast you might want to nail a scrap piece of wood over it."

"Why don't you invite Catherine for the ride? The MacLeod boy will be picking Archie up at the station sometime tomorrow, and until he gets home the two of you could have a little hen party while we put a stop to a skunk's hen party here. You might want to go out of your way a bit and drive slowly by the Hedleys' house."

"That would be cruel," she laughed. "Also, I never did get the stables mucked as I wanted to. The henhouse needs a good clean-out too, but keep that manure in a separate pile to cure. It will burn plants if it's too fresh. We'll need to keep a close watch on the ewes that haven't lambed. They're late, and I don't know why. I left the replacement boards for the pigpen leaning at the barn back door. The ones you were going to use had been painted in some century or other. That paint won't do the pigs any good if they chew on it, and you know they will."

"What would you like us to do in the afternoon?" Daniel asked, but she just ignored him.

Joseph set off to clear a spot for himself in the workshop, Daniel to examine the potential skunk portal into the henhouse, and Susan to prepare supper. After the dishes were done, Susan spent some time with the filly to get her accustomed to her new home, and Daniel took some old quilts to the barn. Before he left, he said, "Joseph, there are serious topics we will talk about tomorrow. They may not be to your fancy, but we'll wait until Mrs. Cameron gets home from Morpeth before I tell you how things are going to be."

Day One

The three watched the sun set from the porch and enjoyed a pork roast that Susan had marinaded in vinegar and herbs. Joseph noticed how Daniel wiped greasy fingers on a cloth napkin and did the same. "Missus Cameron, I ain't enjoyed a meal like dat since I left da Deacon's," he said, "an' dat be a compliment 'cause Deacon's wife, she be 'bout da best cook I ever did encounter. She be deaf an ya couldn't never make out what she tryin' ta say, but she sure know how ta cook."

Susan reported on her outing. "Catherine was delighted to join me, and we pretended we were ladies of leisure instead of just farmers' wives as we entered the village. Both the filly and the gig are a pleasure to drive, Daniel, but then you already know that. Thank you. I'm going to name her Victoria. If Victoria is good enough for the queen, Victoria should be good enough for a horse. And no, we did not pass the Hedleys' slowly. No need to poke the dragon."

"I hope you aren't too upset that we didn't quite complete the week's work you left for us," Daniel said glibly. "After the chores, the first thing we did was cover the potential skunk entrance. Joseph and I finished mucking out both the henhouse and the barn, except for the pigs. We'll replace those broken boards when we tackle the pigpen on Monday. I know that's laundry day, but we'll get the pig clothes to you as soon as the job is done. It won't hurt them to stay on the line overnight. Joseph, tomorrow afternoon we'll rummage around and find you a second set of clothes. We can't have me fresh as a daisy and you wafting porcine perfume. Susan, you weren't even to the Taylors' when the old ewe with the black face lambed. Twins. I know they were a long time coming, but all three seem healthy."

"Twins. That's good news, but not surprising. She's never dropped just one. I'll check in on them later. Nothing cuter than a newborn. I should go out in my new gig every morning. Joseph, how did you fare, your first full day here?"

"Missus Cameron, da work I is used ta an' I ain't afraid a it. Pigs, cattle... ain't got much 'sperience wif sheep, 'cept roundin' 'em up once Massa Lonnegan's front lawn be chewed level. Dat part a da day no problem, but what I'se bin troublin' o'er is, las' night when Massa Cameron brought me da quilts, he said I might not fancy how things gonna be, an' dat has got me a mite anxious."

The Camerons exchanged glances.

"You start," Susan said.

"Joseph, the missus and I discussed you briefly yesterday and immediately we identified two things we find intolerable. Absolutely intolerable. For me, it's 'Massa Cameron'. I am not 'Master Cameron'. I am your employer, and I would like to think I am your benefactor, but I am not your master. When I hear 'Massa', I hear a slave talking. You are not a slave now, not here, and God willing, you never will be again. You said you had never been told you could go wherever and whenever you wished. It's called freedom, Joseph, and you must adjust your mind to it."

Joseph sat silent for a long moment, biting his bottom lip and clenching his left hand in his right. "If I cain't call ya Massa Cameron, d'en what is I supposed ta call ya?" he said quietly.

"'Mister Cameron' will do just fine in more formal company such as when we have guests, but I would prefer 'Daniel' when we're working."

"Massa... Mister Cameron, I doan feel it be appropriate ta call ya Daniel. I ain't quite sure I could get used ta dat. You da boss. We done compromise' on da porch... Kin we compromise on da name? If I 'ddress ya as 'Mister Daniel', would dat sound like I not be thinkin' like a slave?"

Before her husband could respond, Susan said, "Mister Daniel would suit perfectly. Now let's tackle a very serious problem."

"Missus Cameron... Missus Susan... I try real hard ta keep myself from smellin'. It ain't bin easy ta keep cleaned up when I'se bin on da run, but when I git da chance I wash ever' day. Ever' day."

Susan laughed until once again the tears flowed down her cheeks. "Oh, you poor man," she said, wiping her eyes with her napkin, "this is much more important than not finding an opportunity to wash when you are running for your life. No, no, no, no, no... What I am talking about is your dismal command of the English language. Here, it is simply unacceptable to talk as you do. You replace your t h's with a d and you often omit the last letter of a word, especially if it is a g. I've noticed mispronunciation of vowels, double negatives, the frequent use of ain't, always the mark of the lower classes... Can you read?"

Again there was a painful interval before Joseph spoke. "I'se truly sorry dat ya be unhappy wif da way I talk. I ain't known no udder way. All my life I bin 'round folks dat talk like me. No, Missus Susan, I cain't read, an 'cept for Cicero, I doan know any slave dat can."

"Well, that's settled then. If Daniel will do up the dishes, every night after supper you and I will sit at the kitchen table for an hour. You will learn to communicate using the Queen's English while I teach you how to read and write. Do you have any objection to that? I will not hesitate to tell you if you do anything inappropriate in our house. As my husband just told you, you must stop thinking as a slave."

Joseph slumped in his chair and stared at the floor. Finally, he straightened up and said, "I got ta get ma mind used ta changes. I bin hopin' for a long, long time I'd get ta where da Britishers live an' be free. Dat be my dream. Now I got ta ask myself, can I stretch dat dream ta include readin' an' writin'? Missus Susan, I would surely love ta be able ta even sign my own name. If ya can be patient wif me, I will be da hardest workin' learner ya ever heard of. I jus' wish Old Mose and Seth and Ellie could see me now."

The First Week

Fog burned off early on Sunday morning, giving a teasing promise of balmy spring weather to come. Joseph planned on walking to the lake to orient himself to the farm boundaries while the Camerons were at church. It occurred to no one that the new hired man accompany them. To invite Martians to share their worship was more within the scope of their imagination.

The service over, Susan interrogated Anna Leeds about the best way to teach someone to read, and Anna promised to scrounge around for an old primer. Archie threw a bundle of clothing into the buggy as they were leaving. "These should fit him close enough. I can't imagine he'll complain unless he's planning on hobnobbing with high society. Catherine added some new socks I had tucked away in a drawer, so if my feet freeze off and you end up doing my chores for me, we'll know who to blame."

After a late lunch and a productive search for more clothes, the three sat in the porch with coffee, and for two hours Joseph told his story of plantation life, escape, tribulations, the kindnesses of strangers, the false abolitionist, Malachi's murder and Seth's capture, the Deacon, the paddlewheeler, the Underground Railroad, the crossing, Duffy's workshop, and the one constant, fear. He was interrupted many times to answer questions of detail or to repeat something misheard because of his accent.

The telling of the tale helped bring about a catharsis. Joseph finished by saying, "So here I be, right where da t'ree of us hoped ta be. I'se feelin' mighty guilty dat t'was me dat made it when d'em udder two be more deservin'."

The Camerons said nothing as each attempted to comprehend the world Joseph had escaped.

Susan broke the silence by saying, "So how old are you, and what is your full name?"

"I doan rightly know ma age. I 'spect I be nineteen or twenty dereabouts. Not more d'an twenty-one. Ma mudder died a few years back, an' she da only one keepin' track. She taught me my numbers, but she never tell me dat one. Joseph be ma full name. I ain't got no udder name. If you is put on da block ta be sold, sometimes d'ey write da name a yer massa on da bill a sale, but I ain't ever gonna be Joseph Lonnegan."

"The land of the free and the brave," Daniel muttered.

After the cows were milked on Monday morning, while Daniel and Joseph shovelled out the pigpen and repaired broken boards, Susan heated water in the cauldron beside the well for the weekly laundry. She made herself busy dusting the front parlour when it came time for the pig crew to scrub with lye soap to wash out the smell. Manure-streaked work clothes were tossed into the cauldron, and in fresh attire the two men set off after lunch to fell a maple that had barberchaired across the back lane. Susan exercised her new filly while the laundry boiled.

When Joseph saw how Daniel intended to notch the bole, he hesitated to suggest a better way, yet he knew the boss's approach was an invitation to disaster. "Mister Daniel," he said, "I be not feelin' good 'bout dat tree. Da Deacon, he take down a lotta trees fer his sawmill, some hung up an' some on slopes, but he most careful wif a barberchair. He tole me, ya stand where you standin', dat tree come down so fast... One second ya is choppin', da next ya is learnin' ta play a harp."

"If I cut it on the underside of the hinge until it gives, it should shoot straight back."

"Me an' you, we knows it should, but da tree, she doan always know. Ya cut da underside, ya get mashed. Ya cut da backside, ya get mashed. Ya cut da trunk from da side, ya get mashed 'cause it collapse t'ward where it now be weakened."

"Then how do we get this tree down?"

"Mister Daniel, I has done dis before. We put a loggin' chain above da hinge an' pull from one side. Deacon, he use horses ta put pullin' pressure on one side while da axeman, he cut from da udder side, but he never get behind da hinge or underneaf, case it give way. D'ose horses ya got, could one be talked inta givin' steady pressure on da chain?"

"Either. Jacob's probably steadier."

At supper, after the evening milking was done, Daniel recounted their battle for his wife. "Jacob was superb. He seemed to know exactly what we wanted from him. Joseph and I took turns with the axe because we wanted to get the tree down before Jacob started daydreaming and slacked off the pressure. And Susan, that brute came down right where I would have been standing, just like Joseph said it would."

"Dat cuttin' wouldn't a taken so long we used a axe wif a keener edge. I notice' ya only took da one, an' da angle ain't sharp enough fer best cuttin', but it too narrow fer splittin'. Ya need two axes wif two diff'rent blade angles 'round a farm, one for cuttin', one fer splittin'."

"I didn't notice the limbing axe was dulling, but resetting the angle makes sense," Susan said. "We've always used a maul for splitting. Somewhere in the storehouse there are some perfectly good axe heads waiting for someone to carve new handles for them. You should put that on your list, Daniel."

"If ya get some hickory inta my hands, I kin carve da handles fer ya," Joseph said. "If da axeheads be rusty an' dull, an' dat be da only kind I ever see'd waitin' for handles, d'en I need a grindstone an' a file ta get 'em back ta being usable. A file be good for touchin' up a edge, but it be most impossible slow ta set one."

"You and Daniel can root them out tomorrow, maybe tidy things up in there while you're at it. Who knows what treasures are waiting to be rediscovered? It will be a good job for a rainy day."

"Who said it's going to rain?" Daniel asked.

"The chickens say so."

"The chickens," Daniel snorted.

"Ma frien' Malachi, he predict da rain like he feel it already," Joseph added. "He watch da chickens an' da livestock an' feel da air. Said he could tell rain a-comin' from how high da grasshoppers jump."

"We'll see if we can trust the prognostications of chickens," Daniel said, and helped himself to a second helping of everything.

If Joseph thought his work for the day was finished, he was sadly mistaken. Daniel clattered and clanged dishes and pots and pans into submissive piles and began the unfamiliar task of doing the dishes while Susan moved the little white jug of whisky to one side of the table, pulled the coal oil lamp closer, and produced a rag, chalk, and a child's slate. At the end of an hour, Joseph had been exposed to the printed alphabet, both lower and upper case letters, the sounds each letter could produce, and how to recognize his own name. Before he headed off to the barn with Argus, he confessed, "Missus Susan, dat be one a da most long hours a ma life. I worry I may not remember any a dis tomorra."

"You fear you will not, but I predict you will remember some, and then every day a little more, until gradually you will be literate," Susan said.

From the parlour door Daniel added, "The chickens are predicting the very same thing."

"How I know when I be literate?"

"It's very simple. You will be able to pick up a Bible, open it to any page, and read fluently."

"I be countin' on d'ose chickens."

"Better to count chickens than sheep. You won't fall asleep on the job," Daniel said, but Joseph was on his way out the door with a lantern and missed the joke.

Tuesday it rained. After the cows were milked, Susan busied herself with baking and after lunch joined the men tidying up the storehouse. Some items Daniel had set aside to be discarded she rescued, and some she had relegated to a fiery death Daniel re-placed on the indispensable pile.

Last night's alphabet lesson was reviewed and reinforced. Once Susan had shown him how to hold the chalk, Joseph painstakingly copied each letter on the slate and had to identify its sound before it could be erased.

Before Joseph and Argus left for the barn, Daniel remarked, "Get a good night's rest. We're picking stones tomorrow."

"I'se see'd cotton picked an' cherries picked an' peaches picked, but I ain't never see'd stones picked," Joseph said.

"Well, you will tomorrow. It's a job that needs to be done every spring, and I never met anyone who enjoys it. Once Jacob and Jessie see the stoneboat, they get depressed about it too."

"Mister Daniel, if I tole Old Mose I had run off to where d'ey make boats outta stone, he wouldn't believe me, an' Old Mose, he see'd more d'an most. Ya pullin' ma leg 'bout a stone boat?"

"You'll see tomorrow. Don't tell the horses we're picking stones or they won't sleep well either."

By Wednesday, Joseph was getting accustomed to the farm's routine. Bedtime came early, but not before Daniel read a chapter from his Bible. Meals began with a blessing. The kitchen table was the focal point of all farm life; here bills were organized, food consumed, plans made, splinters removed, community events discussed, and decisions reviewed. In contrast, the parlour was dusted frequently and used only for company. Already he had discovered attention to personal cleanliness was best given before bed the previous evening, because until livestock were fed, cows milked, stalls cleaned, manure carted to a pile back of the barn, and fresh straw added, humans did not sit down to their first meal.

After a last-all-day-if-necessary breakfast, Daniel hitched Jacob and Jesse to the four-by-six foot boxed sledge on wooden runners shod with an iron strip on the underside. "Susan will start and stop the horses as we go up and down each field,"

Daniel explained. "You will be on one side, I'll walk the other. Every rock we find that would give grief to the plough, we throw into the stoneboat. When it's full, the horses will drag it to a fence line. The stones we've picked we'll throw in between the stumps and go back for more. You can see why the horses loathe this work."

"Mister Daniel, always d'ere be older, more experience' hands what could plough, so I doan know what kin give a plough grief."

"If a rock is the size of your fist or larger, toss it in the boat."

"Ya say ya got ta do dis ever' year? Once't da rock be gone, don't it stay gone? What d'ey do, migrate back in da spring?"

"It would seem so, but actually the frost heaves them up so there's a new crop each year. Don't you have to pick stones in Tennessee?"

"Ain't got no frost in da ground in Tennessee, so I reckon if a rock be buried, she stay buried."

After he had washed hands and face for supper, Joseph regarded chipped finger nails and said, "Mister Daniel, Missus Susan, next day we pickin' stones, please do me da same favour ya give ta da horses an' doan tell us da night before."

In the lesson hour, every letter of the alphabet was printed, sounded, and printed again.

Thursday, Jessie and Jacob ploughed and Joseph dug the garden plot to prepare for planting. At supper time he confessed to some fatigue but added, "Dat diggin' ain't so bad as slingin' coal or da diggin' I done near da fort an' I had Argus for company. Da garden bin dug before so da soil, I just gotta remind it to loosen up. But at da fort, dat drainage trench be hard diggin' an' deep. When Mister Daniel an' Mister Archie rescue me, I be hearin' someone b'low me talkin' Chinese."

Yesterday's practice with the slate was repeated, then Joseph traced his name over the dots Susan had prepared on a piece of paper. They abandoned the printing early so Joseph could concentrate on what Susan referred to as The Queen's Proper English.

"A t-h combination does not make a 'duh' sound. Place the tip of your tongue under your top teeth, then breathe out as you open your mouth and make a sound with your vocal cords," Susan instructed, demonstrating several times. Joseph found this exceptionally difficult, and eventually the teacher became as frustrated as the student. When he left for the barn with Argus, slouched shoulders betrayed a downcast mind.

For Friday's work, Daniel had planned on harrowing the ground ploughed earlier, but the soil had not dried sufficiently, so the men headed to the forest with chains and horses to wrangle wood felled during the winter. In the late afternoon, they brought back some logs in the buckboard and piled them behind the house for future sawing. At supper, Daniel told Susan the quantity retrieved using two men on the crosscut saw was triple what he could have done alone with the axe.

"One on each side of the stoneboat was three times faster than you pitching rocks on your own," Susan observed. "How he tackled the barberchair, wanting to put a keener edge on the axe, offering to make new handles, making you more efficient... He's conscientious. He's going to be worth the money."

Daniel nodded. "Argus certainly thinks so."

That night Susan had an inspiration. After they had practised the alphabet sounds and name printing, she shoved the materials aside and said, "Joseph, have you ever seen an angry cat?"

"Missus Susan, I 'spect ever'body has see'd a angry cat."

"How do you know a cat is angry?"

"Ya get a cat angry, it hisses at ya, maybe take a swipe at ya wif its claws."

"Imitate an angry cat. Hiss at me."

"Missus Susan, I ain't angry wif..."

"Just hiss at me."

"But..."

"Hiss!"

Joseph hissed.

"No, not like a snake, That will make an s sound. Like a kitten, with its tongue between its teeth. Try again."

Joseph hissed again.

"And again. With your tongue curled a bit."

Later, Joseph would say, "I wager I hissed at Missus Susan about four hundred angry cats worth. Hissing taught my tongue to put itself under my top teeth so it could tackle the t-h sound. That was the absolute most tough part of learning the Queen's English. Nothin' that came after was as ornery as that t-h sound, and if I ever see the queen, I intend to talk to her about it."

Daniel resumed ploughing on Saturday. By Monday, weather permitting, substantial acreage would be ready for harrowing. Joseph wheelbarrowed bags of seed oats, wheat, and barley from their winter storage in the hay mow to a dry, empty stall where Susan sorted them. "Put the barley against the back wall, the oats and wheat in front. We'll plant barley last," she said, "because barley likes a dry seedbed. We intend to plant more wheat this year; the Russian war has driven grain prices up."

By Saturday evening, everyone was looking forward to a day of rest. It was Glencoe's turn was to benefit from Reverend Leeds' ministrations, so the Camerons would attend nearby Trinity on the morrow.

Joseph feared his skull might explode after six intensive hours of Susan's tutorship, but he retired to his straw-on-hardwood bed happy, wishing Old Mose and Seth and Ellie could witness his progress. He knew the alphabet, could sign his name, and with a conscious effort, dis and dat had begun to sound more like this and that. Important to him as well was the cracked pearlware vase he had rescued from the storehouse cleanup. He carefully placed the vase beside the left hind leg of the workbench, but not before he had counted its contents, his week's wages, multiple times.

Aeneas Ragg Encourages His Associates

The captain of the *Linda Ann*, the gigantic man with the turnip fists, and Aeneas Ragg sat in a small room in a dingy, smoke-filled pub in Toledo. Not a word was uttered until the Rubenesque barmaid was depositing beers on the table. "I'll let you know when we need more," Ragg said, "and shut the door behind you as you leave. Remind the proprietor we do not wish to be disturbed." She nodded to indicate she understood. He gave her a pat on her jiggling bottom and received a little giggle in recognition of his attention. What he could not see was how she rolled her eyes on the other side of the door.

Ragg let the silence fester. He took a long draught of his beer and leaned back in his chair, looking at each man separately and intently. Picking up his riding crop from the table, he ran it slowly back and forth between his fingers, back and forth. The captain sipped his beer unconcernedly, but the giant quaffed a third of a glass hurriedly, wiped his mouth with a sleeve, and drank some more, avoiding eye contact with the others.

"You should be nervous, you stupid fucking oaf," Ragg said quietly. "Obviously I need to spell this out for you. You and your equally incompetent partner smash the skull of freight worth more than ten of you on a good day. Freight that has a club foot and couldn't outrun a fucking three-legged toad in loose sand. Does the freight finish back where we can skim some profit? No. The freight finishes up in Lake Erie as a fucking corpse. How could that happen, one might ask? Because some fucking idiot hit him too fucking hard is the answer. Jesus!"

The gigantic man raised his huge hands in protestation, but before he could open his mouth, Ragg roared, "Don't you say a goddamn word, you imbecile! It was you who hit the club-foot, wasn't it? Wasn't it? I send a man to help you and your partner grab a woman and her son. Three of you to grab a woman and a boy. From a barn, for God's sake! And what happens? The freight gets away, the three of you slash some cows 'cause some farmer takes a shot at you in the dark where he can't see the colour of his boots, and this grabs the attention of the whole fucking countryside, including the army pensioners. The farmer is a hero, and you, you are a fucking joke!"

He stopped his tirade to drink some beer. The captain and the giant waited for Ragg to resume, and when he did his voice started calm and steely.

"Even if I ask you, never tell me again how your partner managed to get his guts spread out on a surgeon's slab, because that would set me off again, and I would take a club to *your* head — if I could find one hard enough to do the job. What the fuck did you two think would happen, making so much noise you woke the neighbours? They were waiting for you, you numb dick. What made you think you could grab the top prize in the same spot as the club-foot? Now my sources say he's gone backcountry, and no one knows just exactly where. Gone, goddamn it!"

While Ragg paused to sip his beer, the captain studied the giant, enjoying his discomfiture.

"Make yourself scarce. You have hung around these parts too long," Ragg said, addressing the big man. "My people are telling me no new freight answering our prize's description have come to their attention, so I figure you've frightened him away from the regular bolt holes and farther east, probably farther than the Elgin Settlement or Dresden. Maybe even Blenheim. I have few contacts beyond Chatham, but he'll be a rarity, so he'll be easier to identify. Just find him, and I'll send someone to do the rest. I'll send a goddamn professional this time. You will be his assistant, understand? Don't try to grab the prize on your own. Charm gets answers, so use honey, not vinegar."

The big man drained his beer.

"It wasn't my fault, Mr. Ragg. You're right. They were waiting for us, 'cause we made no more noise than a mouse. It's just bad luck my partner got seen, that's all. I was only able to slip away 'cause they ringed on him. In a way, he saved my life."

"It was your fault if it happened, and it happened. I have paid the captain here a retainer so there will be no more misunderstandings about money. Money! Jesus! This one's personal. How in God's name did a fucking field hand who never was ten fucking miles from home ever get out of fucking Tennessee? That was my mistake, and I'm paying for it. I let the son of a bitch get away, and I sure as hell am gonna catch him. What the hell am I doing this far north? In Ohio, for God's sake. I'm treading water on this one.

We can't rely on Lonnegan's deep pockets to keep paying our expenses if I can't report progress, and we don't make a profit 'til we catch him. Dead or alive, that's the contract. Dead or alive."

The three left separately, the huge man first.

"Burton is right, you know," the captain said as he rose to leave. "It wasn't his fault. He's actually quite a clever lad, though he doesn't look it. It's lack of experience. He doesn't know his own strength. Too bad it was him who tapped the club-foot and not the partner."

"He's only useful to us if we make money," Ragg replied. "I've got a fair number of irons in the fire right now, but as soon as I get some loose ends tied up, I'll send one of my own boys to finish this hunt. One other thing..."

"What's that?" the captain asked, as he opened the door.

"Don't use names."

Metamorphosis

When the school children stopped in for wine and shortbread cookies on Monday afternoon, the Chalmers boy brought two gifts. Anna Leeds had resurrected a dog-eared pre-primer and a First Book of Lessons and passed them on through the neighbour parcel express. That evening, Joseph was introduced to bat, cat, fat, hat, mat, pat, rat, sat and vat. By Wednesday he was up to his ears in letter blends and diphthongs, and by Saturday he was attacking what Susan called connecting words such as articles, prepositions and conjunctions. The following week he memorized thirty common adjectives and adverbs and began comparatives and superlatives. He fretted that he was an imposition on Susan's time and good nature, but she steadfastly maintained that unless one was brain feeble, there was no plausible excuse to be illiterate. Each night she insisted his fingers print some of what his eyes recognized.

She was equally authoritarian about his diction. Dropped g's, an not a before a word beginning with a vowel, verb tenses, "I am" rather than "I be," all were ruthlessly addressed. "You will not indulge in lazy language while you are in our employ," she maintained, and insisted Daniel model an acceptable version when Joseph spoke what she labelled Southern Black. Joseph found the enunciation expectations more difficult than reading and printing because they were imposed outside the perimeters of his nightly lesson hour. Literacy skills were a novelty, whereas his speaking was natural and ingrained since infancy.

One night it happened. They had been reviewing prefixes and suffixes, Susan opened up the first book, and suddenly Joseph was reading about three little kittens who had lost their mittens. He read it through, and then again and again. Susan had him begin in the middle just to make sure he hadn't memorized it in childhood, but by the end of the hour, Joseph had read clearly and fluently. The next evening he read "The Wind and the Sun" haltingly, and the next "The Hare and the Tortoise". "The Little Red Hen" followed, and a week later Susan opened the Bible to The Twenty-third Psalm and watched his eyes glisten as he realized what he had accomplished.

As daylight hours increased, so did the workday. Daniel was a more patient teacher than Susan, reasoning his own workload would be lessened if his hired man mastered essential farming skills. He showed Joseph how to crumble earth between his fingers to determine when the ploughed fields were dry enough to work, and let Jacob and Jessie teach him how to rough up a seedbed with the harrows. With little agricultural experience beyond a cotton plantation and the slaves' garden, much was new to him.

Other tasks demanded attention once the seed was in. The garden was re-spaded and raked, rows marked, and vegetables planted. A cool, breezy day in June was dedicated to shifting the outhouse to a new location, then scattering a year's worth of human waste onto a fallow field.

It was rainy days Joseph looked forward to most. On those days, Daniel retreated to his workbench, cleared the straw off Joseph's bed, and made furniture. In his care of his woodworking tools and his attention to detail, he reminded Joseph of the wheelwright. Although he had several unfinished dressers, washstands, and table and chair sets in progress for customers who had specified certain dimensions, his pace was invariably unhurried. A rudimentary homemade steamer, a small foot-pumped lathe, planes, hammers, chisels, handsaws, a yardstick, a level, pencils, and glue comprised the extent of his tool inventory. Dry hardwood blanks and boards were stacked beside the bull's pen. When Joseph cast a critical eye over them, he knew Michael Duffy would be impressed by their quality.

The first wet day, Joseph was largely ignored when Daniel focused on a washstand. His role was to provide a second pair of hands, wipe up excess glue from drawer corners, and top up the insulation in the icehouse with the sawdust from the floor. On later days, when the boss noted his desire to learn more, he showed him how to use a hand plane, how to construct mortise, tenon, and dovetail joints, and how to smooth a chair leg with a piece of broken glass. Joseph could appreciate why Daniel enjoyed carpentry so much and was attracted to it. The feel of the wood, its aroma, the satisfaction of creating something useful and beautiful, these he savoured and Daniel approved. Both looked to the sky each evening, hoping for impending rain.

It was the summer solstice when the revolution occurred. Supper over, diction practised, the Bible read, they retired to the porch with a cup of tea to watch the sky fade from indigo to violet on the longest day of the year.

Suddenly, Daniel roused himself from his rocking chair, returned to the kitchen, and came back with a candle, a pencil, and a sheet of paper. He hastily scribbled some notes, rocked, admired the expiring sunset, then wrote some more.

Susan studied his odd behaviour. "Well?" she said.

"Well, I've been doing some thinking, and I think we need to make some changes around here."

"Such as?"

"Such as, why do we have so many milk cows? We've got more than enough for butter and cheese, and you only use raw milk when you cook, so why do we spend so much time on morning and evening chores when we could get the chores done lickety-split with fewer milk cows?"

"And?"

"And we could make more money if we ran a herd of beef cattle. They don't need milking, just let them roam in the back fields, look after themselves, sell off in the fall what can't winter in the barn. We could join a beef ring. The Desmonds are in one, and so are the Hedleys and the Chalmers, and Archie has been talking about joining."

"Herefords," Joseph said. "Deacon got really enthused about Herefords. He said a cattle man told him d'ey be efficient eaters, easy to work wif, hardy, produce marbled meat. Dey be prone ta vaginal prolapse, though."

"...they are efficient eaters, easy to work with... They are prone to vaginal prolapse, though..." Susan corrected.

"...they are efficient eaters, easy to work with... They are prone to vaginal prolapse, though..." Joseph repeated.

"You said changes, in the plural. What else do you have in mind?"

"Joseph beds down on my workbench, for goodness sake. Yes, I know, that was an expedient solution to an unexpected situation, but it's no good in the long run. Mind you, he hasn't complained. Still... That's not good when winter comes, and it does tie up my workbench."

"Other than sleeping in an empty stall or the mow, the solution would be...?"

"We could seal off the overhang below the kitchen, double wall it so it's windproof and warmer, put in a door, maybe a window, spike down some planks for a floor, extend the back wall into the basement. Give him his own space, his own room. The outhouse would be closer, the well too. We wouldn't need to move the vertical supports. We've already got the lumber from the old house waiting for some project. Best done before the fall storms."

"Go on."

"Why couldn't we put that little wood stove in there, the one rusting in the storehouse, run a pipe out toward the well..."

"I am not going to sit at my kitchen table and look at smoke drifting past the window. The whole side of the house would blacken!"

"... it could go straight out, eight, ten feet. Only a true south wind would drive smoke back toward the house, and how often does that happen? It wouldn't be seen from the road. We could move some of the woodpile from under the house into the open and stack it on the slope. That's south-facing. It would probably season better, and there's still enough space left under the overhang nearest the lane for a winter's wood. Once we got the materials at hand, Joseph and I — and maybe Archie and Noah and Paul — could bang something together in a day. Levelling the floor might be the toughest part, and Joseph and I could do that beforehand."

"A room under the house, beef cattle, joining a beef ring. What other revelations does your nimble mind have for me?"

"Susan, you are the farmer, more than me. What I know about farming I learned from my father, but he always said if carpentry was good enough for our Lord, it was good enough for him. I guess he passed his preference for working with wood down to me."

"In a nutshell, Daniel."

"In a nutshell, I want to spend more time making furniture. I know, I neglected it last winter, but I was in a blue state and couldn't see any light at the end of the tunnel. It's cash money, not weather dependent money, and we have Joseph now to share the work."

Susan turned to Joseph. "And what are your thoughts on all this?"

He took a long time to answer.

"Missus Susan, I reckon I haven't given much thought to da — to the distant future. Every penny of my wages is in that pearlware vase you gave me. I know my accent makes you cringe sometimes, but Old Mose and Seth and Ellie wouldn't understand me now, speaking the Queen's English as good as I do. I can read and write some, and there isn't a Black soul on Lonnegan's plantation 'cept for Cicero what — that — who can sign their own name."

"In a nutshell, Joseph. I asked for your thoughts on Daniel's ideas."

"In a nutshell, Missus Susan, I don't rightly know. A room of my own, wif — with my own stove, I never imagine' that, or being able to read or write, or earn wages. But I've been told I can go anywhere any time I want, and 'ventually I expect I will want to live wif — find my own home with people my own colour. The wheelwright, he tell me how the Black folks warn off da man what — that came before me, tellin' him he got to prove he not make them embarrassed by him. I couldn't ask for kinder people than you be — are — but you ain't — aren't my folks. If I join da Black folks, I gotta be a worthy person. I gotta be whole. I gotta be able to support myself with farmin' or woodworkin' or somethin'. I gotta be able to read and write and cipher numbers and speak like the queen, so I doan want you to go ta — to all the trouble of setting me up in my own room like Cicero and then...."

"So you are thinking of leaving us?" Daniel asked.

"Oh no, suh! No, sir. Not for a long time, if you'll keep me. I need to learn how to farm — I really enjoy farmin' work, mostly, except for maybe the rock pickin' — picking, but what I would do all the time if I had the choice is be like you, Mister Daniel, and work with wood, makin' stuff."

"Can we count on your help 'til after harvest?" Daniel asked.

"Harvest and beyond, Mister Daniel. There's wood that needs bringin' and sawin' — sawing and stacking an' — and in the winter more trees to take down for next year. Missus Susan, she say — she says you are a crack shot when it come — comes to deer and turkeys and pigeons and geese, and I could help with them. I ain't — I haven't anywhere else to go, not yet, and I doan wanna leave ya — you when you need me or before I has — have learned how to farm and carpenter."

"I doubt you will ever talk like the queen, but then again we won't either," Susan said. "Any more surprises, husband?"

"Two. We are witnessing a revolution in agriculture, yet this farm is behind the times. You and I grew up broadcasting seed by hand, a method that is grossly inefficient compared to the new seed drills. I am wrestling my father's Scottish walking plough while some of our neighbours have purchased one they can sit on. The scythe is honed and ready, thanks to Joseph, yet within a mile we can find farmers using McCormick reapers, which cut the grain while their scythes lean against their barns, leaving nothing to be done but the stooking. Susan, we could double or triple our grain harvest with the same time investment. All this farm's equipment has been inherited and it's now antiquated compared to new machinery that is making its debut."

"Do you have any idea how much this 'revolutionary' machinery costs?"

"Not exactly, no, but we could find out when we go to Chatham."

"Buying a horse and gig in Amherstburg, now farm machinery in Chatham. And the last surprise?"

"I've had a break from the farm, but you haven't. I would like the Taylors and us to set aside a few days after the wheat is threshed and take the train to Windsor. We could stop in Chatham on the way. I'm curious how Michael Duffy and his little wife are faring, and how young Major Emmett is coping as a garrison of one in Her Majesty's fortification. Joseph is here to look after the farm while we're gone, but Angus MacLeod will be heading off to Normal School in September, so Archie and Catherine will be without a hired man if we don't go before the last week in August."

"That would be something to look forward to, but there is so much to be done here. You go with Archie, as long as you don't bring home any more horses to feed. You could invite John Duffy to come with you to visit his brother. That would get Mrs. Hedley's tongue clattering, travelling with an Irish papist."

"Now who wants to poke the dragon?"

Mrs. Hedley Entertains

Little that transpired on the Talbot Line for miles in either direction escaped Abigail Hedley's attention, so when a young man in a buggy two sizes too small for his gigantic frame pulled into the Hedleys' lane, she had already witnessed his approach from the west. He extricated himself from the vehicle with some difficulty and approached the front door, hat in hand, where Mrs. Hedley was waiting.

'Morning, ma'am," he began. "Please do not confuse me with someone who visits with the expectation of selling you a miracle medicine or a household item of dubious quality. I am not a pedlar. Actually, I am come on government business. May I enquire to whom I am speaking?"

Mrs. Hedley was immediately on her guard. "Hedley. Abigail Hedley. Mrs. Abigail Hedley. Government business, you say? And you would be?"

"How clumsy of me, Mrs. Hedley. Please allow me to introduce myself. Burton. Mister Eustace Burton, affiliated with the Department of Land Services and Resettlement."

"I don't see how Land Services and Resettlement would have any business with us," she said curtly.

"Oh, it's quite possible we don't, Mrs. Hedley. My role is to assist certain individuals who may not be aware such assistance is available. In Morpeth, I was informed you are the most knowledgeable in local matters, and now that I have met you in person I can see I was not misdirected."

"Government business, you say. Rather than tell me of it on the threshold, would you care to come in for a cup of tea?"

"Tea would be most refreshing. Thank you, Mrs. Hedley."

Fortunately for the hostess, she had been baking that morning, so the stove could be revived with the addition of a few sticks. While she lifted a massive slice of still warm cake onto one of her better plates and scurried about to make the tea, she could hear the floor boards complain as Mister Burton ambled about the parlour, murmuring approving sounds as he surveyed framed prints that had boasted vibrant colours in some previous decade. She found him admiring a hair wreath as she carried cake, cookies, and tea on a tray to the coffee table.

"I have always maintained the ornamental use of loved ones' locks is such a unique way to keep them treasured in our memory," he said as he sat down and occupied most of the sofa.

"That wreath was woven from hair belonging to my late parents. I agree with you wholeheartedly, Mister Burton. Wholeheartedly. Such a tribute is so touching, so irreplaceable. What government department did you say you were representing?"

"Resettlement and Land... Land Services. It's quite new, so you may not have heard of it, although I suspect that a woman of your intelligence and political acumen stays abreast of all happenings in the legislature."

"Indeed I do. I believe I have heard of the new department, now that you mention it."

"I thought you might. Specifically, I am searching for certain individuals of the Negro race who have entered this part of British North America as fugitives from the United States. They are strangers to our government system and scatter away from the border, unaware there is assistance to aid them in getting established."

"If I knew of any such individuals, what assistance could I inform them they might expect?"

"The price of land in the Elgin Settlement is prohibitive. It's scandalous, really, that speculators gladly take advantage of newcomers to the Negro community. One hundred twenty-five dollars for a fifty acre parcel, at six per cent. Six per cent interest per annum, Mrs. Hedley!"

"Six per cent does seem a bit excessive."

"Seven dollars and fifty cents just for interest. That is where Land Services and Resettlement enters the picture. My department subsidizes the initial outlay so the interest portion of the debt obligation is more manageable."

"This all sounds very complicated."

"However, Mrs. Hedley, there is an expectation the qualifying individuals remain on the land for five years."

Mrs. Hedley poured the tea. "Would you care for a second slice of cake and possibly more shortbread, Mister Burton? I do not wish to sound immodest, but I do believe my shortbread is 'ne plus ultra', as they say in Italy. My secret is to use more butter, a healthy dollop. Mister Hedley sets aside the milk from an Ayrshire for the butter. Also, I sift the flour a minimum of three times. Even so, the end product can only be optimal if the dough is not overworked."

"Very kind of you to offer. Both cake and shortbread are superlative. Wonderfully delicious. Mister Hedley is very fortunate to have found a woman of your abilities."

The second slice disappeared as rapidly as the first. The second generous plate of shortbread was empty soon after.

Mister Burton resumed. "Some think our department's assistance is only for families. Nothing could be farther from the truth. When a young male, for example, takes advantage of our aid, he becomes gainfully employed and much less liable to be indigent or a vagabond. So, naturally, when I heard of your repertoire of knowledge, I immediately came to your door, wondering if you have heard of any such individuals in the area."

Abigail Hedley assumed the posture of one who knows and is gracious enough to share what she knows.

"Mister Burton, it is auspicious that you stopped here. Our neighbours, the Camerons, have taken in a young Black man. I have no idea how long he will be helping around the farm, but he may qualify for your department's assistance. By coincidence, today Mister Hedley is helping Daniel Cameron and some neighbours create a room for the man at the rear of the house, under an overhang. I for one have no idea why anyone would construct a dwelling on the edge of a hill, but that's the Scotch for you."

"Excellent. And just where can I find the Camerons?"

"If you return the way you came, their house will be the first on the left past the road allowance. White, not more than eighty yards in from the road. You can see the hedgerow that marks the road allowance from here."

"Eighty yards. That close to the road."

"More or less. Spruce trees across the front. You can't miss it."

"Under the house, at the back you say. Do they have a dog? Since a child I have been afraid of dogs."

"No need to fear Argus. He's a good watchdog, but he isn't cross if there is family around."

Before Abigail Hedley returned the tray to the kitchen and surveyed her much diminished morning's work, she watched Mister Burton's buggy trot down the Talbot Line. *Odd that he didn't stop in at the Camerons,* she thought. *My directions were quite specific. Possibly Argus was out. He did say he was afraid of dogs.*

John Duffy Recruits

Archie was as enthusiastic as Daniel when the latter floated the idea of another holiday past him. Catherine took the same realistic view as Susan, that there was so much to do this time of year: pickles to put down, preserves to put up, strings of onions to hang, wheat to be milled, pigs to be fattened for slaughter... The whole notion of a multiple days' excursion was quite out of the question, quite laughable really. Their husbands, however, were adamant. It would only be for three or four days, Joseph needed the responsibility of managing on his own, and Angus MacLeod had already proven he was capable of running the Taylor farm. Despite their protestations, the women began to be as excited about the trip as their husbands.

Their departure was delayed by the passing of Paul Desmond's father, followed four days later by his mother. Daniel and Joseph made pine coffins, Noah and Archie helped Paul dig graves at the back of the farm, tables groaned under food the women prepared for the reception after the funeral, and Reverend Leeds was at his sombre best. There was a testy moment when he gently suggested the Desmonds should be buried in sacred ground, and Paul asked him what ground could be more hallowed than the land his parents had worked all their lives. The women wondered aloud, now that he was free of the responsibility of caring for elderly parents, which of the local girls Paul might find time to court.

Late one afternoon, Susan took her gig and filly out for some exercise and met John Duffy coming down the Talbot Line. He pulled his buggy to a halt and held up a hand to indicate he wished to converse. For a woman alone to stop to speak to an unrelated man alone, other than one very senior or a clergyman, bordered on impropriety, but Susan could see Mrs. Hedley at her door and the temptation was too much.

"Good day it is to you, Mrs. Cameron," Mister Duffy began. "I am on my way to speak with both you and your husband, if he would be at home."

"One of us should be, or little work will get done," Mrs. Cameron replied. "You might find him in the near field replacing a board on the hay wagon. But whatever do you wish to speak to me about, Mister Duffy?"

"Ah, t'is a delicate matter, Mrs. Cameron, a delicate matter, but one you may feel qualified to address, you who have lived in the township all your life."

"Well, I'll help if I can. How may I be of assistance?"

"The young wife is due with our first child, a wee bairn you would call it, in a few months, and she — and I — would feel more comfortable knowing there is an experienced midwife available when she is at the end of her confinement, to help with the, the birthing and the, the lying in... and to find a wet-nurse should she be unable to..."

"I understand completely," Mrs Cameron said, trying to put him at his ease. "Unfortunately, except with animals, I have not had the experience of childbirth, either firsthand or vicariously. Is there no one in your church who...?"

"Not that I am aware of, and the new priest is ignorant of anyone to suggest, as you might well imagine. A sister dead of puerperal fever has prompted an understandable nervousness."

Mrs. Cameron had a mischievous inspiration. "Mister Duffy, if there is information to be found about anyone within twenty miles, we are fortuitously near its source. If I were in your position, I would confer with Mrs. Hedley. I have found her most eager to share her vast knowledge of the comings and goings of the township and beyond. If anyone knows of a midwife, she will. I shall inquire among our congregation as well and keep my ears open for any pregnancies. It is common knowledge there is no better remedy for a lost bairn than to suckle a babe, and God takes the wee ones often, some before they exit the womb."

"Mrs. Cameron, I thank you for your advice, and I will consult Mrs. Hedley before the week is out. I shall take no more of your time, but will press on to see Mister Cameron."

"You are welcome to stay for supper. We are having meatloaf and baked potatoes, if that would suit."

"Most kind. Most kind. However, since I am expected, I really should return home. But most kind. Thank you."

"I just chatted with Mrs. Cameron," John Duffy said when he located Daniel. "Your wife can give you the kernel of our conversation. I have come to see you about a totally different matter, a serious matter. A very serious matter."

"Come sit in the porch then. Joseph and Argus can drive in the cows without me."

"The buggy is fine, thank you. This won't take long, but it must remain confidential for reasons which will become apparent."

"If you wish it so, it will be."

"You are aware that my brother Michael and I correspond. You may not be aware he has become involved in a Vigilance Committee. Indeed, it was the Vigilance Committee that was responsible for investigating the first abduction from his workshop, the one with all the blood, and it was the committee that interrupted Joseph's planned abduction. Joseph believes his cries for help awoke Michael, who came to his rescue, but committee members had the workshop under surveillance. There was a, a, a... fatality. A final reckoning, so to speak, and more of the same since."

"Should you be telling me this?" Daniel asked.

"No, not if you do not care about the intolerable situation we previously discussed. Yes, if you wish to see justice brought down on the guilty."

"You know I do," Daniel said.

"I know you do, or you would not have gone down to Malden or taken in Joseph. Through my brother I discovered there are other Vigilance Committees formed, one as close as Chatham."

"My God, that close?"

"That close. The danger is that close."

He paused a moment to let the information sink in.

"Moreover, I have joined it. Our goal is to hunt the hunters. We work outside the law and use violent methods, so you can see why absolute secrecy is essential. To us, bounty hunting is a capital crime. Daniel, we are doing God's work.

Fast and final — that is our motto, and that is why I can provide no further details."

"And you wish me to join, is that it?"

"Yes, we wish you to join."

"John, I'll need to think on this. We're making changes to the farm, trying to start a family... I'm not convinced I have the necessary temperament for that type of work. Your offer requires serious thought."

"Is that a no?"

"No, it's not a no, but it's not a yes either. I'll give you my decision in a week or two. Archie Taylor and the wives and I are planning a short holiday on the new train, thinking of dropping in on your brother, let him know how Joseph is doing, maybe visit the fort, find out if the pensioners are getting off their ass about this issue. Mrs. Cameron suggested we invite you to join us."

"Thank you, but I must decline. We are starting a family as well and my new committee responsibilities will be..."

"I understand. And you can rely on my utmost discretion. One request though. May I share our conversation with Archie Taylor? If I decide to join, I can't see me doing it without him."

"Archie Taylor is as solid and welcome as you are."

The two men shook hands, and Duffy returned home to his swelling young wife. Susan suspected his visit was more than a social call but did not press Daniel for details. He finished the dishes long before Joseph's elocution lesson started and left the kitchen early to read his Bible. He was still reading when Argus and Joseph retired for the night.

Fort Malden Revisited

Daniel and Archie persuaded the women to pack a more modest lunch for their first day and in their capacity as seasoned tourists pointed out the comfort and consistent speed of train travel. In Chatham, they coveted the new farm inventions on display at the equipment dealers and marvelled at their ingenuity. Susan and Catherine recoiled at the prices while Daniel and Archie stuffed brochures into their waistcoats.

Catching the next train, they dined and roomed at the same Windsor hotel Archie and Daniel had discovered previously, hired a spacious double-seated trap from the local livery, and by one o'clock the following day booked rooms and lunched at the yellow-shuttered hotel with the attached stable where Daniel had balked at reserving a room in case they did not require it.

Mister and Mrs. Duffy had been forewarned of their arrival by brother John, and the hospitality was as genuine as before. The new apprentice was working out well they were told, although behind his hand Michael whispered, "He doesn't have an eye for the grain like the club-foot did." Michael made no mention of Vigilance Committees; Daniel and Archie asked no questions. Both the Duffys were pleased to hear that Joseph was safe and seemed to be taking to general farming and carpentry like a duck to water.

Mrs. Duffy was particularly surprised to hear Joseph was learning to read and write. "Knew his numbers he did, so my husband said, but you couldn't hardly understand a word. Good to hear he's becoming intelligible. I for one am glad he's gone. We had nothing but grief from taking in the Darkies."

In the morning, they backtracked from their small hotel to the pensioners' settlement. Sergeant Madill recognized the men immediately and was overly gracious to the ladies, fetching chairs and water and asking if they wished to wait in the shade while he dug about for the major.

Major Emmett greeted them warmly as well. Other than sporting more freckles, he had changed little. He inquired after Joseph and suggested to the sergeant the ladies might be more comfortable imbibing tea or coffee in his officer's quarters. Susan and Catherine took the hint and followed Madill so the men could wander about the grounds and talk in private.

"Before you ask, the answers are yes, no, yes, and no. Yes, to avoid the drudgery of administration, the sergeant major continues his 'picnics', patrolling and reconnoitring. Be assured, sirs, if it comes to a fight, we shall give a good account of ourselves. No, the situation *vis-a-vis* our American neighbour has not changed in the slightest, and we have received no additional resources, including manpower. Yes, we remain unable to address the bounty hunter problem, and no, we have no idea who is responsible for the increasing number of dead bodies washing ashore."

Daniel and Archie exchanged a glance, which Emmett noticed. "Come, gentlemen, if you know something I don't, please share. I have no reason to suspect the locals, so I must assume the bounty hunters have had a falling out, possibly over jurisdiction or money or God knows what and are killing each other off, and that is what I have suggested in my latest report to the governor general."

"What suggests the bodies belong to bounty hunters?" Daniel asked.

"Consistently, they are adult males with American money in their pockets. Equally telling, the few of our citizens who have gone missing have all been accounted for. One, a hunting accident, two drowned when their canoe overturned in the *Riviere-aux-Carnards*, an old man who did not return home for supper, his body found in his woodlot the following day, that sort of thing."

Archie was more gracious this time. "We must collect the ladies before they find life beside the river more pleasant than the farm. It's gratifying to see the fort remains in your capable hands, Major. I wish we could help you with your problems."

"Scuttlebutt has it I will be reassigned soon. There was a hint from the governor in the last dispatch not to get too comfortable. Who knows what poor wretch will all too adequately fill my boots? All I can hope for in the next posting is a surfeit of female companionship."

With wives collected and back in the trap, Archie said, "Our Major Emmett is becoming a man of the world."

"Our Major Emmett is a very sharp young man," Daniel observed. "Did you notice how he produced a plausible explanation for unaccounted bodies, an explanation which preempted possibly the most logical one?"

"What unaccounted bodies?" Catherine asked.

"It's almost impossible to identify the victims when a ship goes down in a storm," Archie said.

"That's true," Daniel said, and nodded sagely.

Noah Hedley Makes a Deal

Joseph was chest-puffing proud that the Camerons had confidence in him to look after the farm for a few days and relieved when Noah Hedley made himself available to help if any emergencies surfaced. For three or four days, he would be not just the hired man, but the farm manager. He wished Old Mose and Seth and Ellie could see how far he had come. Might as well add Bindle and Cicero and Massa and Mistress Lonnegan to the list. If they could only see him now, a free man with his own quarters and his own money and for all intents and purposes, his own dog. He would read to them and speak the Queen's Proper English and watch their jaws drop in astonishment.

Noah rode down the first afternoon to find all in order. He and Joseph talked about how chickens act when rain is coming, and Joseph promised once again to call if he needed an extra set of hands. When Noah returned home he mentioned to Mrs. Hedley how Argus seemed to shadow Joseph, as if he had adopted him.

"Well, it may be Argus to blame that Joseph didn't get the government assistance he may qualify for," Mrs. Hedley sniffed.

"Whatever are you talking about?"

"I am talking about the nice young government man who stopped in for tea and cake and shortbread the day you helped the Camerons make the new room under the house."

"What government man?"

"I'm sure I told you about him. I might have known you weren't listening. As usual. The young man from the Department of Resettlement and Land Services. Or was it Land Services and Resettlement? No, it was Resettlement and Land Services. Yes, I'm sure that was it. It's a new department, the man said. Burton was his name. A charming young man. Very polite. Very large too."

"What in heaven's name has this got to do with Argus and Joseph?"

"Mister Burton asked me if I knew of any young Negro men newly arrived in the community, and of course I told him the Camerons have..."

"For God's sake, Abi, what have you done?"

"Noah, don't you speak to me in that tone of voice! I was only trying to get government assistance in case Joseph wished to purchase fifty acres in the Elgin Settlement and he could get..."

"Abigail, there is no Department of Resettlement and Land Services!"

"Of course there is, or that nice Mister Burton would not have said there was. He asked me where to find the Camerons, and he was intending to stop in, but he drove on by because he is afraid of dogs, so Argus..."

Noah was already reaching for his hat. "That poor bugger. He's all alone. And you... you... you stupid woman! By God, I'll never forgive you if I'm too late. Abi, you've really done it this time!"

The farm manager was in the barn slopping the hogs when Noah arrived. "My wife is naive to the point of girlish innocence," he began, and unravelled what the bounty hunters probably knew. Joseph said nothing, just stood looking at the empty pail in his hand.

"Go get your blankets and a change of clothes," Noah ordered. "It's too dangerous to stay here. You can sleep in the woodshed at my house."

"Mister Hedley, I can't leave. Mister Daniel an' Missus Susan left me in charge. I haven't barely started the chores. Cows need milking, horse stalls need cleanin'. What they gonna think they come home ta find I ain't here? They gonna think I can't be trusted with responsibility, that I'm just sloughin' off, that's what they gonna think."

"Joseph, I'll vouch that you had to leave for your own safety. The Camerons will understand."

"Yes, suh, the Camerons will understand, but will the chickens that ain't yet bin fed or the cows that ain't yet bin milked or the filly that needs to be walked some or…?"

"Your life may be in danger if you stay here!"

"Who I am is in danger if I don't."

"Well, I won't leave you here alone. Here's the deal. I'll help you with your chores, then you come back and help with mine. There's little chance of an attack with the two of us together."

"How the Camerons gonna know I'm at your place?"

"It would be ill-advised to leave a note that just anyone can read. The Camerons aren't likely to come home in the dark."

"Large moon tonight, rising high. They might."

"Here's an idea. Write a note telling them you're staying at my place. We can explain why later. Tie it to the dog's collar. Argus won't let anyone but family read that note."

"Mister Hedley, I wish I'd thought a that. But I got to be here first light to make sure everything just right an' do my chores."

"First light, and I'll come with you. With my new rifle. Same deal. We'll have breakfast at my farm when my chores are done."

Mrs. Hedley Enlightens

It was Mrs. MacPhail's turn to host The Women's Temperance Committee, and she made no pretence of hiding the raspberry cordial. The decanter and its accompanying little glasses were prominently on display beside the napkins and teacups and plates of egg salad sandwiches and shortbread cookies. In the kitchen, in the Scots' custom, a small white ceramic pitcher held down the centre of the table, safe from any disturbance by the ladies. It was generally accepted that whisky was a man's drink to be used medicinally or offered to male visitors. The Temperance Committee ladies would no more drink the Scotch than Mister MacPhail would touch the raspberry cordial.

Among Abigail Hedley's many virtues was the ability to read her audience. She knew they knew she knew, thanks to Noah, more than anyone why the Camerons and Taylors had gone on holiday. Noah, that dear man, had leaked her enough ammunition to subdue any threat to her formidable role as the queen bee of the ladies' circle. Another virtue was her sense of timing. Abigail Hedley could wait for the propitious moment, the exact second, when her information, her revelations, her opinions, her pronouncements, would have optimum impact.

That moment was approaching but not yet imminent. Lesser topics must be dispensed with first. The conversation touched upon the passing of the Desmonds and the universal principle of the elderly, that first one spouse dies, then the other soon after. It was generally acknowledged they were in a better place now, free of suffering, and wasn't it good that the weather had been so cooperative the day of the funeral. Paul's prospects for marriage were discussed, and several possible choices were tabled for consideration. The new teacher was an unknown quantity, so her assessment was postponed to a later date. Someone noted that Angus MacLeod had left for Normal School, but no one knew if he had secured a good boarding house or the cost of such, which must be prohibitive. Wheat was up in price, and all agreed that was a good thing. It was Mrs. Haycroft who gave Mrs. Hedley the springboard from which to soar.

"Mrs. Hedley, the children saw Mister Duffy on the Line a few days ago, and they said it appeared he had come out of your lane. I told them they must be mistaken. 'The Irishman at the Hedley's?' I said. 'Preposterous!' I said, but they were insistent on what they had seen."

Mrs. Hedley took a sip of tea, and for suspenseful effect placed the cup and saucer on the coffee table before she casually said, "The children were quite right, Mrs. Haycroft. Mister Duffy did drop in, allegedly on the recommendation of Mrs. Cameron." She paused, waiting for everyone to think "goodness gracious" and no one to say it.

"Ladies, before you judge, please be mindful of our Lord's admonition to love one's enemies. I was given the opportunity to be of assistance to Mrs. Duffy, whom I have never met, mind you, but who feels she may be in need of a midwife in the future. Mrs. Cameron seemed to think I might know of someone qualified to act in that capacity."

"Do you?" their hostess asked.

"Actually, I thought to ask you ladies if you know of a possible candidate," she answered in a conspiratorial tone. "A wet-nurse may be required as well. Of course, Mister Duffy did not say as much, but I was able to deduce Mrs. Duffy's glands may not be adequate to the task."

She gave the assembly of silenced women time to digest that not only had her expertise in feminine matters been sought out by an Irish Catholic man on the recommendation of a neighbour, but here she was, the paragon of respectability, discussing the functioning of his wife's breasts.

"Mrs Haycroft, I thought you were going to say the children had seen the Camerons' Negro returning home from our place."

Now she had them. She could almost hear ears swivel.

"You have not heard the latest? Oh my!" And again she paused for dramatic effect.

Mrs. Chalmers lunged for the bait. "Why would the Camerons' Negro be at your place?"

"Because he spent the night there. In the woodshed. He couldn't go home because of the danger." She sipped more tea.

Mrs. MacPhail caved. "Abigail, please tell. What in heaven's name is going on?"

One could not improve upon this moment. The request to reign as dispenser of information had been made by their hostess using the familiarity of her Christian name.

"In all fairness, my husband Noah should get some of the credit for saving the Negro's life. His name is Joseph, in case you were not aware. Well, as you know, the Camerons and the Taylors went off on a holiday — Noah says the men wanted to look at some farm machinery — and the Camerons left Joseph to look after the farm in their absence. Noah helped the Camerons and Archie Taylor and the Desmond boy make a room under the house so Joseph didn't need to sleep in the barn. Noah says it is like a tiny apartment with its own small window and a woodstove, if you can believe it.

Anyway, that same day, I got a visit from a government official. I was immediately suspicious. He claimed to represent a department I had never heard of, and when I asked him, Noah confirmed it was totally fictitious. The so-called government man was a smooth talker, and if I had not had experience with that type, I might have been taken in. What was most curious was how he asked about the Negro at the Camerons'.

When we discovered Joseph had been left alone, I reminded Noah about the possibility of bounty hunters, and he immediately rode down to the Cameron farm and practically had to force Joseph to accept our hospitality. The two did up the chores at both farms before the Camerons arrived home, and when they did they were most appreciative. I personally think they were not a day too soon, considering what happened next."

She nibbled a cookie and sipped some tea to hasten its journey. "This shortbread is wonderfully light, Mrs. MacPhail. It's very similar to what Mrs. Chalmers bakes," she said, aware the circle knew she was giving hollow compliments. "So much better than mine. I really must ask you to write out the recipe."

Again it was Mrs. Chalmers. "So what happened next? Are we to assume the Camerons were angry that their Negro had abandoned the farm?"

"Oh, not at all. Not at all. As I said, they were most appreciative and thanked Noah — and indirectly myself — for coming to Joseph's rescue. For our part, we were simply thankful that every day we have been given an opportunity to be a blessing to someone. Although, as it turned out, our rescue was premature."

She indulged in another morsel of shortbread.

"Premature? More happened?" Mrs. Chalmers exclaimed, squirming in her chair.

"Oh yes. Much more. Quite exciting, actually. Lucky that no one got killed — that we know of — although that could still happen. Noah was in the thick of it. He is too much the self-effacing hero, but I managed to overcome his natural reticence to talk about himself, and I wormed the details out of him."

Her audience hung on every word.

"My husband and I and the Camerons calculated that an attempt to abduct Joseph might happen soon. Noah found out a kidnapping had been tried in Amherstburg, but it was thwarted by neighbours such as ourselves who kept an eye on him. Well... Someone suggested we do the same thing here, so Archie Taylor and Paul Desmond were notified of the plan, and for some reason so was Mister Duffy. Noah says the 'modus operandi' — that's Greek for the way someone does things — of the bounty hunters is to make off with their victims during the night, and then they are never seen again. Gives you the shivers, doesn't it?"

She paused while Mrs. MacPhail handed out the little glasses and the decanter was passed around.

"Daniel Cameron and my Noah taught Joseph how to use a firearm and Noah left his old squirrel gun — loaded with fresh powder — beside Joseph's bunk. Every day, the Camerons were especially on their guard, and every night someone stayed in Joseph's little room with him. Argus too. But in a month of Sundays, you'll never guess what happened next."

She took another nibble of shortbread.

"Someone poisoned Argus! Daniel Cameron thinks a passer-by threw some doctored meat into the lane, and of course Argus ate it. He isn't dead, but he wanted to be, he was just that sick. That's when we figured the bounty hunters would strike very soon."

She sipped some cordial, approved, and sipped some more.

"I suppose Mister Cameron was wise in informing Mister Duffy of the plan. Who they were I have no idea, and Noah doesn't either, but Mister Duffy's friends volunteered to get involved, and several of them were Black too.

It happened two days ago, so that is why I thought you would all know. Noah says it was at late dusk, with just enough moon to tease the eyes. It was Archie Taylor's turn to stay with Joseph, and some of Mister Duffy's friends were camped in the barn. Archie's always been a bit impetuous, and maybe that's a good thing, because when they broke in, Joseph clubbed the first one through the door right smartly, stretched him out cold as a mackerel, according to Noah, and Archie let go with his fowling piece. He says he fired high to scare them off. Maybe so, but Noah maintains there was considerable blood on the doorstep."

"How many?" Mrs. Haycroft asked.

"No one knows for sure. Three at least. Maybe more. The one Joseph clubbed was the government man who showed up at our door. Noah doesn't know what happened to him because Mister Duffy's friends took him away in the night. Noah says it took four of them — and you know how strong my Noah is — to get him into the buckboard. Tied up, naturally."

No one could recall a more memorable meeting of the Women's Temperance Committee. Abigail Hedley revelled in the knowledge this had been one of her finest moments and silently thanked Noah for his invaluable assistance.

"Mrs. MacPhail," she said, "I really must get your recipe for that amazing shortbread."

Constance Recruits an Ally

The product of three generations of plantation owners, Constance Lonnegan knew the reality of southern institutions. In their worst manifestation, the males of the aristocratic elite devoted themselves to whoring, hunting and hounds, squandering their inheritances frivolously. Families with poor judgment or lack of foresight married their young girls to these ephemerals with predictable results. In contrast, the best of this class, the men with stability, understood the intricate checks and balances among labour costs, material production, and commodity prices. With the help of the best overseers money could buy, they managed their plantations through an amalgam of grand scale farming as a way of life and proven business principles as a way to profit. The father of a fresher and more vivacious Constance had attached her to Beauregard Lonnegan because he appreciated that Beau's grasp of how matters should be guaranteed for his daughter a comfortable existence among the families of the established gentry.

A comfortable life in an exalted social class was not Constance Lonnegan's problem. Her problem was that Beau's understanding of how things should be differed from hers.

It was expected that Beau hire the overseers, orchestrate planting and harvest, buy and sell slaves, and negotiate the sale of cotton. She, as his wife, was expected to supervise household servants, establish menus, organize foodstuffs, and keep a record of the house's financial outlay. Somehow, little by little, she had lost her place in the great scheme of being a Southern lady, and when she tried to analyse how this had come about, she always arrived at one conclusion. Cicero.

She could not blame Beau for her discomfiture. He had inherited Cicero. But Cicero had become more than what had been intended. His influence was pervasive. He was Beau's manservant, valet, trusted confidant, personal advisor, business delegate, his liaison between the slaves and their owner, a leader of hymns, and most annoyingly, *major-domo* within the plantation house. It was Cicero who delegated tasks, disciplined the servants, kept the household financial records, planned their menus, and supervised the cooks, even when the master and mistress entertained. These were her jobs, her responsibilities, her worries, and she resented losing them to Cicero, no matter how efficient he was. In the mirror she saw nothing more than an ageing woman, children gone, who took brandy in her morning coffee and whose purpose in life was to be amused by fancy chickens.

Ever since she had discovered Beau had fathered Ellie, a new anxiety gnawed at Constance Lonnegan. Any fool could see Beau intended to marry his daughter off to Cicero, guaranteeing a better life than a field hand for his own blood, but a union between her husband's illegitimate daughter and the oily creature she despised would create a monstrous situation for the lady of the house. What little status, what little credibility she retained in domestic responsibilities would totally evaporate. She might as well go live with her chickens.

Constance schemed. Beau would never sell Ellie or Cicero. That Cicero lusted after young, nubile Ellie was obvious. That Ellie loathed Cicero and pined for Joseph, the runaway, was of absolutely no importance. It would have no influence on her husband's decision. But possibly that decision could be put off temporarily.

It was never the practice to consummate a coupling while the girl was still a child, before she began her monthly flow. Constance was aware the household servants were hiding Ellie's menstruation to keep the beast off her, but it was only a matter of time until Cicero discovered the reality. Every laundry day he inspected the personal clothing of the females, looking for signs of blood — or the lack of it. Several years ago he had discovered one of the servants had been impregnated without Beau's permission, by a field hand no less. The man was on the block at Forrest's next auction; the girl and her daughter were still in the fields.

When Constance summoned Ellie, she stood with downcast eyes, hands folded in front, the very picture of submission.

"Ellie, you do not wish Master Lonnegan to pair you with Cicero, do you?"

"No, ma'am."

"Do you still think of Joseph?"

"Yes, ma'am."

"You do realize he is gone from your life, don't you?"

"Yes, ma'am."

"Yet he is still in your thoughts?"

"Yes, ma'am. All the time."

"If he is ever returned, Master Lonnegan will do terrible things to him. Do you remember what he did to Seth?"

"Yes, ma'am."

"Would you like me to help you keep Cicero away as long as possible?"

"Yes, ma'am. Please."

"Take this towel with you. We have many just like it. Wrap your menstrual rags in this towel and bring it to me each month. I will dispose of it without Cicero's knowledge."

"Yes, ma'am. Thank you, ma'am."

"It will be our little secret, so you must tell no one. Agreed?"

"Yes, ma'am. Bless you, ma'am."

On her way to feed her chickens, Mrs. Lonnegan stopped by the kitchen and tasted the soup. "Put less salt in next time," she instructed. "Also, I want a pork loin served for supper tonight. With applesauce. Make sure there is applesauce. I insist on applesauce with the pork loin."

A Message for Aeneas Ragg

A tall, thin man dressed in working man's garb approached the moorings of the *Linda Ann* in the mouth of the Maumee River. "Glad I caught you here," he said to the captain, after being granted permission to come aboard.

"Where did you think I'd be?" the captain asked.

"Never sure. You're an elusive fish. We need to talk."

The captain followed him into the deck cabin, sat at a tiny table, motioned for the visitor to join him, poured both a heartening ration of black rum, and tossed his portion off in one gulp.

"Talk," the captain said.

The thin man pulled a slender brown envelope from a jacket pocket and placed it on the table. "Can you get this to Aeneas? It's important. He'll want to know."

"I can probably find him, given a few days. He's plotting with some of his associates in Sandusky, far as I know. Will he think this important enough to pay my bill for personal delivery?"

"Read it if you want, and decide for yourself."

"If that letter to Ragg is not 'Personal and Confidential', why don't you just tell me what's in it?"

"Good news and bad news he needs to know."

"Start with the good news. I could use some of that."

"We got the woman and the son that escaped us 'cause of that fucking farmer near McGregors' Mills. They were stupid enough to think we'd shot our bolt and put 'em back in the barn. Muffled 'em real good this time. No kicking and screaming, not this time. No shooting this time, neither. You can pick 'em up at the usual spot on the river at your leisure, but the sooner the better 'cause we won't get paid until Aeneas collects the reward money."

"How much?"

"Don't know for certain, but it's sizeable. A young woman, good-looking, young enough to drop more, son old enough for heavy work… It will be like fuckin' Christmas."

"And the bad news?"

"It's really bad. That 'professional' Aeneas sent to get the main prize, the one who was supposed to show us how it was done, well, he got us into the soup real bad. I'm the only one that got away mostly unscathed, and that's only 'cause I was holding a blanket outstretched to throw it over the Darkie's head."

He paused to finish his rum. The captain poured them each another.

"Give me details. Aeneas is going to want to know the details."

"It's all in the letter."

"I'm sure it is, and I'm sure you were very thorough, but you were there and I wasn't, so I want to hear it from you."

"The 'professional' rented a buckboard in Ridgetown, told them we would need it for a week and we would hire someone to return it. Poked around town too much, stayed too long."

"How did you get to Ridgetown?" the Captain interrupted.

"Train, but we sat far apart, then we walked some, hitched on wagons some. The professional had poison with him, said he used it to eliminate dogs 'cause Burton said there was a watchdog. Only thing is, he didn't put enough in the meat, because the dog wasn't dead when we got there. We left the buckboard at the end of the lane. Dusk was just about gone. Tiny sliver of a moon — needed last light to see what we were doing. Everything was where the big man said it was, except the damn dog was in the room under the overhang. Couldn't say he barked, more like a whimper, him bein' sick and all, but that was enough to warn them."

"Them?"

"Them. More than one, that's for sure, 'cause when Burton tore the door off — and Jesus, that didn't take long — he was one mighty strong son of a bitch. Anyway, Burton ripped the door open and barged in, expecting everything to be a surprise. It was a fucking surprise all right! He was no sooner in than he got clubbed 'longside the head, and down he went, like you see a steer drop before the butcher cuts its throat. It sounded like a sledge hammer hitting a hollow stump. Then there's a jet of orange flame and a blast that just about blew my eardrums, I was that close, but I was at the back holdin' the blanket, and that's what saved me. It didn't all go over my head; I got a few chunks of lead to brag about. Looks like bird shot."

"The big man and the professional? Where are they now? Can they sing?"

"I figure Burton was out cold on the floor by this time, so he didn't get any of the shot. The professional, well, his easy huntin' days with the ladies may be over. He was flung back, reelin' and screamin' to beat all, and I half ran, half carried him to the buckboard and we got the hell out, fast like. Nothin' we could do for Burton."

"Once again... Can they sing?"

"I abandoned the buckboard as close to Ridgetown as I dared and left the professional in the back. Someone will find him. I walked 'til dawn, hitched a ride on a hay wagon — don't worry, he didn't see me hop on — and hoofed it some more. Walked to where I could catch a westbound train. No, he won't sing. They won't sweat him for a while anyways. Most of his scalp is gone above the left eye where the lead got him. Jesus, the blood! You wouldn't believe one head holds that much blood. Left eye's dead. Lucky he didn't lose the other one."

"So you have no idea if Burton is dead or alive."

"I just kept my mouth shut and listened to the talk on the train. It's big news. They were sayin' some good Samaritan took the professional to a doctor in Ridgetown. Must of bin a banner day for him, 'cause the big man was dumped at his office as well."

"Dead?"

"No, but all the talk is how the doctor thinks he has swelling of the brain, called it the worst he ever saw, figures the big man will never be the same again, probably be a mental cripple, won't be able to remember his own name on a good day."

"Jesus," the Captain said in a low voice. "How could he know that? What if the big man recuperates? What if they squeeze him for information on the business? He could still point the finger at us."

"That ain't likely to happen from what I heard. The talk on the train was all about how he can't control his bowels and pisses hisself. He has seizures too. One woman said she heard the doctor say that's a sure sign of irreparable brain damage."

"Ragg will not be happy. This one has gotten real personal to him, blames himself he got away, calls him the main prize. Not much is going to plan lately. There was that fuck-up when the cripple died, bad attention near McGregors' Mills, he lost Burton's partner near Amherstburg in the first go, he sends in a ringer to show you and Burton how it's done, and Jesus, now this."

"At least there's the wench and her son."

"They're small potatoes in comparison."

"Are you going to take the letter to him or not?"

"Go back upcountry, keep an eye on things. I'll set sail for Sandusky the moment you're off my ship, and that's in two minutes, as soon as we finish another drink."

As his visitor opened the door to leave the cabin, the captain said, "Maybe you best tell the story a bit different. That professional you're so down on, well, Aeneas Ragg ain't gonna be too happy you left one of his sons in a fuckin' buckboard, all shot up."

Archie's Plan

Susan left the men to fend for themselves and collected Catherine in her gig "to pick up a few things" at the general store in Ridgetown. Joseph was sanding furniture in the barn, and Daniel and Archie were sitting in the Cameron's kitchen, killing off a cherry pie Daniel had chosen for lunch.

"How's Argus?" Archie asked.

"A bit better. Still wobbly. Vomiting clear fluid now, but not as often. How's Archie?"

"Archie is just fine, thank you very much. And why wouldn't Archie be fine?"

"We don't know yet if the big man Joseph clubbed and the one you shot are dead or alive. By all accounts it isn't easy to have someone's death on your conscience."

"My conscience is like Argus, getting better every minute. If it had been your turn on watch, you'd have done the same, and you know it. We didn't have much time to get our ducks in order... Joseph dozing off, or so I thought, and me settling in for a long night in a comfortable chair. Argus was on the floor beside the bunk, raised his head, growled a little, and that Samson had ripped the door open and was through it in less time than it takes to tell about it. Did you know Joseph slept with a club? I didn't."

"It's the handle off a sledge hammer. I gave it to him. Glad he used it. Noah gave him a small bore musket too. His old one. His new one is percussion cap. What did Duffy's committee friends do with the giant?"

"Hedley showed up when he heard the shot, helped them lift him into the buckboard, got the horses hitched up in the dark. Noah says they dropped him off in front of the doctor's office in Ridgetown so someone can find him in the morning."

"Where's the man you shot?"

"No trace. Actually, that's not true. There's a blood trail to the road, then it stops, so he must have had help. No way he could have got away on his own, him being so charitable with all that blood."

Daniel served another piece of Susan's pie, brought two glasses to the table, and filled them with two fingers of Scotch from the white porcelain jug always found in the centre of the table. "That was good work. I just don't want to see a friend have second thoughts about getting involved, that's all."

"In for a penny... Think it through, Daniel. Where would any of us be if we had done nothing?"

"I know. I have thought about it, but probably not as much as Joseph. What do we do now?"

"This is the way I look at it... If one of those sons-a-bitches dies, I see it as justice administered during a crime rather than after, and I will sleep the sleep of the righteous, make no mistake. I figure no one will make another attempt to snatch him for a little while, but hell, Daniel, he's worth a bucket load of money to somebody."

"Somebody who would pay just to hang him."

"True. And I've got a plan..."

Daniel answered a knock at the porch door. "You're out early," he said to the children who had stopped in for wine and shortbread.

It was the littlest Haycroft girl who spilled the beans. "Teacher dismissed us when Mister Desmond came by in his buggy. We figure they're courting."

"Why would you say that?"

"We heard Mister Desmond ask Teacher if she would like to go for a ride to see the American ship in the bay. Then she let us go early so..."

"What's an American ship doing in the bay?" Daniel asked, but the children just shrugged, inhaled their wine and cookies, and set off with the usual "Thank you" to enjoy the precious gift of free time.

"Yes, what is an American ship doing in the bay?" Archie echoed as he refreshed his glass and did the same for Daniel.

"No good reason I can think of. Picking up? Dropping off? Suspicious, isn't it? Good thing Susan's not here," Daniel observed. "You know how she hates Yankees! She'd probably ride her filly right down there and shoot a few."

"Yes, if anyone would, Susan would," Archie agreed.

Daniel added another wee dram to their glasses. "Maybe we should go down there, have a look, see what they're up to."

"No sooner said than done," Archie said, meticulously dividing the last of the jug between the two glasses.

"While I'm hitching up Jacob and Jessie, bring that second pie along. I think it's apple. And bring another bottle of whisky too. You know where it's kept."

Daniel took a little longer than usual to connect horses and buggy. Past the schoolhouse, they turned left and headed for the lake. Not wishing to interfere in Paul's courtship, they pulled up when they reached the bay. There was no sign of Paul or the new school mistress. Each took a long draught from the newly opened bottle. Daniel saw the boat first. It appeared to be anchored close in, but there was no observable activity on board or on the nearby sandy beach.

"That's an American flag all right," Archie said, handing the bottle back to Daniel.

"Good thing Sushan's not here," Daniel said, after enjoying another swallow or two.

"Yup, she'd sink it," Archie said. "I wonder how hard it is to sail a boat like that."

"Can't be all that diffi... difficult," Daniel said. "Once you get the sails up, the wind does the rest."

"True," Archie said. "I suppose all you have to do is steer with that wheel, if it's got one. Some have a tiller."

"Till, tiller, tillest," Daniel said. "Here my frenn, have a drink. Someone who knows as much about sailing ships as my frenn Archie Taylor should have a drink."

"I will if you join me," Archie replied. "It's you who knows about the sails. I only know about the wheel thingamajiggy."

They were quiet for a moment, contemplating the little scurries of water motivated by an easterly breeze.

Archie enjoyed a long swig. Handing the bottle to Daniel, he said, "Might be, could be, poshibly might be the start of an invashion."

Daniel slowly sipped another wee dram.

"Arshie, we might be witnessing hishtory in the making."

"Yup." There was a long pause. "Daniel, you know what we should do? We should steal it."

"Capital idea! Privateers. Shpoils of war," Daniel said. "We'll steal it an' sail down to the fort and hand it over to Major Emmett. Strike the first blow, like Shir Ishaac, Shir Isaac Brock. I've, I've got the pie, you bring the bottle." He half fell out of the buggy, stumbled off down the beach, waded out to the boat, and with considerable difficulty climbed the ladder on the transom.

Archie, carefully keeping the bottle vertical, joined him soon after. Using the wheel for support, he yelled a whisper to Daniel. "Ready to haul up the zails?"

With a show of seamanship that would have given Horatio Nelson apoplexy, the mainsail was raised and tied off with a double knotted bow.

"We're underway!" Daniel yelled just before both men were jolted off their feet as the anchor rope pulled taut.

"It's okay! I didn't spill any!" Archie yelled back, holding the bottle up by its neck as evidence. "I shee the probbem," he continued. He fumbled a folding knife from his pocket and sawed at the anchor rope until its strands separated. The little ship, unencumbered by anchor or knowledgeable crew, set off for the open waters of the lake.

"Nothin' to it, jus' as I predicted," Daniel said, grabbing a rope on the tail end of the swinging boom that threatened to bash the brains out of the inattentive. "Do you want me to raise that little littler littlest sail up in front, Captain Taylor?"

"The wind's picking up, so we'd best leave it alone. Tie that rope somewhere so we can share another wee dram, Captain Cameron."

What had been playful riffles in the bay morphed into sizeable waves in the open lake. With only the main set, the little ship began to pitch and yaw until Captain Archie directed it into the setting sun. "I'll tie the wheel down so it can run before the wind," he said in his best nautical manner. "We should be in Amherstburg before dark."

All headway was lost when the breeze died at sunset. They were not remotely near Amherstburg. Where they were was far enough out in Lake Erie that full daylight would have been necessary to see the shore. Daniel accidentally dropped the bottle overboard when he contributed his half of the apple pie to the lake, but Archie magnanimously forgave him because the bottle was empty.

Becalmed, they had time to contemplate their folly. Libations of lake water slurped from cupped hands began the healing process, but for an ample ration of time neither spoke. By full dark they were almost sober. Finally, Daniel asked, "What do we do now?"

"Not much we can do, not 'til the wind decides to get back to work."

Another ration of time aided sobriety and an appreciation of their situation.

"While we're waiting for the wind, do you remember why you dropped in today?" Daniel asked. "You were saying something about a plan, just as the schoolkids arrived."

"We were saying we know someone would top up a bucket of money to hang Joseph, just to discourage the others. So here's my suggestion. School's back in, and that means we're near the end of harvesting any crops that can be harvested. Hunting season and pig slaughter and salting down and smoking come next. Let's keep Joseph on the move. My leg is almost mended, but now that the MacLeod boy is gone, I could use some help for the heavy work, give the leg a chance to come fully back. Paul and Noah could use an extra set of hands, Duffy for sure when the bairn arrives." He paused to cup several handfuls of water into a fuzzy mouth.

"So the bounty hunters never know where he is, if we're careful."

"Exactly. If we're careful. Anything suspicious, John Duffy's Vigilance Committee can set up the watchers again."

"What you're suggesting sounds like a good idea, except for two things."

"Which are?"

"I pay Joseph a hired man's wages. Cash. I expect everyone to do the same."

"Naturally. Second?"

"You are mighty free sending someone's hired man off to help yourself, among others. What do I do for a hired man when he's gone?"

"I've thought of that, my friend. The Chalmers' oldest boy says he wants to earn a few shekels. He's big enough to be a help. Might not be worth a man's wage and he's still in school, but he could fill in when you needed someone and Joseph was hiding out somewhere else."

"If it's okay with Joseph, it's okay with me. Might give Susan a respite from cooking and baking. He eats as hard as he works."

"Duly noted. I'll warn Catherine and the others."

Whisky-fuelled fatigue and the gentle rocking of the boat lulled them into such a sound sleep they did not notice when the craft ran aground somewhere near Port Alma. At dawn, they woke with a memorable hangover only minimally appeased by lake water. Daniel cut down the American flag to take as a trophy, and they began a plodding trek inland to find a road. Suddenly, Daniel halted in his tracks and said, "I wonder where my horses are."

The Mariners Return

"We thought it might be the vanguard of an invasion," Daniel feebly explained as he rested his elbows on the Taylors' kitchen table. "How did we know there were going to be gale force winds? Maybe if we had had some chickens with us…"

"Don't think you can joke your way out of this debacle," Susan warned.

"If it hadn't been for Archie's superior seamanship, we might have…"

"Superior seamanship? Archie's never been in anything bigger than a canoe in his whole life," Catherine said. "Seamanship indeed!"

"There we were, hazarding our lives in defence of our country, and this is the thanks we get," Archie muttered, shaking his head in disbelief.

"If it's thanks being given out, you might want to share some with Paul and Joseph. When I got home and you were nowhere to be found, Joseph said he saw the two of you heading west. I set out in the gig, and who should I meet but Paul Desmond, who told us you turned toward the bay. Paul picked up Joseph once I had found the team so he could bring them home. Otherwise, those poor horses would have been there all night."

"At feed time, I'll explain why we needed to abandon them for patriotic reasons. Jacob will understand. Jessie will be less forgiving. She doesn't keep abreast of politics as much as he does."

"Are you two still drunk?" Susan demanded.

Archie, eyes closed, chin in hand, nodded a slow negative. Daniel said, "I don't think so. I do have a lingering headache though. Maybe I'm coming down with something."

"Maybe you'll both be coming down with something called incarceration," Catherine said. "Susan and I are expecting the sheriff's knock on the door any moment. Who else knows about this ridiculous escapade?"

"Only the kind folks who let us hitch rides once we found a road," Archie replied. "We were buffeted by the raging gale and high seas for quite some time, and I don't think you girls appreciate how much distance we travelled."

"How many?"

"I'm thinking forty miles minimum, as the crow flies."

"How many kind folks?"

"Four or five or maybe eight or a dozen. We may have talked to someone from Ridgetown. Lucky to get lifts and be home before dark, I'd say."

"You've said quite enough," Catherine observed.

"Our chores are done at home," Susan said, "thanks to Joseph once again. Catherine and I did the chores here. Catherine, thank you for supper. I will be taking my husband home and tucking him in for the night. He may be coming down with something."

Vicky knew the way in the dark. No one spoke on the ride home.

Before breakfast the following morning, Daniel headed to the barn to find their hired man already feeding the livestock. Joseph raised his eyebrows and lowered his head as if peering over spectacles. "I don't want to talk about it," Daniel muttered. "That goes for you too, Argus."

It was the end of the week when Noah Hedley dropped in for coffee. He tossed a copy of the Ridgetown Gazette on the table and sat back to enjoy the reaction as Susan read aloud the article on the front page.

Local Heroes Safe After Rescue Attempt

Monday last, two local inhabitants attempted to rescue a sloop in distress at Rondeau. Mr. Thaddeus Parker of Cleveland, Ohio, and a young woman (purportedly his daughter) had moored in the bay and waded ashore to stretch their legs after an uneventful crossing. Messrs Daniel Cameron and Archibald Taylor of Howard Township were in the vicinity when they noticed the boat had broken its anchor rope and was drifting away from the beach. Both men managed to board the vessel but were unable to prevent it from being blown into the open waters of the lake. Despite a sudden wind shear that tore the flag away and with no visible landmarks for navigation, they successfully landed the boat west of Port Alma after a harrowing night on the water.

Mr. Parker expressed his gratitude to the local heroes for their civic-minded effort to recover his beloved Rebecca.

He also thanked the local authorities for their prompt notification his sloop had been found undamaged.

Obviously suffering from fatigue, both men declined to make a statement. Both modestly rejected the suggestion they were heroes, saying that anyone would have acted as they did in a similar situation.

Susan shook her head in disbelief.

"What did you do with the flag?" Noah asked.

"I found it stuffed in my shirt. Joseph hid it in the hay mow. Susan didn't want to touch it. I suppose I should burn it."

"Yes, you should," Noah said.

"Next time we won't talk to anyone holding a pencil," Archie said.

The newspaper's account fooled no one. For his text in Sunday's sermon, Reverend Leeds chose Matthew 8, verses 23 through 26. *"And when he was entered into a ship, his disciples followed him. And, behold, there arose a great tempest in the sea insomuch the ship was covered with the waves: but he was asleep. And his disciples came to him, and awoke him, saying, Lord, save us: we perish. And he saith unto them, Why are ye fearful, O ye of little faith? Then he arose, and rebuked the winds and the sea; and there was a great calm."* To his congregation Leeds pointed out that God is with us even when we are lacking in good judgment.

In the social time after the service, several mockingly introduced each other to Captain Cameron. "Captain" did not stick, but Archie was known as "Ship Taylor" for the rest of his life.

Shorter Days

The success of Archie's plan could only be gauged if bounty hunters were searching for Joseph and unable to find him. On his circuit, Reverend Leeds requested his flock to keep a weather eye open for any suspicious strangers. To the provincial denizens of Kent County, all strangers were suspicious. In the public mind, newcomers were sorted by gender, age, occupation, marital status, social class, country of origin, and church affiliation. As everywhere in British North America, Canada West enjoyed an abundance of religion but suffered from a dearth of Christianity.

Neighbours all along the Cameron Line viewed any unknown carriage or rider with interest. At Duffy's suggestion, only the last farm that had hosted Joseph and the one where he laboured at present knew his whereabouts. Shunted from one farm to another for two days, then to another for three, to another for two, to another overnight and so on, he became familiar with each farmer's way of doing things. He was surprised how much he missed the nightly lesson with Mrs. Cameron, fearing a regression if he stopped practising his reading and elocution. The greatest casualty of the new routine was Argus.

Paul Desmond was the most indifferent and left him to shift for himself. The most welcoming was Mrs. Hedley. Determined to demonstrate to the community her magnanimity of spirit, she plied her woodshed guest with scrumptious dishes and fresh baking until one night he politely explained he might never be able to enjoy another dessert if she didn't afford him relief from the products of her kitchen. "Joseph, I use centuries-old family recipes, so you can see it's not only the Scotch who can make scones or butter tarts or shortbread," she informed him. "You let me know when you need more food, and if the others don't feed you properly, I'll send some nourishing top-ups with Noah."

With the arrival of colder weather, the focus of farm life changed. Pigs were slaughtered and salted or smoked, the beef ring provided a variety of cuts for the ice house, and preparations were made for the fall hunts. Joseph spent a portion of a week's wages to purchase powder and shot from Noah for his musket and went through it in a day of practice.

The Chalmers boy was enlisted to clean the barrels which would hold the salted cull of the wildfowl migrations. As a hunting dog, Argus was a liability. He would dash about in the woods or on the beach, prematurely rousing the targets, and despite a plethora of varied ancestors, he had inherited no retriever instinct, so on the first day out the men learned to shoot where future meals would fall on land. In theory, wave action would eventually bring a downed bird to shore if it fell into the lake, but in practice even a slight offshore breeze meant a waste of time and lead. When Argus was left tied near the house the second day, he complained so much Susan eventually shut him in the barn so she wouldn't have to listen to him while she processed pigeons, ducks, and geese brought home by her husband and an increasingly accurate Joseph.

The first snows revealed the habits of deer. In mid-December, rather than set up in a stand in the woodlot before dawn and wait for a suitable target as in previous years, Daniel had Joseph, with Argus on a lead, walk toward him from upwind to drive the deer before them. By the end of the second day, two bucks had been harvested, dressed, and hung from tripods outside the back door where Argus could protect them from carnivores.

"When Argus and me was walkin' back," Joseph said, "and you waitin' for us to push the deer ahead, we come across a little building with a stove pipe pokin' through the roof and a pile of wood outside. Why you build a little cabin in the middle of your woods? A witch live there maybe?"

"The supply of witches has dried up of late. It's a sugar shack."

"Mister Daniel, I know sugar be got from cane, and maybe sorghum, that new crop Massa Lonnegan is tryin'. No way you gonna get me to believe sugar is coming out of that little shack."

"Maybe we should call it a syrup shack, but we'll boil down some sugar too. You'll see."

Christmas was a relaxed day in comparison to Hogmanay, the last day of the year. The Taylors invited the Camerons, the MacPhails, the Chalmers, and Paul Desmond to a ceilidh in the Scots' tradition. Catherine added the Hedleys in appreciation of their contribution to Joseph's safety. Abigail Hedley, retreating behind her English heritage, refused to even countenance the idea of attending until Noah pointed out it would be rude to shun an event so important to neighbours, and wouldn't they benefit from her civilizing influence and mouthwatering baked goods, and added he was going even if she did not. She sniffed something about Bacchanalian revels with Oatmeal Savages, but bustled about baking in preparation. Archie and Catherine insisted Joseph come as well, although he was most reluctant.

"Mister Daniel, I don't want to go to Mister Archie's party. What experience do I got with any hog-anything except real-live pigs? I'll be out of place in clothes, speech... everything. I just won't fit in... I'll be uncomfortable."

"Nonsense. That's what whisky is for. Gift-giving for the host is traditional, so I'll give you a bottle for Archie, and I'll take one myself. Susan is baking a fruitcake and taking enough shortbread to feed us all. I know Archie; my friend is a clever man with a practical mind. The ceilidh will go on into the wee hours and then some. Stretch out where you normally do when you're at the Taylors' if you need a break, but be sure you're the first to step across the threshold in the morning. If a man with a dark complexion and black hair first-foots a house on New Years Day, it is believed he brings good luck."

"Nobody gonna beat me on the dark part," Joseph said, "but I'm not sure I can deliver on bringin' the good luck. I truly, really, honestly would prefer to stay here with Argus."

"I told you. Archie has a practical mind. He knows if you're with us, enjoying the music, we know you are safe. Be reasonable. Think of all the aggravation you would cause if you got grabbed while we were enjoying ourselves. Do you truly, really, honestly want to be alone, knowing what those sons of bitches are capable of?"

In the buggy on the way to the Taylors', Joseph looked askance at Daniel in his kilt and Susan in a tartan skirt with matching sash and muttered, "Maybe my clothes not so out of place after all."

"The kilt is from the war; it was his grandfather's," Susan explained. "It's tradition to wear your clan's tartan at social events. Don't worry. You're fine. I married into the clan, so I wear its tartan as well."

"Tartan is the pattern and the colours?" Joseph asked. "You got more than one?"

"Several," Daniel said. "I expect Archie and MacPhail and Chalmers to be wearing the kilt tonight too, so you may see various tartans, but we all belong to the same clan."

"Does that mean you is — you are related?"

Daniel chuckled. "No, it means our ancestors once lived in the same area and shared a relationship with a chief."

"That chief, he like Massa Lonnegan, boss of everyone and everything?"

"In past times he was more of a warlord, an organizer of families who banded together for protection. At one time the clan was a military, economic, and social organization. The chief was a leader who allocated resources, acted as a judge, declared war..."

"Who you need protection from?"

"Other clans, other chiefs. You always have to protect your land."

"How this chief, this warlord, how he keep all these families obeying him, y'all so far from Scotland? He can't whip ya 'cause you so scattered."

Daniel laughed. "Our bond with the clan is maintained voluntarily through a shared history. We show deference to our chief, but never obsequiousness. Although each clansman has the right to call him by his first name, the Cameron custom is to address our chief as Lochiel. It's not at all like you hailing Mister Lonnegan by his first name."

"If I yelled 'Hey, Beauregard', it would be like standing in a barrel of coal oil and lighting two Lucifers, one after the other. I could do it once just fine, but I might not get the chance to do it again real soon."

Joseph became more anxious as they approached the Taylors' house. "Anything else I got to know besides first-footin' before I go to this here kay-lee?" he asked.

"Yes, three rules are mandatory, and you absolutely must obey them," Susan said solemnly. "You must eat, you must drink, and you must have a good time. There may be storytelling, and if you wish to contribute to the entertainment, that would be fine."

"I can eat and drink, but as for the good time and tellin' stories..."

After greetings, the first order of business was to set out the food, buffet style, on an increasingly over-loaded sideboard. When Susan placed a tray of her shortbread on the dessert end, she noticed that there was already shortbread contributed by Mrs. Hedley, Mrs. Chalmers, Mrs. MacPhail, and their hostess.

"Some will be terribly wounded tonight when my shortbread is favoured," she quietly informed Daniel and Joseph, and added magnanimously, "It might be best if you sampled everyone's to avoid hurt feelings. Whatever you do, do not express a preference for mine, even though I know you would like to."

As she placed the fruitcake behind the trays, Joseph and Daniel exchanged glances and the tiniest of nods. When Archie was recruited, he confessed that Catherine had given him the same instructions about hers.

Daniel was right. Except for Paul, Noah, and Joseph, the men wore kilts. Joseph took advantage of the constant offerings of food, starting with roast goose and proceeding eventually to the baked goods. He was intrigued by the exotic dancing, hands in the air, feet precisely placed, so different from what he had experienced on the plantation. From his wallflower chair on one side of the house, he enjoyed watching the respectable Mrs. Hedley trying not to enjoy the evening in her chair on the opposite side. He was dubious about the music of the bagpipes, their chanters masterfully fingered by MacPhail and Chalmers. The whisky he appreciated more as the evening wore on, discovering that, like the bagpipes, it was an acquired taste. The more whisky Archie offered, the less he cared that he was under-dressed for the occasion, and after midnight and Auld Lang Syne and a communal toast to 1858, stuffed with food and topped up with Scotch, he deemed it prudent to head for his cot in the summer kitchen. At that precise moment it was revealed that the quantity of Scotch whisky imbibed while sitting does not equate to the same quantity that permits walking.

Joseph dutifully first-footed the house, and all who had stayed to witness the dawn sombrely downed the breakfast of bacon and eggs Catherine prepared. The water jug placed in the centre of the table she refilled twice. Daniel and Joseph were uncharacteristically quiet on the way home, but both regained some semblance of vertical steadiness after an afternoon nap.

"What did you do with the shortbread you took from each plate?" Daniel asked Joseph when out of range of Susan's hearing.

"When my pockets were full, I got rid of what I couldn't eat when I visited the outhouse, and I made sure to throw it way under the seat so's it won't be seen. You?"

"The same. I filled my sporran twice. First chance I get, I'll empty out any crumbs. I'm worried butter may have leached into the leather. Every time Archie checked the stove, I saw him throw in his share. By *Auld Lang Syne*, all the plates were empty. Leeds would say, 'Blessed are the peacemakers...' if he knew."

At supper, when Susan suggested a toast to a less exciting new year, she noticed that both men poured only a very wee dram for their libation.

After supper they exchanged gifts. Joseph received a new pair of work boots and a pair of pants from Daniel, socks and a shirt from Susan. They had thought their hired man was ignorant of their traditions, so they were pleased when he gave them a wooden bowl he had fashioned on the lathe from a burl.

Winter Realities, Spring Plans

Winter snows arrived to stay, and the men headed to the forest to get fuel for the following year. Once trees were felled, limbed, and cut into manageable lengths, the draft horses sledded the wood closer to the house where it could be attacked with a crosscut saw. The scenario was repeated when Joseph worked at the Taylors' and the Hedleys' and the Duffys' and Paul Desmond's. His logging and saw-sharpening experience at Deacon's mill made him more valuable in the bush. The Chalmers boy was a good worker, but Daniel missed the companionship and strength of an adult when Joseph was at another farm.

One bitterly raw day in February, after he and Joseph had cut and stacked some of the new wood supply piled earlier beside the lane, Daniel suggested they spend the rest of the afternoon in the workshop, out of the biting wind. His latest project was a fancy dining room table for a grain merchant in Highgate, and the freshly planed cherry wood was not of a mind to cooperate. When he called Joseph over from shaping the matching chairs to give a hand, he noticed how fatigued he looked. Quickness had disappeared from his step, and he had the same downcast look as Argus when he was forbidden to accompany the hunting party.

Susan's arrival with coffee gave him an opportunity to take a closer look at his hired man. When she returned to the house, he asked, "Joseph, are you not well? You look like winter may be getting you down. Some are affected by the lack of sunlight, you know. It's quite common to be depressed this time of year. Or are you worn out by how much you're working in the woodlots?"

Joseph studied his coffee for several moments before replying, set it to one side, fished Malachi's knife out of his pocket, and began to whittle a warped pine dowel. "Mister Daniel, it's not bringing in the wood that's the problem. I'm grateful you and the neighbours are trying to fool the bountiers, and when my body hurts I remember they've tried to catch me twice, and I think about Seth and Malachi. I get paid for every day I work, and I don't need to spend any of it, so my vase is almost full. Winter in Tennessee is easier on a body than here, so maybe it is the short days that have lowered my spirits."

He left off whittling for a moment to sip his coffee. Daniel said nothing, waiting for him to resume.

"I should be happy. I have some money, Missus Susan has taught me how to read and write, and unless I get anxious or hurried I can usually talk so the queen would understand."

"You have made amazing progress," Daniel observed. "I notice you are even reading the Gospels. Truly, truly amazing progress. Don't get a swelled head though; you still have quite an accent, even if the words are assembled correctly. Even when you take your time, you aren't sounding like a native yet. When you get excited..."

"I know. You and Missus Susan and the Taylors and MacPhails and Chalmers are the only ones who speak a English the queen would approve of. The Duffys and Mrs. Hedley have an accent too, don't they?"

Daniel laughed out loud. "That's rich, you thinking the queen speaks the same as us. I'll have to share that one with Susan."

"And thanks to you, I am learning how to make furniture, so I am not complaining. I have been luckier than most, again, thanks to you."

He sipped his coffee to stall for time before he bared his soul.

"It seem — it seems to me contentment, happiness, the Promised Land, is always moving ta some place farther on. I thought, if only I can escape slavery and live among the Britishers, I will be happy forever. Then I said, if only I can find a job and make some money, I will be happy forever. Then Missus Susan told me I need to learn to talk like the Britishers and read and write, and I thought, once I can do those things, I will be happy forever. I have accomplished so much, Mister Daniel, with so many people helping me, but I ask myself, what now? I can't stay your hired man until I die — or you do. Then I ask myself, will I feel more comfortable livin' with Black folks? I went to the Taylors' Hogmanay kay-lee like you asked so you could babysit me, but the fling dancing and the whisky and the bagpipes, that will never be who I am, no matter how long I stay."

Daniel swished the remainder of his coffee and thumbed errant grounds from its rim. "Joseph, once the roads allow, why don't we take a trip down to the Elgin Settlement, South Buxton area, just you and me? You can see for yourself how the Blacks have organized a community, maybe get a feel for how you might have a future there. To be a stranger in two worlds would be a lonely life."

"That be mighty kind of ya, Mister Daniel, but no amount of fittin' in with the Black folks is gonna get me to my own Promised Land. Not 'til I figure out some way to get rich."

"You won't get rich on a farm hand's wages, but maybe you could start making furniture once you're on your own and..."

"No, Mister Daniel. You not understandin'. I don't need to get comfortable. I need to get rich!"

"We all want to be rich, Joseph. What has got you so stirred up?"

"Mister Daniel, I got ta get rich so I can hire a abolitionist ta buy Ellie."

After Argus and Joseph had gone to bed, Daniel told Susan of the conversation. "It wouldn't be the first time a young man has pined away for a young girl," he said. "From his description, Ellie sounds like a lovely young woman. He is convinced she would run away with him given a chance, but he fears she has already been given to what sounds like a sinister older man."

"And it wouldn't be the first time love destroyed a man — or a woman. He isn't thinking of do something daft, is he, like trying to return to Tennessee to rescue her?"

"I asked him about that. He said that would waste all the efforts put in by so many good people to rescue him from bondage, said it would be suicide, said he wouldn't get ten miles south of the Ohio River before he was enslaved again.

He got so agitated about his future his language started to slip."

"Maybe you should take him to South Buxton. Maybe there's a girl there who could take his mind off this Ellie that so infatuates him."

"Maybe. Eventually he will have to realize the Tennessee girl is lost to him forever."

"It's amusing he thinks everyone except the queen and us has an accent."

"Didn't she buy a castle in Scotland several years ago? Maybe it's not too late for her to learn to speak properly."

"Maybe."

In the last week in February, Mister Duffy's sleigh pulled into the lane to announce that despite the absence of an experienced midwife, Mrs. Duffy had birthed a healthy girl child. When Susan asked after the condition of the mother, Mister Duffy confessed his concern. "More in bed than out of it, she is. Tired all the time and very weak, poor woman. Falls asleep nursing the babe. That's why I'm here. I was thinking maybe Joseph could do up the chores for a day or two, and I would look after the house so the missus can get some rest."

"We're not sure which farm he's at today," Daniel said. Susan's meaningful glance sent him to hitch her filly to their sleigh while she packed an overnight bag. She did not return for four days.

"The baby is absolutely adorable," she reported. "Mister Duffy wants to name her Bridget after his mother when she's baptized. Just the most perfect little angel you ever laid eyes on."

"And the mother?" Daniel prompted.

"Milk fever. I'm sure it was milk fever. Very painful, very debilitating. I don't think mastitis was very far away. She wanted to refuse the baby her breast, the pain was that severe, but I've seen the same discomfort in a cow right after it freshens, so I suggested she let the baby drain her down. That seemed to work, because she's up and around now. She can't get a good night's rest, what with the baby's demands, but that's normal."

"Did Joseph ever come to help with the chores?"

"The day after I arrived. He had been at the MacPhails', and Mister MacPhail offered to teach him how to play the bagpipes, so he said he was pleased he could help the Duffys. You'll never guess who else showed up."

"The priest."

"No. Abigail Hedley. Yes, the same. She saw Mister Duffy's sleigh go by, then mine, so she put two and two together, and she had Noah drive her over with enough soup, fresh bread, fruit preserves, and shortbread to feed the county. I wonder if her stringent view of Irish papists is mellowing, or if she just wanted to find out what was happening in the township for the next time she holds court."

"Mrs. Hedley does not enjoy an exalted position in your esteem, does she?"

"I have been invited to her tea parties, but I'm too busy for that. Gossip is a game to Abigail, one she plays very well. Still, she went out of her way to help the Duffys. Possibly I have been too harsh. She too found the baby so adorable. Did I mention she is perfect in every detail?"

At the end of February, Daniel, Archie and Joseph took the team and sled down to the lake, where Daniel made a bonfire on the beach. "That's to thaw you out if you fall in," Daniel explained. "Archie's here because this job is best done with more than two. Hard for one to get the other out if he goes into the drink. Three or more is better."

Joseph was taught the slippery art of sawing blocks of ice, hauling the treacherous, dripping rectangular prisms out of the lake with an ice tong without falling in, packing them between strands of straw so they wouldn't refreeze together, and stacking them between layers of sawdust and straw back at the icehouse. He was not yet completely thawed when the exercise was repeated the next day for Archie's icehouse.

The rest of the week, Daniel and Joseph added fresh rows next to the seasoned wood leaning against the south wall of the sugar shack. "For next year," Daniel explained.

Warmer March days made the snow in the bush heavy; Joseph now understood why firewood had been fetched to the house in colder weather. After chores one morning, Daniel emerged from the house with something new to Joseph's eyes. "I hang them on the wall of a closet so the mice won't eat them. Look at the craftsmanship. Superlative, isn't it? I bought these two pair from an Indian pedlar a few years back. I've got the taps, bit, and auger; you bring a hammer, and the pails I've set aside in the storehouse. Not the milk pails. Susan will need those."

"Mister Daniel, I ain't — I have never seen anything like what you're carrying. Are they for some kind of game or somethin'?"

"Snowshoes, Joseph. These are snowshoes, and by the end of the sap run, you will be thankful for them."

The Best-laid Schemes... Gang Aft Agley

"Joseph, it doesn't seem like you've been here over a year, does it?" Susan observed at supper one night as she poured fresh maple syrup over a mound of pancakes. "You have made our life better. I would like to think we have done the same for you."

"Missus Susan, there have been some long days, but I can hardly get my mind to accept it's been a year and a bit since Mister Daniel and Mister Archie rescued me from the fort."

"You're a different person now," Daniel said.

"Indeed I am. I can read, write, carpenter some, farm some. If Old Mose had told me I'd be getting sugar syrup from a tree or practising with my own gun, I would have told him, Old Mose, shake yourself 'cause you has gone completely outta yer head! I wish he could see me now; I wish he could meet you. He wouldn't believe I be livin' under a house with folks that give wine to children and can work this much land with one hired man and no slaves."

"Thinking of this old man, does that make you homesick?" Daniel asked.

"Homesick for labouring for no gratification except Bindle's whip and no future except more of the same?

Nosirree, I ain't homesick, not one little bit, but I do wish I could think of some way to get Ellie out of there."

"Well, there isn't," Susan said. "No way to rescue the thousands of Ellies."

"I suppose I'm a different person too," Daniel mused. "If you had told me I'd have my best friend and my hired man drive off bounty hunters from under my own roof, I would have said, shake yerself 'cause you has gone completely outta yer head!"

Joseph and Susan laughed at his poor imitation and Susan poured them all more coffee. Daniel retrieved a paper and pencil from the sideboard and began to jot down a few notes. "It's time to start listing our priorities," he said. "Joseph and I will buckboard the rest of the seed grain home from Highgate next week, weather permitting. Once that's done, Susan, why don't we traipse down to Chatham and check on when the new machinery will be delivered. I don't want to see the five heifers and the young bull I bought until the back pasture can support them. We have no experience with how much Herefords eat, but I have no intention of their present herdsman driving them over too early just so our grain gets eaten instead of his. You could ride Vicky to check fences. Do you both good. There's no call to supply the neighbours with free beef."

The new plough, seed drill, and reaper arrived at the end of the month. Daniel anticipated a later planting date due to a heavier than average snowpack, but the soil was turned, harrowed, and seeded in half the normal field time, thanks to the new technology,. Purchasing more seed had proved to be a wise decision. Out of curiosity, he hooked Jacob and Jessie to the reaper and wheeled them up the lane and back just to see how this revolutionary contraption worked. All was fine until he pushed the lever that activated the blade. Jacob laid his ears back and balked at the new snick-snick-snick-snick-snick sound, so of course Jessie found it objectionable as well. The horses gradually learned to tolerate the reaper when Daniel put the blade in action, immediately eased off, then put it in gear again, eased off and so on. "Better to familiarize the horses with it now," he said, "than when the wheat is in full head and rain is on the way."

One May evening, just after Susan had fired up the coal oil lamp and remarked on how long the days were getting, they heard horses in the lane. The men set down what they were reading on the kitchen table and were about to reach for their firearms when Daniel said, "Hold on. Argus isn't making a fuss. Must be neighbours."

Susan opened the door in response to Archie Taylor's familiar knock. "We didn't expect you at this hour, Archie," Daniel said. "Is Catherine okay?"

"Catherine is fine, thank you for asking. Actually, I brought someone other than Catherine with me to share your hospitality. Don't fret, he's spending the night with us."

"Any friend of yours is a friend of mine," Daniel said.

"He's a friend of yours as well," Archie grinned, and stepped aside so Major Emmett could enter.

Susan regained composure first. "Come in, come in, come in," she insisted. "Tea or coffee? There may be some cake left if Daniel..."

"Tea would suit me fine," Emmett said, hanging his coat on a hook behind the door and taking a seat at the table. "I find coffee disturbs my sleep if I imbibe too late."

Archie pulled up a chair as well, and said, "Daniel, do I need to offer you a chair in your own kitchen? The good major is here on official business."

"Quite a surprise!" Daniel exclaimed when he regained his voice.

Befitting one who is accustomed to authority, the major took control of the conversation immediately, asked after everyone's health, chatted with Joseph about his life since the fort, and generally made himself the congenial visitor. When Joseph excused himself to go to bed, the major requested that he stay. When all had tea and cake in front of them, he began.

"Although Mister Taylor has been given a brief preview of what I have to communicate, I have saved the details for this assembly. You will notice I am not in uniform. That is because I am no longer Major Emmett. I have resigned my commission. I will be travelling in the United States for several weeks..."

He paused to take a sip of tea,

"And you are coming with me."

Part Seven

ON HER MAJESTY'S SECRET SERVICE

Emmett Explains

The recent major stopped talking to enjoy his cake. No one spoke, all waiting in shock for him to explain his thunderbolt. When the cake was finished, his teacup replenished, and his chair pushed back from the table, the thin, red-haired young man began a monologue.

"Mrs. Cameron, that was most enjoyable. I should not have indulged, considering how I attacked the wonderful repast Mrs. Taylor provided at supper. Still a growing boy and all that... Well, I shall explain the plan and how you fit in. You understand this is hush-hush, of course.

Some bigwig back home has woken up to appreciate that the machinations south of us will undoubtedly have repercussions. Lines of cleavage in the republic may result in war between the states. Questions arise. How soon could this happen? Would a northern army, predictably the speedy winner of such a conflict, wheel its victorious armies northward to seize Her Majesty's colonies in fulfillment of the Manifest Destiny chimera? Will Mister Buchanan, their latest king, think to invade us to divert attention from domestic issues? Nothing so re-focuses public opinion as a convenient war.

My mission is to ignore the official rhetoric and travel south of the border, talk with the populace, get a feel for what the common man thinks, discover if he believes a war is coming, how soon, and his level of enthusiasm for it. His Excellency's instruction was quite explicit: 'Put an ear to the ground to detect the hum of future strife.' All very unscientific, but one can learn much from listening, so I'm told. Upon my return, I shall share my findings with the governor general, who will pass them on to Westminster.

That is why I was required to resign my commission. If I travelled in uniform, no one would talk with the candour we require. If I travel out of uniform but with my commission, I could be shot as a spy, which would inconvenience me and limit my usefulness. The understanding is that I will carry out my interrogations as an interested private citizen. However, upon my return, I will assume an officer's commission once again, but with a cash honorarium and possibly a higher rank as a reward for my services. That would no doubt please my parents, who will obtain a good return on their investment, for it was they who purchased my initial rank as a birthday present upon my fifteenth."

He paused as if waiting for comment. Every eye was on him, and no one ventured a word.

"I intend to zigzag about, into a southern state or two as well as the north, but my role must be above suspicion or the common sort will not confide in me. So... I shall be the manservant of one of you gentlemen, Mister Taylor or Mister Cameron, and Joseph will be believable as the personal servant of the other. Ostensibly, your reason for travelling is to sell cattle. As cattle traders, you will be of particular interest to those who believe a civil war is inevitable and wish to be in a position to profit from it. They will have a deeper interest in its genesis."

He leaned back in his chair, quite proud of his presentation. "You can see I've given this a great deal of thought. Oh, and I should mention, expenses will be covered."

There was a very long pause. Daniel broke the strained silence first. "Major... Mister... Emmett, it won't work. It just won't work."

Emmett looked pained, as if someone had accused him of cheating at cards. "Of course it will work. Whyever not, if everyone acts his part?"

"First, both Archie and I have farms that need us. We can't just drop everything and go off on a bogus cattle trading expedition. Second, you have an unmistakable English accent. That, along with a certain manner, possibly the result of the habit of command or, dare I say, class consciousness, would make you unbelievable as a servant."

"The habit of command? A certain manner? Mister Cameron, whatever do you mean by 'a certain manner'?"

Susan answered for Daniel. "The word my husband is looking for is imperious. Your manner is imperious. A sense of authority emanates from you naturally. Don't misunderstand me, Major Emmett. That is a most desirable virtue in a military commander. Less so in a servant. I simply cannot picture you taking brusque instructions from your employer with the necessary meek and subservient demeanour."

"Were you thinking of the wives coming along as party to this ruse?" Daniel asked. "I doubt wives normally tag along on business trips."

Emmett began to sputter. "Well, yes, I did... I did consider the womenfolk would afford good cover for our little act... Whether that is normal..."

"And why did you think Joseph would ever wish to return to where he might be re-enslaved?"

Emmett was on surer ground with his answer. "Mister Taylor informed me Joseph has made tremendous strides learning how to speak English as it ought to be spoken, also that he is now literate. Frankly, I hope to use Joseph's knowledge of the cultural topography. In short, he has been there and we have not. As for any danger of being taken once again into bondage, what are the odds that anyone would recognize him in the role of a gentleman's servant, a servant who speaks proper English?"

Susan said, "Major or Mister Emmett, whatever your title of address, your plan has merit, but it requires serious modification."

Daniel interrupted. "Susan, you cannot seriously entertain the idea we can be involved in this harebrained scheme in any way, shape or form!"

"We, no. You, why not? Does not this conversation remind you of another we had some time ago? The reasons remain valid: a break from the farm, your need for adventure, an opportunity to discover the direction in which that republic I abhor so much is moving. What Mister Emmett is offering is no less than an opportunity to do our patriotic duty. Did I not manage before? And this time, the months between seed time and harvest, I have the Chalmers boy. Let the new cattle turn the grass directly to beef. If we have fewer milk cows there is less need for winter hay; we can deal with that when you return. The only obstacle I can see is that Catherine would have no one to help if Archie were to go with you."

"My seeding is done. Catherine might relish a break from me, but I wouldn't consider leaving if I couldn't persuade Paul Desmond to help in an emergency, or Noah Hedley."

"Archie, you can't possibly be thinking of taking Major Emmett up on his offer!" Daniel exclaimed. "It's madness!"

"Oh, to be sure. In its present form. But what an opportunity, Daniel. What excitement! Just think of it! Travelling with a manservant, expenses paid..."

"Madness?" Emmett exclaimed. "Surely you can not mean that! My plan is ironclad — subject to you all playing your parts. I heard 'modifications'. How can you possibly make it better?"

Daniel started counting on his fingers. "First, what do Archie and I know about selling cattle? I just bought six Herefords and probably paid too much for them. I wouldn't have known the breed had a predisposition to vaginal prolapse if Joseph had not told me. An experienced cattle trader would expose me as a fraud in two minutes. Second..."

"The cattle you are selling are fictitious," Emmett interrupted. "You and Archie would tell prospective buyers you are exploring opportunities in the event a war breaks out. Establish a ridiculously high price. Everyone understands greed — it's as universal as music and violence. We'll make up bogus business cards. See... I've thought this through."

"Second," Daniel continued, "you may think Joseph can be our guide in certain matters, understanding the language possibly, but I have no intention of putting him in mortal danger all because I'm off on some ridiculous caper designed by, with all due respect, Major, a young man who has seen little of life outside the army. Third, you would be the weak link for reasons my wife has pointed out. Fourth…"

Emmett held up a hand to prevent further elucidation. "I take your points. Indeed, I take them rather too well. Please give me a moment or two to examine your objections."

Susan took this hiatus to steep more tea. Joseph, Archie, and Daniel looked at one another in silence. With elbows on the table and his head in his hands, Emmett appeared the personification of despair. As Susan refilled cups, the young man righted himself, sighed, and resumed the discussion.

"Mister Cameron, I shall imitate your habit of numbering the points you wish to make. First, the mission is important. Second, it must succeed. Third, funds have been provided to advance its progress. Fourth, you are unanimous in believing I am unable to pass as a servant. You see what I do not. What then would you suggest?"

"Why not pose, not as someone of the lower classes, but someone higher up?" Archie asked. "The certain manner already mentioned is more suitable to, let's say, an aristocrat or a member of the landed gentry. Couldn't you be Lord Emmett or Viscount Emmett or something like that?"

"You are looking for investment opportunities, and that is why you are interested in whether and when there will be a war," Susan added.

"Brilliant, that last part," Emmett said. "However, to claim aristocratic status is preposterous. Unthinkable. Just not done, you see."

"Where were you born?" Susan asked.

"Little to do with anything, but Shropshire. Why do you ask?"

"Then travel as Sir Shropshire Emmett. If there is no such person, what is the harm? Americans are easily dazzled by class snobbery — and money."

"That word 'snobbery' suggests a plebeian jealousy, but yes, Mrs. Cameron, Sir Shropshire Emmett might do no harm." Sir Shropshire Emmett drummed the fingers of his right hand on the table. "This persona I am to be would not travel without some sort of valet or servant. Totally out of character." He turned to Joseph. "Mister Cameron's reservations concerning your participation have merit, but should you join in this endeavour, you would round out the *dramatis personae* admirably. My appeal for your assistance comes with an offer of double the monetary reward you presently receive from Mister Cameron."

Joseph examined the pattern on his teacup. Seconds went by, then a minute. Finally, he placed the cup back on its saucer, half turned to the young man, and said, "Major, mister, sir, I do not know what *dramatis personae*" mean. If I understand you correctly, your job is to help the Britishers best be ready in case the Americans decide to take over."

"That puts it in its simplest form," Emmett replied.

"If the Britishers lose, this all becomes the United States?"

"Heaven forbid, but yes."

"And in the United States the law says a runaway slave who is caught is to be returned to its owner?"

"Yes, the *Fugitive Slave Act* is contentious and not uniformly enforced, but yes, to my knowledge that law has not been repealed."

"So if I help you, I be helping the Britishers keep the Americans out if there be a war."

"Yes. Knowledge is power. We must be prepared for any eventuality, so yes, you would be helping us be prepared in case there is an invasion."

"Major Emmett, I tremble in my very soul when I think of going back into bondage, so I got conditions before I agrees ta help."

"And they would be...?"

"No disrespect sir, but you are ignorant of how easy it would be for a slave trader or a bounty hunter to snatch me away. I'd be gone, and what could you do about it? So, I don't want to have any part in this expedition unless I be safe, and that means Mister Daniel and Mister Archie come along. Then I got three ta be a manservant to, and that means three times more work, and I don't know exactly what a manservant does other than carry bags and shine boots, but I also got three looking out for me and knowing where I is — where I am all the time."

"Incredible! The Empire loses its North American colonies all because Daniel Cameron refuses to go gallivanting," Daniel muttered.

"Shush!" Susan whispered. "This is important."

"That makes perfect sense," Emmett said. "Anything else?"

"Yes. Do you know where you will be going so you can talk to all these common folk?"

"I thought of striking a balance between cities and the countryside, possibly frequenting the occasional public house, chatting with a spectrum of society on a train, nothing too specific. I definitely wish to obtain the feminine point-of-view. It is a fact men are influenced by their womenfolk. Why do you ask?"

"Could we retrace the path I took, more or less, from Lonnegan's plantation to the border? That would give you the balance you seek, and it would take you into slave states."

Daniel interrupted. "Joseph, I can see where you are headed in this conversation. No! Absolutely not! We cannot rescue your Ellie, and you might as well get the idea out of your head right now! Even getting near your previous plantation would place you in indescribable danger."

Emmett held up a forefinger to indicate he would pronounce judgment on the idea. "The route might be ideal. Ohio and Kentucky, a mixed bag of opinions. Any state below the Mason-Dixon Line, Tennessee for example, gives us exposure to the Southern point-of-view. As for this girl, though, that might be totally out of the question."

"I want to add my two pence worth," Archie said. "Notice Daniel said, 'we' cannot rescue your Ellie. 'We' means he is already thinking of himself as part of the expedition. Major Emmett, if you can make this work, I want to be involved. As for Ellie, at least we could find out what her owner would sell her for, and possibly give Joseph some hope she isn't lost to him forever."

He turned to his friend. "Come on, Daniel. I'll be damned if I'm left out. We'll never get another chance like this."

"You would need to take great care when you got near the Lonnegan plantation," Susan said.

"Good God! Am I to be dragooned into this venture by my wife, my best friend, my hired man?" Daniel exclaimed.

"No one is dragooning anyone," Emmett said. "I understand there are valid reasons for Mrs. Taylor and Mrs. Cameron to remain at home, and if others choose not to accompany me, I shall go on my own."

"Horses," Joseph said, looking at the major.

"I beg your pardon. Did you say 'horses'?"

"Horses. Not cattle, horses. Mister Daniel and Mister Archie should sell horses. Deacon, he was a smart businessman. He was banking on a war and the need for beef. Others thinking like him, he said, a lot in Ohio, he said. So what else do an army need? Horses. Can't ever have too many. And Mister Cameron may not be an expert cattle man, but he got a sure eye for a good horse. That filly he bought Missus Susan, you won't find one to beat that filly."

"Victoria is a purebred Canadian horse, and Joseph is absolutely correct when he says my husband knows a good horse when he sees it," Susan confirmed.

"This Canadian horse, are we talking about a separate breed?" Emmett asked.

"Yes, created from stock brought over from France originally, lots more in Canada East than here, unfortunately," Daniel replied.

"What makes it special? Could we fool the Americans into thinking they might want some?"

"We wouldn't need to fool anyone. And we're just testing the waters to see if there's a market, remember?"

"There's that 'we' again," Archie whispered to Susan. "He's hooked."

"The Canadian horse is very versatile," Daniel continued. "That's what makes it special. It jumps, it pulls, it has a pleasing gait for its rider, it looks stylish. Its breeders call it The Little Iron Horse. It may be the perfect horse for the military in North America because it's intelligent, willing to work, usually about fourteen or fifteen hands, but robust, an efficient eater..."

"I'm sold already!" Emmett exclaimed, and slapped the table. "Horse traders you are!"

"Isn't trying to sell horses in Kentucky something like selling ice to Eskimos?" Archie asked.

"It won't matter. War requires horses, horses, and more horses. Kentucky will supply what it has in the event of war, but will that be to the South or the North? Smart money always invests in future conflicts. We'll push the equine rather than the bovine. Mister Taylor, if it's not too presumptuous, I propose we sleep on this and meet tomorrow night at your house to iron out details, embellish our ideas, polish our approach…"

As Emmett and Archie headed out the door, Daniel said, "I have not committed to anything."

No one paid him the slightest attention.

Cameron and Taylor: Horse Traders

After breakfast the following morning, Joseph walked to the Taylors' to help Archie repair some fencing. Throughout the day, the Camerons avoided any allusion to the previous evening's discussion, each waiting for the other to broach what threatened to be a contentious topic. It was when Vicky pulled the gig out of their lane on the way to the Taylors' that Susan began, dominated, and terminated the conversation.

"What I have to say is a repetition of a previous conversation, but I would appreciate it if you did not interrupt until I have finished. Daniel, I understand your concerns about me and the farm if you go away. My heart knows I wish to farm on this land. You may wish to farm or be a carpenter or something else, but your present restless spirit needs nourishment. Don't miss out on this opportunity to serve our country with your best friend. Archie needs this as much as you do. Amherstburg whetted your appetites for adventure in a bigger world. What would it serve if you moped about for the rest of our lives wondering what might have been? Go, stay away as long as you are needed, and be safe. But you must go until you know what you want and where you fit. Otherwise, it will be me who spends the rest of her life wondering if you married the girl next door for the sake of convenience. Daniel, you can have security or you can have adventure, but you can't have both. I will provide the security you can come home to. If you were gone a year I would worry, but I would understand. You insult me if you think I cannot maintain the farm on my own. I am not going to starve to death." She flicked the reins to have Vicky break into a trot. "I'm glad we got that settled."

"Paul said his fields are in, insisted all Catherine needed to do was ask and he would help where needed," Archie informed the group once they were seated around the Taylors' kitchen table. "If the Chalmers boy helps Susan, that should free Daniel and me for four or five weeks or more."

"We will require cards of introduction," Emmett said. "For myself, I was thinking of something non-committal yet sophisticated, possibly a simple 'Shropshire Emmett, Esquire', underlined by flowing scroll-work. In gold, naturally. Your cards should be of a more plain sort, befitting your station."

"See," Susan interrupted. "There's that class consciousness again. That 'befitting your station' doesn't sit well here and will rankle even more south of the border."

"I fail to see..." Emmett began in a condescending voice, but Catherine jumped in to help her friend.

"That's just it. You are a foreign transplant and fail to see how all that has been left behind. There is a more egalitarian tone in North America. If that 'befitting your station' talk reinforces the image of the snobbish Englishman you are trying to convey, fine, but if it's overdone, it will draw unwelcome attention to the four of you."

Unaccustomed to being rebuffed, Emmett was silent for a long moment. Finally, in a mollified voice, he said, "There's that word 'snobbish' again. Ladies, this is why we are convening, to anticipate any impediments to the success of our mission. I appreciate your point about achieving a balance in the role." He turned to Daniel. "You have had time to ponder your commitment, Mister Cameron. I go alone if necessary. More of a lark with the rest of you, though. I daresay more chance of success as well. Are you in or out?"

Daniel forced a wry laugh. "My best friend craves adventure, my wife packs me off swaddled in a patriot's flag, and my hired man harbours fantastical notions of somehow rescuing the love of his life. If this expedition results in misadventure, you five are witness that I feel more volunteered than volunteer. Very well, I admit it. I cannot permit Archie to go off on this escapade without me, I see the military necessity of Major Emmett's mission, and if I am not along, I worry Joseph may do something incredibly ill-advised to free this girl, Ellie. So... I am in." He received a short round of applause from the others.

Emmett turned to Joseph. "I too see you as a possible weak link. What happens if you inadvertently forget yourself and begin to speak... to talk like... to...?"

"To speak Southern Black?" Susan prompted.

"Exactly. Southern Black could..."

"Could get me returned to Master Lonnegan and get me hanged," Joseph said, finishing Emmett's sentence for him. "You will be Sir Emmett and Misters Taylor and Cameron, and I will shine your shoes and carry your luggage and be the most inconspicus servant anyone could wish for. For me to try and find an abolitionist to buy or steal Ellie would be ridiculous, so I must rely upon the three of you to make discreet inquiries if an opportunity presents itself." He half-turned to face her and said, "Missus Susan, this is how I will talk, slowly and precisely, in my very best Queen's English? Will it pass for a Britisher?"

Susan laughed. "Not by a long shot. The word is inconspicuous, not inconspicus. To us, you still have a pronounced accent, but the way you structure your sentences may fool some Americans. I would have said, 'This is how I shall talk.' My advice is, say as little as possible. Appear to know, nod, and say 'hmmm' rather than construct a reply. Much can be said with silence." The others nodded agreement.

"It must appear we have fallen into each other's travelling company by happen-chance, so I suggest we meet in Detroit, Monday mid-day next," Emmett said. "I shall leave exact rendezvous information at your Windsor hotel. My horse is well rested, so I shall dash off at first light." He rose from the table and shook hands with Archie and Daniel to indicate the meeting was terminated.

The next two days were consumed with luggage packing and attending to everything that would contribute to making farm work as easy as possible for the women. Paul Desmond dropped them off at the train station, encumbered as usual by more food than they could hope to consume in two days. At the hotel, Joseph was told there was no accommodation for coloured folk, but he was welcome to bed down at the nearby livery; the desk clerk thought to arrange for a breakfast to be delivered. Daniel balked at the price demanded for a boat ride across the river to Detroit until he saw the current. On the far shore, a carriage waiting for hire took them to the address Emmett had left for them, a tavern near the waterfront.

Joseph took a chair by the door. They found Emmett sitting disconsolately in a corner booth, poking at a pork pie and nursing a beer. The reason for his forlorn demeanour was soon confessed. "While I was retrieving a beer, I attempted to engage some gentlemen at the bar in conversation about the possibility of a war. My beginning here has not been propitious. My manner of speaking drew scorn, and the barkeep suggested I might be a Nancy, to everyone's great merriment. To be honest, I did not foresee my mission starting out with such a cock-up."

"In the military, you are accustomed to the skeleton of an enterprise first, then you flesh it out with details," Daniel explained. "In the greater society, with strangers, one engages in lighthearted conversation about mundane topics such as the weather before one bores into the heart of serious issues."

"Feathers first, then the meat of the bird," Archie said. "This is what we meant by 'a certain manner.' First day, and you have already drawn unwelcome attention to yourself, you have exposed what information you seek, and you are sitting in a public house referring to your mission."

"Gentlemen, you have hit the mark as always. There are rooms reserved for us at an establishment south of Detroit. I suggest you procure some nourishment before we rent a conveyance. We shall spend the evening establishing our route, our level of acquaintance, and so on."

By the end of supper at a modest hotel, Emmett was in a less self-recriminatory frame of mind. He produced maps of the states he planned to visit, and while Joseph blackened leather boots and organized clothes for the following day, he traced a back-and-forth route from Toledo to Cincinnati. Daniel and Archie suggested more train, less horse, and the conviviality of taverns in order to survey public opinion, and since Joseph's clandestine journeys north from Columbus had been usually at night and hidden from view, he was of no help at all.

"I had some business cards printed for you. We must be consistent in our story. A substantial inheritance was bequeathed by my only relative, an eccentric uncle, on the occasion of his passing. I first made your acquaintance at a tavern in Detroit as I was setting out to search for investment opportunities in America. As we seemed to be congenial companions, I thought I might tag along as you plumbed the waters in search of markets for Canadian horses in the event of war. However, you must never refer to me as 'major' under any circumstance."

Daniel and Archie nodded agreement. Sir Shropshire Emmett turned to Joseph. "We need to discuss the protocol for travelling with a Black servant, here and in the slave states, if we intend to permit no harm to befall you."

"The farther we go south, the more distance 'tween master an' servant or master an' slave. It be — it's complicated. Massa Lonnegan often send Cicero to deliver business documents for him, negotiate if he can get a better price for cotton in Natchez or N'Orleans, find out the price of shipping, that sort of thing. When Massa Lonnegan do — does business in person, Cicero wait at the door, listenin' but not sayin' nothin'. But if a field hand so much as put a toe off da plantation without permission, you gonna hear the whip, no doubt about it. So it all depend on…"

"Your Queen's English is slipping. Are you nervous about your role in this venture now that we're across the border? Are you reconsidering your commitment?" Daniel asked.

"Yes, Mister Daniel, for sure I am nervous and anxious and scared —but not so much I can't carry on. As long as I can keep my mouth shut, and as long as one of you is nearby to vouch that I am your servant, then... That's the problem. Lots of places won't let Black folk stay with the white folk. Same as Canada West. I'll be sent to a stable or somewheres, so you won't know when I've been snatched. Even on a train, I may have to ride with the baggage or in a cattle car. You can bet the Queen's English gonna suffer then, when I'm alone."

"Where did they tell you you could sleep tonight?" Archie asked.

"Fewer problems this far north. I'll sleep outside your room, across the door. That way, nobody can get to you without steppin' on me. Nobody gonna question a Black servant sleepin' outside a door."

Emmett cut the letterhead from a piece of hotel stationery and began to write. He handed the finished copy to Joseph and said, "Is there anything I should add before Daniel and Archie sign this?"

Joseph read out loud. "To Whom It May Concern. The bearer, Joseph of Morpeth, Canada West, formerly Upper Canada, is a British Subject and a Free Man acting in the capacity of Servant to Mess'rs Daniel Cameron and Archibald Taylor, Businessmen, Purveyors of Fine Equine Stock."

Eyes moistening, Joseph handed the paper to Daniel, who passed it to Archie for his signature as well.

Joseph returned to the boots and the others to their plans.

"What is that arrow in the corner of each map?" Daniel asked.

"Good God!" Emmett exclaimed, slapping his forehead. "That's a British Ordnance stamp indicating the item has been approved for official government use. You may have seen the arrow in cannon, usually above the touch hole. Well done, Daniel. That might have given our little game away to an alert observer. I shall cut the borders off the maps and burn them before we retire."

No one slept particularly well that night, especially Joseph, who was disturbed by other guests stumbling to and from a shared water closet at the end of the hall. Emmett had secured more expensive rooms serviced by a chambermaid, so his own people were not among the traffic. After a hearty breakfast, they set off in a hire for the waterfront, where a sloop was waiting to carry them to Toledo and what Emmett claimed would be a more luxurious hotel.

Shortly after casting off, the crew of two set the sails to take advantage of a following wind and relaxed at their stations. The skipper identified for Archie the various types of ships encountered, explained the virtues of his sloop over a cutter, and pointed out the subtle differences between a yawl and a ketch. For fifteen minutes, he let a grinning Archie work the wheel to reward his interest in nautical matters. Emmett chatted with first the co-owner deckhand and later the skipper about the fickle weather at this end of the lake, the average sailing time from Detroit to Toledo, and if a war broke out between the states, how it might impact shipping on the lakes. Daniel studied the horizon in an attempt to retain his breakfast.

A Letter to Aeneas

Dear Pa. I am in Michigan. Little brother is with me but he ain't capable of much just yet. He has bin recooperating at a rundown inn across the border. He sure got himself shot up some. There ain't no hope the left eye will work agin. That side from his nose to the top of his head looks like somebody held his face inta a fire. I cant see how he can be of much use in the business for awhile after getting himself shot all to hell like that. Looks like I'm the only good-looking one in the family now. Ha Ha I got Burton across to. Wasnt easy. The docter in that little shithole Ridge town had pawned him off on a biblethumping dogooder. He is in a hell of a situation to. He shits himself on a reglar bases and smells like a pisspot all the time. Didnt recognize me and can not remember any thing before today. You know how a punkin can grow lopsided like thats what Burtons head is a lopsided punkin. What do you want me to do with him. Am getting low on money specialy after paying little brothers bill. There aint no chance he'll put us in a aukword position if any one poking round finds him specialy now that he's in the good ole USA. I aint forgot about the main prize. Sniffed around the talbot line near where Burton found our runner holed up. Theres a sweet little gal teaching school who told me all I wanted to know. I told her I wanted to pay up some money I owed mister Cameron and could she tell me were he lives she says sure but you wont find him or his darkie hired man at home cause theyve disappeard and whats curious is his best friend has disappeard to. Name of Taylor. She says her young man is helping out at his farm till he gets back and her young man reckons their disappearins got something to do with mister L's runaway so you tell me what the hell is going on. I sent mesagges to our people at Detroit and Toledo and the captain to keep an eye out for any thing suspistious. Little brothers already got a eye out. Ha ha. Get it. Tell me what you want done with Burton. I figure little brother can travel in a week once he finishes scabbin' up. Your loving son W.

The Team Practises

The winds that deposited them in Toledo were more benevolent than their surly hotelier. "I thought you said we would bide in more comfort tonight," Daniel remarked, once they had been shown to their stale, dowdy rooms by a bellhop who impatiently opened and closed his palm for a tip. "Why should he expect a nickel from me when Joseph is getting paid to be the servant?"

"When in Rome," Emmett said, then added, "This is the last of the arrangements set up by our friends this side of the border. After tonight we shall be on our own, so I have no doubt we will sniff out finer establishments more befitting a young gentleman who has come into a sizeable inheritance."

"By 'friends', do you mean spies?" Archie asked.

"By friends I mean friends."

Archie did not question the distinction.

Joseph took his supper seated outside the door, the others in the smoke-filled bar. Emmett was about to speak to an overly-whiskered gentleman about the accuracy of his expectorations at a nearby spittoon when Daniel placed a warning hand on his arm. Nodding in the direction of a mass of regulars, he quietly observed, "Possibly the friend who recommended this hotel was more canny than we supposed. What do you notice about our fellow drinkers, including the old geezer who can't spit straight?"

"Workmen. Ordinary chaps. Why?"

"Judging from their work caps, I would wager there is a high proportion of navvies. Here's your chance to interview the common man, Emmett, and possibly learn about recent railway construction. A bit off topic for our purposes, but information that would be welcomed by our side. Does our budget include drinks for the house?"

"Of course it does — within reason. When we run low, my signature at a state bank will draw more. I told you, this is a serious enterprise. The governor general will provide; he did not get his appointment just from knowing the right people."

"Then this is the perfect spot to practise. Let the crowd enjoy their pints while we finish our supper," Archie said. "Daniel and I will start a conversation if we can. You follow our lead."

That evening they established a pattern and polished it each day. Rather than dine at their hotel among a few guests, evenings found them in a gregarious tavern where they could mingle among a greater number of going and coming patrons, each more or less uninhibited by alcohol. Daniel and Archie would amiably approach a likely prospect or small group, remark on the weather, introduce themselves as purveyors of quality Canadian horses, ask advice about the optimum route for the next day, and casually mention they were travelling in the company of a young man searching for sound investments. If he was not already in a conversation, Emmett would be signalled over. He would gush a hand-pumping hail-fellow-well-met-jolly-good-so-pleased greeting and order a round for his new-found acquaintances. Alcohol and conviviality invariably widened the circle of participants. Eventually, they would return the topic of the moment to the purposes of their respective motives for travelling and what did everyone think about the probability of a war between the states. Insights, opinions, points-of-view, conjectures, and convictions invariably coalesced into agreements, reasoned disagreements, heated arguments, apoplectic shout-downs, and on one occasion, a fist fight.

From their discussion with the navvies, they discovered Ohio's rail network was comprised of several fledgling railroads and more companies waiting in the wings. This suited Emmett. They would board for half day excursions, then angle back to approximate a north to south progression. On trains, they focused on more affluent travellers to balance their research in the taverns. At first, they talked to many who shared Yankee anti-slavery views, but farther south, these were outnumbered by pro-South Butternuts.

If there was already a Black person in an establishment, Joseph accompanied his employers. If, when the four entered, a silence fell upon the room, Joseph would take his post outside the door. In some hotels and on trains, signs indicated the "Coloured" and "Negro" sections. In keeping with his identity of free British subject, Joseph was particularly mindful of the Queen's English in those areas when he asked fellow Blacks to foretell the future, and duly reported their pessimism back to Emmett.

Joseph had seen a portion of the bustling city before, and Emmett had been to London, but a metropolis the size and grandeur of Cincinnati was a new experience for Daniel and Archie. Agape, heads swivelling, they marvelled at the height of buildings and the ubiquitous crowds. Daniel was aghast at the price Emmett paid for rooms for two nights at an upscale hotel near the Ohio River. "It's not you paying the piper," Archie reminded him. "Dinna fash yersel."

Before supper, Emmett the mission superintendent left to buy steamboat tickets and Emmett the boy returned with a walnut handled revolver in a wooden case. "As I passed a gunsmith's shop, it occurred to me we should have some ordnance in case of emergency," he said, aiming the firearm at objects around the room. "Five shots, self cocking, rotating cylinder, cap and ball. It comes with a cleaning brush, and I also had the smith throw in fifty caps and cartridges at a penny apiece. He maintains this is the latest design, an import, he said, made by Adams. I liked the solid weight and balance of a navy revolver as well, but I was quite taken with this little beauty, although she's got a hefty feel to her. Should be hefty for a forty-four. I bought this holster too. If you leave the smaller strap on, it slips over your shoulder and under your arm so one can wear it under a jacket. Unbuckle the strap and it can be worn on the waist over a belt. Quite clever, eh what? I'll leave it in my bag so as not to draw attention."

The following day, after sending a breakfast to Joseph in the basement, Daniel and Archie started their morning meal while waiting for Emmett. "A kid with a new toy," Archie said. "He's probably late coming down because he's pretending to shoot buffalo or Russians."

"I hope it stays a toy," Daniel replied. "Using it will only draw attention to us. We must give the boy credit, though. It's a practical purchase, and I admit I myself might have drawn up sharp at a gunsmith's shop. Ironic that it's Joseph who needs it most, yet he's the one who would never be armed."

"Emmett is a remarkable young man," Archie said. "He's quick-witted, never hesitates, just assumes he knows what to do and charges ahead. I can't see myself doing what he's doing when I was his age a few years ago."

"It's called confidence. I suspect he was born with the habit of command, just as some are born with the habit of unquestioning obedience."

Emmett, face raw from inexperienced shaving, joined them. He fanned four steamship tickets out on the table. "Early breakfast tomorrow. Need to be at the pier by nine. Sternwheeler. Large boat. Draws two fathoms almost. She'll stop at Louisville long enough to exchange passengers and freight, then we're off to Paducah, where we disembark. Won't take long — we're with the current. I thought we might just drift some, but the ticket agent said no, she must always have a head of steam to manoeuvre."

They spent the day exploring the city, chatting with receptive strangers, offering to sell imaginary horses, wondering aloud if river steamboats were lucrative investments. Joseph fretted that Emmett might have purchased tickets for the boat on which he had worked his upriver passage, but this one was twice its size. A wave of apprehension hit as the Ohio River pulled them away from the wharf and carried him closer to his previous life. When they discovered servants were expected to wait on employers in their staterooms, he felt more comfortable.

The days were consumed in subtle but probing conversations. The consensus seemed to be that until the North refused to honour the *Fugitive Slave Law*, the South held out some hope its economy and way-of-life could be maintained. Most believed the North underappreciated the

Southern conviction that slaves were property protected by law, and the South underappreciated the indifference of all but a minority in the North.

Only one, a talkative cattleman who boarded at Louisville, seemed to think war was inevitable. When Emmett exchanged pleasantries while lingering over breakfast coffee, he sat down at his table uninvited, introduced himself as Walter Smale from "a frog's jump upstream, but north of the river," and when Emmett revealed he was second guessing himself about investing in a fragile nation, Smale claimed he understood and could give forty reasons why a war between the states would erupt soon.

Later, as they leaned on the rail to watch the scenery float by and with Joseph waiting in attendance, Emmett recounted the conversation for the benefit of the others. "As he extolled his analysis, I found his logic seductive. Mister Smale has obviously followed the drama of his country's tensions with scrupulous attention, and seems utterly convinced that it will only require one incident to spark a conflagration. He told me with some dismay he is not prepared for it, and when I requested elucidation, he confessed he and others in his area have suffered losses to the herds they were building up in order to cash in when war creates a demand for beef."

Daniel motioned for Joseph to join them at the rail. "That sounds familiar. Didn't the man you worked for at a sawmill plan to get into cattle for the same reason?"

"The Deacon? Yes, Mister Daniel, that was Deacon's thinking too."

"At dinner we should seek out Mister Smale, find out more," Emmett said, addressing the riverbank. "This smacks of preplanned war profiteering. Even general information about railways or the food supply in the northern states will be welcomed by our people who evaluate these things."

During the afternoon, several of the passengers produced their sidearms and for amusement fired at targets on the bank. Emmett used the opportunity to fire off two dozen rounds without excessive embarrassment and retired to his stateroom to clean his new acquisition.

It took little to persuade the backslapping Mister Smale to join them. Emmett introduced Daniel and Archie as horse traders who, similar to the cattleman, wished to profit from a coming war. "Fortuitous it is that you are in horses, gentlemen. Now if you were in cattle, you would be in despair, that is if you are from up near my way. It is why I am on this boat."

"Despair? Despair is a heavy word," Archie said.

"Blackleg, gentlemen, blackleg. Not just my herd. Every herd in the area. Stay in horses. That's where the money will be."

"I am not acquainted with blackleg. Please educate me," Emmett said.

"I'm certain, the others too, it's not anthrax. Anthrax hasn't hit for a decade or more. Livestock get it from deer, you know. Anthrax kills them all. No gentlemen, this is blackleg. A neighbour says someone nearby brought in a breeding bull from Lebanon and brought the Shakers' curse with it. I've no reason to doubt him. The calves still on the teat are fine, the older cattle too. But any weaned and less than two or three years, they lose energy, become stupefied, get feverish, the joints swell, they go lame — then they're dead. It hits fast. Nope, it's not anthrax, it's blackleg."

"You say blackleg is why you are on this boat?" Daniel prodded.

"Yup. Herd numbers are down, and we need to jack them back up, what with the war coming. I'm scout for a dozen or so. Quite a responsibility, actually. We'll buy some young, healthy, distanced stock, graze them on fresh pasture, separate the herds for a year, maybe two. That's how to beat blackleg — if you believe the old folks."

"Then you're travelling far from home to…"

"Yup. Can't take any chances buying contaminated beasts local. Once I find what we're looking for, we'll ship them on cattle boats upriver and rail them home."

"I am glad we decided not to be in the cattle business," Daniel said knowingly to the others.

After lunch, Joseph approached Daniel and Emmett before the group began to socialize with other passengers. "Mister Daniel, could this be an opportunity to pay back Deacon some? If we could send this man in his direction, maybe…"

"A capital idea, and one I have not considered. What do you think, Emmett?"

"How can we find this Deacon?"

"I don't know. On the run, I never knew where I was exactly and didn't care, so long as I was runnin' north. I did hear Deacon say the wife bought clothes in Mayfield."

"Then we'll tell Mister Smale we have heard a sawmill owner within a day of Mayfield may have breeding stock for sale and has been recommended."

"Thank you, Mister Daniel, Mister Emmett. I owe Deacon a debt."

"What goes around comes around," Daniel said.

"I hope the Americans remember that when they toy with the idea of invading," Emmett muttered.

It was raining the morning they docked in Paducah.

"Emmett's heading out to find us accommodations, so we should shelter from this rain in the first eating establishment we find," Daniel said, as Joseph collected their luggage on the dock. "Then he's off to find an adequate conveyance for an extended time. I'm going to suggest we get the hell out of Paducah as soon as we can. I notice your Queen's English is slipping the farther from home we travel. It wouldn't do to sound too much like the locals if you're a British subject from Canada West."

"Paducah is a dangerous town for me, so I reckon my brain is remindin' my tongue how nervous I am about being here," Joseph said.

"See? Back home you would have said 'I figure' or 'I guess' rather than 'I reckon', which is what the locals would say."

"This is where Deacon sold squared timber for a church," Joseph reminded Daniel. "I got real mixed feelings 'bout this town 'cause Deacon was tempted by the Devil here, but we got an upstream boat that took me to the Promised Land here too. There's people here who have seen me runnin', an' if I get recognized, they won't care about figurin' or reckonin' or anything other than twelve hundred dollars."

Emmett found his companions loitering in a tavern's dining room near the waterfront when he returned. They all enjoyed roast beef riding on a thick slab of bread accompanied by mashed potatoes, everything floating in gravy. Joseph took his meal on a chair beside the door, close enough he could hear Emmett's report.

"I rented two rooms, expensive for the quality of the establishment, but I suppose that's normal for a busy waterway town. Joseph, the proprietor said it's the stable for you, but I insisted that since our servant is tending for three, we wanted him at our beck and call. It required a generous gratuity, but he finally relented, grudgingly, so you may sleep across a doorway. My intention is to chat with the good people of this fair town," he said with a rueful laugh as he regarded water pouring from the eaves, "and tomorrow we will set out dry and early."

"What were you able to find for the next stage of our journey?" Archie asked

"Unfortunately, the establishment would rent no vehicle for an extended time so I had no alternative but to purchase one. It's a canary yellow, large-wheeled phaeton, originally custom made to deliver mail I'm told; the suspension should be adequate, and it's spacious enough for our bags. I secured a commitment that by the time I pick it up after breakfast tomorrow, it will be outfitted with two front facing seats. Back home, we would say it's in the Victoria style, since the rear half has a collapsible leather hood that can be raised in weather such as this. In retrospect, I should have checked the concertina top more carefully; if there are cracks or holes, the rain will find us if it hasn't stopped. For the price, I insisted they throw in four blankets as well."

"Canary yellow? Are you going out of your way to draw attention to us?" Daniel asked.

"Why not? Others will see a wealthy, potentially profligate young man who has just inherited a fortune. We must not deviate from our assigned roles. The colour reminds me of a post-chaise, a 'Yellow Bounder', from my childhood, so that is what I shall name my acquisition. The Yellow Bounder. The horses look on the haggard side of prime, but the phaeton appears solid."

He mopped up the last of his gravy with another slice of bread. "We absolutely must stay in character, or I would have suggested one of you horse traders work the transaction. I know I paid too much, but that cannot be helped if we wish to progress."

The meal over, they slogged through the muddy streets in the rain, clothes heavier every second. Joseph suddenly halted in front of the inn and set down the luggage he was carrying on the boardwalk. "Mister Emmett, I cain't stay here! I recognize dat green door. Deacon and me, this be da place we run from ta take da boat ta Cincinnati. I bin here before."

A Letter From the Ferret

Aeneas;

I am sending this message to the captain first because he will know where to forward it to you as soon as possible.

There is news to our mutual benefit. Lonnegans runaway name of Joseph is in the same town where he gave us the slip when he buggered off with that shyster lumberman before I could round up our people to nab him. I had a close look with a lantern in the stable and this is the same one although I did not recognize him at first never expecting him to ever return here for God's sake. He has added ten pounds so the client will be pleased when we cart him back healthy.

Our friend at The Green Door gave me the heads up so we will need to throw him a bone. A charitable gesture motivates other eyes.

Lonnegans runaway is acting as servant to three travellers. One is a homely red-haired young Englishman who created a scene with our friend the innkeeper, insisting his travelling associates found the inn unacceptable and all would seek lodging elsewhere. While the limey was dripping and squelching mud on the carpet and expecting his money back in full no less, I had a good look from the tap room at our main prize and I am one hundred percent sure this one is Lonnegans. Our friend says he remembers him and that rigid spined timber merchant who absconded with him so that puts the heat to the wax.

I gave our friend the nod and he returned the money for the rooms but not the tip he got for permitting the so-called servant to sleep inside. I had a boy follow them to an inn close to the waterfront and he says the limey booked two rooms for one night so I reckon they're hoping to dry out and head out tomorrow and I will hire a fella I know with time on his hands to follow a few hours behind until we can round up the right help. The runner knows what I look like so I will stay in the background so he won't take off like a scared jackrabbit again.

Regards

To Mayfield and Deacon's Mill

The morning dawned drier than the four individuals who set out south from Paducah. No one had slept well. Clothes were still damp. Daniel's observation that they smelled like wet dogs was accepted as truth rather than an attempt at humour. A hot breakfast and multiple cups of coffee were only partial restoratives of higher spirits, and it did not help that Joseph could not find the road Deacon had used to transport the finished lumber. Emmett did not wish to trumpet their intended route by asking for directions to Mayfield in the town, and it wasn't until they had backtracked from a false lead and Joseph saw the church where Deacon had first brought his squared timbers that the Yellow Bounder was finally turned in the right direction.

The fair weather did not last. For two days, the expedition was troubled by intermittent rain, thunderstorms, mediocre food, and a dearth of inns. Conversations with the locals were invariably short and unproductive. Some waved off the suggestion Kentucky might be unable to provide an adequate supply of horses in wartime, while others maintained that by the time horses from British North America were shipped, the war would be over. Not one had heard of the virtues of the Canadian Horse. No one suggested there would be no war; the debate was over when and what would trigger it, and if Kentucky would jump north or south.

It was of no consequence if Joseph remembered only some of the route. A simple "Is this the road to Mayfield?" gave oncoming travellers an opportunity to share knowledge and advice about road conditions ahead, and road conditions were consistently bad. "Rain first, then the humidity," a local farmer told them. "Best we can do once't the humidity sets up shop is hope for a breezy day." Each night, Daniel and Archie ensured the horses received more than adequate rations, even if it meant a few pennies more for extra oats. By the time they pulled into the modest town of Mayfield, the team was not pretty but was coping well.

The sawmill was three hours south by southwest. Joseph felt less anxiety the farther they journeyed from Paducah, as if the mill were a place of sanctuary. Except for rail fences enclosing dozens of white-faced red cattle where before there had been open, bottom-land meadow, the place was exactly as he remembered it. Pa was toting freshly rinsed lunch dishes to the drying rack on the porch when they arrived in the early afternoon, and Red and Blue were preparing to return to work. Deacon and his wife and children emerged from the house at the sound of their approach, and all seven surrounded the unique, colourful phaeton bringing such unexpected visitors.

"Lordy! Lordy! Lordy!" was all Pa could say. Red and Blue backslapped Joseph half way to the barn, they were so jubilant at seeing him, and Deacon kept exclaiming, "So, you made it after all... You made it after all... Who would have thought?" in disbelief. His wife scurried back inside the house.

It took a full twenty minutes to make the introductions and explain the nature of their horse business and investment investigations. Deacon shooed the children away, said his wife was already "throwing something together" for a late lunch, insisted they stay for supper, and offered the barn for the night's accommodations. Joseph disappeared with Pa and the twins to paddock the team and catch them up on his adventures, and the Deacon, Daniel, Archie, and Emmett conversed on the porch while the newcomers enjoyed their sandwiches.

Deacon was most curious about Joseph's escape, but the others insisted he should tell his story for himself. Daniel and Archie mentioned a cattle buyer from farther east, a Mister Smale, might possibly show up on Joseph's recommendation in an effort to pay his debt. When the visitors apologized for interrupting the Deacon's work, he dismissed their concerns, saying Pa and the twins would have everything under control until the morrow, when they needed to stack an order of black locust timbers that were destined for bridge pilings down toward Dyersburg.

Emmett asked about his burgeoning cattle enterprise. Deacon admitted he had found good stock in Ohio, but the cost of transportation was prohibitive, so he had tracked down animals much closer to home, and on the advice of the cattleman on the boat to Cincinnati. he had purchased from several herds to mix bloodlines. The most difficult part of setting up his operation, Deacon pointed out, was building fences where needed and putting in enough hay. He had purchased two wagon loads from neighbours to get the herd through the winter and had lost no animal. Indeed, the herd had increased by sixty percent and was healthy and thriving. Pa, now the most enthusiastic of them all, had taken on the supervision of newborns.

Before supper, the visitors set up sleeping arrangements. Joseph and Pa planned on sleeping in the twins' quarters to free up the second living area for the others. Daniel had just finished stuffing a doubled-over rectangle of canvas with straw when Joseph timidly approached and asked if he could speak to him about a delicate matter. Archie and Emmett wandered off to wash up, curious but too courteous to eavesdrop. With Joseph's permission, Daniel shared their conversation before they exited the barn.

The wife and children set up trestle tables on the lane for the evening meal, and after the Deacon boomed out a grace Reverend Leeds would have envied, everyone enjoyed copious amounts of warm biscuits, fried chicken, potatoes, and greens, with pie for dessert. With a glare and a horizontal swipe of his fingers, Deacon shut down the little girls' questions about why they were eating with the slaves. Archie, Daniel, and Emmett complimented Deacon's beautiful wife, saying that Joseph had not exaggerated in the slightest when he extolled her culinary virtues. Remembering her disability, they pointed to their plates, kissed their fingers, and held them over their hearts. She smiled shyly and bobbed her head to each in acknowledgement.

The long days meant enough light to enjoy coffee and conversation after the meal. The children were told to help the wife with everyone's dishes so that Pa and the twins could hear of Joseph's escape as well. Noticing Deacon did not have an after-dinner smoke, Daniel and Archie abstained from their pipes. Deacon told of rough looking, threatening men who had invaded the little valley while he and the boys were on their way to Paducah, and of how thorough they had been in their search. He gave credit to Pa's silence and his wife's gibberish hurled in anger that finally persuaded them to leave empty-handed, and he ended by saying he was surprised Butch had not had a heart attack from the anxiety of seeing his mistress so distressed.

For the next half hour, Joseph recounted his experiences being freighted from one safe house to another through Ohio and into Michigan, and the frigid rowboat ride across the Detroit River, his near abductions at the wheelwright's and the Camerons', and finally the challenges of mastering the Queen's English.

"You do not sound like the young man who left here," Deacon observed. "So you can read and write as well?"

"Thanks to Missus Cameron, I can. Not as good as Mister Daniel yet, but I figure he got a head start."

"He doesn't sound like the fugitive we took on as our hired man either. He's been a great help to the wife and me. I think he has saved every penny he has earned," Daniel said, shifting the conversation. "Speaking of money, Joseph tells us you are quite the businessman."

"I pride myself in providing well for my family. I have no debts."

"You are a man after our own hearts, Deacon, so you will appreciate what Joseph was trying to do, sending Mister Smale this way, assuming he shows."

"The boy has a good heart."

"The man has wages squirrelled away too." Daniel looked at Joseph, then back to Deacon. "He has asked me for a cash advance with his nest egg as collateral." He pulled his billfold from a back pocket and counted out thirty-six dollars on the table. "That is what is owing on Pa's account, we are told. He's getting up there, and Joseph does not wish to see him die in bondage." He counted out a second pile of bills. "That money is to buy out Red's indebtedness."

Archie counted out a third pile. "I cannot permit my friend to have a more generous heart than mine," he said. "That will release Blue from slavery as well — unless of course, Deacon, you are not a man of your word."

Deacon and his slaves stared at the cash dumbfounded. Finally, Pa muttered "Lordy Lordy Lordy" and Deacon shifted in his seat, never taking his eyes off the table.

"I did not anticipate this day for quite some time yet," he said. "You insult me, Mister Taylor. I most certainly am a man of my word, so I will sign the requisite manumission papers. An unexpected surprise indeed. However, this is coming at me at an awkward moment if Pa and the boys decide to leave post-haste. Without their help, I will be unable to fulfill a contract for timbers that are scheduled to leave tomorrow."

"Are we to understand the load is going south?" Emmett asked.

"Yes. Into Tennessee. Black locust... An absolutely wonderful wood, although there are those who think it burnishes up less pretty than some others. Many who don't know their woods go for the larger diameter oaks, but black locust is stronger than ironwood, more rot resistant than cedar. It will last a hundred years in the ground and still bear weight. It grows in batches, and we've got more than two dozen groves. That's what we took to Paducah, and if I can, that's what we're taking tomorrow for a bridge. It's black locust that brings in a handsome profit."

Before he could rhapsodize further about the merits of black locust to influence his slaves about their future, Emmett said, "I have an additional business proposition that may interest you. You can only profit handsomely from it if you accept my offer. Shall I continue?"

At "profit handsomely", Deacon absentmindedly stacked the money and jammed it into a back pocket. He turned to Emmett and said nothing, still reeling from the turn of events.

"I wish to examine whether cotton production might be a money-making venture, especially in light of a war which you are convinced is coming. My country is dependent on southern cotton, the supply of which would be curtailed by a blockade of the Mississippi. I speak for Taylor and Cameron when I say a market for horses has not been fully explored, and Joseph has a debt to pay in Tennessee. It is to our advantage to travel together. You would still have the labour of the twins. You would pose as the owner of the three, thus preventing the potential re-enslavement of free men by opportunists. I relieve you of out-of-pocket expenses including food and lodging, and I pay Red and Blue a labourer's daily wage plus fifteen cents, which I believe is more than charitable. The journey would provide a chance for them to think of staying on or leaving your employ. Pa would stay here, paid by you at a freeman's wage. You pay for services for your horses, we pay for ours."

Deacon pondered the offer, then extended his hand across the table. Emmett made no move. "Deacon, the offer is made on one condition. You will immediately draw up three dated individual articles of manumission for each man. Mister Cameron and I will write a true copy, you will sign all nine, and Mister Taylor, Mister Cameron, and I will sign as witnesses. Pa gets one set to hide, your wife gets one — in case of any difficulties in the future — and I take the third. Only then will I shake on the bargain."

"You are as suspicious of my honour as is Mister Taylor," Deacon complained.

"Sir, we are strangers travelling in a country where slavery remains legal. Honour may be a relative commodity."

An hour later they shook hands.

No one except the wife and the girls could capture sleep. Pa and the twins were in elated shock at finding themselves freed so unexpectedly. Deacon's brain was too busy with thoughts of the future, and the others were too excited about what they had accomplished and what adventures might await to permit slumber.

Into Tennessee

Breakfast dishes had not been finished when Walter Smale arrived. The gregarious talker on the boat was now a laconic businessman, eager to look over the herd with Deacon as escort. While Daniel, Archie, Joseph, and the twins ramped black locust timbers onto the wagon, Smale wandered about the pastures, patting flanks, palpitating throat muscles, looking deep into bovine eyes, examining hooves, studying manure patties, and in general casting his own critical eye over the whole. At the lunch table he produced a small notebook, wrote some figures, ripped out the page, and handed it without comment to Deacon.

Deacon gave a low whistle and stared at the paper.

"What you have here is not an ideal cattle operation. I didn't expect such from an amateur trying to get into the business. To be honest, sir, you need to move your cattle more. Mobility builds muscle and muscle eats well. Yours are a trifle chubby, but fat produces flavour, so there's a trade-off. You are treating those beasts like pets. Don't let them graze down one pasture before you move them to the next; the first will regenerate quicker. However, as you can see, I am giving you a generous offer for forty head of the young crop — of my choosing. You have purchased top quality, healthy stock, sir, and we are in the market for such and right now. That price you see is the going rate for prime animals plus five percent, and that is more than I have offered any on the way here. If we have a deal, I will mark the animals I want today and write a cheque, which will clear the bank before my drovers arrive to cut out my choices and drive them for river transport. I am glad I was told of your herd. Do we have a deal?"

"Mister Smale, we have a deal," Deacon said enthusiastically and extended his hand.

Lunch over, Smale returned from his trap with a can of paint and a brush. Wearing a splattered leather apron, he revisited the herd and painted a swath of blue on the shoulder of each of the chosen while Deacon tallied the count.

It was mid-afternoon by the time Smale had departed and the wagon load was roped secure. "Not much point in setting out before dawn tomorrow," Deacon said, and went into the house to inform his wife their guests would be staying another night.

That evening, rest came more quickly to everyone except Deacon and Emmett. Deacon lay awake, still astounded by the rate of return on his original outlay and wondering if a war might be of greater benefit than he had previously anticipated. *God rewards the righteous* was his last coherent thought before he fell asleep.

Emmett dozed off wondering if his expenditures might be seen by the governor general as exceeding his mandate.

At dawn, when the draft horses beheld the spectre of the loaded wagon, the result was a reluctant hookup. The twins piled bags of oats on top of the lumber and more in the back of the Yellow Bounder with the luggage. Lunches packed by the wife reminded Daniel and Archie of their first ride on the Great Western. Joseph suggested that since they did not know the route, the phaeton should follow the wagon, and that way they could help push on the hills, something that had not occurred to the others.

Rested horses and dry roads made the journey to drop off the black locust timbers efficient and uneventful. The first night out, they "lived rough" as Emmett put it, and camped under the wagon or under canvas, thankful for the blankets Emmett had seen fit to include. By evening of the second day they had reached their destination, unloaded the timbers, and were happily ensconced in The Sleepy Goat, a tidy little inn run by a rotund widow in her late thirties who laughed much, cooked well, and was adamant there would be no war. When she discovered he was the only eligible bachelor in the group, to the amusement of all she warned Emmett he would be robbing the cradle if she ran away with him, and to their surprise she allowed Joseph, Red, and Blue to sleep in the stable for no extra charge. Since there were no other guests, the Blacks were permitted to eat breakfast in the tiny dining room the following morning.

Coffee finished, Blue wandered over to a map of western Tennessee pinned to a wall. "My late husband tacked that up to help our guests make sense of the roads, what few there are," the portly woman said as she began to clear the dishes. "Very confusing, this part of the world is," she continued. "So many swamps and marshes and streams to turn you around, it's easy to become disoriented if the sun's not out."

Blue motioned for Joseph to join him. "About there," Blue said, finger on the map. "It was 'bout there Pa picked you up on the road. It was there," and he stabbed his finger higher on the map, "it was there we stopped for the night. See, the road follows the river for miles."

After that, it was easy. Joseph sketched a crude facsimile of the road connections, and with lunches packed by the proprietress and a generous exchange of money, they were off with rested horses and a sense of purpose.

At a larger inn that evening, Daniel had an inspiration. "Deacon," he said, "we need you because no one would believe these Blacks are our slaves, but we don't need the heavy wagon and the draft horses now. Why don't you persuade Emmett to rent a team and double-seated buggy from this livery for you and the boys, and leave your horses to be picked up on our return? Without the wagon, we could trot along four times as fast. Fewer nights on the road would save Emmett money in food and accommodations, and it would save wear and tear on your wagon and team."

Emmett was enthusiastic about anything that would show frugality. Daniel was proven right about their rate of speed, and by noon they were on the road where Pa had invited Joseph to hop on the empty wagon. He had no difficulty locating the precise spot Malachi was shot. Daniel, Archie, Red, and Blue helped search the steep bank, and Joseph showed them the rock overhang where he had taken shelter from the brown boots. There was no sign of a body, not so much as a scrap of clothing. Joseph lamented that he had been unable to even throw a token handful of soil over Malachi's corpse, reluctantly admitted there was nothing more to be done, and returned to the vehicles. He sat lost in memory for the next hour, silent and brooding.

They found a dismal little inn about half a mile past the intersection where the abolitionist's wagon had been set on fire. Daniel and Archie took their meal outside to eat with Joseph and the twins.

"This is your decision," Daniel said, "but it may turn out to be a bad one. Joseph, are you sure you want to go through with this? I would like to talk you out of it."

"Mister Daniel, Mister Archie, I will never, ever have another chance to stop what happens up that road. I'm the one that got away. Malachi was shot because that old man betrayed us. Whatever Massa Lonnegan has done to Seth, it's all because of him. He is a murderer, Mister Daniel. A murderer. The twins said they'd come with me and act as bait to see if that Judas is still in business 'cause he would recognize me right off. All I ask is Deacon say we belong to him if I get caught, or you vouch I be a free subject of the queen."

Daniel leaned against the Yellow Bounder and studied something on the other side of the horizon. "Either will be uncomfortable to explain, so don't get caught. Leeds would say 'Vengeance is mine, saith the Lord,' so I suppose this will make me an accomplice." He hesitated a moment before going on. "But damn it, I am not Leeds. The way I'm seeing it, I will be enabling the man responsible for your friend's murder to continue his wicked ways if I do not help you. 'The only thing necessary for evil to triumph is for good people to do nothing,' as Susan would say. If I help you and something happens, I have you on my conscience. If I don't help you, Joseph, that is on my conscience. I'm in an impossible situation."

Archie said nothing as he carried their supper dishes inside and returned to help harness the horses. Looking hard at Daniel, he said, "Your Sunday lessons are interfering with what you know should be done. I've forgotten how old Wickerson pronounced it in Latin; *Nemo me lacessit impugne*, or something like that. It translates to: No one harms me with impunity." He stuffed a cardboard box of Lucifer matches into Daniel's shirt pocket and pushed a lantern in between the twins. "It's borrowed from the stable," he said, "so don't break it." Looking at Joseph he said, "Forgiveness is for weaklings."

"From what you say, the cabin where this old man lives isn't many miles up the left fork," Daniel said. "If we used what light is left, and I dropped you off..."

"Mister Daniel, that cabin is a long way up that road when you're walkin' at night and tremblin' at what's coming 'round every bend, but it can't be that far with horses. Better moon tonight than what we had."

The Hamlet

Daniel dropped them off on the near side of the hamlet and waited in the Yellow Bounder. Several dogs barked at their passage. No one came to his door to observe the three traverse the bleak outposts, yet someone in one of those squalid little houses looking out from the brooding forest, primordial in the fading light, owned a scruffy little white terrier, the two of them confederates of the one-legged man.

The isolated, crumbling log cabin on the far side showed no sign of light or life or dog in the gloom. A smell of decay, of accumulated filth, of body wastes, of rotten food, of sickness, issued from the open door. Joseph hung back so as not to be recognized. With Red at his back, Blue rapped knuckles on the warping doorframe, waited, then knocked again. From inside a weak voice demanded, "What do you want?"

The twins stepped back from the stench. "My massa has sent us with a message fer Mista Polaris, an' we has lost our way. We be mighty obliged if you could tell us where ta find Mista Polaris," Blue said.

"Just a minute."

They could hear someone rummaging about. A coal oil lamp was lit. There was a repeated thumping as the old man, leaning on crude crutches, came to the door in only a short, tattered, once-white cotton nightshirt, backlit by the lamp. He had not attached his wooden leg, and the stump was raw and suppurating a vile, stinking black pus.

The old man supported himself against the doorframe with his right shoulder. "What makes you think this house might know where Mister Polaris is?" The voice was less feeble.

"You was recommended to us, suh."

"Tell me who recommended this particular house?"

"I did," Joseph said, and stepped closer to the open door so he could be seen in the faint light.

In an instant, the old man produced an antique flintlock pistol from behind the doorframe. As he pulled the hammer back to cock it, his thumb slipped and it fired prematurely into the straw dogbed. With stunning speed, he slammed the door. A latch dropped and they were left standing in the near dark, listening to the thump of crutches, a chair overturning, the weight of a body falling, and the unmistakable sound of breaking glass.

Joseph pulled the twins back from the door. "Could be he's got more than one gun. Talk low so he can't find a target by sound."

They heard banging and thumping from inside, then coughing. It was Red who first smelled the smoke, and soon they could see it lazily swirling through the cracks in the door, illuminated by an orange light. Intermittent coughing became continuous coughing. The twins heaved shoulders against the frail door four times before the rotting leather hinges gave way to reveal an evolving disaster.

The dog's straw was in flames. Hundreds of sparks drifted randomly, spreading the fire with mind-boggling speed. The stinking blanket on the bed was already smouldering. Through the smoke that was filling the cabin they could see the old man, on his side on the floor, his raw stump glistening black and gold in the firelight, his left hand grasping the nearer end of his filthy mattress in an apparent attempt to raise himself. Coal oil from the lamp, which had smashed when the old man fell, suddenly ignited to pool flame throughout the small space. Red entered the cabin, flipped the blanket, and threw it over him to smother the flames burning through his shirt and skin. He grabbed his ankle and began to back toward the door, pulling the screaming old man, who maintained a vice-like grip on the mattress. Overcome by the heat and smoke, Red was forced to let go and retreat to outside air.

Blue took a deep breath and dashed in, but at first could not find the leg to grab in the dense smoke. Eventually, he too ran out, falling onto his back as he came. In between coughs and gasps, he said, "I got him within a yard, but I can't pull him farther. Something's holding him back."

Suddenly, Joseph suspected why there was an impediment.

Inhaling deeply, then holding his breath, he plunged through the door and past the figure prone on the floor. He seized the smoking mattress and turning, pulled it and the body clutching it out the door and into the road. Before the mattress could burst into flames, he stomped out any remaining sparks.

Flames from the interior illuminated a horrendous sight. Most of the body was blackened, but in places charred skin had sloughed away to reveal bloody raw flesh, like crackling pulled from a roast pig. Hair and eyebrows were bristles only. His eyes focused on something distant. Shallow breathing and sporadic shallow coughs showed he was still alive. Slowly, he turned his smoking head to watch his cabin burn. Gradually, then faster and faster, the moss chinking between the logs burned away, letting orange light leak out as though the cabin were a giant jack-o-lantern.

There was a rumble of wheels on the road behind them. Daniel pulled up in the Yellow Bounder, with the buggy containing Emmett and Archie close behind. Once the vehicles were turned around, the three newcomers joined the triangle to peer down at the blackened body. "Couldn't let you have this all to yourself," Archie muttered in Joseph's ear.

"They showed up shortly after I dropped you off," Daniel explained. "Deacon stayed at the inn to explain to anyone curious that we decided to go for a ride after supper, and we must have got turned around."

From his pocket, Joseph pulled the knife he had taken from Malachi, knelt, cut the mattress down its centre, felt through the stinking feather stuffing, and one by one extracted several small grey canvas bags. Oblivious to his burns, the dying man watched with horror. He pursed cracked lips as if to spit at him.

"My good man, it doesn't appear you have enough saliva left in your wicked body to form spittle," Emmett said. "Do you truly wish your last act to be spitting on a man you have so wronged? I recommend you expend your energy straightaway on pleading for God's forgiveness."

The blackened man turned his head ever so slowly to look at Emmett. "Redcoat," he whispered. "A redcoat. A goddamned fucking redco..."

They studied the dead man until Daniel reminded them of their involvement in his death. "It must appear he scrabbled out of his burning cabin before he died. We must leave no evidence we were here."

"Then we best be on our way," Emmett said, "lest we raise the hamlet. There is no magnet like a fire."

Archie dragged the ripped mattress off the road and threw it into the burning cabin, while Daniel tossed the canvas bags into the phaeton. Emmett produced his revolver from under his jacket. "In case anyone tries to stop us."

Candles appeared in windows as they trotted through under a clear moon. Safely back at the inn, Deacon guarded the stable door while Archie and Daniel unharnessed the horses. Once Joseph had a smoky fire started in a brazier near the outdoor tables on a flagstone patio, Emmett stuck his head into the tap room to inform everyone his party intended to enjoy the balmy evening with a fire, and anyone who wished to join them was welcome. Now comfortably into their beer, there were no takers.

They waited long enough to allow the fire to permeate the area with smoke, and then they abandoned it and gathered around the little mound of canvas bags on the stable floor. Joseph untied the drawstring of one and dumped out a stack of paper money, neatly bound with hemp cord. He carefully severed the string with Malachi's clasp knife, and slowly counted out one thousand pounds in Bank of England notes. Daniel and Archie each counted out the same exact amount from two similar bags. A lighter bag, counted by the Deacon, contained five hundred and thirty-five pounds.

No one had ever seen that much cash in one spot. They studied the pile of money without speaking, no one wishing to break the spell of sudden wealth. Finally, Daniel said, "Decisions must be made. We can't stand in a stable all night.

Joseph, some of this must be from the betrayal of your friends, so you have a greater claim on it than the rest of us. Does this sit well with you? Since Deacon and Emmett share a room, and since Emmett has a revolver, I propose the money be left with them overnight. Emmett can carry it in his bag when we leave tomorrow morning. We dare not talk about anything but the weather at breakfast. The first chance to be alone, we'll stop and discuss this windfall."

"Mister Daniel, that sound smart to me." The others nodded in agreement. "I'm just wonderin' how many runaway slaves that Judas betrayed over the years to earn such a heap a money."

"And who paid him?" Deacon added.

No one slept well.

Aeneas Revisits the Sawmill

Pa was slouching over the top rail of a paddock fence, foot propped on the bottom rail, watching newborns jerk heads into mothers' udders to prompt more milk, when four horsemen cantered up to the house. He recognized all but one. The stocky man in the knee-high, brown riding boots and a slim, younger man with long hair threw open the door of the house and barged inside. He heard Deacon's wife scream and the faint sound of a slap and more screaming and more slaps and then children crying. There was nothing he could do to stop the outrage because the other two, a portly man with a narrow, pinched face and a young ruffian as slim as his brother, were striding to the paddock for him. The ferret-faced stranger watched indifferently while his companion pinned the old man's shoulder against the top rail and punched him repeatedly with his free hand. When he was unconscious, they dragged him to the porch and tossed him in a heap beside the sobbing mother and children.

Aeneas Ragg swept his hand to encompass the barn, stable, sawmill, and cattle-strewn fields. He spoke to his companions, not to the cowering inhabitants. "This here is where he's supposed to be, and what do I see? Nothing! Again! Absolutely fucking nothing! No man of the house, no main prize, nothing! This is the second time I have had the pleasure of looking for Lonnegan's runner here, and I can tell you I'm getting fucking tired of it." He focused on the portly ferret face. "Are you sure your man heard right? You better be absolutely one hundred percent certain you got the story straight, 'cause I've got too much invested in this fucking case to waste any more time on wild goose chases."

In a meek voice, the ferret face solemnly said, "Aeneas, you know I would not have contacted you if I had not been positive. My man followed them to Mayfield. That's where they asked specific directions to this sawmill. This sawmill. Doesn't the fact that the owner and the slaves and the limey and his friends are not here prove they've taken off with the main prize?"

Ragg calmed a little. "Maybe it does. Maybe it proves dick all."

He turned to the older son. "I don't think you'll find anything, but take a look around anyway. Be careful. Remember what happened to Burton. Then shoot the cattle, just to make a point. I'll help you, to speed things up."

To the disfigured son he said, "If you want to, you can knock the old man around a bit more to help him remember better. I doubt you'll get anything out of him, though. These fucking upright citizens would be too smart to tell him where they're headed, even if the old coot wasn't so far gone."

He pointed to the cowering females, "Lock these inside. Don't touch the woman. She's addle-brained. Before we leave, give the kids a couple of smart slaps so if we ever need to come back they'll show some respect."

A half hour later, the one-eyed son adjusted his suspenders and sauntered onto the porch when he heard the others on their horses. The Deacon's wife had not heard the gunshots, nor could she hear her children sobbing in the barricaded bedroom, but she could see the door vibrating from their hammering fists. She left them there until she could wash and remove her torn dress. Beyond repair, she set fire to it in the fireplace. Not until she had propped Pa's body into a sleeping position on a porch rocking chair did she open the door of the girls' bedroom.

Aeneas rode beside his one-eyed son. "Why did the main prize return back here? Why did the limey and the others bring him right here? He sure as hell ain't running away any more, not if he's travellin' south from Paducah. You tell me why three white men show up here with him. This does beat all. I gotta figure out where they're runnin' to."

"Ain't likely he's hitchin' a ride with strangers, hired on as their servant, is it?" the son asked.

"No, there's more to it, and why back here? After that last fuck-up, you'd think he'd scurry deeper into Canada, where he'd feel safer."

They rode in silence and reined in at the main road. Ragg suddenly smacked his right fist into his left palm. "Jesus, I wonder if he's going back to where we nabbed the other two. Maybe he thinks the little one got away. Maybe he's lookin' ta find out what happened to him. By God, that could be it! Anyone got a better idea?"

There was no response.

You," he said to the ferret-faced man, "go back to Paducah and carry on as normal. There'll be others heading over the

Ohio. My boys and me, we'll head south and west. In the off chance the main prize backtracks, send a message by packet to my office in Memphis if there's no telegraph."

As they watched the associate trot away with a backward wave, Ragg spat on the ground and said, "I can't promise we'll be comfortable tonight, but I know of a little inn, The Sleepy Goat, that'll put us up farther down the road. Nothing fancy. Logs on a cobblestone foundation, stable, a dining area with whiskey and strong beer. Not many rooms, but you'll have clean sheets, if that matters. A jolly dame who's as podgy as our departing friend runs the place. She laughs at everything and cooks a good meal."

Spoils Divided

The next morning, they halted beside a grove of red oaks and sat on the dewy grass to discuss their good fortune. Daniel said, "Let's go 'round the circle, throw out some ideas... Nothing binding until we all agree. That all right with everyone?" The rest nodded. "Joseph, you've got as much claim as anyone. You start."

"Mister Daniel, I surely think Red and Blue should get a chunk of this money. They risked their lives to save that Judas from his hellfire on this earth, and that should be worth something. Everyone should get some. We have all invested something to get this far, but we haven't risked our lives like the twins did."

Although he was not beside Joseph, Deacon said, "As for me, I do not wish one penny of this ill-gotten, filthy lucre. My God will reward me through hard work, not from money taken through deception. Split it six ways if you wish, but I will touch none of it. I would take money from gambling before I would hazard my eternal soul by accepting a sou."

"A portion to Red and Blue would give them a sound basis for what comes next as free men," Emmett pointed out.

"I will not delude you into thinking I do not covet a portion. However, any coming my way would be used to underwrite expenses. I fear I have been rather profligate of late with the resources at my disposal," He looked at Daniel and Archie.

"Your portion could be used to buy land in the Black settlement or carpenters' tools," Daniel said to Joseph.

Joseph stared at the ground, pulled at blades of grass, shook his head, and quietly said, "No, Mister Daniel. Ellie."

Red spoke up. "Me and Blue, we talkin' last night before sleep, thinking 'bout all that money. Deacon, we know you worry 'bout yer business if you can't get anyone who can do what we're doin', cause you said so, so if your God doesn't see it right to have any come our way, we'll stay with you until you can replace us or we find somethin' that pays more profitable. Us being bought free caught us by surprise as much as you, but we won't leave you and the missus and the little ones in the lurch."

"Thank you, boys," Deacon said. "I much appreciate that. See, gentlemen. My God provides, and he has surrounded me with people who seek his ways and walk in righteousness."

"Does this sound fair?" Daniel began tentatively. "Blue and Red get five hundred apiece, as do each of the rest of us except for Joseph, who gets a thousand. Our whole business here would not be possible without Joseph," he said with deliberate vagueness, "so he should profit most. There is also the issue of the loss of his friends. If the rest of you agree to my suggestion, I intend to give half my share to Joseph so we can buy the girl. Farm machinery will chew through the rest."

"Damn it all to hell! It sure gets goddamn expensive not being outdone by a friend like you, Mister Cameron," Archie exclaimed. "If the rest of you agree, I'll match Daniel." He shook his head in disgust. "I can't believe I just said that." Deacon winced at the irreverence.

Emmett added, "I will make no such commitment, but whatever remains after our extravagant expenses are paid might as well be invested in carpenters' tools as wine..." He was about to say "for the officers' mess" but caught himself in time.

When put to a vote, Daniel's proposal was accepted unanimously. Everyone but Deacon was to receive five hundred pounds, except Joseph, whose share would be fifteen hundred, counting the banknotes coming from Daniel and Archie. The remaining thirty-five pounds would go toward maintenance of the horses and lodgings.

"Deacon," Red said, "we was hopin' some a that filthy money might drift our way. Course, we had no way a knowin' God would think to give us as much as He did. We has always said you were a good businessman, and we ain't likely ta find a better one just down the road. Besides, what else do we know other than timberin', although maybe we startin' to know a little 'bout raising cattle..."

"What Red is tryin' ta get around to is," Blue interjected, "if we invested our money in the squared lumber and Hereford business, would you take us on as...?"

"As shareholders, yes, as partners, not yet, not until we saw how this arrangement worked. I would always be the senior partner, naturally. We would require a lawyer to draw up a contract. Lawyers don't work cheap, you know."

"That's okay. We got some money," Red said, and everyone laughed.

"We need to decide where we go from here," Daniel pointed out. "Emmett will continue to look for investment opportunities I predict, and Joseph has his heart set on buying this girl he's convinced adores him. The way I see it, we are in a slave state, so we still need you, Deacon, to claim the Blacks are yours. Joseph dare not get anywhere near Lonnegan's plantation, so if the four of you retrace our route and den up at an inn, then Emmett, Archie, and I can travel down to Lonnegan's, buy the girl, and meet you. Then we all get the hell out of Tennessee so the Blacks can breathe free."

"Possibly Mr. Lonnegan will not sell the girl for a reasonable amount, if he was willing to pay twelve hundred dollars to get Joseph back," Archie noted.

"There is something else we should talk about," Emmett said. "Even if Deacon said true about the money being filthy lucre, it's the canvas bags from that stinking mattress that are fouling my luggage. They are most convenient, but they must be laundered at the first opportunity. Let's divide the money here and now. Blue, Red... Deacon should carry your shares because there would be embarrassing questions asked if slaves were found with that much money. Joseph, obviously your portion should go with us for the purchase."

"Deacon, on your return, you should not stop at the inn where we stayed last night," Archie advised. "News travels fast, and we emanate a smoky aroma that might prompt someone to connect you to last night's going's-on, despite our precautions. Where will you wait for us? I can't imagine we will take long to do business with Lonnegan."

Deacon thought for a moment. "Why don't the boys and I drop off the buggy, retrieve the wagon and team, and head home. Emmett and I can settle up when you get back to the sawmill. Joseph's debt with the old Judas is marked paid, any plantation on the river will be able to direct you to

Lonnegan's, and Joseph will be safer with me. The Sleepy Goat, that little inn where the widow fed us so well, will suit for a rendezvous if your errand is expeditious. It appears to have few guests, and she was good to the boys. If we're not there, you'll know we've pushed on. With an empty wagon, we might be able to make it home in a long day, if the roads stay dry and we start at first light."

"That sounds logical to me," Daniel said. "Give us two or three days and we'll be along with the girl."

Constance Acts

Lonnegan had not expected his wife to storm into his office before her second brandied coffee. It had been so long since she had asked about plantation affairs he could not remember the last time she had entered his inner sanctum. Assertive planting of the feet and a slamming of the door trumpeted her mood, and there she stood in her usual uniform, the grey morning dress with the lace cuffs. Rather than anticipate why she was so animated, he swivelled his office chair to face the front of his desk and waited for her to begin.

"Intolerable! Beauregard, I will not, I can not, tolerate any more of that man's sanctimonious condescension! He reorganizes, contradicts, second guesses every decision I make. Every one!"

"Now Connie, you know Cicero has proven invaluable to my business. I'm sorry if his efficiency ruffles your feathers."

"Don't 'Connie' me! Ruffled feathers be damned! You have molly-coddled that man to the point he has forgotten his place. It's a wonder he isn't telling you who to buy and sell."

"How long has this venom been fermenting? He's said nothing to me concerning any dissension."

"For heaven's sake, Beauregard, why would he, when he knows you permit no challenge to his authority in this house? He knows you will condone whatever he does."

"Do you expect me to choose sides between my wife and my house steward, for God's sake?"

"That is exactly what I expect. I am your wife. He is a slave. Or have you forgotten?"

"At least I can rely on Cicero not to be fuzzy-headed by noon. Furthermore, it appears he is able to maintain discipline in the servants without striking them."

"Maybe I wouldn't need to get 'fuzzy' if I could fulfill my proper role here. That includes the bedroom, Beau."

"Jesus Christ, what is twisting your tail to bring on an adolescent tantrum like this?"

"Don't you dare talk to me like I was one of your field hands! I have put up with his meddling in the kitchen and not said a word, because I'll admit he constructs a good menu. I even bit my tongue when he corrected a tiny addition error in the monthly house accounts. But as God is my witness, he has overstepped this time."

Lonnegan said nothing. As if she had been away for a great length of time and he wished to catch up on the changes, he took a closer look at the mother of his children. He noted the ample girth, the ageing skin, the sagging arms, the fleshy face. Trying to picture her as the radiant young beauty who had once captivated him, he leaned back with his elbows on the arms of his chair and held his hands open, thumbs up, as if waiting to catch the incoming explanation.

"Ellie is sickened by the very thought you will marry her off to Cicero."

"Who I marry Ellie to is none of Ellie's business."

"That may be true, but I have made it my business. I may be fuzzy by noon, but I'm not stupid even when I'm fuzzy. I know why you want to secure Ellie's place among the servants. Does she even suspect you are her father? So, God damn you, Beauregard, I have made this sordid situation my business, and I'm telling you I would rather see Ellie married to a barrow wight than that oily serpent who has insinuated himself so deeply in our affairs."

"You have deliberately taken us off topic so you could trot out your revelation about a toss that also is none of your concern. You haven't yet told me the specifics of why Cicero has you so incensed."

"I told Ellie I would help her hide the evidence of her womanly maturation so as to delay any pairing you might be planning with that hovering beast who is twice her age."

"Now who is meddling?"

"She was to bring the blooded rags to me, and I would send them out with my laundry. Now I find that Cicero has been pawing through my small clothes to find what he can find. I won't have it! I simply won't have it!"

"Who told you this?"

"Ellie was the first. I know what you're thinking. Yes, she has a motive, but I quietly broached the topic of this, this, this... outrage with the other servants, and each verified it."

Lonnegan leaned forward in his chair, hands clasped on the desk, in the posture a bank manager would assume when explaining to a supplicant why his loan application has been denied.

"Cicero acts on my instructions. I had put aside my man's urgency about that pairing for a time, but now you have made the decision for me. I own this plantation, I run this plantation, and I will not have you or Cicero or Bindle or Ellie or your goddamned chickens tell me what will transpire on it. I tell you what will happen, you don't tell me. You should have had enough time to get used to the idea by now."

"Who is the Devil incarnate? You? Or is it Cicero? Or Bindle? Which is the Dark One, and who are his angels?"

"Cicero and Ellie will consummate at the autumnal equinox. That will appease Cicero and give Ellie — and you — time to resign yourself to the fact that your wishes carry no more weight on my management of this plantation than the throat feather of a fucking hummingbird. Now leave me to my work. Go and get drunk — if you already aren't."

"Beauregard, mark my words; this is a decision that will come back to haunt you."

"What will haunt me is if we can't get our cotton to Britain, that's what will haunt me. Are you so busy with your chickens and your laundry and your detective work you don't realize there is a war coming? Go and tell Cicero and Ellie the good news. The autumn equinox."

The immediate beneficiaries of the morning conversation with her husband were Mrs. Lonnegan's exotic chickens. She had scattered twice their daily allotment of grain before she was able to attract the attention of a little boy too young for the fields.

"Child, do you know where Mister Bindle is at the moment?"

"Yes, ma'am. Mister Bindle be gettin' a new shoe fer his horse, ma'am."

"Would you like to earn a sweet?"

"Oh yes, ma'am, I surely would."

"This rolled up piece of paper contains a message for Mister Bindle. At the bottom is the instruction it is to be returned to you, and you will return it to me, and when you do, I will give you a sweet. Do you understand?"

"Yes ma'am. I get a sweet when I bring da paper back ta you."

"Can you keep a secret?"

"Yes, ma'am."

"If you tell no one you carried this message to or from Mister Bindle, I will give you more sweets — and maybe more messages — in the future. I don't suppose you can read."

"Only da massa and Mister Bindle an' Mister Cicero kin read, ma'am."

"Quite so. Off you go. I shall wait right here until you come back."

God Rewards the Deacon

Just as at home, Deacon insisted on an early start each day. His retrieved team had been well cared for and made such good time with the empty wagon that they arrived at The Sleepy Goat an hour and a half before supper. As before, there were no overnight guests, although their hostess did say there had been three the previous night and that some of the locals might drop in for a drop or two later. Until they arrived, she permitted Joseph, Blue and Red to eat in the little dining area.

"I'm always happy to see someone return for another stay," the portly woman said. "I hope it means they enjoyed my inn, or maybe it means this inn is the only one they could find when dark overtakes 'em." She laughed as if this were a novel and quite clever idea. "Now you take last night's people. A father and two sons. The father's been here before, so he's introducing his sons to me as if The Sleepy Goat is a posh hotel in N'Orleans. Very complimentary, but as for me, I hope they pass by the next time they pass by." She giggled at her own wordplay.

"I must admit, I would be some chilled if I met them on a dark road. They make you feel like you're the mouse and they're the snake. The son with the scarred face and an eye patch, well, if he doesn't look the very image of a pirate, I don't know what a pirate looks like. The father is more intimidating than the sons, if that's possible, does all the talking, maybe all the thinking, for the three of them." She prattled on while setting the table. Deacon wondered what tomorrow night's guests might hear about him.

At their departure, they discovered she had prepared lunches for their travel and had provided earthenware jugs of water. "Once the sun burns off this morning fog, you'll get thirsty. There's plenty of stagnant water, but you may not be near a fresh flowing stream when you need it. Drop the jugs off the next time you're through," she said, looking at Deacon.

Having taken this way recently, there was no need to ask directions. At high noon, they rested the horses in the shade at a lazy watercourse that was of questionable quality for humans and toasted the foresight of their hostess. Traffic was unexpectedly heavy with farm wagons and the occasional buggy. On several occasions, slower, loaded wagons pulled off on a firm edge to let them pass; Deacon acknowledged the courtesy with a wave and a hollered "much appreciated" or "much obliged."

Deacon's hope that in a long day they could push through to the sawmill was dashed when the wheel horse on the gee side pulled up lame. By the time the offending embedded pebble was located and with difficulty extracted from the frog and the now-tender leg bound for support, the light was spent. Disappointed that they must camp rough so close to home, Red, Blue, and Deacon made the best of it and crawled under the wagon early. Joseph, gazing into the remnant coals of their cooking fire, stayed awake longer, wondering how

Daniel, Archie, and Emmett were faring. Once asleep, he dreamt of Ellie and Cicero walking side by side through a spring flower meadow, with him running after them and never quite catching up.

A damp, foggy dawn found the horse still limping. Reluctant to let pulling aggravate the injury, Deacon tied him to the rear rack and harnessed only three to the wagon. Figuring to get a late breakfast at home, they set off with empty bellies at a speed slow enough to accommodate a hurting horse.

An uncharacteristically cool morning kept them chilled and clammy. Somewhere a sun must be attempting to dissipate the dense fog, yet at ground level they could see only a few yards. Deacon, trusting their homing instincts, gave the horses their head. It was almost noon when the wagon turned into a familiar lane, and still a weak sun had not mustered enough warmth to shoo away the fog.

Deacon reined in the horses at the stable doors, jumped down, and was about to say something when he straightened and became motionless. Everyone stopped to listen. There was no bird song, no movement, no welcome, no sound of animals or children. He picked up three pieces of paper littering the ground, examined them, and crumpled them in his hand. Almost whispering, reluctant to disturb the silence, he said, "These are from a Bible."

As if on cue, a subtle eddy of a breeze shredded the vapour to reveal the horror. Red and Blue walked slowly to the porch, where Pa's lifeless body slouched in a rocking chair. Red knelt by the old man. Blue suddenly dashed into the house, followed by Joseph, who re-emerged with Malachi's knife in hand to cut the rope Deacon's wife had used to hang herself and the tablecloth to cover her naked body. Balancing on the same chair she had kicked away from under her, Deacon wrapped the body stiff with *rigor mortis*, supported its weight with his left arm while his right sawed at the rope knotted around a porch beam, and gently lowered this once beautiful woman to the porch floor.

"Beaten ta death, Pa was," Red said quietly. "Beaten ta death." He walked around the body lying on the porch floor, and he too entered the house.

In shock, Deacon gazed at the crooked-neck tragedy at his feet. As if awakening from a dream he murmured "the children" and moved toward the door. Blue met him inside. "Deacon, it better you not come in just yet." Deacon ignored him and pushed past. In five strides he was in their bedroom, looking down at his two little girls, sleeping side by side with hands folded across their chests, faces up, eyes closed. He studied the angelic faces, then with no sign of emotion, he bent down, kissed each on the forehead, and drew a quilt over their heads.

"We will bury them this afternoon. This afternoon, before they change from the way I want to remember them," Deacon said in a low voice. "If you boys retrieve shovels, I'll wrap the bodies. I'll leave them resting on the porch until I determine the best place for their eternal repose."

Joseph helped Red and Blue dig Pa's grave beside their mother's. "I fret for Deacon's mind," Red said. "Look at him just sitting there, 'side his family, yet he ain't said nothin', ain't shed a tear... No sign of grief, no sign of mourning."

"You boys holdin' up okay?" Joseph asked.

"Pa lived a good life. Bad — real, real bad it had to end this way," Blue replied. "Time for grievin' coming, once my mind catches up to what my heart is tryin' to tell it. At the moment, best to concentrate on the work we've got to do."

Deacon chose high, sunny ground on the far side of the creek for the graves. He would not permit the others to help. "This belongs to me. Thank you, but this belongs to me," he said. "We'll require something for supper if you want to assist in some way. Take a look around. See if there are any cattle left alive. Any wounded, put them out of their misery. We'll try to decipher what happened once we're finished here."

One at a time he carried the three bodies across the bridge and placed each in the grave he had dug, his wife first, one child on each side. The others were not called to attend. He simply stood beside the fresh mound of earth for a time, then turned away with no words of closure uttered.

The Dam Bursts

While the twins collected eggs, Joseph recovered wood from the scrap pile and constructed three crosses, one twice the size of the others. It would be Deacon's prerogative to drive them into the soil at the head of the fresh graves, so he left them leaning against the house near where Pa had been found. He picked up several more pages ripped from a Bible and stuffed them into a pocket. They met at the house door like ball bearings drawn to a magnet. Deacon and the twins had also found pages scattered about.

"It's time to find out what happened," Deacon said. "You might as well come in. I tried to keep the girls away from your world while this was the centre of mine... but now... you might as well come in."

Deacon wandered about the kitchen, seeing the familiar but sensing disharmony. Blue drew his attention to the kitchen counter, where scrub marks obliterated most of a long, thin blood stain, which he studied like a trapper reading an animal track. A teacup containing a broken egg sat at the back of the counter. Near the stone fireplace he bent down to study some flower petals the same yellow colour as the half dozen black-eyed Susans in the vase on the round oak table.

"Joseph, where did you find the tablecloth you brought me for a winding sheet?"

"On the table. I grabbed the vase so as not to break it, and I snatched the tablecloth off the table and put the vase back down."

Deacon examined the vase. "There is a chip broken out of the rim and mended with egg white." He scrutinized the kitchen chairs. "These two have been thrown about. See the scuff marks on the top of this one and a scrape along the seat of that one, the one that's starting to come apart." He wandered back to the hearth and pulled from the ashes a singed dress remnant and half burnt Bible pages that had been used to light the fire.

"Why would the murderer try to hide his crime?" Red wondered.

"He didn't," Deacon said. "Whatever happened here, my wife put it all in order before she... before she... she... She placed the chairs around the table, mended the vase, straightened the tablecloth, tried to get rid of the blood. She did all this either before or after she smothered her babies."

He sat down, placed his elbows on the table, and put his head in his hands. Joseph brought him a piece of paper, neatly folded into quarters. "Deacon, this was behind the coal oil lamp on the mantelpiece. It's Pa's manumission; there's printing on the back."

Deacon ignored him for long seconds, started to reach for it, put his head back in his hands and said, "I can't. Read it to me."

"Deacon, it's not my place..."

"I said, read it to me!"

In a monotone, Joseph read

*"please forgive me children
did not suffer pillow cannot go on this evil world shamed
violated God forsakes me evil evil evil
here before here before here before two brothers thin
one eye burned face forced shame violated fought
fought fought fought hurt fought fought I hurt fought
older high brown boots brown vest brown hat brown
brown brown kill them kill them kill them kill them kill
one fat rat faced fat rat
sorry sorry shame sorry sorry sorry
girls did not suffer suffer sorry suffer sorry pillow
Butch tied tied Butch kill kill kill
no God here no God here no God here no God here
God forsakes us sorry kill kill kill sorry
can not go on forgive me fought"*

Deacon continued to stare at the table. As if he had not heard Joseph's recitation, he said, "We can't bury the cattle. Tomorrow morning we'll use the horses to drag the carcasses into a pile, and while I report what happened to the sheriff, you can burn them."

The Blacks left Deacon staring at the table, head in his hands, his wife's suicide note at his elbow, and retreated to the barn.

"Don't want to pack away Pa's things just yet," Red said. "There's time enough for that tomorrow. Hell of a way for an old man to die. He couldn't a bin a threat to whoever..."

Blue interrupted. "For certain Pa's death is a shocker, but we knew this day was coming, only not this soon and not this way. There is nothing good to say except, he didn't die a slave. On the other hand, Deacon, how could he foresee he would lose his wife and children and his new business in one day. Yet we ain't seen one tear, heard one broken breath, not one glimmer of sorrow. No grieving."

"That's true, but it's comin'," Joseph added. "It may take a while, but that dam's gonna burst."

Deacon brought a gargantuan omelette, bread, butter, and coffee to the barn for supper. "This won't be as tasty as my good woman makes, but it will keep body and soul together for a few hours. I can't sleep in the house. I'll take Pa's bunk and join you in your world tonight. My world is gone."

All slept fitfully. At dawn, Red pulled the cooling bucket out of the well so they could fry bacon and eggs for breakfast. The lame horse was given the day off, Deacon hitched up the buckboard and headed for the county seat, and the remaining horse was put to work dragging carcasses to the area of highest concentration. With only one horse, the mound of dead cattle was not complete until mid-afternoon. Slab lumber and cutoffs from the scrap pile were heaped around and over.

"It must be Deacon that lights this," Blue said. "Not ours to burn. Maybe never could be."

The buckboard returned at dusk. "I stopped in at the neighbours, told them not to fret if they saw smoke, "Deacon said, "and I told them to come day after tomorrow and take whatever critters they can use. Pigs, chickens, geese... If you can catch 'em, you can have 'em, I said. I dropped into the bank as well, before I pushed on to buy some things. You boys eaten yet?"

He unloaded a can of coal oil, three wooden boxes of groceries, and a firearm wrapped in a canvas sock. After a late supper of sausages with sauerkraut and store-bought muffins, they carried chairs to the field to watch the spectacle. Deacon splashed the dead livestock with coal oil and ignited the funeral pyre. Eventually, the dense black smoke and the stench drove them back. It was going on midnight when the Blacks retired, leaving Deacon immobile, staring into the fire.

"He's up to somethin'," Red observed. "We've never had a gun on the place before, and now neighbours told to help themselves."

"I reckon we'll find out tomorrow," Blue said.

The day started calm enough; later, Joseph would blame himself. Washed up to face the day, breakfast tucked away and the dishes done, Deacon suggested they meet on the porch with coffee to discuss the future.

"Did you find the sheriff?" Joseph asked.

"The sheriff was all full of kind words and sympathy but says he only has jurisdiction in the county. If the perpetrators turn up in the county, he will pursue their capture and conviction with energy. Those were his exact words. Capture and conviction with energy. In short, my visit with the sheriff was a waste of time."

"What you boys gonna do now?" Deacon asked bluntly. "Joseph, you'll be going back with Cameron and Taylor and Emmett, and hopefully, the girl. But Red, Blue, what are you going to do now?"

It was Red who replied. "We ain't had much time to digest this here new situation we're in, so Deacon, what we're gonna do maybe depends on what you're gonna do. Maybe get more cattle... Maybe work on just the lumberin' 'til next year... Maybe..."

"Boys, I haven't slept much since... since we got home, thinking about just that, 'mongst other things." Taking care not to spill his coffee, he rose from his chair to stretch his legs, leaned against a post, and looked out over the creek to where Butch dozed on a mound of fresh dirt. No one said anything. After a minute, as he turned away to resume his seat, he noticed the three crosses. They were the trigger. Coffee arced skyward as he threw the mug into the yard and fetched the crosses a kick that sent them skittering down the porch and onto the grass. He followed after, stomping them in a rage until they were kindling. The enamelled coffee mug felt his wrath next. He kicked it from where it had landed toward the mill. Breathing heavily, he resumed his chair and continued to gaze straight ahead. The next words had to be his.

He waited until his breathing had settled down to normal, uttering the first words in a low voice. "Boys, my good wife was right. We have no god; He has deserted us. What god is indifferent to a loving, beautiful woman so assailed by evil she must destroy the fruits of her womb?"

His breath hitched and there was a moment's pause. When he resumed his voice was louder and more resolute.

"On Sundays, I have stood before our congregation as a man of faith. Never again. I will never again claim to be a man of faith. I have not stolen, borne false witness, cheated, whipped my slaves... I have fought the sins of the flesh and the weakness of the spirit. Despite that, Satan came here in the body, yet where was my God? Aloof, indifferent, uncaring... Where was my God when she needed Him? Not here. Satan was here, Satan could find us, but not Him. I have tried to be a good man, living by the tenets of a loving and merciful God.

I do not want a merciful God. I must have a vengeful God. And boys, He has not shown up for work. He was not here when He was needed, and that makes Him an accomplice."

Deacon entwined his fingers into one large fist and rested his elbows on the arms of the rocking chair. "Did I not say, not long ago in my days of innocence, my God provides? And look what He has provided! Did I not say, He has surrounded me with people who seek His ways and walk in righteousness? If they wish to walk in righteousness, they damn well better not travel with me, because I am going to hunt down the... the... the degenerate fiends who did this, and... And I will kill them!"

He unclasped his hands, got out of his chair, stood on the edge of the porch and, looking at the sky, shook his fist and shouted, "Do you hear me, God? Can you hear me?" He stepped off the porch onto the grass. "I'm going to kill them! Did you hear her? Did she call out to you for help? Did she? Well, I don't need your fucking help! I can kill them all on my own without it!"

Deacon turned away with a noise that sounded like a sob, leaving the others to absorb what had just happened. It was twenty minutes before he returned with another mug and the coffee pot. In a matter-of-fact voice, as he filled their cups, he said, "I'll follow their trail from The Sleepy Goat. The widow may know more about them than she told us. The rat face in the wife's note must be the slave trader, the one Joseph escaped from in Paducah. I'll kill him last. You boys are free to do whatever you want. I've got one more thing to do before I pack up. I'm leaving tomorrow morning, first thing."

"Deacon, Red and me, we got no chance to avenge our Pa on our own. Travellin' just us, two Black men, askin' questions... No chance at all. But if we was to tag along with you, we all for the vengeance part. The only problem I got with watching someone crack open a skull like a dropped watermelon is that I'd get more satisfaction from doing it myself."

Red nodded his affirmation. "Old Black man beaten to death... We only hope his heart gave up before the beating was done. There be someone out there who thinks he can beat an old man to death and nothing gonna come of it. If you'll take us with you, we'll show what's gonna come of it. Just need to find him."

"Joseph, what about you? I can't see leaving you here by yourself. It wouldn't be safe. We'll probably meet the others coming this way even before we get to the widow's inn, but you have to make your own decision."

"Deacon, the description in your wife's note sure does fit the bounty hunters that killed Malachi and grabbed little Seth. When the others come along, I'll go back with them, but if we overtake your family's and Malachi's killers, don't expect me to be squeamish about sending any one of them to Hell. Mister Archie claims there's times justice needs to be done when the crime is fresh, and I can't find no fault with that. I may have already done for one when I clubbed that Goliath who tried to catch me at the Camerons'. So, if I could travel with you until..."

"It's settled then. Leave the lame horse and his partner to browse in the pasture. They can get water from the creek. Pack light and put everything you need in the buckboard. We leave at dawn and breakfast on the road. I'll organize the groceries I bought to keep us for a day or two, but before I do I have one more chore."

A TALE FROM THE CAMERON LINE

Deacon crossed the bridge. They saw him dig a hole at the foot of the fresh mound, but those who looked forward to smashing the skulls of their fellow man could not watch when the new rifled musket was placed against the head of his wife's faithful old yellow dog.

"Lot can happen in a week," Blue said. "You tell me a week ago I see Deacon bury his family, burn his cattle, shoot old Butch, curse his God, set out on a blood trail, I would a told you to clear out 'cause you plumb crazy."

Part Eight

PRICES TO BE PAID

The Understanding

"It is good of you to meet me," Constance Lonnegan said from the shadows of the stable door. "Our conversation will be mutually confidential, you understand. Mutually beneficial as well."

Bindle lifted Bellerophon's left front leg and meticulously examined its hoof. "Understood, ma'am. Mutually beneficial. However, confidential will be difficult, what with so many coming and going. I suggest our 'conversation' is best enjoyed when your horse slips a shoe this afternoon. Tell someone where you intend to ride, and when you are late returning, I'll volunteer to go look for you. The boys can handle things on their own. I'll predict a loose shoe problem that I noticed this morning and bring a hammer and nails with me. That way, Bellerophon can return good as new."

"East fields, at the forest edge where it intersects the creek on its north side."

Bindle tipped his hat to her as she returned to the house for an early lunch.

"I reckon we got half an hour," Bindle said, as he dismounted and moved both horses into the shadow of the trees.

"We share a problem, Mister Bindle, and we can share its solution if you choose."

"Enlighten me, if you please."

"Although you have not been with us for a great length of time, I regard you, as does my husband, as the ideal overseer. The plantation thrives only because your methods get efficiency from the slaves, and despite the issue of the runaways, you maintain the perfect balance between fear and discipline."

"I do not yet see the problem, Mrs. Lonnegan."

"The problem is you are not in a position to implement your talents within the big house. Mister Lonnegan is tenderhearted to a fault, and his susceptibility to subtle blandishments blinds him to the dangers created by his compassionate nature."

"Dangers?"

"Dangers, Mister Bindle. Cicero is a slave. A slave, Mister Bindle! Yet he has been permitted to become over-mighty, insinuating his way into my husband's trust. It is Cicero who runs the household. He determines the menu, checks my accounts, disciplines the servants, accompanies my husband on business trips. My God, he has even been sent on his own to do business on behalf of the plantation."

"So the problem..."

"The problem is that there is unrest, and that needs watching. Already there is a young wench, Ellie, who lacks proper subservience. She flaunts my authority and acts as though she enjoys a privileged status. Such an attitude can only foster murmurings among the others."

"I know who you mean. For her race, Ellie has blossomed into a beauty. You say she is troublesome?"

"You would deal with such a rebellious attitude in the field immediately, but Cicero's unnatural position prevents me from smacking that insolent puppy into line. Cicero wants her, and that son of a bitch will get her unless we stop this insubordination from growing. Surely three runaways are a sign it is already among the field hands. Simply put, Mister Bindle, our slaves are questioning their God-ordained place in the order of things, and that makes it your concern."

"What solution do you suggest? The field hands answer right smartly to the whip, but if Cicero is getting too big for his britches, you're right, he must be reduced to his proper level. However, if he's the apple of your husband's eye..."

"As is the girl. I propose a conspiracy of two, you and me. I have convinced this girl I want reduced that I am her ally. Ellie is naive enough to actually think I am helping her avoid marriage to Cicero, so I'll suggest she run away, with my assistance of course. I will even help her get to a location where you can pounce, and that, sir, can only enhance your professional standing with my husband."

"It wouldn't hurt it."

"Runaways are always whipped, are they not?"

"Invariably. Whipped first, often more to follow."

"She would not need to be whipped much. There would be no need to disrobe her; a few stings through her clothes would be sufficient. You could justify your mercy by pointing out she's worth more on the block if she's unblemished. Seeing his intended scourged and hopefully banished to the fields, or possibly even sold, will trigger Cicero into doing something rash."

"Such as challenging authority?"

"Such as challenging authority. Ideally, this would be best done when Mister Lonnegan is away on business. As I said, his benevolent nature..."

"I understand. You humble Cicero before he can get paired with Ellie, and vexatious Ellie is removed from the house... You said this would be mutually beneficial. What do I get out of this?"

"Mister Bindle, I will be honest with you. Beauregard may fume and he may threaten, but he will never sell Ellie. Never. However, if she is banished from the house, how could he marry Cicero to a field hand? My dear man, don't you see? You get the girl."

Messages

The Lonnegans were enjoying an afternoon libation on the front porch when a lone rider trotted up, dismounted, and with no word of greeting handed Master Lonnegan a letter. "If there is a reply, sir, I will wait."

Beauregard opened the letter to read:

Dear Mister Lonnegan;

One of my associates is riding down to Forrest's auction so I hope this letter he's carrying reaches you before I do. Good news. My people have discovered your property has returned. A Limey and two travelling with him have taken him on as a servant and most suspicious they almost for certain was at that sawmill where he skedaddled out of to head north but he ain't there now and me and my boys made sure they won't be helping themselves to another man's property again soon. We think he may have returned to where we intercepted your other two just to find out what happened to them but thats only a guess. One of my most productive associates I told you about him the peg leg one well his cabin got itself burned down and he is dead so we don't know if your property had anything to do with that or not but it happened

A TALE FROM THE CAMERON LINE

near the time of him coming close to the state line so maybe it was no coincidence. You know this one is personal and is causing me a parcel of trouble and I would rather catch this one then ten others because he don't fit the pattern. Why would a runner come back to where he run from I ask. We figure he is somewhere between where we nabbed the two and your plantation so it ain't that far as the crow flies a matter of a couple of days straight riding three tops if the roads are wet. Me and my boys we're on our way back to Memphis to collect from other matters and we will drop in on our way to see you once we scurry about and beat some bushes before we head home.

Best regards
Aeneas Ragg

Cicero, waiting silently just inside the door, had writing materials at the ready. Lonnegan read the return letter to the rider before sealing it.

THE ONLY THING NECESSARY

My Dear Mister Ragg;

I commend you on your perseverance. Last year's expansion of tillable land has necessitated a commensurate expansion of the work force. On the morrow I am boating down to Memphis to purchase four or five field hands. Mister Forrest usually has some in stock. My expectation is to be home in several days; however, if I should miss your most welcome visit, please rest reinforced in your conviction that I remain confident of your resolve. Good hunting.

Your Most Humble Servant,
Beauregard Lonnegan

"Please be good enough to leave my reply at Mister Ragg's office with a note that I shall drop in before I catch an upstream boat, in the event he has arrived in Memphis before my departure."

The rider touched a forefinger to his hat and trotted back down the lane.

As Lonnegan handed the writing materials to Cicero, he said, "Pack an overnight bag for me. Two days, possibly three. I'll catch an early boat. If Ragg shows up here, be hospitable, but there's no need to set out our best wine or the fine China. Pearls before swine."

Ellie Runs Away

Bindle enjoyed the lingering feel of firm breasts and buttocks as he manhandled a trussed Ellie against the front of the box. Taking a red handkerchief from his pocket, he scrubbed tears from her face as she thrashed it back and forth in avoidance. When she bit his hand, he slapped her hard and grabbed her firmly by the chin until she stopped moving. The others acknowledged his wave to ride on as he took up the reins from the seat of the buckboard.

"Didn't get very far, did you? You hardly ever do. The way Mrs. Lonnegan tells it, you ran away so as not to have Cicero fuck you. Jesus, girl, you think you can decide these things? I reckon you've put an end to that sweet life you've enjoyed in the main house. First thing we got to do is toughen up those soft little hands. You won't meet your quota with the hands on ya now."

Ellie squirmed against the rope, testing the knots, tightening them so they might permit the extraction of a hand.

"Don't bother. I know how to tie a rope," Bindle said, chuckling. "Whyever did you think neighbours would help you? You always hide in the hay. It's like an immutable law of the universe. No one would ever think of looking in the hay for a runaway, you always think, and that's always where we catch you." He chuckled again, appreciating his own insight. "Christ, you didn't get ten miles."

Ellie maintained a stoic silence. One ankle was tethered to the tailgate, so even if she could fling herself overboard, she would be dragged behind the buckboard before she could dash for freedom.

"You got about an hour to think this situation through, Ellie. You stupid girl, you bite me again, I'll lay your back open 'til I see bone. You think on that. You think on what was left of Seth when Mister Lonnegan was finished with him. Remember how he wanted Lonnegan to hang him? Compared to me, Lonnegan's skill with a whip is childlike. You won't tell him that though, will you?" He laughed. "That would hurt his feelings."

Bindle gave Ellie time to think.

After another mile, he said, "This is what is going to happen. You run away, you get whipped. That's a fact. Whether you get whipped a little or a death sentence depends on the master, but he's in Memphis at the moment, so it's up to me. You be real nice to me, real polite, no kickin' or bitin', I'll just give you a taste to sort of let you savour what braided leather can do. You get uncooperative, I'll rip your dress off and whip you tits to the breeze until even Lonnegan's drooling Black lackey won't want to mount you."

He stopped the buckboard within sight of the plantation house.

"For our mutual benefit, I hope you've made the right decision. You see, you can play the part of the rebellious slave. On that Ellie, I use the tip of the whip. I pull the butt back at just the right moment — takes practice — but the tip keeps going until it's yanked back suddenly — that's what makes the snap — and the tip cuts like a knife. It will flay your back 'til I'll see your ribs through raw meat. You'll be so busy with screaming and thrashing about you probably won't feel the blood running down your legs. Now for the docile, repentant Ellie, I hold both the tip and the handle in my hand so that the whip folds back on itself. You get lashed with the thicker part. Oh, it will still hurt. You will cry. But after five or six, once I see that you have resolved to never again commit the sin of disobedience, I will stop. So which do I whip? The rebellious Ellie? That's choice number one. Or the repentant Ellie? Choice number two. Which is it?"

Almost whispering, Ellie said, "Number two."

Any hope of rescue by the mistress evaporated as she saw Constance Lonnegan survey the buckboard's arrival from the porch, turn, and disappear into the house. As the slaves assembled, Bindle moved the dilapidated yellow chair holding Malachi's and Seth's skulls to the far side of the ear tree, out of the way. A rope from one wrist was passed around the tree and re-tied to the other. There was no need for any sentence to be read. Everyone knew retribution for leaving Lonnegan's plantation without permission was harsh and immediate. Bindle checked that his subordinate overseers were positioned behind the crowd, ready to deal with any remonstrances, and affirmed Cicero was at the head of the household servants.

True to his word, Bindle doubled the whip back on itself. Ellie flinched under the first blow but did not whimper. The whimper did not come until the seventh. Not until Bindle saw tears coursing down her face and her knees begin to buckle did he coil his whip.

"Now get back to work!" he ordered the semi-circle, and with the faintest of murmurings the slaves shuffled off. Cicero approached the tree with a kitchen knife in hand and began to cut at the rope.

"What the hell do you think you're doing?" Bindle bellowed. "Did I say you could cut the wench down?"

"There was no need to give her so many!" Cicero yelled back, knife still raised.

"You scuttle back inside your white shell this instant, or I'll have you on the tree next!"

"Mister Lonnegan would never..."

"Mister Lonnegan is not here! I'm here, and I'm in charge of discipline when he is not here! And since Mister Lonnegan is not here, I am telling you to get your scrawny Black fucking ass into the house right now!"

Even the subordinate overseers could not see if it was his fist to Cicero's jaw that caused the knife to slice Bindle's left arm above the elbow or if Cicero had already started to move and the fist was in self-defence. Cicero fell backwards under the blow, and Bindle slapped his right hand over the wound in surprise. The subordinates dragged the semiconscious majordomo to the stable and tossed him into an empty stall while Bindle walked to the plantation house for first aid.

"I do believe that arrogant son of a bitch intended to stab me through the heart if I'd given him the chance," Bindle said through gritted teeth.

"Look on the bright side," Constance Lonnegan replied as she attempted without success to thread a needle. "Our plan could not have worked better. We all saw Cicero attack you with a knife, Ellie wears the stigma of an ungrateful runaway, and Beauregard comes home to a *fait accompli*. What do you intend to do with Ellie?"

"Leave her on the tree. At dark, I'll have my men lock her in the honey storehouse. As for Cicero, we'll rough him up so he looks the part when your husband returns."

"No, Beauregard and Cicero are too close. Leave him as he is. We don't want to elicit any undeserved sympathy. I've told you, my husband has a blind spot with that slave."

"As you wish. You know him better."

"Will Ellie need attending to? Salt and vinegar to prevent infection, maybe?"

"No. I didn't cut her. She'll be bruised for a couple of weeks, but that'll serve to remind her of what she is. And who I am. Ellie and I will get along just fine from now on."

"The honey storehouse is a good idea." She swirled the needle in a glass of rum, drizzled some over the wound, and passed the rest to Bindle. "Drink, then bite down on this rag. This is going to hurt."

Lonnegan Returns From Memphis

Beau Lonnegan was not a happy man. Ragg was not at his Memphis office when Lonnegan had dropped in for a progress report, so that time was wasted. On reflection, he convinced himself he had paid Forrest too much for a gangling twentyish field hand and a family of four. The father and mother would suit, but the son was too young for heavy work, and the chubby, unattractive daughter might be dimwitted. He rationalized that at least there was minimal chance of a family running away. At the moment, runaways were a sore topic indeed. On his return, he was informed by his wife of Cicero's attack on Bindle and why Ellie was imprisoned in the honey storehouse.

Beau Lonnegan's temper was of the slow fuse variety. He had no intention of losing composure in a knee-jerk fit of rage, but he was determined to dig out the kernel of truth in the whole affair, and someone in the near future was going to pay for this fuck-up.

The subordinate overseers were interviewed first. Each declared that Cicero had attempted to stab Bindle when the latter had stopped him from cutting the rope, and that was what had necessitated Bindle's act of self-defence. When Bindle was on the carpet, he set out the facts in a terse, businesslike manner. Lonnegan admitted a runaway's punishment must be immediate and public and agreed the overseer had followed traditional practice appropriately. Bindle invited Lonnegan to examine Ellie's back; he claimed that out of compassion for her youth and sympathy for her dislike of Cicero, he had administered light blows with insufficient force to break the skin. When Mrs. Lonnegan helped Ellie undo her dress to the waist and draped a shawl over her breasts for the sake of virginal modesty, close examination confirmed purple welts but no broken skin.

He received only one word answers from Ellie. Yes, she admitted to running away. No, she did not have help from any of the slaves. Yes, she ran away to escape a future with Cicero. Yes, she understood why such behaviour merited punishment. Yes, she realized that if she was kept on as a house servant, justice would not be seen to be done.

Constance verified Bindle's account and maintained that it was obvious to all present Cicero's knife thrust was meant to be fatal. As she left his office, she added, "I told you he was getting too uppity. Maybe he knows his place better now."

Cicero was last. He told the story differently, suggesting Mrs. Lonnegan had engineered the escape, capture, and punishment for motives he did not fully comprehend. He denied any attempt on Bindle's life, saying the knife was to rescue his betrothed from excessive punishment. Of all the participants, Cicero was the only one Lonnegan believed was telling the truth, yet when Cicero bowed out of his office, something in their relationship had broken, and both knew it could never be repaired.

Lonnegan lit a cigar and yearned for the wisdom of Solomon. He could see no path forward that would not create a problem in the future. In the end, he permitted Cicero to resume his house steward duties under the guise that the entire episode had been a misunderstanding, and to extinguish any thoughts that Bindle did not act with total authority, he complimented Bindle on his actions in front of the slaves. It was understood house servants were automatically demoted to the communal cabins and heavy labour if they ran away, yet the fields would destroy Ellie, and Lonnegan retained hopes of eventually giving the girl to Cicero. So, for a fortnight Ellie was banished to the honey storehouse to sleep on loose straw and subsist on bread and water. To ensure the other slaves witnessed her punishment, she was assigned to mucking out the hen houses, the pig pens, and the stables. Lonnegan hoped that after this public humiliation a quiet reintegration into the household would go unnoticed.

Thoughts of domestic turmoil faded when the master focused on agricultural affairs. There was always something clamouring for attention. This afternoon he had inspected the roof on the storehouse that housed ready-for-transport cotton bales. If there was any building that must have a leak-proof roof, it was that one, and he was debating in his mind when its replacement should begin when Cicero glided to his office door and cleared his throat.

"Visitors, Master Lonnegan. Three. On the front porch being greeted by Mrs. Lonnegan."

"Ragg and his sons?"

"No, sir. Foreigners, driving an extended phaeton. One is a rather unattractive English young man who claims he wishes to learn more about cotton. The others have said little."

"Three. One English. The other two will be the travelling companions." Lonnegan looked at the floor and bit the corner of his lip in concentration. "Have Mrs. Lonnegan insist our guests dine with us this evening and then spend the night. Notify the kitchen. I'll leave the wine to you, but don't hold back. When you assign the guest rooms, separate the trio if possible. Tell Bindle to send riders north and south to find Ragg and tell him to get his ass here at the gallop. I don't know what the hell is going on, but I bloody well intend to find out."

At the Lonnegan Plantation

Daniel surveyed the Arctic vastness of linen tablecloth as he pulled out an exquisitely ornate chair to take his indicated place at a mahogany table long enough to accommodate three times their number. Mahogany wainscotting warmed the room. Matching serving tables held decanters, crystal glasses in several configurations, extra linen napkins, a gravy boat, a tureen, ladles, and a gleaming silver tray in waiting, patiently holding tea spoons and teacups patterned with oriental themes. There was adequate space in the dining room for two servants to pass each other between the serving tables and the diners' chairs. A chandelier twinkled above each end and cast sparkles of light on fine china, gleaming silverware, and the snow white ceiling.

At the far end sat their host, distinguished looking in a finely tailored suit of light burgundy highlighted with satin lapels, his moustache, goatee, and hair perfectly trimmed. To Daniel's right Mrs. Lonnegan reigned, demure in a fully hooped, dove grey evening dress set off by a lace collar, lace cuffs, and diamonds comfortably nestled in a silver pendant. Daniel compared his house to the Lonnegans' and wondered how he could ever explain such opulence to Susan. He pictured her coming in from the barn in a cotton print dress, throwing her kerchief over a hook, checking the cat's dish, pumping water into an enamel basin to wash up after chores, setting the table with pewter tableware and blue-scalloped dishes, and removing ironstone bowls from the cupboard to prepare supper.

He later pondered how he would describe the exotic dishes to Susan without using inflated superlatives. There was a civilized gap between courses to permit unhurried digestion and conversation, with the result the gourmet offering lasted for hours. Cicero topped up wine glasses as the last of the dishes were cleared by a plain, chubby girl who, from Joseph's description, could not possibly be Ellie. Lonnegan passed out cigars, chairs were pushed back from the table, stomachs were patted, Mrs. Lonnegan not-at-alled the effusive compliments on Southern hospitality, and the small talk about weather and the state of the roads died its natural death.

"So what, or who, do we have to thank for the pleasure of your company?" Lonnegan began.

Lonnegan noticed Mister Cameron and Mister Taylor seemed quite content to let young Emmett do most of the talking.

"For the last three days everyone said to stop in at the Lonnegan plantation if you wish to find out about cotton, what Beauregard Lonnegan doesn't know about cotton is not worth knowing, and so on. So here we are, rather travel worn and unable to dress appropriately for such dining but eager to hear your opinion of the cotton market and the future."

"I hope you will not be disappointed by any shallowness of knowledge, Mister Emmett, but may I ask, what is your relationship to the cotton market?"

"I do not wish to sound immodest, sir, but I am reaping an encouraging rate of return from my investments in the textile industries of Great Britain. Silent partners can exert a certain modicum of influence, but I find total ownership has more advantages. If my benefactor, my late uncle, cares to observe my progress from his lofty perch," and Emmett pointed his cigar to the ceiling, "I would like to think he approves of me becoming familiar with future opportunities as well as the behaviour of bequeathed stocks, bonds, and property."

Emmett took a long draw from his cigar and took time to exhale.

"Such endeavours sound very wise to me," Mrs. Lonnegan said.

"Yes, well you see, I believe passionately in diversification of one's assets, many eggs in many baskets, that sort of thing, but what is the point of owning a factory that spins cotton if said factory has no access to cotton? So that is why I am here, to analyse the future of cotton availability in these United States before I invest. You will appreciate that the three of us have been grilling the locals on the probability of a war breaking out between the states. What is the point of investing in a plantation if that plantation cannot get its cotton to the aforementioned mill in England? All your enemy needs to do is blockade the Mississippi and my mill will close for want of raw material, and my hypothetical plantation will wither for want of a market."

Lonnegan turned his attention to the others. "Mister Cameron, Mister Taylor, do you share this young man's interest in cotton?"

"Not at all, sir," Daniel replied. "In Canada West — you may know it better as Upper Canada — Mister Taylor and I enjoy access to a respectable number of horses, many of them Canadians. The Canadian is a jack-of-all trades in the spectrum of breeds, and if a war erupts and we are able to supply quality horses... I'm sure you can see how profitable that might be. And that, sir, is how we fell into each other's company. Business decisions must be based on sound information, so, like Emmett here, we value your insight concerning a possible war."

At a subtle nod from Lonnegan, Cicero refilled wine glasses. Daniel noticed he shielded Mrs. Lonnegan's glass when he topped it to the brim. The same happened when they switched to more potent spirits.

"If I understand you correctly, a war would be advantageous to you but disadvantageous to Mister Emmett," Lonnegan observed.

"Exactly," Archie said. "Is war coming?"

"Yes. No one knows exactly when, but yes, it is. However, my advice, gentlemen, is to sell your horses quickly, because the war will be short. The South has what the French call *elan*, and we will be fiercely united in our fight for our property rights. In contrast, the North is divided and irresolute. It will claim the South has no right to break from the union, but even the village idiot understands that fundamentally the clash will be about slavery, an institution without which the South cannot thrive. However, how many in the North are willing to die to free the Negro? Damn few, gentlemen, damn few."

He sipped his wine and took several puffs on his cigar.

"Mister Emmett, don't fret about a Mississippi blockade. The war will go on until the North realizes it cannot defeat the South and not a day longer. If the North were to stop the shipment of King Cotton, it is in Britain's interest to intercede. Your navy would break any blockade of the Mississippi to safeguard its — your — industries."

"Do you find my husband's prediction reassuring, Mister Emmett?" Mrs. Lonnegan asked.

"Quite. However, if I pull up short on a specific commitment, it is because my tobacco operation in the Carolinas is presently not economically viable, not in the long term, so it's a case of once bitten... I suspect my superintendent is either skimming the profits or is too lax with the slaves. I should ask your advice about buying slaves while I'm here, Mister Lonnegan. Do you sell slaves? I'm in the market for one or two."

"Occasionally. Cotton has been high, so I have bought more than I've sold. The plantation is expanding. As for investing, my advice to anyone who will be an absentee landlord is the same for cotton as it is for indigo or tobacco or any other commodity: avoid buying an entirety and trying to govern from a distance with a manager. Better to buy into a modest start-up operation where someone with a stake in its success will keep a close eye on your mutual investment. Then there is no harm in being a silent partner who does not enjoy immediate oversight, because the active partner will act in your best interest.

If you have no experience in the slave market, why don't you gentlemen stay for a day or two? I shall give you a tour tomorrow so you can see first hand that properly disciplined slaves are a necessity but constitute only a fraction of a profitable plantation."

"Yes, do!" said Mrs. Lonnegan. "We won't take no for an answer. You are putting us to no inconvenience, and I, for one, would welcome seeing my husband converse with civilized folk from the outside world. Cicero will show you to your rooms when you are ready to retire. Let him know if there is anything you require; he runs the house for us." She smiled sweetly at her husband.

Connie, you play your part well, thought Lonnegan. *Enough of this charade. Time to exert some pressure, find out if we're dealing with charlatans or the real McCoy.* He twirled a forefinger and said, "Cicero, a nightcap for us all. Gentlemen, I must admit your arrival is not totally unexpected."

"Indeed," Daniel said.

"Possibly you can tell me why you were travelling in the company of a fugitive slave. My fugitive slave, to be exact."

"You are misinformed, sir. Sir, we have travelled in the company of no slaves," Archie asserted. "Mister Cameron and I do not own slaves, and Mister Emmett's are on his holdings."

"Come, come gentlemen. Agents in my employ inform me my runaway slave, Joseph by name, accompanied you to a sawmill not overly far from the Tennessee-Kentucky state line. I am told the proprietor of this sawmill, an abolitionist sympathizer who is called The Deacon by all who know him, willingly provided him with assistance in his escape."

"This is most interesting," Daniel said. "It will make for an entertaining tale back home. We hired on a Black named Joseph as a manservant, but we believed him to be free."

"So how was it that, in all of Kentucky, you happened to visit where he had received help?"

Archie gave a little laugh. "Emmett, Cameron, it seems our Darkie may have played us. Mister Lonnegan, in our search for opinions about the coming war, we simply wandered about as tourists, so when our servant suggested a particular direction or a particular road, we had no reason to go another. It seems our path was not as whimsical as we thought." Emmett and Cameron chuckled and nodded an agreement.

"So then our route was not spontaneous," Emmett mused. "Gentlemen, we have been warned the African race can be devious in the extreme, but I do believe we have now experienced it firsthand. Yes, Mister Taylor, your assessment is quite correct. We have been hoodwinked by a scoundrel into thinking our route was arbitrary. Joseph's previous connection explains our warm welcome at the sawmill."

"An amazing coincidence that you hire my runaway and then happen upon our little Eden," Lonnegan observed dryly. "Amazing."

"Yes, truly," Daniel agreed. "However, I suspect it was inevitable that the trajectory of Mister Emmett's wanderings in search of cotton enlightenment would bring us to this preeminent plantation sooner or later." He confirmed the last dribble of his libation had been drained, mashed the stub of his cigar in an ashtray, and stood. "Mister, Mrs. Lonnegan, I, for one, am fatigued from travel. I shall retire to sleep in the bosom of your magnanimous hospitality to three total strangers." He gave a little bow to the head chair as he said, "I look forward to tomorrow's promised tour, sir."

Taylor and Emmett excused themselves as well. As Cicero was showing Archie to his room, Daniel whispered, "Masterful fabrications, Emmett, absolutely masterful."

Downstairs, Lonnegan said to his wife, "I wish I knew where the hell Ragg was. Maybe he has discovered why Joseph has returned. This evening has proved nothing, but if these are con men, they are goddamn good at it. We must figure out some way to delay their departure until Ragg arrives."

"Leave that to me," Constance Lonnegan replied. "Leave that to me."

Master Lonnegan Gives a Tour

At breakfast, Mrs. Lonnegan waited until Cicero was refilling coffee cups to make a suggestion. "I trust your slumber helped restore you from your travels, but possibly you have not had an opportunity to provide the same courtesy to your laundry. It has been my experience that clothing, once worn, does not improve in luggage. While Mister Lonnegan takes you on a tour of his operation, why don't you leave any socks, shirts, small clothes, whatever you need freshened, for Cicero to look after?" She smiled at her husband. "He is very good at sorting clothes."

Lonnegan ignored the sarcasm. "Gentlemen, I will require some time to organize the construction of a new roof for a warehouse, material costs, that sort of thing, so in the meantime, amble about, take a peek at whatever arouses your curiosity until I can join you."

The trio piled soiled clothing behind each bedroom door and began their familiarization walk. As soon as Cicero had the opportunity, he reported to Lonnegan's office. "Nothing out of the ordinary in the horse traders' bags. The young gentleman has a revolver and ammunition in his, stowed in the top pocket for easy access. I felt about in each. Mister Emmett has the only luggage with a secret compartment."

"I hope you were careful to leave all in an original state."

Cicero gave him a sideways look as though he were insulted by any suggestion of clumsiness. "Naturally. The compartment is created by a false bottom, easily removed if one knows what one is looking for."

"And you found...?"

"Three manumission documents and packets of money. A great deal of money, apparently all in English pounds. It was impossible to count without disturbance, but the Englishman is toting a surfeit of hidden cash."

"Have the girl hang out the laundry when it's washed, but be in no hurry about it. Any queries about why it took so long to dry, suggest the tardiness of slaves. If necessary, we will use the excuse that their laundry is still damp to keep them here another day."

Daniel and Archie waited at the stable for a green Emmett to catch up. "Sorry, gents," he wheezed. "You go ahead. I intend to take a brisk walk down the road and back to purge the gunge from my lungs. Who knew cigars could turn one's tongue into a desiccated corn cob?"

"So the bottle of wine did not exert a medicinal healing influence?" Archie asked. Daniel added, "Or the bourbon?" and both laughed at his discomfiture.

The unique construction of a chicken coop behind the house garden attracted Daniel's interest. Fancy chickens of various subspecies were confined in a wire-fenced area around the little red building as brightly painted as the barn. A wide door at its front was propped open, but manured straw was being tossed out the back into a wheelbarrow. He discovered the coop had been designed so the rear could be opened on hinged doors to facilitate cleaning.

"Are you a chicken fancier, Mister Cameron?" a voice behind him said, and he turned to find Constance Lonnegan, a pan of grain in her hand, walking toward him through the garden.

"Actually, I know far less about chickens than my wife," he replied. "She would be jealous of this flock. They're for show, are they not? I can't imagine any of these pampered fowl ending up in the pot."

"Not if they behave themselves. I'm more concerned with foxes or skunks. Mister Lonnegan claims I have hen fever. The Appenzeller Spitzhaubens came from Switzerland, the Brabanters from Holland, and chanticleer nearest the front door is an Ayam Cemani I imported from Java. I'm hoping to produce a tasty hybrid that will be hardy and a good egg layer."

"Goodness gracious. Java. Imagine. Any luck so far?"

"The Europeans seem to be hardy enough to cope with weather fluctuations. It's too early to say about the Javanese; I just got him. His wings won't need to be clipped; he'll stay close to the hens. Egg production is adequate but not out of the ordinary, and the eggs tend to be small."

"It wasn't your chickens that piqued my curiosity as much as the way the coop can be opened at the back."

"Ellie, the girl in there, is being punished and has not been assigned this menial job before, so I am visiting my sweethearts early to ensure she scrapes down the floor as thoroughly as I demand the field hands do before she adds fresh straw. This coop was not constructed to make it easier for slaves to clean; it opens to permit access to sun and air.

Winters can be rainy here, and fowl do not thrive where there is mould."

The girl emerged from the coop, balanced her shovel across the top of the load, and wheeled it toward the gate. Daniel thought better than to open it for her and studied her from a distance. A simple canvas dress was stained with filth, as were her hands and face and bare feet. He caught a glimpse of delicious breasts when she bent to shoo a potential escapee back into the enclosure, closed the gate, and laboriously wheeled the load toward the main manure pile behind the stable. In Joseph's description, Ellie's statuesque body radiated an ethereal beauty; under the dirt, this girl would be attractive, but at the moment all she radiated was the acrid odour of chicken droppings.

"So she's not a field hand?" Daniel asked. "She looks and smells like one."

Constance Lonnegan laughed. "Far from it. At one time, Beauregard planned on having her learn the culinary arts, but that was before she tried to run away. I suspect he still plans to marry her to Cicero, if she ever learns her lesson."

"If she serves in the house, possibly Emmett would find her suitable. He says he's looking for a capable domestic. What could he expect to pay for her?"

"Ellie? I don't know what she would fetch in the Memphis market, but it's an academic question. Mr. Lonnegan would never sell her, or Cicero for that matter. Personally, I resent the airs she puts on trying to be dignified. She's a slave, for God's sake. I resent her attitude, and I would sell her tomorrow if I had my druthers. Insolent slaves belong on the block. Of course, Mister Bindle has ways of cowing the field hands. You will no doubt meet him this morning."

Daniel said nothing, trying to stall for time until he could figure out next steps. As Archie's footsteps approached, he put a hand to his side and flexed it backward several times to warn him off.

"Mrs. Lonnegan, while we are on our tour, could I trouble you to jot down the various kinds of chickens you maintain? Susan, my wife, will be most interested, although I don't want her to get any ideas about buying chickens from Java."

"No trouble at all. I'm always happy to share my hobby with others."

As Ellie attempted to open the gate, wheel in the empty barrow, and close the gate behind her, all the while not letting any escape, Daniel made a pretense of helping keep the flock in its pen. By moving to the gate, he hoped Ellie would overhear their conversation.

"I do find it remarkable that we travelled in the company of a fugitive slave that came from your plantation," he said, changing the topic. "What are the mathematical odds of a coincidence like that happening?"

"Beauregard will hang him for sure when he's returned. Three escaped, Mister Cameron, three, but as long as one remains on the run, the others live vicariously through him. So he must be caught to prevent disquiet brought on by false hope."

"Pardon my ignorance, but do many escape? You must remember I am not from the south."

"There is no way of knowing how many run away throughout the South, but I can tell you for a surety, few escape."

"The manservant we employed, this Joseph, he seems to have got away."

"Some take longer than others to retrieve. Beauregard has the best bounty hunters in Tennessee on his trail, so you see, it's only a matter of time." She turned toward the chicken coop and yelled, "Missy, I haven't heard a sound from that shovel in a while! Do I need to summon Mister Bindle for a reminder?"

From the back door of the plantation house, Beauregard Lonnegan called out, "I'll meet everyone at the stable." Daniel excused himself to join a healthier looking Emmett and a quizzical Archie. "Later," he said.

"Fine, fine horseflesh you have," Archie remarked as Lonnegan strode up to the trio. "While my friend Daniel investigated the noble art of raising chickens, I took the opportunity to look over your equine stock, and I can't find a utilitarian nag among them."

"Nor will you. I pride myself on keeping track of my bloodlines. Mister Emmett, Mister Cameron, please give me your opinion of my horses while I have a stable boy harness a carriage."

"Not a peep from me, sir, not while I'm in the company of three who know far more about what constitutes a quality animal than I do," Emmett said as they entered the building.

A child would be able to see that all Lonnegan's animals were the best money could buy and well cared for, so the compliments were frequent and genuine. When the carriage was brought to the door, Lonnegan drove it himself, stopping often to point out the kitchen for the hands, the gin, various storehouses, the cattle barn, the pigsty, the granary, the blacksmith's and carpenter's workshops, the smokehouse, the slave cabins, the slaves' garden, the bee yard, and the extensive fields. He introduced them to Bindle, who acknowledged them with a tip of his hat, explained his plans to increase production on fresh acreage, pointed out how a proper division of labour made for efficiency, ignored Daniel's query about the babies slung on mothers' backs, and analysed the attributes of some of his recent acquisitions to justify their purchase. Emmett hung on his every word and queried him about the life cycle of a cotton plant, its unique properties, weevils, and its propensity to exhaust soil.

"You say you wish to invest in a source of cotton for your mill..." Lonnegan said.

"Mills," Emmett corrected.

"Mills. You say you wish to invest in a source of cotton for your mills," Lonnegan continued. "What do you import? Long staple? Short staple?"

Lonnegan is setting a trap, Daniel thought, and considered feigning a coughing fit to give Emmett time to think, but the young man skated through the hazard without a second's hesitation.

"Both. We import from Egypt as well as the United States. I assume some may come from India. I have no idea what percentage of each we process. It wasn't all that long ago my dear uncle passed, so please be patient with me; I am very much the novice in this study."

Lonnegan circled the carriage back to a large wooden building and disembarked, followed by his guests. "The success of your entire operation will depend on the machine you see here," and he led them into a combination workshop and storehouse. "This is a cotton gin. Its sole purpose is to remove the seeds from the bolls. When assessing an investment, start here, Mister Emmett. Notice how uniform the hooks are in my machine. I insist upon precise settings for the hooks and brushes. There are two pitfalls with this machine. Never, ever permit anyone to use the gin if there is the slightest moisture in the raw cotton. Second, slaves have a tendency to overfeed the hopper to achieve their quota more rapidly, and the result is snagging and therefore inefficiency. The machine cannot be hurried, so punish any slave who does not follow instructions to the letter. I sometimes think they deliberately stress the process just to avoid work when the gin clogs."

Lonnegan turned the carriage down the lane, the trio assuming they were heading to his holdings across the road. "Also, you mentioned a superintendent in the Carolinas may be too lax with your slaves. Without sounding presumptuous or patronizing, may I suggest you may be guilty of a certain generosity of spirit that comes with youth. Simply put, your superintendent may be taking advantage of you because you are too lax in your relationship with him."

He stopped the carriage part way to the road. "There is no room for sentimentality in business, Mister Emmett, and no substitute for a clear-headed exercise of power." He led them across the grass to a large maple tree and pointed to a dilapidated old chair, its rungs warped, its yellow paint almost gone. On it, facing north, sat one large and one small human skull. "These two attempted to escape with the manservant you hired. Didn't Machiavelli advise it is better to rule through fear than love? Love can be withdrawn, but fear is involuntary."

No one replied. Unsuccessfully, each tried to look away, to ignore the message, yet each pictured a third skull on the chair, as if it would round out a collection. As they climbed back into the carriage, Lonnegan said, "Everyone on my plantation understands my expectations."

The same boy who had harnessed it met the carriage at the stable door and spoke a few words to Lonnegan. "I appreciate that you gentlemen are on a business trip of sorts, but it appears your laundry is not yet dry. Please stay another night, or better yet, stay a few days, get a feel for what's involved in growing cotton. My wife said she liked to see me converse with the outside world, when actually it is she who needs contact with civil people who do not exhibit the rough edges we often see hereabouts. I will have Cicero organize a barbecue on the front lawn and we can eat 'al fresco' on the porch. A few rum punches will not go amiss, will they, Mister Emmett?" and he laughed at the young man's embarrassment.

"Very good of you, Mister Lonnegan," Archie replied. "We really should push on tomorrow, but your offer sounds too good to pass up. I just hope we can extend the same warm hospitality to you if you ever visit Canada West."

"Or England," Emmett added.

"I must abandon you this afternoon, but please feel free to enjoy a bit of a holiday. Cicero will look after everything; even Mrs. Lonnegan stays out of his way when he orchestrates our meals. As for me, I wish to greet the upstream boat. A trader in Memphis was supposed to have a parcel of slaves delivered by now, and yet I have not seen hide nor hair. Before I go, I suggest we grab a sandwich or two on the front porch to see us through to supper."

Lunch, Supper and Breakfast

There were rum punches at lunch. Daniel took special notice of Mrs. Lonnegan's consumption, which appeared to be double anyone else's. Lonnegan was too sharp to be unaware, so Daniel assumed he condoned his wife's drinking.

Daniel began the probe. "Mister Lonnegan, your wife tells me the girl I observed at the chicken coop has domestic experience; however, she was unable to tell me what someone like that would be worth. Emmett might like to get an idea of value for money, wouldn't you Emmett? Would someone like that suit?"

"Probably. Scrubbed up, of course. Exactly what I am looking for is a youngish female who can fit seamlessly into a busy entrepreneurial household, a quick learner who would naturally assume a subordinate position, but who might eventually take over the kitchen. Would your girl fit the bill?"

"Ellie would 'fit the bill,' as you rather crudely put it, Mister Emmett, but the man I recommend is Mister Nathan Forrest in Memphis, a trader diligent in the care of a wide range of merchandise. The girl is not for sale."

"Mrs. Lonnegan predicted your response to Mister Cameron. How much for Cicero? He appears smoothly competent — a bit old for what I expect from a house steward, but then he would not require breaking in, as the girl would. I shall pay your price for Cicero, if it's not overly extravagant."

The major-domo stood rigid at the doorway.

You claim to be in the market for slaves, yet manumission papers in your possession show three have been released from bondage recently, Lonnegan mused. *Most curious.*

"Mister Emmett, neither Cicero nor the girl are for sale."

"I'm jesting, sir. I was just sounding the waters when I offered to buy Cicero. He truly is too far advanced in years for what I have in mind. I like to look ahead, Mister Lonnegan. In twenty-five years, I shall begin the inevitable descent from my prime, so I ask myself, in a quarter century, will I wish to be searching for a replacement house steward or chef or valet? No, with a view to the long road in the kitchen, a young, malleable female is the route to go."

Daniel and Archie leaned back in their chairs, pretending to be disinterested bystanders, astounded by Emmett's ability to play the role, and tuned in as acutely as Cicero.

"Within reason, the money is no object, Mister Lonnegan," Emmett said casually. "I offer you five hundred English pounds for the girl."

"The girl is not for sale."

"Seven hundred."

"No."

"Eight fifty."

"No."

"One thousand. Before you decline the offer, please consider: Mister Cameron was informed the girl was suffering punishment for running away. If — when — the girl runs away again, you will be out the girl and a thousand pounds

— Bank of England pounds, Mister Lonnegan, not your ephemeral, suitable for wallpaper dollars issued by the latest johnny-come-lately-and-soon-to-be-gone-again state bank. A thousand Bank of England pounds is a sizeable sum, sir."

"Yes, yes it is Mister Emmett. You can offer me twenty thousand pounds, and the answer will be the same. No."

Lonnegan wiped his mouth with his napkin, drained his glass, and pushed himself away from the table. "Now, if you'll excuse me, I am off to track down a shipment. Enjoy a pleasant afternoon, gentlemen."

Cicero glided about the table with a bottle poised. Daniel, Archie, and Emmett waved a hand over their glasses; Mrs. Lonnegan's was again refreshed. "That will be all, Cicero. You may go. Please attend to the laundry these gentlemen left in your care. They may not enjoy the same trust I do in your ability to sort clothes. Leave the bottle." Cicero bowed ever so slightly and disappeared into the house.

"Gentlemen, would you care to see my fancy chickens?"

"That would be delightful, Mrs. Lonnegan," Archie said. "Mister Cameron becomes insufferable when he is knowledgeable about a topic and he is aware others are not."

Carrying her glass with steady hands, their hostess walked them through the house garden to the chicken coop, looked about to make sure they were alone, and took a sip of her drink.

"Since we have no idea how much time we have for discussion, I will not be circumspect. As I told Mister Cameron this morning, Mister Lonnegan will not sell Ellie. I will."

For emphasis, she tapped her sternum with a forefinger and repeated, "I will. For one thousand Bank of England pounds, Mister Emmett, you can have her. However, a cheque is useless to me; I must have cash."

"That is not an impediment, Mrs. Lonnegan," Emmett said. "Not an impediment."

"You see, if you take her off my hands, I rid myself of an ungrateful vexation, that unctuous house steward is put in his place, and for reasons best known to myself, I get revenge for my husband's transgressions. I am assuming the offer is still open?"

"Of course," Emmett said.

"Then the transaction must be done as I dictate, or we do not have a deal. Ellie must appear to run away a second time. In exchange for sweets, a small boy runs errands for me, so communication is not a problem; for such a small boy, he is very discreet. I will send her shoes with him. He will unlock the honey storehouse door and return the key to me. He will tell her to leave the door ajar behind her and to hide at the end of the lane of the farm where she took refuge previously. For the pick-up I can draw you a map."

Daniel marvelled how this woman who had consumed so much alcohol at lunch was able to think and talk coherently. It occurred to him she had become accustomed to copious quantities of spirits over years of an aristocratic lifestyle.

"Why not lock the door behind her?" Archie asked.

"I may be able to stall for time if I say I think I saw her heading to finish the pig pen or the stable or whatever. That way someone will think someone else let her out. If possible, you should be on your way before her escape is noticed."

"A hurried departure will raise suspicion," Daniel said. "We should tarry over breakfast coffee, ask your husband if there is any possibility he may change his mind about Emmett's offer, say our good-byes at leisure..."

"True. But however this transpires, Beauregard must not discover it is I who has the thousand pounds and it is he who is paying for his sins. As for Cicero..."

Emmett said, "Where shall I give you the money? We don't want anyone to witness the exchange."

"Heavens, no. Put the money in a laundry bag and toss it into my room as you come down for supper. I shall squirrel it away and follow you. As soon as we go in, I will draw you a map so you can immediately recognize the farm. Turn left from our lane, and it is straight down the road about seven or eight miles. On your right hand side you will see two dead trees, one hollow and wind-snapped about half way up, the other leaning over the lane. If you pass over a bridge longer than a team and wagon, you have gone too far."

When Lonnegan returned with his recent acquisitions, he spent time with Bindle assigning them their cabin and getting them ready for work the following day. With Cicero directing preparations for the barbecue, the money transfer was easily accomplished. This night's meal was less formal than the previous. After dessert and liqueurs, the men sat around a bonfire, enjoying the life of the idle rich. Lonnegan expressed polite regret when he learned the trio planned to depart in the morning, but said he admired their sense of purpose and hoped he had been of some small assistance in helping them appreciate the situation in the South and particularly the cultivation of cotton.

Breakfast was consumed leisurely as planned. At any moment the conspirators feared Ellie's absence would be discovered, but they loitered over coffee, expressed their gratitude to the Lonnegans for their most charitable hospitality as Cicero loaded their luggage into the Yellow Bounder, and forced themselves to appear reluctant to leave. At mid-morning, Archie drove their horses past the ear tree and onto the road heading north. Each involuntarily let out a sigh of relief once the plantation disappeared from view.

When Archie stopped the team three miles down the road, Daniel asked if he was listening for sounds of pursuit. "No, damn it, I just realized where our plan falls apart."

"Where?" Daniel and Emmett asked simultaneously.

"Think it through, gentlemen. We can only hope Ellie has escaped, but she knows her life will be hell if she is caught a second time, so… She will do everything in her power not to be seen. She doesn't know us from Adam, and Daniel, you say you tried to talk loud enough she would hear Joseph's name, but there is no guarantee she did. Worse, she has no idea she has not simply been sold to another owner. Mrs. Lonnegan thinks that, so why would she tell her different? What if she decides to take her chances as a fugitive and not be at the rendezvous point? Who could blame her?"

"We have to believe she has realized by now that Mrs. Lonnegan intends for her to never return," Daniel replied, "so she may take her chances with a new owner. But what the hell would go through your mind if you were in her shoes? Fear of a life of backbreaking drudgery in the fields? We have no alternative but to carry on and hope for the best."

There was no one waiting at the landmark trees.

Anxious lest a traveller come upon them stopped for no apparent reason, or worse, a pursuit party from Lonnegans', they searched through roadside bushes and called out Ellie's name. Archie suggested only Daniel should speak, since Ellie had hopefully heard him at the chicken coop. He yelled that Joseph was waiting for her and that they were friends of Joseph and that they were trying to rescue her from slavery and she must come out of hiding immediately or there was a good chance she would be caught again, and so on.

No response. A quarter of an hour elapsed and still there was no Ellie. Daniel impatiently paced back and forth at the head of the lane, scanning the local farm house and the adjoining fields. Suddenly he stopped, retreated to a point between the signal trees, walked over to the snapped one, got down on his knees, and peered up the hollow bole. Words disappeared into the darkness. He stood, dusted off his knees, and waited. Two full minutes passed before the others in the phaeton witnessed a tentative shoe on the ground, then two, then the bottom of a canvas dress, then the whole Ellie wriggling out of the tree.

She stood stiffly, evaluating the situation. Daniel took a step back to make her more comfortable. "Ellie," he said in a calm and unpressing tone, "we can explain as we go, but we must go now. This instant. You are free with us until you are caught, but if they catch up, we cannot protect you. My name is Cameron, that is Taylor, the skinny red haired one is Emmett. Do you remember Joseph? I am Joseph's employer. Joseph is waiting for you. We're on the run, so hop up beside Emmett. Please. We absolutely must put miles between us and Lonnegans'. Once you hear the whole story, you will understand."

Archie flicked the reins, and off they set at a pace he thought the horses could sustain. Several miles later, with still no sound of pursuit, he turned to Daniel and asked, "How did you know she had climbed up into the tree?"

"Mrs. Lonnegan said the girl needed to finish the pig pen. Remember? I smelled pigs. Archie, my dear friend, there is no odour quite like the smell of pigs."

At the Sleepy Goat

Spoons poised, Joseph, Red, and Blue watched the widow ladle a generous helping of grits into their bowls. She pushed a jar across the table. "Don't let Deacon hog all the brown sugar. Can't have grits without brown sugar."

"Top rate, ma'am," Deacon said, "and I am used to good food, as the boys can attest."

"If I had known you were coming... Too late for lunch, but grits may hold you over 'til supper. There's a roast on."

The widow topped up each coffee mug, including her own, and took a chair opposite him. "It's good to see you again. I surely wish I could give you more information about the men you seek. Speaking God's truth, I didn't have much to say to them when they were here, and they didn't say much to me, other than to yell for more food and whiskey. They did like their whiskey. The father even put some in his porridge, he did. A terrible waste of corn mash, I thought, although he can add it to pig swill for all I care, since he's the paying customer. Nasty customers, demanding customers, hard to please customers, and welcome customers the way they topped up the bill so charitably. You wouldn't think they're the type to think about a poor widow who's trying to coax a little inn into the future."

"So you have seen only the father before?"

"Only the father. As I told you, he acted like this was where the president overnighted when he was in the neighbourhood."

"You have no idea where they were going from here?"

"Just down the road, southerly. But if I was chasing them, well, first, I wouldn't, but if I was chasing them I might head toward Memphis."

"Why Memphis?"

"I heard one of the sons, not the one with the scarred face, t'other one, say he hoped they got a better price in Memphis next time 'cause he figured they coulda done better from Forrest on the last delivery."

"Forrest?"

"Forrest. He said Forrest was talking about going out of the business. If you ask me, I think those three are bounty hunters."

"What makes you think so?"

"In their talk they mentioned all sorts of places they've been. Far away places... Michigan, Indiana, Ohio... Why else would three men be travelling back and forth across the countryside, each toting a gun he could trade for the best horse at any tavern? Besides, when they unsaddled to look to their horses, and you could see from a distance those were handsome horses... Most look after their own mounts because the local boy who helps in the stable can't be here all the time, and no one expects a poor widow woman to work the livery too... Anyways, when the saddlebags were dropped, I heard the sound of chains or manacles or some such heavy hardware. Wasn't crystal wine glasses, you can bet on that. So I says to myself, bounty hunters, and if they want whiskey, they get whiskey, and if they want steak and kidney pie, they get steak and kidney pie."

Deacon said, "Have I got this right? The name is Ragg. The father is Aeneas; he's shorter but stockier, more muscular than the sons. He's the one that wears the high brown boots. The sons are tall and lanky, one has a severely scarred face, both wear their hair long... Anything else? What about the horses?"

"Two bays for the boys, if I remember, a dappled grey for the father. Of him I'm certain; he was a handsome animal. Better than most we see hereabouts, and we see some of the best."

"If we could trouble you for an early breakfast tomorrow. We have far to go. Lunches too, if that's possible. The last ones came in mighty handy, and I'm much obliged you thought to send them with us. Add those to the bill. And if you can spare, a bag of oats."

"I thank you, Deacon. The Sleepy Goat would not survive without come-ag'in business. Your boys will find the oats right beside the stall they'll bed down in." She turned to Joseph and the twins. "Once the locals have drunk up and sung themselves home, you boys feel free to come in for a late snack. If I'm gone to bed, I'll leave the raisin pie on top of the breadbox. You finish it off, what's left. There's ginger cookies beside the box too, in case the corners need filling."

Voicing their gratitude, they cleared the table while the widow retrieved the coffee pot and tipped more into all their mugs.

"Deacon, if I may ask, why are you so all-fired interested in those particular customers?"

"You may ask. Those men are responsible for the deaths of my wife and my children. I am going to kill them." He sipped his coffee, added some cream and brown sugar, and said, "I appreciate you being so kind to the boys."

Clothes for Ellie

"First village or town, we need to rest the horses, acquire some travelling food, get our story straight if we're overtaken," Emmett fretted.

"The story is pretty well told if we're caught helping a slave run away," Daniel said. "A favourite slave, I might add."

"They hang horse thieves here. I choose not to contemplate our fate if we're apprehended stealing a person," Archie said.

Emmett shook his head in disbelief. "Gentlemen, did you think I would omit this necessity?" He fished about in a shirt pocket for a piece of paper and waved it about. "Behold, a signed and dated receipt. Ellie is technically my property. Well, maybe legally she's still Lonnegan's property because she was sold by his wife without his consent, but the people we meet won't know that. I asked for it to be signed simply 'Lonnegan'.

This is why we must get the details meticulously correct; for the sake of all parties, consistency is essential should anyone question what transpired."

Daniel gave a low whistle. "Emmett, you never cease to amaze. At the plantation, your superlative ability as a convincing liar of the first order was positively faultless. *Ad lib* fabrication is a God-given talent, sir, and I stand in awe. And now I see you had the presence of mind to coax a receipt from that pathetic, scheming, alcohol soaked woman. Again, I am in awe."

"As am I," Archie added. "Well done."

"I thank you, gentlemen. You were excellent foils in our little drama. I propose we continue to play the assigned roles. Should anyone ask, I have purchased Ellie to serve as a domestic. If the anyone is importunate, we are not from the South, and we had no idea Mrs. Lonnegan did not have the right to sell off a family asset, so we are suitably contrite, nay, mortified, if we have contributed in any way to dissension between our most hospitable hosts. However, I must be on my way if I am to return to England before the storms of autumn. Therefore we wish to press on in haste, thank you very much..."

"We don't want to draw unwanted attention. Is it appropriate for three men to travel with a young female slave?" Daniel wondered. "If not, what is our alternative?"

"I can tell you it is not appropriate to travel with any woman of any age sporting a canvas dress which reeks of ordure. Pig manure especially. Is malodorous canvas to be the theme of our expedition?" Emmett asked. "I beg your pardon, Ellie. Not meaning to be rude, but you do stink."

Ellie hung her head in embarrassment. "I'm sorry," she said.

"Are you hungry?" Daniel asked. She nodded. "When did you eat last?"

"Some bread. Early this morning."

"Good gawd!" Archie exclaimed. "My stomach is already so empty it's clicking against my ribs like a little boy's stick on a picket fence, and we had a full breakfast. You must be famished."

The next hamlet they passed through boasted no amenities. It was hours before they entered a village with a general store.

"Emmett, it would look best if you kept an eye on your property. Archie, if you could find some oats for the team, with a fresh infusion of Emmett's cash I shall see if I can rustle up something to eat."

Fifteen minutes later, Daniel emerged from the general store with a heaping armload of purchases; for privacy, they drove to the edge of town. He passed beef jerky all round and with a new can opener prised open a can of corned beef for Ellie. He handed her a spoon and a small paper bag as well.

"Cookies. And a few sweets. Do not share them, no matter how much Archie pleads."

Ellie sat in the rear seat of the phaeton, spooning out chunks of meat, eyes glistening with tears. When she had finished the whole can of beef and was starting on the cookies, Daniel unfolded a crimson red dress with a bright yellow diagonal stripe and placed it on the seat beside her. 'It's pretty much all they had — except for brown and grey. I asked myself what Susan — that's my wife — what Susan would recommend, and the red one jumped out at me. It may be too large, but it will have to do until we can get you something better."

"Don't don the dress until we can find somewhere to get you cleaned up," Emmett suggested. The somewhere happened to be two miles down the road. Daniel handed Ellie a fresh bar of yellow soap from the mound of purchases, and the men waited patiently on a bridge while she scrubbed herself in the stream underneath. A canvas dress floated away on the current. It was a fair time before she re-emerged, but when she did, there had been a transformation. The manure-stained girl clad in odoriferous sailcloth had been replaced by a youthful beauty, vivacious in her red dress.

"Ah, Joseph, now I understand," Daniel muttered.

"We had no idea you were in the vanguard of vogue," Archie said. "Imagine, Daniel Cameron picking out that stunner all on his own."

"I haven't Emmett's skill at prevaricating, so I must confess the truth. When in doubt, rely on the wisdom of old ladies. There were several in the store, and I simply asked their advice — not that there was much selection in colour or size, mind you. Each agreed: if the woman is married and over thirty, buy a dull one; if unmarried and less than thirty, the red."

"Damn clever," Emmett said.

"Emmett, the ease with which you toy with the truth is corrupting me; in the store, I concocted a lie on the instant. I told the ladies I was travelling with a friend who had recently acquired a young female slave, but his mother who had been accompanying our party took ill and was unable to continue. So, I asked, what is the proper etiquette in this situation? People everywhere love to be asked for advice."

"And?"

"And they were of one mind. If the owner is not married, no one will notice. After all, one said, she is his property. But they all agreed that if the man were married, he should avoid public indiscretions."

"Anything else?" Archie asked.

"Yes. One suggested that while travelling, if she is a new purchase, the girl should sleep outside his door with one end of a length of stout cord knotted to her foot and the other to his."

Emmett laughed. "Did you buy a ball of cord as well? It will be difficult to explain a runaway slave running away."

Daniel turned to the girl. "You have had a rather busy day of it, Ellie. Will you try to give us the slip? It would break Joseph's heart if we showed up without you. We can't promise you won't get caught. All we can promise is that we will try to get you to freedom."

She clasped her hands under her chin and looked him in the eye. "I will die before I let Cicero touch me."

"Let's be off," Archie said, picking up the reins. "I intend to push the horses to put miles between us and Lonnegan. We won't reach The Sleepy Goat tonight, and inns are few and far between."

They might have reached the next inn before dusk had Archie not taken a wrong road. By the time he realized his error and backtracked, night was upon them. The innkeeper informed them he could provide enough supper to fill empty bellies until morning if they were content with the scrapings from a roast of beef piled on a slab of bread. There was no problem finding rice pudding for dessert; it had not been as popular as he hoped. However, sleeping accommodations were out of the question; all rooms were rented. He suggested the stable as the only alternative. So, on her first night out of bondage, Ellie found herself under a horse blanket in her new dress, once again on straw, in a corner of a vacant horse stall, while her three liberators in the next stall told jokes, laughed, and threatened snoring or flatulence with dire consequences. She heard Daniel say, "...an elevated level of language compared to Joseph," and Archie reply, "She's lived in the house with the gentry," and Emmett say, "I wonder if she can read." Just as she fell asleep, she heard Emmett again. "By Jove, wouldn't she look smashing at the officers' ball in that red dress?"

Breakfast was adequate. Although the sky promised rain, Ellie chose to eat in the Yellow Bounder. For a change, they did not wish to engage in conversation with the locals, although the locals were quite content to ask all about them. Daniel shooed the travellers out the door when a gap-toothed, tobacco chewing country bumpkin asked how much they wanted for the wench. They left with no lunches packed, dependent on the provisions from the general store.

"Today we put as many miles behind us as we can," Archie said, as he and Daniel struggled to put up the concertinaed leather top. "We'll take turns driving, but even if we get to The Sleepy Goat tonight, I can't imagine Joseph, Deacon and the twins haven't already pushed on to the sawmill."

By noon, the rain that had started out mid-morning as a drizzle, now driven by an unrelenting southwest wind, had soaked all to the skin. Ellie, aware that her saturated dress had become translucent, wrapped herself in a carriage blanket and curled up in one corner of the back seat.

"You look positively uncomfortable," Daniel remarked.

"I have never been off the plantation before for more than a few miles, so I don't mind that I'm wet. This is all new. I have heard of towns, of course, but I had no idea they had stores where a white man could just walk in and buy a dress if he wanted."

"Remarkable," Emmett muttered.

"Mister Cameron, I have a favour to ask, if it's not too much... I don't want to appear ungrateful..."

"I can't think of any favour that would make you appear ungrateful. What is it?"

"If it's not too much trouble, could you buy me a brown or dark blue dress?"

"Don't you like the one I picked out for you to replace that canvas monstrosity?"

"I love it! I absolutely love it! This is the first dress I ever had anyone buy me in my whole life. I've always had to sew my own. It's just that... just that... it's too bright. Everyone will think I'm a harlot, 'specially travellin' with three men. And it draws attention to me — to us — and I don't want anyone lookin' at me and startin' to think..."

"She makes a good point," Emmett admitted. "Next town, Mister Cameron can apply his vast fashion knowledge and buy you another in a more subdued colour. However, I seem to remember I'm the one who footed the bill for this one, so the next one can come out of his pocket."

"Thank you," Ellie said. "But not a grey one. I'd look like a ghost in a grey one — and a grey one would remind me of Mistress Lonnegan."

Lonnegan Learns of the Conspiracy

"Mister Bindle, not all that long ago you stood in front of my desk, hat in hand, to bring me news three field hands had escaped. That tale has not yet played out. I return from Memphis and commend you on Ellie's speedy recovery from her little jaunt. Here you are once again, telling me Ellie is missing and nowhere to be found."

Lonnegan sat back in his chair, intertwined his fingers, and said, "If I understand you correctly, the storehouse door was left open all yesterday, each of you supposing someone else had unlocked it, and no one thought to check where she was supposed to be. Now I hear someone locked it last night, again each of you thinking someone else was responsible. Then this morning, when you unlock the door, lo and behold, no Ellie. A door that was confining a girl who was being punished for running away was unlocked by someone and someone locked it again to make all appear normal. Now, who the hell was it?"

Bindle fidgeted with his hat. "Mister Lonnegan, I checked before I darkened your door. Not me or my men unlocked that door or locked it last night, and only us has the key, 'cept for the master set in the house."

"Jesus H Christ, are you suggesting someone from the house let her out? Cicero? The other kitchen wench? Cook?"

"I don't know who let her out; I only know our keys are accounted for."

"What are you doing about catching her, other than twirling your hat in my office?"

"My men are on the road right now to see if anyone's seen her; one is checking with neighbours to the south, the other has gone north to see if she's hiding in the barn where she holed up before. She might think we wouldn't suspect the same place twice."

"If Ellie was hiding in a specific barn, how in God's name did you find her?"

The hat twirled faster. "We were given a tip."

"Who gave you this tip? A specific barn on a specific farm suggests knowledge beforehand."

The hat continued to rotate as Bindle looked at the floor.

"Goddamn it man, who?"

"I would rather not say, Mister Lonnegan."

"You would rather not say... You would rather not say... Maybe you would rather not work. Bindle, you will not have a job here or anywhere within a hundred miles if I don't hear the truth out of your mouth the next words you speak. Now, who — gave — you — the — tip?"

Lonnegan allowed him time to consider his options. Finally, he said, "Mrs. Lonnegan."

Lonnegan took two cigars from the box, handed one to Bindle, indicated he should take a seat, and lit for both. "There now, that wasn't so hard, was it?" Leaning back in his chair, he placed his elbows on the arms, pressed the tips of his fingers together, and blew smoke above Bindle's head. "Tell me everything. No detail is too insignificant."

In the next few minutes, Lonnegan learned of his wife's overture to a conspiracy, how Bindle examined Bellerophon's hoof to manufacture an excuse for a rendezvous, the resulting conversation, and how his wife wanted to orchestrate a divide among her husband, Cicero, and Ellie by having the girl banned from household service.

Lonnegan and Bindle smoked in silence for several minutes.

"How did she communicate?"

"She has a small boy run errands for her."

"Could the child have unlocked the door and re-locked it last night?"

"Yes. With difficulty, yes."

"Is Cicero's assault with the knife what really happened?"

"Yes."

"Is my wife behind the girl's second escape?"

"I have no way of knowing, one way or the other. Possibly, but this time she has not confided in me. If she has helped the girl, she has not involved me in any way."

"I find it curious that Ellie goes missing close to the time our guests make their departure. Do you think they may have anything to do with her escape?"

"I have no way of knowing, one way or the other. It's possible, I suppose."

"Goddamn right it's possible! Pull that tassel for me. I want Cicero. As for you, Mister Bindle, I never punish honesty. However, a word of advice. Don't be late with it again. Carry on and keep me posted. Find the girl! She can't have gone far."

By the time Bindle extinguished his cigar and backed out of the office, Cicero had appeared.

"I have a hunch, but before I make a fool of myself, Cicero, I want you to search Mrs. Lonnegan's room. Normally I only ask you to report on hidden bottles to keep an eye on surreptitious drinking. This time, be more thorough. Discreet, but thorough."

Cicero returned in less than ten minutes. He placed one thousand Bank of England pounds on Lonnegan's desk and said, "Under the mattress." As he bowed himself out, Lonnegan said, "Tell Bindle I wish to see him again."

Constance Lonnegan had no premonition of upheaval when she breakfasted the following morning. While her husband ate his poached eggs on toast with crisp bacon and English style muffins slathered with jam, he remarked on how quiet the house was without visitors and how the rain seemed to have passed to the north. As normal, he inquired how she planned to spend her day, although she knew he did not give a tinker's dam how she planned to spend her day. It wasn't until her second coffee, when Cicero did not meet her eye to receive a glanced thank-you for the brandy, did she sense something was amiss. She detected the faintest hint of smoke. Beau Lonnegan shoved his dirty dishes aside, moved his chair back from the table, crossed his left knee over his right, and studied his wife.

"Do you smell smoke?" she asked.

"Yes, I do," he said.

"Aren't you going to track it down?"

"I already know where it's coming from."

"You do?"

"Outside."

She pushed herself erect and exited through the back door. An opaque pall of grey smoke was rising from behind the garden. It took her several moments to grasp the scene before her. The clothesline curved under the weight of her chickens, tied by one leg and headless. Flames emanating from the open door of the chicken coop had totally engulfed the interior and were licking at the roof. A sob of pain escaped her, and she put a hand over her mouth as she watched the horror.

Lonnegan stood beside her and gazed at the conflagration with disinterest. "You are free to walk the grassed grounds. You may not venture farther. Christ, Constance, how did you ever think you could get away with it?"

She turned and raised her hand as if to strike him.

"If you touch me, I will break your jaw. Feel free to leave if you wish. I can replace you with a young belle in a day."

She dropped her hand and stared at him, her head moving ever so slightly back and forth in disbelief. Lonnegan snapped his fingers; Cicero hurried to his side and handed him a small canvas bag from which he removed bundles of money tied with butcher cord.

"A thousand English pounds? You pissed all this away for a thousand English pounds? Under your fucking mattress? You stupid, stupid, stupid, drunken, unimaginative woman."

He dropped the bundles back into the bag.

"She's still mine, you know. You cannot sell what belongs to me. She is still my property. I will get her back."

He handed the bag to Cicero, turned, and beckoned to the stable door.

"Excuse me, Constance. There is one more thing I need to do."

He strode over to the stable from which Bindle emerged, carrying a navy revolver and leading Bellerophon.

"Thank you Mister Bindle," Lonnegan said, taking the revolver from him. "I will do this myself."

The Raggs Visit

By late afternoon, the coop was a pile of glowing embers digesting any remaining charred lumber to ash. Constance Lonnegan stood at the window of her bedroom, empty glass in hand, and in vain hoped the fire would consume her husband's empire, even though a slave standing beside a cluster of water buckets guaranteed its containment. When field hands carrying decapitated Spitzhaubens dashed to their kitchen, her inebriated brain was too numb to protest.

She heard hooves before she saw the three riders. The leader, a short, heavily muscled man wearing a brown leather vest and knee-high brown riding boots, pulled up at the stable door. She watched as her husband engaged them in conversation, worried his left ear as was his habit, and pointed north. They dismounted, surrendered their mounts to the stable boys, and followed him toward the back door of the house. She heard him yell, "Cicero, three for supper and to spend the night," and moments later there was the sound of the kitchen help readying a tray of glasses and bottles to be brought to the front porch.

"*I am ill. Do not disturb. Supper in my room. Down for breakfast.*" she wrote on a piece of flowered stationery and left it in the hall outside her door.

Retiring to her bed to sleep it off, she was unable to think of a future beyond the twin prisons of husband and bottle. She sank into a fitful sleep eventually and dreamt she was riding Bellerophon around and around and around a crystal palace. About midnight, she was wakened by the raucous laughter of drunken men. When she returned to her dream, the crystal palace had melted into a crimson pool of bloody feathers.

She was downstairs later than usual for breakfast. The overnighters had cantered down the lane an hour after first light, leaving their dirty dishes stacked on a serving tray ready for removal. Lonnegan rose from the table, deposited his empty coffee cup on the tray, and began to leave the room with no acknowledgement of her presence. He stopped at the door, turned as if he had forgotten something, and said, "Since we are a house servant short, until Ellie returns you can do up those dishes to help the kitchen staff."

She gasped, and a hand went to her throat. "You monstrous son of a bitch... If you think..."

"I cautioned you about meddling in how I run this plantation, but you wouldn't listen. You despise Ellie, yet you don't want her married to Cicero. You aid her escape, not once but twice. You drink yourself into a fog every day. You conspire with my overseer. Cicero finds one thousand pounds, under your mattress no less, and we are supposed to believe Ellie ran away on a whim? How fucking dim do you think I am? Now do the goddamn dishes!"

Heading South, Heading North

Always Deacon sat on the driver's seat beside Red or Blue, who took turns with the reins. A shoulder cradled the rifled musket. Joseph and the alternate driver amused themselves by peering about to make doubly sure the observers at the front had not missed any evidence of their quarry. For Deacon and the twins, it was Ragg and his sons; for Joseph, it was Daniel and Archie and Emmett with Ellie.

Deacon insisted on a slow pace. "We have all the time we need," he said. "This job must be done right, and it will take longer if we pass them by while they're taking a piss or watering their horses. We don't even know they will stay on this road." He asked oncoming travellers if they had encountered three men, two long-haired, rawboned and slim, on bays, one of them scarred, the third shorter on a dappled grey. After each negative response he would say, "No hurry. We have all the time we need."

He made inquiries at every town, every village, every hamlet, every inn and every tavern. Occasionally, someone would venture the trio had been seen going south, but no one could say just when. "At least we know they are still on the road to Memphis," he would say. "No hurry. We have all the time we need."

They camped close to the main road so that travellers must pass their scrutiny. The first night out from The Sleepy Goat, Joseph squatted beside Deacon, who was watching Red fry up some ham for their late supper.

"Deacon, I've got a question for you. I don't suppose anyone will be travellin' in the dark, but let's just suppose Ragg and his sons was to come by..."

"Okay, suppose Ragg and his sons come by... What's your question?"

"Those murderin' three can't get worse, and we got four of us here itchin' to send 'em to Hell. The problem is, they got three guns, maybe more. We got one gun, cooking knives, and an axe for firewood."

"So your question is, how am I going to kill them, three guns to one?"

"My question is, how are we going to kill them, one gun to three?"

"There was a time when I would have said 'Have faith. My God will protect the righteous.' Now I'm not so sure. He seems to be busy somewhere else."

"Mister Daniel taught me how to shoot. I'm not as good as him, but I can shoot. I got a steady hand, and he showed me how to lead a moving target."

"We are in the South, Joseph. There have been slave risings, so folks get mighty uncomfortable if they see Darkies and guns together."

"Here's what I'm thinkin'. Let's say you get one of them, but then one of them gets you. That's not a fair trade 'cause there are still two of the sons-a-bitches left, and that means

Red, Blue will be back in bondage and I'll be in Gloryland, after some real bad experiences on the way."

"You're the only one of us they've ever seen, and that was running, so what are the chances of being recognized?"

"Deacon, I can't let them take me alive, and they won't care to 'cause I'm worth the same to them dead. I don't want to go back to Massa Lonnegan with my head in a canvas bag, and even if they don't know who we are, the odds are as ugly as a constipated rattlesnake. Three guns to one."

"All right. First opportunity, I'll buy a handgun for you... under two conditions. The first is you pay me for it when Emmett comes 'round with your money. The second is you keep it hidden and out of sight. Deal?"

"Deal. Deacon, for such a good businessman, I worry you don't understand some kinds of arithmetic."

Next morning, they entered a town whose local gunsmith offered a limited selection. Deacon knew the asking price of the rusting revolver was ridiculously inflated; he attempted to deaden the pain by a low bid, but the smith would have none of it, only offering to throw in some ammunition. "Double the ammunition, a cleaning pick, a bottle of gun oil, and you've made a sale," Deacon said reluctantly. He returned to the buckboard embarrassed by his lack of leverage in the negotiation, even though he rationalized it was not his money and Joseph would be enthusiastic about any firearm.

He was. He examined the piece in detail, hefted it, sighted on imaginary targets, and caressed the corroded barrel with his fingers. "It ain't been loved much, but Deacon, it's beautiful. Where's the trigger?"

"Cock the hammer back. See, it magically appears. The smith said this was made in New Jersey by Mister Colt. Thirty-six calibre. Might have a kick. But accurate, the man said. Rifled barrel. You say Cameron taught you how to shoot? Loose black powder or cartridge and percussion cap?"

"Both. How come you know so much about shootin' all of a sudden? The twins said you never had a gun on the place, you being a man of God and all."

"Meat on the table with my father's musket in my youth, and I just bought this from someone who knows about it, so if I parrot what he said I may fool somebody. As for being a man of God... I thought my Jesus suffered little children to come unto him. It turns out my Jesus is the one on the rampage in the temple, taking action when he sees the defilement of something holy, and I can't think of any greater defilement than how my family..." He could not finish the sentence.

"You sayin' we got all the time we need. Then we got time for some target practice once I get the oil to this. Wouldn't do ta find the powder has clumped or the gun jumps to one side when we need it."

An hour later, Deacon pulled the team up near a stream. Joseph wedged a piece of bark in the crotch of a willow, and for the next half hour Deacon with his rifled musket and Joseph with the rusty Colt revolver shot all around the target. Finally, their eyes reddened by gun smoke and their spirits lifted by noise, they cleaned the firearms and proceeded south, in agreement that the Ragg family must meet its fate at close range.

Seven miles to the south, Daniel, Archie, Emmett, and Ellie were making slow progress. Their first and second delays were minor; they had stopped at a general store that stocked a suitable brown dress and replenished food supplies. While Ellie exchanged red for brown under the first appropriate bridge, the men wrestled the leather top into its collapsed position. Their consistently slow pace was due to dense forest that prevented the sun from drying out the rutted roads, still puddle-wet after the recent rains, so the extra effort to pull a vehicle with four people and luggage through mud sometimes boot high was exacting its toll from the team. It was Emmett's turn to take the reins. Ellie sat beside him, taking in everything novel. Daniel and Archie sat in the back seat, ready to bail out and grunt the Yellow Bounder out of wheel-sucking wallows when necessary. Other than cursing wet boots, wet pant legs, and wet roads, there was minimal conversation.

After a period of silence, Archie said, "I wonder how the women are getting on. I'll bet they're thinking we're having the time of our lives, traipsing around a foreign country and livin' high on the hog."

"Well, that is sort of what we have been doing, thanks to her Britannic Majesty's Government. How to explain it all in context so they understand there's more to it... That will be the problem when we get home."

"Home. I'm thinking I can't get home fast enough. We're seeing some spectacularly magnificent country, more picturesque than the flatness of Kent County, but..."

"But it's not home..." Daniel finished the thought for him.

"Catherine and Susan will be different, more independent, more confident in themselves, if all has gone well," Archie said.

"I can't imagine Susan getting more independent. We'll be different too. You know, I used to read my Bible every night. I haven't read a word since Michigan, and now I spew curses that would have earned me a mouthful of soap a few years ago."

Archie nodded agreement. "True for both of us. Just listening to us today churning through this hell-sent mud would make a drunken sailor blush."

Daniel leaned toward the front. "I won't ask you, Ellie, if you're homesick. How about you, Emmett. Eager to get back?"

"Yes. I'm enjoying this mission immeasurably, and I'm trusting my report to the governor general will justify my expense account. It's been quite a lark at times, eh what?" He glanced at Ellie. "However, I am concerned we are still so far from The Sleepy Goat. If we are playing Hare and Hounds with Lonnegan, the hare is wheezing badly."

"Can't be helped," Archie said. "Not much we can do about the mud."

"Even so, it wouldn't do to be caught in the open. Do me a favour, Daniel, and hand me my revolver and a pocket's worth of ammunition from my luggage."

With a smirk on his face, Aeneas Ragg descended the steps of the general store. He left the grey's reins thrown round the hitching rail and said, "We've got a hard ride comin' up, so you boys climb down for a spell and give your ass a break. Last night we thought we're looking for a red dress. Man inside said he sold a brown one earlier today to a man what had a large, yellow phaeton waitin' for him. Bright yellow, with over-sized wheels, he said, just like Lonnegan described. Bought biscuits and cheese and pickles and a ham too. Didn't have to prompt him. I just asked about strangers passing through, and he was real helpful and jawed on about the rain comin' so fierce and the road. I reckon we should be able to catch up a pullin' team 'fore dark."

The Gunfight at the Bridge

Archie was not ten minutes into his turn to drive when punky crosspieces on a suspect little bridge let the back right wheel slip between two stringers. Daniel surveyed the problem. "Archie, it's two thirds to the axle, and the horses might be able to free it up with a good heave, but there's always the chance the wheel may break. Before you flick the reins, Emmett and I will try to lift the axle, take some of the pressure off."

"We could take some stress off the wheel if we could lever the axle higher," Emmett affirmed. "Give me five minutes to find a serviceable piece of wood. Daniel, if you can scrounge up a fulcrum..."

Ellie stood on the far side of the bridge to lighten the load. Daniel returned with a flat rock before Emmett was able to wrestle free a broken branch that was thick enough to do the job.

"Now!" they yelled as the axle reached its apogee above the boards. Archie prompted the horses ahead, the wheel rolled free, and once off the bridge he stopped the team to collect his passengers. It was while Daniel was examining the wheel for damage that they heard the sound of approaching horses. Just to err on the side of caution, Emmett slipped off the road to the left and ducked lower than the planking.

Daniel was about to climb into the back and Ellie was reseated in the front when up trotted three riders, each carrying a musket. With sinking hearts, everyone realized the pursuit they feared had materialized.

They were so concentrated on the drama unfolding they did not hear a buckboard approaching from the north.

The man on the grey horse said, "Red dress, brown dress, no dress —don't matter. You'll be coming with us, Ellie."

Knowing it would not work, Daniel tried a bluff anyway. "You must have been sent by Beauregard Lonnegan. Did he not tell you this girl has been purchased by our friend? He has a receipt signed by Lonnegan himself."

"No he don't! He's got a receipt signed by Mrs. Lonnegan, if he's got one, and that one's fraudulent 'cause she ain't got the right to sell what ain't hers. Where is he anyway?"

"I believe he stepped into the bush to relieve himself. He should return any..."

The older son fired his musket into the air, startling everyone.

"Enough of this bullshit! Receipt, no receipt, doesn't matter! She's coming back with us!"

Spurring his horse over the bridge and around the fidgety team, he reined up beside Ellie and reached down to pull her out of the phaeton. She grabbed on to Archie with two arms. He circled his horse. Again he leaned into the carriage, stretched out an arm...

The second bullet was not fired indiscriminately into the air. At a velocity approaching the speed of sound, it smashed through the skull above the right ear, creating a tidy hole less than one inch in diameter, turned the temporal lobe to porridge in its travel, and exited behind the left ear, leaving a jagged hole roughly two inches wide. Quite dead, his body slumped over his horse, which headed back over the bridge. The younger son fired into the cloud of smoke drifting from the north toward the bridge, while the father attempted to locate the shooter and danced his horse about to create a moving target.

The right hind leg of the dead man's prancing bay plunged into the hole in the planks and the horse fell sideways, its leg producing an audible snap as it pinned its dead rider on the bridge beneath. Rather than try to reload, the younger son, yelling, threw his musket to one side, and pulling a handgun from his belt, spurred his mount forward as he levelled his pistol. A fourth bullet came from Emmett at board level. It missed the charging rider, but spun his hat into the air, prompting him to rethink direction. He whirled about, and as his horse too began to prance, he fired the pistol at another smoke cloud coming from the far side of the bridge, a cloud formed from the discharge of a rusty Colt revolver. This bullet took a tiny notch a quarter of an inch wide out of Aeneas Ragg's left ear.

The older Ragg had heard three different firearms from two different directions. Two men scrambled into the back seat of the phaeton. As one turned to fire at him with a revolver, the team leapt forward, spoiling his aim, and the bullet whistled somewhere over his target's head. The canary yellow phaeton fled up the road, and Aeneas Ragg was left to hold a handkerchief to an ear, shoot a horse with a broken leg, and bury a son.

"Hold on!" Archie yelled, as he prepared to swing the team around a buckboard drawn across the road within a hundred feet of the bridge. A Black man with a blue bandana ran into the middle of the road and waved him on. "No one comin'! We'll move outta your way, you push on like you'se on fire, an' we'll follow ya."

With exhausted horses, both phaeton and buckboard were pulled up miles later on the far side of yet another narrow bridge. There was no sound of pursuit. This was as defensible a spot as any, although the dense forest would require a constant vigilant eye to prevent outflanking.

Joseph and Deacon sat in the back of the buckboard, leaning on the tailgate. Deacon was ghost pale and barely conscious. Using his jacket as a dressing, Joseph was pressing it against Deacon's right side, which was saturated with bright red blood. There was a trickle of blood from a wound on the right side of his scalp as well.

"They were using buck and ball, and I figure it was the buck that furrowed above the ear," Joseph said. "That wound isn't serious, unless he's planning to grow hair there. The other's more concerning. I don't want to roll him to see if there's an exit hole, but I think the bullet's still in him. Maybe someone can reach in behind and feel for blood."

Before anyone could move, it was Ellie who took charge. She climbed into the box, felt from Deacon's left for blood, and withdrew a dry hand. "Don't take the jacket away," she said. "Keep it firm against him." She climbed down, retrieved her red dress from the phaeton, used Archie's pocket knife to rip it into long strips, and with the twins' help pushed them behind Deacon so they could be knotted over the wound.

Deacon nodded a feeble thank-you. He was able to murmur, "You got the girl. Good for you," before he lost consciousness.

They held a brief council. Daniel said, "We know one is dead. That may earn us a brief breathing space before we are caught up again. If we are going to move Deacon, now is the time, when he can't feel anything. I propose we secure him to the Bounder's back seat. He won't be any less comfortable there than the buckboard. If I drive and Ellie rides with me, she can keep an eye on him. That leaves Archie, Emmett, Joseph, Red, and Blue in the buckboard. Anyone got a better idea?"

"Yes," Archie said, "I do. You're a better shot than me. I'll drive the Bounder, you take Deacon's gun, then we've got three that can fire at anyone coming at us."

"Good thought," Emmett said. "Let's get the hell out of here."

To The Sleepy Goat

Progress was slow. Occasionally, Deacon would moan and Ellie and Archie would think he was rejoining them, then he would fade again into a blessed oblivion. They found no town, no doctor, no inn or tavern, and no dry place to take shelter. As dusk approached, Archie looked for open, high ground where they could overnight. The best he could find in the miles of forest and wetlands was a two acre meadow near the road.

After Red and Blue watered the horses at the inevitable nearby stream, the teams were supplied with nosebags full of oats. The plan was they would be tethered but left hitched to the vehicles to facilitate a quick getaway if necessary. Firearms were cleaned and loaded. Everyone gathered around the Yellow Bounder to get caught up on the other group's adventures. Leaving out the details, the short term course of events was soon told. Red explained that Pa and the Deacon's family had been killed by Ragg and his sons, so Deacon and the twins were on a vengeance hunt. They were just short of the gunfight bridge when they saw three riders approaching a stationary, canary yellow phaeton. Deacon and Joseph had used the buckboard for cover while the twins sheltered behind nearby trees. Blue verified it was Deacon who killed the son attempting to drag Ellie out of the phaeton. Joseph had fired, but no one saw him hit anything.

"The Deacon's was a pretty shot from someone who only fired that gun a few dozen times," Red observed.

"A lucky shot, even at that range," Blue said. "They got off a lucky shot too. Not lucky for Deacon. Look at the buckboard. I figure the bullet was slantin' downwards 'cause it was fired from a horse, and it went through the side boards just where the boss was standin'. Maybe that's why the bullet didn't go out his other side, 'cause the wood slowed it down."

"But hallelujah, we got one of 'em. Looks like you've been successful too," Red said.

"We got Ellie," Daniel said. "We can explain later, but basically we ran off with her. You just witnessed how badly Lonnegan wants her back."

Joseph and Elllie had said not a word to each other. Too shy to even look at one another directly, they stole surreptitious glances in each other's direction, hurriedly looking away when caught. When the others were preoccupied searching for dry wood, Joseph finally found the courage to approach her vigil beside Deacon.

"Seth?" he asked.

Ellie did not look up. "Hanged. Massa Lonnegan left him on the rope 'til it was hard to tell he'd bin human. He forced us to watch when he cut off his head. He boiled it, Joseph!" She paused to suppress her disgust. "He boiled it and put it on Old Mose's chair at the ear tree 'longside Malachi's."

"Old Mose's chair not at the cemetery?"

"Old Mose is dead. Bindle found him, said it looked like a heart attack, but we all wonderin' what Bindle was doin' visitin' the cemetery."

Everyone remembered it as a miserable night. The twins took ten minutes longer than an eternity to get a fire started behind the barrier of downed logs and branches Daniel and Archie constructed, a fire that smoked so prodigiously it would attract the notice of any passer-by, even if the barrier shielded the flames. Daniel's, Archie's, Emmett's, and Joseph's bedrolls became increasingly damp as they sponged up moisture from the ground. The twins' bed in the buckboard was only marginally more comfortable. Ellie's sleep on the front seat of the phaeton was disrupted by Deacon's moans and his calls for his wife and children. Each time she awoke, she re-positioned his blanket which his writhing had tossed aside.

Day dawned clear. A rushed breakfast of ham with cheese and biscuits was eaten cold because it was evident to all that Deacon, feverish and incoherent in his mutterings, was worse. Ellie was able to coax a few sips of water down his throat before they set out, the Yellow Bounder leading. Although no one mentioned the need for medical attention, Archie pushed the horses as fast as was prudent on the rutted roads. They recognized the next town from their previous travels, but hopes for medical expertise were soon dashed. The local physician had recently deceased and there was no one with more experience with gunshot wounds than themselves.

A drying breeze continued throughout the day, firming roads and permitting a faster rate of travel. Still there was no sign of pursuit. It was late afternoon when they pulled up at The Sleepy Goat.

When the twins carried Deacon in, the widow was everywhere at once. She cleared off a dining room table so they could lay him out in better light, brought warm water and clean sheets for bandages, took five seconds to check on the night's supper, grabbed a bottle of rum on the go, and checked to make sure the closest room was ready for her patient. Elbowing Ellie aside, she unwrapped the strips of red dress and pulled Joseph's jacket from the wound. It looked ugly. Fresh, bright red blood seeped through a dun-coloured ring of dried clots.

Other than half-open eyes, there was no sign Deacon was conscious. He lay inert, uttering no sound, even when the twins turned him on his side to look for an exit wound. The widow ran a hand down his back, once, then again, then a third time, and pronounced her diagnosis.

"The bullet penetrated below the last rib, so that's the good news. There's no doubt in my mind it got to see some of his liver on the way, and that would explain the colour of the blood. He's already got a thunderin' fever, so there's no hope unless we can get the bullet out. However," and she hesitated, "however, I think the bullet in his back is just under the skin. I think I can feel it."

Deacon was completely unconscious now.

Daniel ran a hand along Deacon's back. "Yes. I can feel it too. It's right there."

"How the hell are we going to extract it?" Emmett asked in a low voice.

"We'll cut from the back..." the widow said.

"...and we'll do it right now, while he's still out," Archie added.

The widow fetched a wicked-looking carving knife from the kitchen and, ignoring the floor, splashed it with rum. The twins rolled him on to his left side, right arm and right leg extended to balance him on the table. Joseph held the right wrist in the event he regained consciousness. The widow emptied more of the rum over Deacon's back, dribbled some over her own hands, and again wet the knife.

"More rum on that blade than he's tasted in his life," Red muttered.

"Everyone okay seein' more blood?" the widow asked.

Archie pointed to Daniel and himself. "We've slaughtered livestock," and Emmett added, "It can't be worse than an autopsy I witnessed."

"If I cut an X, maybe we can pop the ball out better," the widow said, knife poised.

"Maybe, but it will take a dog's age to heal," Emmett observed. "That's why bayonets are triangular, to make a nasty wound that doesn't seal."

"We should take a chance on a simple cut that we can close with a bandage," Daniel said.

Ellie said, "He's already lost a heap a blood."

The widow puckered the flesh with two fingers and cut quick and deep. Pushing on each side of the incision with her thumbs, she produced nothing but more blood. Ellie emptied the rest of the rum bottle on her own hands and leaned over the Deacon. She pulled the incision apart while the widow probed with a finger, and suddenly the musket ball pushed to the surface. Everyone exhaled at the same time.

"We'll let it bleed a bit to wash any infection out," the widow said as she prepared a dressing cut from a sheet. Before the dressing was knotted, the Deacon was rolled onto his back so the entry wound could be examined. Recent movement had opened it, and it was seeping freely.

"Look there," Ellie said, pointing.

The widow peered into the bloody mess, reached in, and removed an inch long splinter of wood and then a second one. She gently pressed on the surface of the wound and all around it and said, "I can't feel any more. If we got the ball and half the buckboard out of him, he should mend okay, but if he isn't better by tomorrow morning, we'll know we didn't get it all."

As if this were part of every day's routine, the widow tied more strips of bedsheet to hold the dressings in place and checked on supper while the twins, Joseph, and Daniel carried Deacon to the bed prepared.

Ellie helped the widow with supper. Several travellers were told all the rooms were taken, but a meal was available if they wished, and later the local regulars found their way home once they had consumed their quota of beer and whiskey. "You can sleep on the floor in my room, Ellie," the widow said. Joseph and the twins retired to their customary stall in the stable. Emmett paid for separate rooms for himself, Daniel and Archie. "If there's an attack in the night, it's safer if we're not bunched up," he explained. Deacon's rifled musket Daniel placed within arm's reach of his own bed.

In the morning, Deacon was conscious, his fever had subsided, and he was able to slurp some chicken soup specially made by his hostess. He was remarkably pale and slept for hours, but by noon he was sufficiently recovered to be amused by the musket ball in a glass on the nightstand and hungry enough to enjoy half a sandwich and more soup. He was strong enough to walk to the commode on his own, then slept most of the afternoon. The widow pulled a rocking chair into his bedroom and napped beside him, cat on lap.

Emmett called everyone together and held a forefinger to his lips. "We'll keep our voices down. Who knows how tempted our hostess might be to make this inn solvent on Lonnegan's money? Now, we need to decide on what we do next."

Various scenarios were discussed. It was finally decided Emmett, Daniel, and Archie would rummage through the Deacon's belongings for the twins' money just in case his wound turned septic, Blue would stay with the Deacon and the buckboard until the invalid was well enough to travel, and Red would return with the others to the sawmill to ready it for his arrival. The others would then push north as fast as possible.

No one noticed the cat take up its place in an afternoon window, and no one noticed their hostess creep out of the bedroom and listen from the kitchen.

"I have a better idea," she said, startling them. "You leave Deacon here in my care; I'll nurse him until he can travel. It's safer if the twins take the buckboard home with Ellie and Joseph and the whites."

When no one said anything, she added, "If Ragg returns, I can cover for one person better than two, and he'll just keep going if he doesn't find Ellie or Joseph here." When still no one uttered a word, she said, "Your whole story you haven't shared with me, but I give you more credit for that. It's safer. I'm never going to help a lout like Ragg, not for all the tea in China."

Emmett paid for one more night plus food. After a crack-of-dawn breakfast the seven departed before Deacon awoke. The widow waved good-bye from the door and yelled, "Don't worry! He's in good hands! I'll look after him."

Aeneas Returns to the Plantation

"We buried the boy beside a stream. Quiet spot. He'd a liked that. His brother said a few words over him." Aeneas Ragg drained his glass and set it to one side for Cicero's attention. Lonnegan noticed the fresh scab on Ragg's ear and let him talk.

"Here's what's happenin', Mister Lonnegan. I've sent my younger son to the landing to catch the first upstream boat. It's a race now. You and I both know they'll head north hell-bent-for-election fast, trying to get across into British territory. If they were smart, they'd disappear on the back roads, go overland to Louisville, then maybe cross into Ohio from Covington, but they know and we know getting to a free state doesn't mean you're scot-free. They'll beeline to the Ohio, Paducah almost for sure, grab a boat to Cincinnati, take a train north. That's the fastest route and most logical."

Ragg drank half the refilled glass.

"Can't count on this new telegraph thing stretchin' where we need it, so the boy is gonna beat them to the border, rouse up our people, be there waitin' for 'em where the net narrows."

"They've got a head start," Lonnegan said.

"True. Leastways they think they do, and that's in our favour. They got a head start travellin' by road to Paducah, but a steamship will get my boy to Cincinnati by the time they're in Paducah, and he'll be on a train to Toledo by the time they get to Cincinnati."

"Will you be joining him?"

"Later possibly. I'm going down to Memphis to look after other business. You're not my only client, Mr. Lonnegan, but you're the client I most want to be successful with."

"It's become personal, hasn't it?"

"One son ambushed and shot down just doin' his job, the younger son, an eye gone and scarred for life, one of my associates hunted down and killed like an animal with his back to a river, one burned to death, another associate with his brain mashed so bad he pisses hisself and can't tell you his name... Yes sir, you might say it's personal. Very, very fucking personal." He drained his glass.

"It's personal for me too, Mister Ragg. This has cost me more than money or the temporary loss of the two remaining slaves. You're certain Ellie was in the phaeton with the Limey and the horse traders?"

"The boy had his hands on her when he was shot down in cold blood. It was a beautifully prepared ambush — and we rode right into it. The gunsmoke never did let us see who was firin' at us t'other side of that bridge."

"Hear that whistle. That's a boat leaving the landing. Your boy will be on his way by now. Would you care to spend the night, get an early start for Memphis in the morning?"

"Mister Lonnegan, I would greatly appreciate that. You are a true Southern gentleman, sir."

"After Cicero fills our glasses and we drink to future success, he will set a place for you at supper. Mrs. Lonnegan is indisposed and will not be joining us."

Part Nine

JUSTICE

Running North

A pleasant surprise awaited at the sawmill; neighbours had not taken the remaining animals. Chickens had scratched out a living somehow, and with a cacophony of clucking surrounded the buckboard in expectation of grain. The pigs, which had been let out to wander freely, came on the run. The horses were more reserved; there was no sign of a limp on the one left to mend.

Two of the chickens had been premature in their joy at the twins' return. There was no time to hang them to dry once they had been cleaned by Blue; Red dismembered them and fried the pieces in their own fat. Greens from the garden gave balance to the meal. When Ellie volunteered to wash the dishes, Joseph grabbed a tea towel. Still new with each other, neither spoke or looked directly at the other.

"Feels strange to be eatin' in the house," Red said. "You can figure out the sleeping arrangements on your own 'cause Blue and me, we're in our own beds tonight." Ellie took the girls' room, Emmett the Deacon's, and Daniel and Archie claimed the beds in Pa's quarters. Joseph insisted straw and a blanket in the buckboard would feel just like home.

"But first, now that we're all together and settled, we need to figure out where we go from here," Daniel said. "For us, I suggest the straightest line is back to Paducah, sell the team and Yellow Bounder, hop a boat to Cincinnatti, take a train to Toledo, jump from there into British North America, and waste no time doing it. You boys okay with us heading out tomorrow morning? Sooner or later, Ragg is going to show up in a rage, but we can't sit around waiting for him."

"You gotta go," Red said. "For Joseph's and Ellie's safety, you gotta go. I'd say go tonight, but that ain't practical."

"What worries me is that you're defenceless if, when, Ragg shows up, and you can bet he won't come alone. I'll leave Deacon's musket with you, and it wouldn't hurt to practise some. Will your manumission papers be recognized?" Daniel asked. "Why don't the two of you come with us to Mayfield in the buckboard? No one will question whites buying guns, and you can scurry back here with them and no one's the wiser. For a short time that also leaves no one here for Ragg to encounter, and gives you more protection."

In Mayfield, Daniel and Archie purchased rifled muskets identical to Deacon's and topped up the ammunition supply. As the northbound travellers waved good-bye to the twins, Archie said, "Remember sitting around the table back home, thinking our little excursion would be a holiday, an adventure of sorts? I sure as hell hope their future is more adventure than tragedy. We were so innocent. My God, what a broken country." Daniel nodded in agreement.

As Joseph pointed out, this was his third time travelling between Mayfield and Paducah, so there was no anxiety about the route or where to find an inn with a livery. He worried about Ellie's accommodations needlessly; in most inns a separate room was set aside for Black servants travelling with their mistresses. Ellie only spoke when spoken to. The geography, the sense of freedom, the accents... All was new and different; even though she had been a house servant, she was unsure what to say or how to act around these people, and she feared she might embarrass herself in front of Joseph.

The plan was to arrive early in the morning, sell the horses and the Yellow Bounder back to their original owner, and board an upstream boat as soon as possible. The plan melted away when they arrived in Paducah at noon, and as before, it was raining. The livery where Emmett had purchased the team and phaeton had no intention of negotiating a fair price with someone in a hurry to sell; he left with half what he had anticipated. At the ticket office, he was told an upstream boat was still within sight and they had missed it by minutes; passage on an early boat the following morning was the best he could do.

"Next time, we drop luggage and everyone off at the inn before Emmett sells the phaeton," Archie grumbled, and Daniel said, "There won't be a next time."

A portly, ferret-faced gentleman studied the bedraggled party as it shuffled battered luggage through muddy streets past The Green Door to the alternative inn. The next downstream boat large enough to stop at Memphis on its way to New Orleans carried an envelope addressed to "Ragg and Associates".

A second letter left Paducah. Before he joined the others for supper, the postal service received a hefty sum from Emmett to send a letter to an address in Detroit. It read, *"Forward the following to Sgt Madill at Fort Malden stat. Sergeant; Please be good enough to relay to His Excellency,*

'*Mission Accomplished. Your most obedient servant*' etc. Also, a consignment has been located, purchased, and is on its way within the week." He left it unsigned.

That night, after Ellie hung wet laundry on drying racks in each room and while Joseph cleaned and dried boots, he introduced the topic of the future. "It took me some time Ellie, and I ain't sure I'm all the way there yet, but now my mind is more in freedom than in bondage. Mister Cameron, he don't permit me to call him Master, an' Missus Susan, well, she'd be right down disgusted with me sayin' ain't, or dropping off a g from a word. The Queen's English I'm still working on, and some days it seems I'll never get there. Of course, it will be easier for you, being in the house and hearing how the white gentry talked and all, not like a field hand, but..."

"We on the wrong side of the River Jordan, Joseph. I can't let myself hope Massa Lonnegan gonna let us get away. Somethin' gonna go wrong, an' my life gonna be in the fields an' havin' babies that'll work in the fields too. Maybe these men we're travellin' with, maybe they sell us first chance or we gotta be beholdin' to them, work for them like Lonnegan."

Joseph laughed and rubbed the inside of a boot with a dry rag. He held it up for inspection. "See this here boot. On the plantation, what kind of job would get done on it? Enough not to get punished, that's what. This is Mister Emmett's boot, and I want it to be as dry and shiny as I can make it when he steps inta it tomorra morning, just like I did Mister Daniel's and Mister Archie's, 'cause Ellie, I am getting paid money for the job. Actual, in my hand money, Ellie. You're right about the wrong side of the river. Except, this ain't the River Jordan. You and me, we're a long ways yet from the Promised Land. I know 'cause I bin there."

"I can't see anyone ever leavin' the Promised Land, ever, once they there. Why'd you come back?"

"To keep it the Promised Land. And I was hopin' somehow to get you free... Wasn't sure how to do it..."

"Your white gentlemen, they did a cracker job of runnin' off with me, didn't they? I'm truly sorry Deacon got himself shot."

"They surely did, but we've got a heap more runnin' to do. Maybe more shootin' too. Ellie, I was thinkin' of you every day."

"I never forgot you either, Joseph. I was ponderin' over the least painful way to kill myself if Cicero... If there's a lot of runnin' left, I'm glad I'm runnin' with you."

Ellie spread shirts and trousers to expose the maximum area to the air, and Joseph began work on the second of Emmett's boots. Neither spoke, each afraid to venture into unknown territory. At last, Ellie said, "Do you plan on jumpin' over the broom with me?" Joseph waited so long to reply she feared she might have misread their conversation.

"I do. The thought of you with Cicero, well, that was a terrible burden my mind was carryin'. Cicero or anybody else, doesn't matter, I want you for me. Trouble is, I can't marry just yet, maybe for a long time."

Ellie turned to look at him. "Why not? What's stopping us once... if... we reach the Promised Land?"

"Where we goin' is not the plantation, Ellie. We ain't slaves no more. We gotta be able to look after ourselves now, make a livin'. You don't understand... Mister Daniel, he teachin' me how to carpenter an' how ta farm, but I'm closer to startin' than finishin', and I'm not good enough at either to make a place in society, Black or white. There ain't no fit for us in the Black community if we ain't respectable, if we're just ragtag runaways with nothin' to add except more 'I told you so's' from the ones who don't want us."

"That don't matter to me."

"Well, it matters to me. I got no land, no trade, no tools. Listen to how I'm talkin'. I should have said, 'I have no land,' and 'There is no place for us in the Black community if we are not respectable.' If Missus Susan was here right now, she would plump herself down at that little table and hang her head in embarrassment, all my learnin' disappearing like that. Can you read?"

"I know the letters. I can recognize my own name."

"It's a start, as Mister Duffy would say."

"Who's Mister Duffy?"

"A wheelwright, a man who gave me a job once I crossed the river."

"Black?"

"No, white. I told you. Where we're goin' is different from the plantation, and if some Britishers want to keep us in our place, at least it's a different place from Lonnegan's. I have been helped mostly by whites, all along the line, and Blacks when they could, like food brought by a boy early on when we first started runnin'."

He paused to cast a critical eye over the second boot.

"Wait 'til you meet Missus Susan. Mister Daniel say she come from warrior stock, an' I believe him. When she say, 'A C looks like a cookie with a bite out of it,' you'll remember that after you've forgotten left and right. Her and Mistress Lonnegan, they be about three planets apart."

Next morning's dual-stacked upstream boat was a cousin to the sternwheeler that had carried the four men from Cincinnati. The whites watched from the rail as little riverside towns and villages emerged from the verdant forest and passed into anonymity. Skiffs and rafts scurried out of the way like drunken waterstriders, their occupants' mouths gaping at the magnificent power of the smoke-belching, churning leviathan. Occasionally, oxygen-depleted warm water drove fish to the surface to be shot at for amusement. Everyone agreed there would never be a grander way to travel, not even by train. By preparing the staterooms and clothing for their patrons, Joseph and Ellie played out their roles.

In Cincinnati, Daniel suggested they should keep a low profile. "No telling what wolves, Ragg's or others, are lurking about to steal valuable sheep," he said. "Joseph and Ellie should stay in the hotel." He, however, asked Emmett for directions to the gunsmith, and reappeared several hours later with an Adams revolver that was a twin to Emmett's. "I bought it out of my farm machinery money," he explained. "To tell the truth, I was angry and frustrated that I could do nothing at the bridge. Deacon, Emmett, even Joseph, were answering back, while I was watching everyone else spring into action. That will not happen again."

Their previous wandering through Ohio had given them a good idea of the best railroad route to Toledo. Emmett was able to purchase tickets for Joseph and Ellie to ride in the "Coloured" section, so Joseph avoided the baggage car. If Ellie had been impressed by Paducah, she was left awed by the steamboat ride, a hotel stay in a major metropolis, and now a train.

When they detrained in Toledo, it was mid-afternoon. They decided to stay close to the harbour at the same rundown hotel as before, and Emmett agreed with Daniel that they should immediately hold a council.

"The way I see it, we have three choices," Emmett said. "When I registered, I asked the desk clerk why we were unable to purchase a train connection to Detroit on the new Detroit, Monroe and Toledo. He doesn't know the details, but he's not sure it's complete. He's heard rumours about a washed out track or maybe a bridge, but he says it's more probable lawyers are slowing everything because it crosses a state line. That leaves renting a carriage or chartering a boat with its own skipper."

"If we rent a carriage, we have the same problem as at Paducah," Archie pointed out. "It's not practical to buy a team and carriage and sell them again..."

"At a loss," Emmett interjected.

"...and sell them again in two or three days," Archie continued. "Not practical to hire a driver with a team either. More money and time gone, and one more person who can tell someone where we are."

"I hate to suggest it," Daniel said, "and I dread the thought, but chartering a boat might be our fastest way into British territory."

"It's settled then. Archie, if you can find somewhere to buy two days worth of groceries, things that travel well, and Daniel, if you can keep an eye on Ellie and Joseph and maybe order supper to be served in our rooms, I'll march myself down to the waterfront and see if I can scare up a boat for tomorrow."

The same grasping bellhop who had irritated Daniel previously was lugging trays with bowls of coagulated grey stew and bread pudding to their rooms when Archie and

Emmett returned. Daniel waved off the extended hand, and informed the young man he might receive a small gratuity if and when the party was satisfied with the food and when the dirty dishes were removed. Everyone met in Emmett's room. The conversation diverted attention away from the sorry meal.

"The pirate is here," Archie announced, "scarred face, black eye patch and all. I saw him heading toward the harbour. I looked into my purchases so he wouldn't pay me any attention; eye contact invites eye contact. I didn't worry about a one-eyed man recognizing you, Emmett, seeing as how at your last meeting you introduced yourself by blowing his hat off. Anyway, he's here, and you can bet the lint in your pockets he's looking for Ellie and Joseph."

"He'll need to look jolly well early if he wants to catch us up," Emmett said, "because we will be on board a thirty-six foot sloop, the *Billie Jo*, before dawn tomorrow. The captain says there's no fuss or bother getting us to British North America. His son crews for him. They didn't want to leave before the wind comes up, but I insisted it was imperative our departure be discreet."

"Wouldn't it have been wiser to mingle with outgoing boats later in the morning?" Daniel asked. "To mention we do not wish to draw attention to our departure is one way to draw attention to our departure."

"I think we are dealing with an honest man," Emmett said. "The boat seemed stout to me, clean lines, recently varnished, all ship shape as we say in the navy. The second half of the fee, a grossly excessive fee I might add, is motivation to have us step ashore safe on British soil."

"Joseph says this is the narrow end of the net," Archie said, "and I agree with him. I, for one, do not want any surprises this close to home, so I suggest we keep a two hour watch from a chair in the hall. I'll take the first, wake Daniel for the second, then Emmett, then me again."

Joseph shook his head. "You want to have a sentry in the hall, and you don't think that will draw attention to us?"

"Have you got a better idea?" Archie asked, a bit peeved that Joseph's point undermined his suggestion.

Joseph thought for a moment. "How about this? I sleep on guard in the hall. Nothing special about a Black manservant sleepin' outside his employers' rooms, and from there I can keep an eye on Ellie's door."

"Okay, but I'd rest better if we didn't wake up to find you spirited away in the night. Why don't we loop some string around your ankle and pass it under Daniel's door, so if anyone comes to grab you, his ankle can tell him. That idea we got from some old ladies in a general store."

"Oh no, string around my ankle will have no effect on a good night's sleep," Daniel remarked sardonically, "Dinna fash yersel'. I won't be getting much rest anyway, what with tossing and turning tonight, thinking about tossing and turning tomorrow. Maybe I should skip breakfast, assuming we've got something for it on the boat."

Emmett turned to Joseph. "Tell Ellie to wedge a chair against her door."

"So Daniel, you really think we're out of the woods?" Archie began. "If the pirate..."

Daniel held up a hand in resignation, sighed, and said, "Fine. When the boy comes for the dishes, I'll send him for a ball of string."

The Billie Jo Sails North

The sky had barely begun to lighten when Daniel roused the others. "I couldn't sleep. I think I'm already seasick from anticipation of the day." The walk from the inn to the harbour took less than five minutes. As they handed their luggage from the dock to the captain, who passed it to his son to stow below, he noticed Joseph and Ellie. "Ahhh, that explains it. I should have twigged with the English accent. No problem. Abolitionist money is as good as any."

The son held a finger to his lips to indicate silence and pointed Joseph and Ellie to the cabin behind a slatted door. He pushed the *Billie Jo* off the dock with an oar, and went forward to hoist a triangular foresail while his father worked the wheel. The sail hung limp, and their progress was so annoyingly slow Daniel whispered, "Maybe we should offer to paddle."

It took a full hour to clear the harbour. The eastern sky was pink now. "Too calm this early to fill the sails," the captain said. "It's the Maumee current we're riding into the lake. Not much to it, but it's there." He pointed to the bigger water of Lake Erie. "See that riffle. That's where we'll leave this Irish hurricane and catch an offshore breeze. Might blow up some good puffs later if that sky is telling the truth."

"Wonderful," Daniel muttered. "Just wonderful."

The sun was above the horizon when the wind strengthened enough to push the hull against the water. The mainsail was hoisted, the son winched the sheets to maximum efficiency, and with a forefinger pointing straight ahead and a nod, the captain expressed pleasure at their speed.

"Wind from the west, am I right?" Archie asked. "Is that good? From the south would be better, wouldn't it?"

"We'll take what we can get. If a west wind pushes us too far, it may mean the boy will be kept busy with more tacks. Whenever we come about, you keep your heads below that boom if you want to keep 'em."

The day warmed, the coast became a fainter line on the horizon, and all but one relaxed. A freshening wind produced a small chop. Daniel declined Archie's offering of salt pork sandwiches. "Best to look at the horizon if you don't sailor well," the captain suggested.

"Our cargo is coping nicely. New experience for them. You can thank Ellie for the sandwiches," Archie said.

Between the *Billie Jo* and the Ohio horizon, Daniel noticed a ship. Twenty minutes later it was perceptibly closer and still on the same course, dead astern. Fearing the captain might return to Ohio if he became alarmed, Daniel slid next to Emmett and said, "There's a boat behind that may be following us. Wouldn't hurt to have our revolvers handy and loaded with fresh caps, maybe some extra ammo in our pockets."

"I'll warn Joseph," Emmett said. When he returned from the cabin, he pointed out the closing ship to the captain and asked, "Can we outrun it?"

"We're at least an hour ahead, so who knows?" the captain replied. "Maybe she's heading the same place we are."

"If you can get any more speed out of the *Billie Jo*, please do," Archie said quietly. "Do you have any firearms aboard?"

"There's an old musket strapped to the port wall in the cabin. We store the powder and wadding in the table drawer to keep it dry. Balls are in a little canvas bag, same drawer. Surely it won't come to that... The *Billie Jo* didn't sign on for a shootout."

"We simply want to be prepared," Emmett said offhandedly, to soothe the captain.

To Daniel's discomfort, the wind picked up as the hours passed. By the time the sun was well past the middle of the western sky, the following ship was within a quarter mile and gaining.

"Yup, that's a brigantine for sure," the captain confirmed through his telescope. "Square foresail. Probably gaff-rigged at the stern. Double the tonnage of us. Faster than us too, 'cause she carries more sail. If she orders us to heave to, we'll go into irons."

"Which means...?" Daniel asked.

"We'll turn into the wind, empty the sails, simply float with no forward momentum. She flies no flag, but if that's an American ship, there is nothing they can do. We're in British water now. Look fore. That coast is Canada West."

"Sir, on that boat there's a man who wouldn't care if we were sitting in the Thames River watching the Lords go into the House."

"They're after the Darkies, aren't they?"

"Yes, and revenge," Archie said. "Captain, we don't have time for the story. You simply must trust us when we tell you... If that man overtakes us, he will try to kill us all."

"Can't you just give him the Negroes? Just give him the runaways you're helping. That's what he wants, isn't it? The Darkies?"

Daniel said slowly and deliberately, "Sir, even if we did that — and we will not — he will still kill us. He won't care the *Billie Jo* is a chartered boat. He thinks he can take the Blacks for the reward and not leave any witnesses alive. You understand revenge, don't you? He killed the best friends of the man in the cabin, and that Black man in your cabin will not let himself or the girl be captured alive. That man chasing us is wanted in Canada West for kidnapping and possible murder."

After a short pause he added, "And we killed his brother."

The captain studied the British shore. "Then it's run or fight." He looked back at the brigantine. "Or it's run and fight." Turning to Emmett, he said, "Take my glass, and see if they've got a cannon on that brig while I keep the sails filled. She's big enough to carry a small one."

Emmett focused the telescope, collapsed it, and placed it beside his hip. "A jolly good club if we go to hand-to-hand," he said. "No cannon. She's the *Linda Ann*. Undoubtedly the same *Linda Something* that abducted the club-foot from the wheelwright's workshop. Blue hull, red stripe... Ragg's son is in front of the foresail, sitting straddle on the bowsprit, and he's holding a musket, obviously waiting to get within range before he fires."

"That won't be long now," Daniel observed. "Sooner if that musket is rifled."

"Ready about!" the captain yelled. "Helm's-a-lee!"

"Good God, that was close," Daniel said in a voice louder than necessary, as the boom swung over his head and the *Billie Jo* rolled to alter direction.

"Course correction," the captain replied calmly. "We'll run due north on the steepest keel angle a west wind allows. They're fast, but maybe they can't change course on a hard tack like a smaller boat, what with that square foresail, so I'm gambling we're more nimble."

Daniel immediately discovered that a steep keel angle left the starboard gunnel only inches above the water. He moved his revolver from behind to the front of his belt to avoid the occasional splash.

The *Linda Ann* had come about seconds slower than the *Billie Jo* but the former's speed soon made up the few yards gained. "Heads down and ready about. Helm's-a-lee!" the captain called, and again they gained a few yards, which were just as quickly made up by the brigantine. To the fore, trees were visible. "*To be so close...*" Daniel thought.

Again and then again the captain came about, his son expertly winching the sheets to an optimal adjustment of the sails. "The wind is shifting northerly," the captain said. "The more the better, 'cause If the breeze cooperates we can close-haul, and maybe run a point or two closer than that brig."

Individual trees could now be distinguished, and at about three hundred twenty degrees they could see where the Detroit River widened into the lake. Their pursuer closed to within two hundred yards.

"Joseph," Archie yelled, "if I can see you through those slats, then an unlucky bullet can find you. Best put something between you two and the cabin door, and keep it closed."

"Damn!" the captain exclaimed. "The air can't seem to make up its mind where it wants to go."

"Will that give us any advantage?" Daniel asked.

"Maybe. Maybe not. They sit higher with taller masts, so it's probable they'll catch more wind. The question is, can we sail closer to it."

One hundred yards.

"We'll present a tempting target if we come about again," the captain said. "I'll take her in on a straight run. Erie is a shallow lake, so the waves can be impressive. With any luck, they'll run aground, and without their draft we'll surf right in on the rollers."

Seventy-five yards.

"Never in my wildest dreams did I ever think I would be praying for higher waves," Daniel said.

Fifty yards.

A bullet carved a furrow of wood off the boom, and from the brigantine came a puff of smoke and the crack of a rifle. Archie crouched on the port side of the wheel, the flintlock's barrel resting on the transom, its brass powder flask protruding from his pocket. Daniel and Emmett vainly attempted to keep their heads below the gunwales, Daniel's more exposed on the port tack.

There was the sound of a hammer on meat, and before they heard the shot the captain jerked forward, his right shoulder holed by a musket ball. The sloop yawed. Archie grabbed the wheel and straightened her toward shore as Daniel slid from his bench and wrestled off the captain's jacket and half his shirt to expose the wound. The son, feeling the boat lose way, came aft to find his father semiconscious and bleeding beside the wheel. "It's clean. The ball's gone in and out again," Daniel yelled. "He's in shock. Take him below. The girl will know what to do."

They could see the shoreline clearly now, and the shadows of the trees stretching out from a setting sun. Cattails flanked to the left and right of a small beach, where Archie could see tiny figures running.

Twenty-five yards.

"I have to keep us on course!" Archie yelled. "How close?"

"They're going to try and board us," Emmett said calmly. "There's an older man at the helm, two with grappling hooks at the ready. The pirate has moved behind the foremast for cover, maybe to steady his musket for another shot."

'Pray your powder's dry," Daniel said. "Emmett, you take the front man, I've got the second. Wait until they're right alongside. If the pirate shows himself, I've got the better shot."

The man at the front rail suddenly swung his grappling hook and flung it over the far side of the sloop. He leaped backward out of Emmett's line of fire and pulled the rope taut across the cabin door. The sailor closer to the stern threw his hook with the same sudden motion. It caught on the transom and both ropes together pulled the sloop beside the hull of the *Linda Ann*.

"I can't hold her!" Archie yelled. He pulled his knife, opened the blade, and sawed clumsily at the aft rope with one hand, the other on the wheel. Joseph, peering through the slats of the cabin door, realized the smaller ship would remain captive if it was held in thrall. Against the pressure of the forward rope, he forced the cabin door open a finger's width, and using Malachi's knife, sliced it. The bow of the *Billie Jo* swung to starboard, the stern still held in check by the aft rope.

Emmett looked up to see Ragg's son aiming at Archie. The reflexive shot Emmett fired off missed the man but hit the stock of the firearm, spinning it out of his hands and into the water.

Daniel risked a shot at his target as the stern grappler tied his rope off on the rail. It missed and splintered wood beside the head of another sailor coming to his assistance.

"At least five on that boat," Daniel yelled.

"Bloody hell!" he heard Archie say, and Emmett added, "Enough to go around."

The *Linda Ann* swung to starboard, scraping hulls. The pirate and the two who had used the grappling hooks with such effect dropped onto the *Billie Jo*, Ragg's son brandishing a foot long blade perfect for close-in butchery. The others carried pistols. As the brigantine arrested its rise on a crest and the sloop reached the bottom of a trough, there was the briefest moment when each ship stopped its vertical movement. The sailor still on the *Linda Ann* who Daniel had almost hit fired a pistol at Daniel, and before the missile had finished fizzing into the lake, he whirled to his left and sent a bullet through the man's head. It entered his throat on an upward trajectory and exited the cranium north of the optic nerve. Daniel's victim fell slowly over the rail, glanced off the *Billie Jo's* transom, and, leaving a plume of blood from a partially severed tongue, disappeared in the blue-green water.

As Daniel turned to face the three who had successfully boarded, he saw the aft grappler's pistol belch fire as Emmett swept it away from his face. His assailant smacked the smoking pistol against the young man's head just as Emmett fired his revolver into his belly. Emmett collapsed onto the deck in front of the wheel to join the dying man writhing in his own blood.

The aft rope Archie had so frantically attacked gave way; the *Billie Jo* swung free, and with only the helmsman to sail the ship, the *Linda Ann* veered to port. Archie stabilized the wheel with his left hand while with his right he groped behind him in an attempt to grab the old musket, which he intended to use as a club if it would not fire. The deck levelled.

Daniel had no time to fire his revolver a second time before the tall, eye-patched son was on him, knife in hand. He dropped it to one side and, head low, flung himself at his adversary, grasped the knife arm by the wrist, and held him close so the man could not slip out of his control. Back and forth the two struggled, twisting and turning. Archie, behind the wheel, realizing he had no shot, abandoned any idea of recovering the musket,. Even if the powder in the pan ignited the main charge, a full second could go by, and in that time either of the dancers might be facing him.

The fore grappler had no such hesitation. As he raised his pistol to fire at Daniel, Joseph shoved the barrel of his revolver through a slat of the cabin door and fired a thirty-six calibre ball through his heart at a range of three feet. Instantly dead, he made no sound as he joined his groaning gut-shot partner and Emmett on the deck.

Daniel smashed the pirate's hand once, twice, three, four times against the wheel until the knife dropped. Archie roared, "Ready about!" and in an instant he understood. Ignoring the thin man's hands on his throat, he grabbed him around the waist and lifted. Archie yelled "Helm's-a-lee" and flung the wheel hard to port. For a moment sails emptied, then filled on the opposite tack. The boom swung across and caught Ragg's remaining son on the ear with a skull-shattering crunch, followed by an audible snap. Daniel let the dead man, his head hanging like a rag doll, slip to the deck to join the others, and collapsed with relief on the starboard bench.

"After the *Linda Ann* slanted off, I might have got her in. Really, I might have, but when the captain's son emerged from the cabin, I turned the wheel over to him," Archie would explain later. "With the boy at the helm, I figured he'd get the blame, or the glory, riding the *Billie Joe* in on the rollers, to get us as near as we could to that beach before she grounded. He turned her into the wind the second she started to scrape, the waves flipped her on her starboard side as she hit, and there we were, keeled over, sails in the water, swaying back and forth as pretty as a mermaid's hair."

Reports to be Written

Archie was examining Emmett's bruised forehead and a powder burn on his cheek when help arrived from the beach in the person of Sergeant Madill, who waded out until the water was up to his armpits and waves lifted him off his feet. The other end of the rope he attached to the *Billie Jo* was held by the fisherman and the wheelwright on the beach. A fourth man, using the rope to steady himself, came out to help.

With the sloop on her side and the cabin half full of water, it was only with great difficulty Joseph, Ellie, and the boy were able to pass the captain to the others. They had ripped apart a pillow case to provide a dressing and had used his belt to immobilize the right arm in a sling. The wound was wet with lake water, which kept the entry and exit holes seeping fresh blood. "The bullet went right through," Ellie confirmed, "but it shattered the collar bone. Please, try to keep the bandage dry." The request was patently impossible.

Starting with the wounded captain, Madill half carried, half floated the *Billie Jo's* occupants to shallower water where others, clinging to the guide rope, could help them ashore. Ellie was his second cargo; treacherous waves of a large lake were beyond her experience. Terrified, she held on to Madill's neck with a death grip. The now fully conscious Emmett came next, followed by Joseph, a non-swimmer, then Archie and Daniel.

The captain's son was reluctant to leave the sloop until Madill reassured him it would not be claimed under the rules of salvage. "By all the saints, every one of us will vouch you never abandoned her. She's tethered to the shore, see? We'll call that a right proper anchor. At first light we'll send a detail to pull her into deeper water where she can be righted, and we'll have her bailed and moored up the river by nightfall tomorrow."

Seeing the sergeant was nearing exhaustion from his efforts, two men unknown to Archie and Daniel pulled themselves hand over hand out to the stranded vessel and tied a separate rope to the foot of a dead man so he could be hauled to the beach. It was almost dark by the time the three corpses were laid out side by side, faces covered by a shared blanket.

Fatigued, their adrenalin expended, the *Billie Jo's* survivors huddled on the sand.

"Sergeant, how in heaven's name did you know to be here when we needed you most?" Daniel asked. "If ever there was a miracle..."

"We received a letter from the major saying we could expect you with cargo within the week. Of course, we expected you'd be coming across to the town dock from Detroit. That's where the committee took turns watching for you. It was our best sentry who saw there was something going on out in the deeper water."

"Your best sentry?"

"An old woman who walks her dog by the lake every day. There is no better sentry than a nosy old woman. Now let's get the wounded shoulder up to the fort so the doctor can take a run at him." The sergeant turned to the man who had helped nearest the sloop. "May we throw the corpses on your wagon? I suspect the others would rather not ride with them."

"The missus and I have room in the workshop if any need looking after," the wheelwright volunteered.

"That's very Christian of you, Mister Duffy, but I'm sure we can make arrangements. The doctor needs to look at these two," he said, pointing to the captain and Emmett. "Am I right about the fort, Major Emmett?"

"Just Emmett for the moment, Sergeant, but you are quite right. British subjects fired on by an American boat in British waters. Military business if there ever was."

"We've been missing you, sir."

"Thank you, Madill. I've missed you too. I wish we'd had you with us. Nip and tuck at times. It's been a jolly good lark."

The doctor was not gentle with the captain's injury. By lantern light he washed it, put on a fresh dressing, and guaranteed more discomfort in the morning. "You will sleep here in the infirmary tonight," he brusquely informed his patient. "Madill can tidy up a spot for you. Your son may keep you company, to fetch and carry should you require anything. That wound must be reexamined in better light. A bullet fired at close range, especially from a rifled barrel, may be hot enough to cauterize the blood vessels in its passage, but you have successfully contaminated the entry and egress holes with lake water. I'll disinfect again in the morning, after I have had an opportunity to probe for bone splinters."

The others enjoyed a more comfortable night. The doctor had smeared an evil smelling salve on his blistered cheek, and Emmett claimed the hearing in his left ear was almost back to normal. A pensioner's wife took Ellie under her wing and set up a cot for her in her cabin. Emmett insisted on sleeping in the abandoned barracks with Joseph, Archie and Daniel. "For the moment I am a civilian and therefore not entitled," he said, to counter Sergeant Madill's insistence he sleep in the officers' quarters, which his replacement now occupied.

After breakfast in the town, the able-bodied returned to the infirmary for a progress report on the captain's condition. They found Emmett's replacement already there, telling the doctor it was imperative the patient be repatriated as soon as possible. He introduced himself as Captain Peabody, shook hands with the men, enquired after their health, chatted briefly about the weather, stated he would send a formal letter of explanation to the U.S. authorities when a detail rowed the corpses to the Michigan side, asked for specifics of the brigantine which had attacked them, and offered transportation to the railway station the following day. He wished the group well, told the son he would show him where to find breakfast for himself and his father, excused himself, and left with the boy in tow.

"A most efficient officer," Archie remarked.

Yes, quite efficient," the doctor remarked indifferently. "As for you, Major Emmett, you will not be leaving my care until I am convinced that face wound is healing on its own. The many blood vessels in the face promote rapid recovery with minimal scarring; still, we'll keep an eye on you."

Captain Peabody poked a head back inside the infirmary door. "My apologies, gentlemen. I was remiss in my duty and quite forgot to mention I shall need a full account from each of you as to how we are in possession of three American corpses and three American citizens, one wounded, one a minor, and one possibly a fugitive. Rest assured the other side will express curiosity about the details. Who knows what pretext an ambitious power may use to embellish this into an international incident, so we must demonstrate we have taken every step to ensure full transparency. I wish those accounts written in separate rooms for comparisons, and once they are on my desk I shall arrange that together we dine tonight in the town."

The doctor finished drying an enamelled basin he had used when flushing the captain's wound, and without looking at the door, said, "Sir, possibly you could clear up some details for Emmett's report."

Peabody stepped into the infirmary and closed the door behind him. "What do you require 'clearing up' for anyone's report, Doctor?"

"When the duty sentry was notified of shots heard on the water and Madill and I drove down to the lake, interested citizens were already gathered to watch the sloop evade her pursuer. I never thought to record the names of any witnesses, and I can vouch Madill did not either. So may we assume you do not need the names of the people on the beach?"

"If they had no part in the conflict between the two boats, there would be no need for names? Anything else?"

"I am led to believe the girl is betrothed to Joseph, the man standing next to you, a British subject employed by Mister Cameron and who lives at his residence. Surely there is no necessity to mention her in our reports. Providing first aid to the captain was her sole contribution."

"I see no need to clutter up the individual accounts with trivial superfluity. Is that all?"

"Sir," Daniel said, "we were planning on departing today, but now there is little chance. Is it possible we could send a letter home to advise of our safe arrival?"

"Of course. I am sending a dispatch to the governor general via the mail service later this morning. If you can have any correspondence to Sergeant Madill within the hour, he'll see it catches the train. I will inform him when I see him forthwith to enquire what fruit is on sale this week."

Before anyone could react, Peabody drew a forefinger down the middle of his nose to the bottom of his chin. The finger hesitated for the briefest moment in front of his lips. He nodded to the doctor, then to Emmett, and exited the infirmary for the second time.

Home

Susan and Catherine were waiting on the platform when the train pulled in. Luggage was tossed, and with a fuss of steam and grinding iron, the train was again on its way. There was an indefinable awkwardness when they embraced their husbands, as if they were unsure how to act with acquaintances they had not seen for a very long time.

"I brought our buggy and Catherine theirs, to accommodate everyone and the luggage," Susan explained. "Where are Joseph and Emmett? Did you leave Emmett at the fort?"

"We said our good-byes on the train. But first things first," Archie said, and motioned a shy and demure Ellie over to be introduced. "Catherine, Ellie is staying with us for a time. If the Camerons take her in, Abigail Hedley will explode in a fit of righteous indignation."

"Well we can't have that," Catherine said. "My dear, I am so glad you are safely here. I can hardly wait to hear your story, but I hope it isn't as exciting as Joseph's. For the moment, be at ease. We are only a few hours from home."

"This won't be as comfortable as the train," Archie said, as he turned his team into the road.

"But where are...?" Susan began, as Daniel threw his luggage behind the seat and climbed up to take the reins.

"You aren't going to believe this, Susan," Daniel said, clicking Jessie and Jacob into motion. "Joseph will not be returning for days. At Fort Malden, Emmett received a missive to present his report — in person, no less — to the governor general, who will be in Kingston near the end of the week. Naturally, Emmett wanted to arrive in a style befitting an officer and a gentleman, so he has hired Joseph on as his manservant at a ridiculous rate of pay."

"So Joseph has rescued his true love and will be in attendance at Major Emmett's meeting with His Excellency, where they will discuss matters of great importance to the Empire."

"Exactly."

"I hope he uses good English."

"He got a bit careless in stressful times, but my language suffered more. It will take some time to tell the tale."

"How much time?"

"A full bottle of whisky, then maybe another one."

"Is there going to be a war between the states?"

"Yes, there is going to be a war between the states."

They rode the rest of the way in silence.

Argus did not wait for the buggy to halt before he made a total fool of himself, running in circles and random oblongs, then knocking the prodigal son down as he attempted to alight. "Will bacon and eggs do for supper?" Susan asked, retrieving the luggage from behind the seat. "I'll put some on while you tend to the horses. It's a good thing they aren't as exuberant as Argus when one of his heroes returns."

As nervous as newlyweds, supper talk was of the weather and Vicky and the state of the roads. Neutral topics. Daniel dried the dishes which Susan stacked on the drainboard. "Coffee or tea?" Susan asked. Daniel shook his head no. She retrieved two glasses and a bottle of whisky from the sideboard, set them on the table, and poured a charitable quantity.

"How's the farm?" he asked. "Are you okay? I worried about you."

"I'm fine. The usual small hiccups we're used to. There are skunk tracks around the henhouse again. Those Herefords you bought, well... That was a good idea. They're thriving in the back pasture and no trouble at all, but they've gone wild, so they'll be deucedly difficult to work with come winter."

She took a tiny sip of Scotch. "What about you? How are you? I worried all the time about you too."

"In God's grand scheme, I haven't been gone all that long. Longer than we thought maybe, but not all that long. But it changed me, Susan. It changed me."

"Isn't there an oriental proverb that says we cannot step into the same river twice?"

"Just the country we traversed would be enough to stretch my world, and my words will be inadequate to describe it to you — or the places we stayed and the meals we ate and the people we met. It's something else, above and beyond all that."

She said nothing, waiting for him to organize his thoughts.

"Susan, I have seen wickedness in the flesh... pure, unapologetic evil, and I will never be the same."

"We have evil here too."

"Not like I've witnessed. Babies strapped to mothers' backs in the fields, human skulls on a chair, the appalling slave cabins... You start to get some idea of the depravity when you see the slave cabins."

He drank some whisky.

"Don't think for a second we got Ellie away scot-free. There was a price higher than money. We killed people, Susan. I shot one, and Archie helped me kill the second. Joseph got one that was about to shoot me. The one Emmett killed almost shot him first."

"So it was self-defence. Even God accepts killing in self-defence."

"You misunderstand. I have no one's death on my conscience. I enjoyed killing those sons of bitches. They were vermin. This whisky is not to dull a gnawing conscience. I drink in celebration, a toast to myself. 'The only thing necessary for evil to triumph...' Well, I did something... and I would do it again in a heartbeat."

His wife let him talk without interruption.

"The first one was a lucky shot with an untried firearm, but don't tell anyone that. The others give me more credit for marksmanship than I merit. I fired at just the right moment... One boat had stopped rising, the other falling. The second... I'm so glad it was me that killed him. I will be proud of that to my dying day. He was a monster, Susan. An absolute monster. He raped a lovely woman, left her mind so unhinged she killed her own children in shame because she couldn't fight him off. So my days of sitting in Sunday service and listening to Leeds pound the Bible and tell me to fear damnation of my eternal soul if I break any commandments, well, those days are gone, because in the next life God will reward me for crushing that filthy animal's head like an eggshell. I have never heard a sweeter sound."

He finished the glass of whisky.

"I don't know why I took my Bible with me. I haven't opened it in a month. It's possible I may never open it again. Red and Blue said Deacon thought God was asleep too, there's so much rot in the world. Are we purified in our struggles against the Devil, are they designed to make us worthy? Maybe the Greeks had it right... Maybe our struggles are just for God's entertainment."

"Red, Blue, Deacon... I want to hear every minute detail when we have time. Can you be content here now? Will your world require expansion again in a month or two or a year? Will you be like Ulysses, unable to rest from travel?"

"You pushed me to have an adventure, to see the world so I would not regret not having a go at it when I got old. I know you wanted confirmation I had not married the girl next door for the sake of convenience, confirmation of my love..."

"And...?"

"Adventure is a useful word. It wraps a ribbon around times of discomfort, pain, danger, terror, panic — a word that packages them to make them drawing room acceptable. I suppose it pretties up the ugliness. Susan, I saw jaw-dropping beautiful places with forests and rivers and hills and valleys too splendid for human eyes and towns where the taverns pour into the wee hours and women who share until the money is gone, and there is a war coming for sure, yet there is nowhere I would rather be than right here. Joseph calls this the Promised Land, and you know, I think he's right."

He paused and looked directly at her. "I love you and I want to be right here, with you, forever, and if you're not here with me, then my Promised Land will be like Joseph's without Ellie. Incomplete."

She reached across the table and put a hand on his. "I love you too," she said.

"I missed the farm, but I missed working with the wood more. The seasons dictate what must be done, and no one can argue with that, but when the farm can spare me, it's the wood that calls."

"I understand," she said. "For me, it's the land I hear. The land and you. I was so worried I would lose you, because this land, this farm, without you here with me... If there's no *us*, it's unthinkable."

"We should go to bed," he said.

"Yes, we should."

Two Tables

It was an evening after harvest when the Camerons, the Taylors, and Emmett were able to get together. They met around the Camerons' kitchen table to enjoy tea, pie, one another's society, and talk of the future.

"So Emmett, how should we address you now? Major? Colonel? Field Marshal?" Daniel asked.

"Still Major. I was informed I am too young and lacking in combat experience to assume the responsibility of a regiment, so colonel will have to wait. I suspect field marshal is a few years beyond that."

"I thought you were offered a rise in rank if..." Catherine began.

"I was, and it's coming. However, no one committed to precisely when. I'm not complaining. The pay for my services on our little excursion was charitable beyond my expectations, and I have received a juicy posting to boot."

"Well, don't keep us in suspense," Susan exclaimed. "Where are they sending you?"

"Gibraltar. From there, who knows? Perhaps India."

Archie said, "I hope they paid you heaps. You'll need heaps to keep you in the lifestyle you affected as Sir Shropshire

Emmett, potential investor in cotton plantations and owner of mills."

Emmett chuckled. "Yes, I rather fancied being scandalously rich like that, and I suspect a lady's romantic passions are not diminished when she discovers a possible object of her affections is a man of means. And I've been told I play the snob frightfully well, eh what?"

Everyone laughed, and the men complimented the hostess by attacking a second piece of pie.

"Enough about a poor English officer who survived a posting in the wilds of British North America, travels into the republic, and the friendship of what I believe your neighbour calls 'oatmeal savages'. Where are Joseph and Ellie, and how have the Camerons and Taylors been faring?"

It was Catherine who answered. "Joseph has purchased land near the Elgin Settlement, over by South Buxton. That's where he is right now, finding materials so the men can throw up a small cabin before winter. Daniel and my husband went down there with him to pick out good farmland. It seems dashing off on holidays has become a habit with our menfolk."

"I don't consider digging soil samples a vacation," Archie replied, "but it may be more of a holiday than the bee in a couple of weeks. Daniel, Noah, Paul, John Duffy, and I will be there — that's unless the Blacks want to do it. We're told the Blacks like to look after their own, once they're accepted into the community."

"If he can find enough of what he needs, he's planning a structure about twelve by sixteen, big enough to become a workshop when he tacks a proper house to the side," Daniel said. "We'll take him the lumber left over from his room under the overhang, and he might as well have the little box stove too. Naturally, the first priority will be an outhouse. Until he can dig a well, he'll need to tote water from the closest stream."

"He hit a snag when he tried to register a legal title," Archie added. "The county told him he needed a last name, and he said he wanted it to be someone who helped get him this far. We didn't realize he was pulling our leg when he suggested Argus, until he laughed when we tried to talk him out of it. Then he said, 'Dinna fash yersel,' and he maintained he might be expected to wear a kilt and learn the bagpipes if he chose Cameron or Taylor. He settled on Emmett and threw in Moses for a middle name — to remind him of someone from his childhood. I hope you don't mind."

"Mind? I'm flattered. Honoured actually, that he thought I contributed to his progress. And Ellie?"

"Ellie is back at the house supervising our cookstove. I must say she is now indispensable at the Taylors," Archie said with a straight face. "She remembers various recipes from the plantation, and as soon as she walked into the kitchen the cuisine notched up noticeably." He leaned away from Catherine's attempt to cuff him across the head. "Yup, sure glad that girl came to the rescue. I'll probably starve to death when she's gone, now that I know what food is supposed to taste like," and he dodged another playful smack. "I might need to hire more help until this one is old enough to pitch in," he said as he patted his wife's stomach.

"You too?" Daniel asked. "That's wonderful news. We should ask Mrs. Hedley if she can find a midwife for Susan and Catherine when they come to term."

"Don't you dare!" Catherine laughed. "What if she tried to help us herself?"

"She would show up with a hundredweight of shortbread," Susan said.

"That's the best argument I've heard yet to ask her," Daniel said, and ducked to avoid a flicked backhand from his wife.

"Well then, congratulations all round," Emmett said. "Archie, as someone who has enjoyed your hospitality, I doubt you will suffer from any deprivation of good cooking, but you say Ellie is leaving?"

"Ellie and Joseph are getting married next month," Daniel explained.

Emmett pushed a tiny crumb around his plate with his fork until it disintegrated. Studying the wreckage, he said, "You know, I was quite taken by the girl, but I never imagined she would become Mrs. Emmett under these circumstances."

"When he saw Leeds about performing the ceremony, the reverend asked him who he had approached to be his best man. That set him back. He fretted that if he asked me, Archie would be offended, and we all know how thin-skinned Archie can be. He settled on Noah Hedley so as to acknowledge his friendship when the bounty hunters showed up."

"Mrs. Hedley has taken over the preparations," Susan added. "She delegates and supervises and makes lists and has poor Noah running in ten directions at once. He's been sent to God knows where to purchase notions and a bolt of cloth, and no matter what he brings back, it won't be right and he'll be off again. Abigail has made it clear no one else has the skill to make a dress for Ellie, and she has already baked enough shortbread to feed a fort garrison for a week."

Catherine nodded in agreement. "And you can bet there will be more to come. Shortbread keeps, though."

"I haven't noticed that in this house," Susan remarked, looking at Daniel.

"It's the school children who diminish the supply. And mice."

"Incredible," she said.

"If Mrs. Hedley brought shortbread, we could give ours to the children and the mice and then we would have…"

"Whoa! Stop right there! Are you telling me you would give my shortbread to rodents because you prefer Abigail Hedley's?"

"When Daniel and Joseph and I cleaned up the plates at the ceilidh so no one's feelings would get hurt, we sampled everybody's, and… and Mrs. Hedley's *was* remarkably good," Archie said in an attempt to rescue his friend.

"Better than mine?" Catherine asked.

"And mine?" Susan asked. "Daniel, are you confessing that you don't like my shortbread as much as Mrs. Hedley's?"

"Archie Taylor, give us your thoughts on how my recipe compares to Mrs. Hedley's," Catherine commanded, in an exaggerated sweet voice.

With a dismissive shrug, Daniel said, "Perhaps Abigail just happened to hit something close to perfection on that particular baking day."

Archie nodded his head in agreement. "Yes, that must be it. That ambrosia was probably an accident."

"Ambrosia?" Susan and Catherine said in unison, glaring at their husbands.

Susan clenched her fists. "Daniel, if you say Abigail Hedley's shortbread is food for the gods while mine is fit for mice, I will..."

"I wish I could tell you we need shortbread to welcome a new garrison at Malden," Emmett interjected in an attempt to deescalate the growing domestic tension. "The fort is now finished as a military installation. They're turning it into a lunatic asylum."

"Surely you jest!" Daniel exclaimed, seizing the opportunity to change the subject.

"I do not. It's always about money... Speaking of which, I'll contribute to a wedding present. I could buy the material for the dress. Ellie looks stunning in red."

Susan shook her head. "Interfering at this late stage will only annoy the dragon."

"If you want to chip in, we're buying tools for Joseph," Archie said. "I'm off to Chatham to find a vice, Daniel's buying a set of chisels, Noah's buying a plane, Paul a saw, John Duffy a hammer. A level is always useful."

"Done," said Emmett, reaching for his wallet.

Catherine looked at Susan and muttered, "I smell another holiday coming up."

Susan nodded and whispered, "When they're away, let's drop in on Abigail. Maybe if we flatter her enough..."

Aeneas Ragg placed a well-travelled envelope on the table. "There's the last advance you sent me for expenses, Mister Lonnegan, and it pains me more than I can tell that I am obliged to give it back. It's an admission of defeat, and I ain't never liked the taste of defeat."

Cicero refilled Ragg's glass to help dilute the taste.

"Am I to understand you have decided to get out of the business?"

"Yes, out before the world goes more to hell in a handbasket. I sent a man up to the sawmill where the holy roller helped your boy escape, just to see what he might see. No sign of the owner, but there was fresh young cattle in the field, and propped ag'inst a kitchen window was two manumission papers. Copies, of course, but what the hell is the world coming to when a man throws away property each worth seven, maybe eight hundred dollars? I gotta try my hand at somethin' else before I get too old to learn new tricks. I hear Forrest is thinkin' of closing shop; maybe I'll see if there's a business opportunity in the space he leaves."

"Sir, you once told me I would not be disappointed in your efforts. I have found that to be true, so I am hearing bad news. If I should need similar services in the future, is there anyone you would recommend?"

"The johnny-come-latelies may think there's easy money huntin' runaway Negras but no, I know of no one who will replace 'Ragg and Associates'. I ran my own network with the thought I would eventually hand it over to my sons. There's no chance of that now."

"Is there no subordinate interested in stepping into the breach?"

Ragg drained his glass and set it down on the table with a thump.

"Subordinates, Mister Lonnegan? No, there are no subordinates left that could fill that bill. No sons now to carry on the business. I'll be frank with you, Mister Lonnegan. It is on your account I can't afford any more. I'll itemize it for you. My first son gunned down in an ambush, the old peg-leg burned, one killed by vigilantes early on, his partner left a slobbering basket case, one feeding the fish in Lake Erie, my younger son with his head bashed in and two more shot up, all sent home in pine coffins by the fucking British. The latest was my eyes and ears up on the Ohio. A sternwheeler setting off from Paducah found him tied to one of the paddleblades, gutted like a fish. He'd been in the water overnight, so I reckon he wasn't hangin' on for the thrill of a morning boat ride."

Lonnegan picked up the envelope and tucked it into the right pocket of his jacket.

"Mister Ragg, I am truly pained by your misfortunes. I share your dismay. The world is an evil place when the escape of three illiterate, ignorant, ungrateful field hands reverberates in so much suffering. Will you stay for supper and beyond? The early boat in the morning can accommodate your horse. Might that suit? We can retire to the porch for a libation while the table is set."

"That would be quite convenient and I thank you. You have always been the kindest and most civilized of my clients."

"Roast duck is on tonight's menu, with a light red from the south of France as accompaniment. Or, should you prefer, a less acidic white. Unfortunately, Mrs. Lonnegan will be unable to join us. She is prone to intense, recurring headaches and has taken laudanum."

Gettysburg

July 6th, 1863
Dearest wife;

You will have heard by now of our tremendous victory so just a brief note to tell I have survived and am well. Today I ladled at the cook station assigned to feed the burial parties. The 3rd was very hot and it rained the afternoon of the 4th which didn't help the Negroes planting the dead. They work dawn to dusk and you've never smelled such a green putrid stink as when they break for a meal. They're using doors for stretchers to move the corpses now because those left are stiff as a board and bloating and hard to handle.

The casualties on our side are horrendous. Many more for the South. So many more there's a rumour some officers are riled with General Meade for not counter-attacking once we smashed Johnny Reb's attack. A missed opportunity they're calling it.

If I live to be a hundred I'll never again see anything like it. I had a front row seat because even the cooks got sent to the center of our line. That's where Meade predicted Lee would attack and Lee obliged him. Everyone knew they were coming because the Rebs' artillery banged away at the center for long enough. Most went over our heads and did more damage behind than in front. Our infantry grumbled because they thought our guns should be giving them what-for right back but Hunt, he's the general in charge of our artillery, he's a fox. He ordered our guns to cease fire one at a time so Johnny would think they'd been knocked out. That saved ammunition too. We knew we were in for it when their cannons went silent and the smoke cleared.

There's a stone wall that makes an elbow right where the 71st was placed, with the 69th on their flank and that's where I was put. We had lots of time to watch their infantry form and jaw about what was going to come up that slope. The man in front of me was middle-aged like me, and I asked him where he was from in Pennsylvania and he said he was from Kentucky and was new to the 71st. I told him my name was George and I would load for him as fast as I could and he told me everyone called him Deacon and we shook hands. He said he was paired to a widow who owned a little inn south of the line but had joined the Bluebellies because he couldn't see any future for the Gray.

Where'd you get that old beat-up piece he asked and I told him ammunition and muskets were doled out to the cooks and I was sent here. I brought my own he said but we had better make sure our calibres are the same because a lodged ball might prove unfortunate in a few minutes. I saw how he flipped the flap of his ammunition pouch over for easy access and so I did the same. We both put a handful of caps in our pockets and I said we better pray our powder isn't damp and he said I don't pray and I said I do.

THE ONLY THING NECESSARY

We didn't talk much once the Rebs started coming. At first all we could make out was thousands and thousands across the better part of a mile and marching slow toward us. I said doesn't it look like every one of those Johnny Rebs is bent on this here exact spot and he said it does seem that way. That gray and brown mass just kept oozing towards us and then we could see their battle flags and Deacon said the ones right in front of us were from Virginia and Tennessee. An officer passed behind us and someone said he had never witnessed raw courage like those Rebs crossing open ground like that and the officer said then we must match it and add some more.

Our artillery opened up and the shot ripped gap after gap in their lines, but they just closed up and kept walking. When they were about a third of a mile out General Hunt ordered canister and from then on the carnage was terrible. You could see there wasn't as many as before and at about three hundred yards you couldn't keep a cow alive on the grass between the bodies. Three hundred was where the 71st started firing and then I thought I was a goner because most of our boys pulled out of the line. I have no idea why, but they moved somewhere else. Dozens stayed at the wall because maybe they didn't hear the order but I couldn't skedaddle because of my bad leg and besides Deacon was taking his time picking his targets, making every shot, and if I left he had no one to load for him so I stayed.

Some of the Rebs got to the wall and over it and then it was hand to hand on each side of us, the bullets still buzzing around our heads. Deacon stood up and peered down the slope and that's when he got hit through the body. There was a phft sound and I saw him take a step back. One more shot he said, I must make one more shot, and I handed him his own gun and he leaned across the wall and concentrated on one man. I looked to see what he was aiming at and right in front of us was a short, stocky man with a tattered brown vest running up to the wall.

I might not have picked him out from a thousand other Rebs except he was wearing knee-high brown riding boots. It was Ragg, the man who burnt our barn, I am sure of it. I heard another phft and Deacon was hit again but still he had a bead on Ragg. He yelled out Ragg! and Ragg turned toward us at the sound of his name and sort of snarled and Deacon shot him just as he reached the wall. The bullet caught him in the teeth and blood sprayed out for a yard or more behind his head. It wasn't three seconds later Deacon caught a third bullet and slumped over the wall and all the while I never got so much as a scratch.

I was exhausted after all that and collapsed with my back against the wall once the shooting was in the distance and then something very odd happened. An officer in a red tunic and the officer who said we must match the Rebs' courage walked along the wall, tallying the dead and wounded. The Union officer said, Colonel, I wish you had remained farther back; even foreign observers are not immune to an errant bullet. The red coated one didn't reply. He stopped where Deacon was on the wall and he turned his head the better to see the face. I knew this man he said, and he ran a finger along a hairline scar I hadn't even noticed before. He was a tragic figure he said and walked on. I guess we'll never know how Deacon knew Ragg and how the colonel knew Deacon.

I hope this finds you in good health. Give my regards to young George and tell him I am proud he is doing well at the college. My leg pains but it would anywhere. No one has any idea when this will be over but the good news for me is that we have our own wagons so everyone involved with feeding the army rides. I cherish your letters. Mail is slow but it will catch up at some point so please write.

Your loving husband,
George

Author's Notes

"The Only Thing Necessary: A Tale from the Cameron Line" began with a dead mouse. This particular mouse was demised on brick fired in 1819 by a United Empire Loyalist ancestor for the birth of what eventually became Daniel and Susan Cameron's home. My second cousin, Irene Cameron, was conducting a tour of this historic house for my children and confessed her old cat was such a poor hunter it was necessary to set traps.

"I'll take that mouse," I said, meaning I would dispose of it for her.

"What do you want it for?" she asked, and in that moment I appreciated the Scottishness in our blood.

As we resumed the tour, I left the mouse because, as Irene pointed out, I had no immediate use for it. "And that's where we kept the Negroes," she said, and pointed to a portion of the basement at the rear of the house. These seven words were the spark that ignited research into a chapter of my family's history that remains frustratingly obscure. But if we know there is a story and we don't know the story, then we can either wallow in "what if's" or make up a story.

What do we know for sure? We know that a Cameron family who lived in this house sheltered Black refugees for a reason, and that reason was to protect them from bounty hunters. We know that some of the neighbours knew of this. We know some citizens near Amherstburg were so incensed that fugitive slaves were being kidnapped and returned to the United States they formed an extra-legal "Vigilance Committee" to forcibly put a stop to the practice. We know bounty hunting was curtailed dramatically once the vigilantes took action.

At first I found the Cameron involvement a conundrum. Their location in Kent County on the Talbot Line near present day Kenesserie Road was too far east to be associated with the Essex County vigilantes. Then I discovered a similar Vigilance Committee had been organized in Chatham, a mere forty kilometres away, less by crow flight. That vigilantes were active so far east speaks to the magnitude of the bounty hunter problem. It was the Chatham committee that achieved notoriety and everlasting glory in 1858 by preventing the delivery into slavery of young Sylvanus Demarest.

This story is a work of fiction, and I claim a fiction writer's prerogative to play fast and loose with the characters and their roles.

My great-grandfather, the real Daniel Cameron, was a farmer and a pretty fair carpenter, but he would have been a few years too young to participate in this story. My great-grandmother, nee Susan Green, sincere in her belief milk was harmful to the young, provided homemade wine and cookies for the schoolchildren who stopped in each day. To avoid confusion with other families' genealogy, I have named Daniel's best friend Archie, although he was almost certainly the John Taylor who married Catherine Hackney. Cameron and Taylor did steal an American boat, each thinking the other knew how to sail. Alcohol was involved. All are buried in the Trinity churchyard.

I needed Abigail Hedley to communicate the narrow minded, provincial prejudices found in early rural communities. My great-grandfather suffered censure when he stopped his buggy to chat with an Irishman of the Roman Catholic persuasion. Most of the characters are the product of my imagination and have no tie to anyone living or dead. Leeds is an amalgam of several circuit riders, but Father Daudet and Nathan Forrest the slave trader are historical figures.

The period from 1848 to 1860 is a minefield for writers who strive for historical accuracy. Nationalism and liberalism, dominant themes of the century, provided a backdrop to technological revolutions in transportation, communication, agriculture and weaponry. One farmer might still be swinging a scythe while his next door neighbour was sitting on a mechanical reaper. Purists will froth at the mouth when they encounter a reference to a rifled musket rather than a rifle or a musket, but at the time a muzzle loading musket with a rifled barrel could be referred to as either or both. The modern breechloader was in its infancy and such a rare commodity it was unknown to the average citizen.

I have shamelessly simplified the complex geography of western Tennessee and Kentucky, much altered during the Depression by the Tennessee Valley Conservation Authority. For the sake of the story, roads have been added and water subtracted. In earlier days travel times were influenced by a plethora of factors. The river road between Amherstburg and Windsor can now be driven in less than an hour; the drive between Dyersburg and Mayfield will take a few hours. In the 1850's, a heavy rain could turn dirt roads into squelching nightmares for man and horse alike. Proper care of horses was as important as food and shelter for human travellers, and with inns infrequent, it was not uncommon for travellers to seek sustenance for both from the locals, many of whom opened their houses and barns to passers-by in exchange for a contribution. We are witnessing a resurgence of that practice in our time, commercialized through bed and breakfasts or temporary rentals in private homes.

The plight of the slave in America is well-documented. For a fascinating glimpse of the Black experience in Canada West, read Dr. Lorene Brigden-Lennie's University of Waterloo PhD thesis, "Lifting As We Climb: The Emergence of an African-Canadian Civil Society in Southern Ontario (1840-1901)."

The people who would create the Dominion of Canada found the idea of human bondage repugnant earlier than our neighbours to the south. Thousands of the somewhere between 30 000 and 40 000 citizens of British North America who fought for the North in the American Civil War died in that titanic struggle.

References to the Cameron Line allude to my own blood ties to Clan Cameron and to the portion of the Talbot Trail/Highway 3 where at one time my Cameron ancestors lived.

The only thing necessary for evil to triumph is for good people to do nothing. Someone in my family tree understood that... and did something. Someone said, "Not on my watch!"

I am proud of that.

David Cameron Shepherd

Manufactured by Amazon.ca
Bolton, ON

41044236R00351